Mark Wallington was born in Dorset, and had a variety of jobs before becoming a travel journalist and scriptwriter. He is the author of *Five Hundred Mile Walkies*, *Destination Lapland* and *Boogie Up the River*.

Married with two children, he now lives in St Albans, and is a regular contributor to the *Daily Mail*, the *Sunday Times*, *The Guardian* and *Cosmopolitan*. *The Missing Postman* is his first novel.

'Mark Wallington brings a small-town postman triumphantly to life, investing the commonplace with much humour and unexpected detail.'
*Daily Mail*

'This book deserves to be read.'
*Northern Echo*

'A beautifully observed and original first novel.'
*Today*

# MARK WALLINGTON

**WARNER BOOKS**

A *Warner* Book

First published in Great Britain in 1992
by Hutchinson

Published by Warner Books in 1993

Copyright © Mark Wallington 1992

The right of Mark Wallington to be identified as Author
of this work has been asserted by Mark Wallington in
accordance with the Copyright, Designs and Patent Act, 1988.

A CIP catalogue record for this book
is available from the British Library.

ISBN 0 7515 0087 9

Phototypeset by Intype, London
Printed and bound in Great Britain by
Richard Clay Ltd, Bungay, Suffolk

Warner Books
A Division of
Little, Brown and Company (UK) Limited
165 Great Dover Street
London SE1 4YA

For Catherine

# 1

It was Winston Churchill who was responsible for Clive Peacock becoming a postman.

When Churchill resigned the premiership in 1955 he was succeeded by his deputy, Anthony Eden. Eden's post at the Foreign Office was filled by Harold Macmillan, who in turn vacated the Ministry of Defence. Selwyn Lloyd, the Minister of Supply, was moved across to Defence, and Reginald Maudling from the Treasury was moved to Supply. Sir Edward Boyle, the Parliamentary Secretary in Supply, took over Mr Maudling's job, and F. J. Errol MP stepped up into Boyle's.

Unable now to devote enough time to his responsibilities on the board of Ashanti Goldfields, Mr Errol resigned his directorship of that company. Ashanti Goldfields quickly found his successor in Mr Leonard Fowey, an accountant with Financial Consultants Mayhew and Barber. Mayhew and Barber advertised for a replacement in *The Times*. Robert Haines from Norfolk applied and was appointed. He announced his departure from the post of Financial Manager at Simpsons Glue Manufacturers of Norwich with unrestrained glee, telling them they could stick their job, which was an old company joke but he couldn't resist it.

The vacancy at Simpsons was duly advertised and it caught the eye of one David Eames, a senior rep from Huntley and Palmer Biscuits in Reading. Tired of a salesman's life on the road, and looking for something more office-based, David Eames applied to Simpsons, was interviewed and was told he was totally unsuitable. However, they did have another vacancy in quality control which they thought he might like. David said he would like it very much thank you, and he and his family left Reading to put down roots in Norfolk.

Huntley and Palmer promoted an area rep to the position of senior rep. A junior rep was promoted to area rep, thus leaving a vacancy for a junior rep. Huntley and Palmer gave it to the local employment exchange to fill. The job eventually went to Patrick Bolger from South Wales, a man who had secretly always wanted to work with biscuits.

Bolger's job in a car showroom on the outskirts of Swansea was filled by Eddie Rowley, an assistant delivery manager from a Royal Mail sorting office on the Dorset coast, who had moved to South Wales when his wife inherited a guesthouse there. His job at the sorting office was filled by internal promotion, by the chief facer-canceller. A postman higher-grade was promoted to the facer-canceller tables. A postman lower-grade was promoted to postman higher-grade. This left a vacancy for a postman lower-grade. The job was advertised in the local press and a woman named Gwen Peacock drew a circle around it and shoved it under the nose of her seventeen-year-old, Clive.

Clive Peacock wrote off just to please his mother. An application form came back. Under hobbies Clive wrote cycling and natural history. He made up the bit about natural history.

He was called for an interview. He borrowed his friend Ralph's suit whose trousers were three inches too long for him. Before he went into the interview room he removed his National Health spectacles, out of vanity.

The interview went smoothly enough. The recruitment officer was impressed by Clive's enthusiasm for cycling. He was puzzled by his ignorance of natural history, but since it was a cycle-postman the GPO were looking for rather than a botanist, he wasn't overly concerned. The only tricky part of the interview came at the end when Clive, unsure whether it was time to leave or not, stumbled over an ashtray stand. He was never sure if it was his borrowed trousers or his eyesight that was to blame.

Three days later, ten months and one week since Winston Churchill had stepped down, the job chain ended when Clive received a letter offering him the position of postman. He accepted. It was his first real job and, he quickly realised, the only one he would ever want.

# 2

CLIVE PEACOCK LOST his job at the Post Office thirty-five years later, on a bright but unsettled morning in the second week of July, the morning the Optical Speedsort machine arrived.

It lay silent at one end of the sorting office, a machine the size of a locomotive, painted battleship grey and with red and green buttons. It could sort 45,000 letters an hour. It could read typeface. It could sort letters into postal zones, then into streets, then into house numbers. Clive stood a safe distance away and fiddled with the change in his pocket.

The morning shift was in progress. The barn of the sorting office was warm with the friction of letters running along conveyor belts. Everyone worked in shirtsleeves. Barney Loxton called out to Clive. Clive couldn't hear him above the noise, but he nodded anyway.

He walked round the Optical Speedsort machine. It was greased and oiled and had sharp edges. He nodded and smacked his lips and dared himself to reach out and touch it.

'What do you reckon then, Clive?' said Peter Robson, making him jump. Clive cocked his head, inflated and slowly deflated his cheeks.

'It arrived during the night. Came on a juggernaut from Swindon with a police escort. Wide Load written all over it.' Peter Robson ran a finger along the side and tutted. 'It's got scratched, look.'

Clive nodded and said: 'Phew, some machine.'

'Forty-five thousand letters an hour, Clive. She'll read the addresses on the envelopes, for heaven's sake. Comes with her own engineer – Desmond over there.' Peter Robson nodded towards a man sitting on a stool reading a newspaper. 'That's progress staring you in the face, that is.'

Clive searched the Optical Speedsort machine for a face. Most machines had faces if you looked for them. The canceller tables had two insect eyes where the lights grew out of the beam. The coding desks had a conveyor belt of a mouth and a stop-button for a nose. The pre-sorters had a long chin and sad smile, and the automatic sorters had a curled lip.

But this one, this Optical Speedsort machine, it was expressionless. And when Clive did reach out and touch it the metal was cold.

'We might have to move again you know, Clive. There are 34,000 square feet here but it's not big enough. They're going to have to put one of the canceller tables in the snooker room as it is. Still, that's progress.'

Clive shook his head, then nodded.

'Anyway,' said Peter Robson, 'I'm glad I caught you before you went out. Come into my office. I've some good news for you.'

Peter Robson was Delivery Manager and he was under stress. That was what he told everyone anyway. He said to Clive: 'Introducing new technology into the sorting process is the best and worst part of my job, you know.'

On his desk was a model of Concorde and on the wall a picture of Norway. Peter Robson had been brought in by the Post Office a year ago. He had a reputation as a coordinator; he was an ergonomist. That was what he told everyone anyway. He had a smell about him that Clive imagined was the smell of Norway – a sort of toothpaste smell.

As Delivery Manager Peter Robson had his own electric cordless kettle. He made some tea with milk from the miniature fridge he'd had installed at his own expense. Then he pulled out a key-ring on a piece of string from his pocket, unlocked a drawer in his desk and took out a

Tupperware box in which he kept a packet of shortbread; an elastic band over the top kept the biscuits extra fresh.

'Tea and biscuits,' said Peter Robson. 'Nothing beats it, but technology, in the form of Tupperware containers and cordless kettles, can improve it.'

He put two biscuits on a plate, wrapped the packet up carefully, put the elastic band back on, returned the packet to the Tupperware box and the Tupperware box to the drawer. Then he locked the drawer and put the key-ring back in his trouser pocket. There had once been a debate in the canteen over whether Peter Robson ironed his under-pants.

'Oh yes, that's a wonderful machine they've invented there,' said Peter Robson, following a route in his mind's eye out of his office, down the corridor, left at the entrance to Parcels and back out on to the letter sorting floor. 'You know how it works?'

'No,' said Clive, 'not exactly.' But then Clive didn't know how Concorde worked either, nor the fridge, nor the telephone on the desk.

'A computerised eye, that's how.' Peter Robson leaned forward as if he was about to deliver the Six O'Clock News. 'It'll increase efficiency almost fifty per cent, that's what they forecast.'

Increased efficiency. That was a phrase Clive had heard many times in the previous thirty-five years. And yet he still came in to work every morning at five-thirty, sorted his first delivery, delivered it to Beaconsfield Hill on his bicycle, emptied the box at the end of the round, returned to the sorting office for breakfast, then repeated the whole operation and went home. The only effect increased efficiency had had on him was that, because the new premises needed to house all the machinery were out of town, he was now allowed to take his bike home at night.

'You can't stand in the way of progress, can you?' said Peter Robson.

'Not these days,' said Clive.

'And this is just the start. Fifty-one million letters, on

average, the Post Office handles every day, delivering to 24 million delivery points, via 100,000 mail collection points.'

On the notice board above Peter Robson's head was the announcement of the trainee sorters versus supervisors football match. Clive recalled the last time he played for the postmen's side. They lost sixteen–nil against the frankers. He scored an own goal. It was after that match that he realised there was something badly wrong with his eyes.

'I mean,' went on Peter Robson, now sitting back with his arms behind his head, 'the volume of mail is increasing phenomenally. They said fax machines would be the death of us, but no way. By 1995 every household will get three pieces of unsolicited mail a day. Think about that.'

Clive thought about it. For thirty-five years he had done as he was told down at the sorting office. Clive liked to know where he had to stand.

'I read somewhere,' said Peter Robson – now stood up in front of the picture of Norway so that his head was framed by fjords – 'that they're working on robot postmen. Each street will have grooves and each house will have a sort of . . . slip rail I suppose, and every morning after the letters have been through the computerised sorting machines they'll be deposited in little computerised metal postmen who will set off and pop the letters through the letterboxes. Like you do now.'

Clive corrugated his brow. Peter Robson sat down again. He suddenly seemed nervous; he was stalling. He said: 'Invest and reinvest in technology, that's always the best policy. That Optical Speedsort machine out there will mean that this sorting office will be able to handle twice as many letters per day as it could before. Any letter that comes in here will go out again at twice the speed. Any idea what that will mean, Clive?'

'Well . . .' said Clive.

'It will mean that all outward letters will leave this office twice as quickly. Every van will leave this depot with twice as many letters. All inward mail will be sorted at double the rate. When postmen come into work each morning there will be twice as many letters waiting. You know what that means?'

'You're going to need more postmen.'

'Wrong. Less postmen, but more efficient ones.'

Clive nodded.

'So. The rest of the country may be having a hard time of it, but things have never looked better for the Post Office.'

'Good,' said Clive.

'And it means good news for you, Clive.'

'Good,' said Clive.

'Well, you've been here a long time. You have seniority of position among our delivery staff.'

'Thank you, Peter.'

'Postman of the Year, two years running – correct?'

'1967, and '68.'

'Exactly.'

Peter Robson leaned forward again.

'The thing is, Clive, you don't have a driving licence, do you?'

'No,' nodded Clive.

'And you see, that machine is going to churn letters out by the vanload – literally. Bicycles just aren't going to be able to cope any more. Bicycles are being phased out. Two-hundredweight Leyland Dafs are being phased in.'

'Well, yes,' said Clive and remembered he had to call in at the bike shop on the way home and buy a new spoke key.

'It's going to mean redundancies for some folk, unfortunately.'

Clive swallowed. They wouldn't . . .

'Not for you though, you lucky devil.'

'No, I didn't think . . .'

'No, of course not. Not you. You're going to get early retirement.'

'Early retirement,' echoed Clive, and his legs started to shake.

'You've earned it, Clive.'

He could feel his face drain, and then his leg was banging the underside of the desk. Everyone had been warned that the new technology would mean job losses, but they were always on the sorting office floor. No one had ever suggested the delivery staff was in danger. How could it be? No matter how fast they sorted the letters, they always needed people to shove the things through doors.

Peter Robson was looking at him, expecting him to say something, so Clive said: 'I'd like some time to think about it, please, Peter.'

Peter Robson clicked his tongue and then laughed. 'You're a card, Clive. Early retirement is what everyone your age dreams about.'

Clive said: 'I don't know, Peter. Early retirement.'

'I don't believe you, Clive. You're fifty-two! You've been here thirty-five years; you're all paid up. You'd be barmy not to take it. You don't get chances like this very often.'

Early retirement. It had been the last thing on his mind when he'd climbed on his bike that morning. He'd seen colleagues drool at the sound of those two words, and yet Clive had never understood the attraction. 'What are the other cyclists doing?' he asked.

'They can all drive.'

'How about a walk? I could do a walk instead.'

'We've got all the walkers we need, you see. Of course we could relocate you if you were that keen. You'd have to move to another area and everything though. Wouldn't really be worth it.'

'I could learn to drive. I've been meaning to.'

Peter Robson said: 'Do you really think the old eyesight is up to it, Clive?' and he smiled carefully. Clive smiled with him. He knew more about Peter Robson than Peter Robson realised. He knew the sort of tactics he was capable of. When the Robson family arrived a year ago they had lived on Beaconsfield Hill for a time before they moved over to the Westcliff, and Clive had been their postman. Clive knew, for instance, that Peter Robson had moles in his front lawn, and he knew that Peter Robson used to put

9

two traffic bollards outside his house each morning to reserve his parking space. He also knew that the way Peter Robson had solved both problems was to concrete his front lawn and park his car on it.

'Just how early would my early retirement be, Peter?' said Clive, bringing his knee under control.

'Well, you could stay until the end of the month, but they're switching the Optical Speedsort on proper next Tuesday. So you might as well go after Monday. You've earned it.'

Clive was still nodding. Peter Robson said: 'So. Congratulations.'

'Thank you very much.'

Peter Robson was looking at him blankly. Clive's problem of not knowing when to leave hadn't improved over the years. Throughout his life he had wondered whether he should have left earlier or stayed longer.

'We had to get this machine, you see,' said Peter Robson. 'It reads the addresses.'

Clive thought: I can read the addresses too, you know. My eyesight isn't that bad.

'And don't worry about retirement, Clive. You'll love it. Look at Kevin Ellis, got retirement last month. He's found himself a nice little part-time job somewhere, and he's taken up wood-carving. You should see the decoy ducks he does. Never been happier.'

Now was the time to leave, Clive decided. He made a move in his chair, and immediately Peter Robson was on his feet and Clive realised he should have left about two minutes earlier. He stood up and his hand moved automatically towards his pocket in search of some loose change to play with. Peter Robson thought he was reaching out to shake hands and so he stretched out his own. When Clive put his hand in his pocket Peter grinned and withdrew, pretending to button his coat, but by that time Clive had realised Peter Robson wanted to shake hands and had pulled his hand out of his pocket again and was offering it

10

to be shaken. This time Peter Robson grabbed it and shook it firmly. His grin was like a U-bend.

Clive positioned himself at his sorting box, legs apart, stomach in, shoulders back, perfectly balanced. After thirty-five years he could sort his mail as smoothly as any machine.

'Did you see that new mini-series last night?' said Nigel Sweeney from the neighbouring booth. 'The one about prostitutes in Russia?'

'No, I missed it,' said Clive.

Margaret Rogerson, his other neighbour, said: 'I taped it – probably never get round to watching it though. That's the trouble with a video.'

Above them a computerised newsreel flashed red letters around the room: 'Congratulations to all!!! Area Sorting Office of the Month for the third time in two years.'

Barney Loxton shouted to Clive again from his pre-sorter machine. Clive still couldn't hear him. This time he shook his head.

'Calling all blood donors,' flashed the newsreel. 'The mobile unit will be in the car park from midday today.'

Clive wrapped his letters in elastic bands, stowed them in his bag and hurried out. He didn't want to tell anyone just yet. He needed to get outside.

In the yard he climbed on his bike and rode over the traffic humps and out of the depot. He cycled through the industrial estate, across the bypass via the Eucalyptus roundabout – trees donated by Twin Town Livorno, north-west Italy – and joined the one-way system through town. The traffic was clogged, choking on its own exhaust. Clive wound his way through the jam until he reached the hospital, where he ducked under a barrier and pedalled through the car park to Maternity, then down an alleyway past Radiology, until he emerged at Casualty where he joined the hospital's own one-way system. This led him over three more traffic humps to the exit. He waved to Stanley on the gate, then turned left down to the harbour.

11

Now he could hear gulls, and smell seaweed. He put his head back, breathed deeply, and pedalled along the waterfront towards Beaconsfield Hill. He usually began to accelerate fifty yards before the incline but today it was a hundred. His jacket filled with the breeze; he hit the slope flying and he was up that hill in under thirty seconds, just as he had been twice a day for the last thirty-five years. At the top he stopped and gazed over the rise to the estuary and the mudflats. He felt as fit as the day he had joined the Post Office. His slim frame was just as supple; his lungs still filled every corner of his chest.

He slotted a bank statement through the Lemsfords' box and a brochure from Distant Dreams Holidays through Mr Denbigh's. He slipped a letter from Cardiff through Mrs Wheatley's on Holme Road, and a postcard from Portugal through the Haddens' – he couldn't help reading the line 'Frank says he has had his pocket picked twice so far'.

At Mr Parfitt's on Tarr Avenue, where there was a No Smoking sign on the front gate, he delivered a bill from British Telecom. At Mr Hardy-Lewis's house, set back from the others on top of the hill, he put a large white manila envelope into the metal-plated cavity in the wall. Two Dobermans insulted him from behind electronic gates. It started to rain and he pulled his hood up.

He poked a blood donor reminder card through the door of Mr Pitman on Rockley Road and then there was one for his own house opposite, a DIY catalogue for his wife. He squeezed past the concrete mixer on the front path and slipped the catalogue as gently as he could through the box, making sure the lid didn't slam. Christine worked nights and would only just have gone to bed.

An hour later he had two letters left. The address on one was 'Ken (the house on the corner) Wyman Crescent?' But that was good enough for Clive. He knew Ken – Ken Tidy. Ken and Clive were members of the same Neighbourhood Watch.

The other letter was for Gayle Hovis, 38 Prospect Road,

and he always liked delivering letters to Gayle Hovis. He reached the bungalow and strode down the garden path. The Hovises had lived there twenty-four years. Clive had delivered the congratulations telegrams the day Gayle was born. He'd walked down that path with her birthday cards and valentine cards, with letters from the kibbutz she once went to work on, and, for the last three years, letters from the University of Lancaster. Now he had hold of a smart white envelope marked Board of Examiners.

Clive weighed the letter in his hand. It was a pass, he knew it was. He'd been a postman long enough to recognise a letter bearing good news rather than bad. He hesitated briefly then dropped the envelope through the door and hurried away – he could hear footsteps on the stairs. He imagined Gayle in her dressing gown, picking up the letter and knowing what it contained. She'd prop it up against the cereal box as she ate breakfast – no, she'd be too nervous to eat breakfast – she'd just look at the envelope, her parents sitting by her in support. Then she'd find the courage to open it and she'd shriek and her parents would hug her, and there'd be a few tears and then a bottle of champagne perhaps. It was frightening what a letter could do if it put its mind to it.

He cycled back along the harbour. The thought that all this was going to end on Monday made him search for some reaction, that knot in his stomach, but all he had was the urge to get off his bicycle and walk for a while.

Someone called out from the Harbour Lights, 'What's up with the bike, Clive?' Clive couldn't see properly who it was but he called back, 'Puncture.'

Later, sitting in the mobile blood donor caravan, with his sleeve rolled up, and the needle sparkling in the corner of his vision, it occurred to him that that was exactly how he felt – punctured. And, instead of turning away from the needle, he looked, and he could see the blood being slowly drained out of him.

# 3

AT ONE O'CLOCK he left the sorting office and cycled home. On a lamppost at the bottom of his road a notice had been attached: 'Notice is hereby given that the District Council, after consultation with the Chief Officer of Police and in accordance with Section 90c of the Highways Act 1980, intend to establish one road hump on Rockley Road. Any objection to the proposed hump should be made to Mrs E. Hartford, Chief Divisional Executive (Humps). Extension 36.'

Clive thought of Mrs E. Hartford sitting at her desk, waiting for objections to her humps. He had never written any graffiti before in his life but he felt the urge now. He wanted to write: 'Mrs E. Hartford I love your humps.' But he controlled himself.

As he approached his house he saw Christine up on the roof. She was replacing the ridge tiles with some ornamental Victorian equivalents she'd salvaged from somewhere. The Peacocks' house consisted largely of Victorian equivalents Christine had salvaged from somewhere.

Clive called up to her: 'I've got some news.'

She turned her radio down and screwed up her nose.

He called louder. 'I've got some good news.'

Christine gave a precise shrug – I'll talk to you later; I'll be up here for a while yet. Then she turned her radio back up .

Clive went indoors and pulled the *Examiner* out of the letterbox. 'Wednesday is One-Way Day' read the headline, and Clive tripped over the antique umbrella-stand Christine had bought in a boot sale: price £12, value £120.

He hissed, and rubbed his shin. She'd been rearranging the furniture again. Clive felt like a stranger in his own home sometimes, but this was because Christine was forever rearranging the furniture.

14

In the sitting room he pulled back the curtains and sat down with the *Examiner*. 'Man Drives Car Through Travel Agent's Window'. 'Local Woman Sneezes For Two Weeks'. From beneath the chaise longue across the room Christine's breakfast plate and cup waved at him.

On page four was a picture of Mayor Eddie Hicks, balanced on an exercise bicycle, at the start of his Slima-thon – proceeds in aid of a Variety Club sunshine bus. Underneath his picture the caption read: 'Local woman swims Channel'.

On page five was a picture of Mrs Rita Pilling from 23 Beech Road emerging from the water at Calais with an unconvincing grin. Underneath was the caption 'Mayor gets on bike for charity'.

Pages eight and nine were the ones that interested Clive, though. They contained a map of the revised one-way system, and he sighed when he saw that the harbour was to be included in the new scheme. It would mean that to get to work now he would have a lengthy detour down . . . but then he remembered that after Monday he wouldn't be going to work any more.

There was a photograph underneath the map. It was of Raymond Catterall, the Town Surveyor. He had bags under his eyes. On either side of him stood his staff. Third from the left was Mrs E. Hartford from Humps.

Clive picked up the Edwardian telephone, the one Christine had salvaged when they demolished the railway station: cost £5, value £45. He called the civic centre and asked for extension 36.

'Humps,' said a woman's voice. And Clive gently hung up.

Retirement will mean more time in the garden, he thought, as he surveyed the fourteen spring onions that occupied the row between his eighteen carrots and his five potato plants.

But he didn't need more time in the garden. The plot was tiny – reduced to ten feet by fifteen feet after Christine had put up a sun lounge extension – and it yielded as much as it possibly could. The previous year he had lost only two (out of nine) leeks, and one potato plant (out of six) had been a bit of a disappointment; otherwise he'd reaped all he'd sown. Precision, that was the watchword of the small-scale gardener. And discipline, of course.

He realigned his one courgette fractionally, and corrected a potential tangle in the two runner bean shoots. Gardening was like housework really. He often had the urge to vacuum the soil.

Christine was still up on the roof with her radio; she had a Thermos flask up there. Clive waved to her and she waved back. He was going on to the mudflats, he mimed. The wind dropped briefly and Clive could hear the radio and the Malcolm Dixon phone-in show for sexual, marital and emotional problems. Christine was up on the roof listening to sexual, marital and emotional problems from all over the country.

'I can't stand the deceit any more,' cried Elizabeth from Chester, and Malcolm Dixon's advice was lost as the wind picked up again.

Clive climbed down the low cliffs behind the house and joined the footpath that swung around the mudflats. He took his glasses off and scanned the distance. The sun was bright but a cloud bank was mustering out to sea. Someone called out his name, and there was Ralph upstream, a figure in wellingtons wearing headphones and being led by a metal detector as if he was walking a dog.

Clive walked slowly towards him. The evening was peaceful with familiar noises: the burp of his footsteps in the mud, the hum of the traffic on the ring road beyond the industrial estate.

Ralph and Clive greeted each other with their eyebrows. 'You did this patch last week,' said Clive.

'The mud shifts, Clive.' Ralph yelled to compensate for his headphones. 'No patch of ground is ever the same two days running. That's the joy of metal detecting.'

They wandered upstream. A heron loped under the elec-

16

tricity cables and landed in the mud up to its knees. The sun shone on the Bejam factory and then was suddenly gone as the cloud bank swallowed it whole. Clive and Ralph didn't say much. They had grown up together. Clive could never remember not knowing Ralph; he was always there in the background of every memory.

'Guess what,' announced Clive. 'I'm being given early retirement.'

Ralph considered this, then shouted: 'Congratulations.'

'Thank you,' said Clive.

'No, really,' said Ralph, and he took his headphones off as a sign of respect. 'What does Christine say?'

'I haven't told her yet.'

'You've got to tell her.'

'Of course I'm going to tell her. She was up on the roof when I got home.'

'You're a lucky man, Clive.'

'I'm not prepared for it, you know. It's come as a shock.'

'I meant you're a lucky man having Christine as a wife.'

'Oh,' said Clive.

'You'll have more time with her now you're retired.'

'Yes, I know.'

Ralph put his headphones back on. He yelled: 'You'll love it, Clive. When I retired from Securicor my life began. I've got much more time for metal detecting now.'

A wind began to swing in off the sea. It bounced off the back of the carburettor factory and whistled inland, a warm wind. And now the cloud bank was clearly a storm, drifting in over the sea trailing chains of rain. How beautiful it looked against the red sky to the west. Clive had a sudden desire to be on his bicycle cycling along a coastal road with a letter to deliver somewhere nice.

'I mean, you're all right for money, aren't you?' bellowed Ralph.

'I suppose so.'

'And if you want more, you could probably get a job down at Superburger with me. I'll ask them for you tomorrow if you like. Then you can get yourself a metal detector.

17

You can get a good Fieldmaster like this second-hand for about sixty quid, one of them with a full ferrous disc, auto or . . .' Ralph stiffened and adjusted his headphones. A Long Vehicle applied air brakes on the ring road with a scream, but Ralph's concentration was total. Ralph had a theory that the Viking King Raedrik had been buried on these mudflats in AD 879 with all his jewels, treasures and articles of war. He'd been looking for the site for four years now, and for four years all he'd found was ring-pull tops. This hadn't discouraged him though, as now he swept the mud with his detector and homed in on one spot which looked just like all the other spots but which, from the expression on Ralph's face, was undoubtedly the spot where King Raedrik lay buried.

Clive held the metal detector as Ralph pulled on his gardening kneepads and knelt on the mud. From his pocket he pulled a trowel and slowly began to excavate.

The dusk came. The storm seemed to be anchored out over the bay. The river turned inky and the tide bore in. Ralph probed with the precision of a surgeon. Eventually he emerged with a ring-pull top from a Diet Pepsi can. 'Bugger,' he said, and put it in his pocket with the others.

As they walked back to the road there was a clap of thunder in the distance, but the cloud bank was moving away now and the downpour would fall further up the coast. Clive thought of the night when as Boy Scouts he and Ralph had come down to the beach for a sausage beano. They'd lit fires and wrapped apples up in silver paper to bake, but a thunderstorm had rolled in, and the Akela had said they were too unsheltered, and so they packed up and left the apples uneaten in the bottom of the fire. Akela had lived up the hill on the opposite side of the bay with her husband, who was wheelchair-bound. He taught at the school but lost his job when he struck one of the boys, who had made a joke about his handicap, although no one really knew what his handicap was. The boy was Michael Blight. It was Michael Blight who sold Clive his first bicycle. On that bicycle Clive joined the

18

cycling club with Ralph in 1954. They went on outings every Saturday and Sunday. Clive saved from his Post Office wages and bought a speedometer for his Raleigh. Once he clocked up forty-five miles an hour coming down the hill from the lighthouse. He told everyone at the club but they didn't believe him. So they set up a speed trial. Clive flung himself down the hill and clocked up thirty-eight miles an hour before he hit a rut and flew over his handlebars. He ended up in hospital with a broken arm, off work for a month. The injury still gave him trouble now and again . . .

A rumble of thunder pulled him out of his daydream. Ralph said to him: 'You know that arm you broke when you fell off your bike doing that speed trial?'

'Yes.'

'Do you ever get any trouble from it?'

'Now and again, why?'

'Just wondered,' said Ralph.

When Clive got home, downstairs was in darkness – just the red light from Christine's electric screwdriver recharging in the socket under the stairs, and the glow from two more free newspapers dumped on the doormat.

Christine was in the bath – Clive could hear the radio up there. He put a bowl of lentil and bacon stew into the microwave and watched the timer for two minutes, then carried a tray up the creaking stairs. The staircase had once been part of the town's old courtroom. Christine had wandered inside when they were dismantling it and asked if she could have sections. It hadn't creaked when she put it in but she soon fixed that.

On the landing he called out, 'It's me,' and pushed open the door of the bathroom.

Light splashed out and caught him with his trouser legs still tucked into his socks. Christine was sat in a bath of murky water, her arms and neck suntanned to the T-shirt line, her long back pale. Clive sat on the edge of the bath with his lentils on his lap.

'Finished?' he asked.

'Finished,' she said and poured a jar of water over her head. 'They'll need cementing in though.' And she sank beneath the water again.

The bathroom was the only room in the house that Christine hadn't altered in some way. There were old white tiles, a lino floor and green paintwork. It had been like this for the eight years they had lived here. Clive liked it because it was the only room in the house that he truly recognised.

Christine resurfaced. There was a ring of scum forming round the edge of the enamel. She'd worked hard all day and now she was going out to work all night. She poured another jar over her head and said: 'How would you feel about moving house?'

Clive stopped chewing. He couldn't believe what he'd heard. He said: 'What do you mean, move house? Why on earth should you want to move house? You've put so much work into this house . . .'

'I don't mean change house, I mean move house – change locations. I've heard of this firm in America that actually digs up your house and moves it for you.'

'Moves it where?'

'Wherever you like – up the street, down the street. We could move off Beaconsfield Hill and put this house up on Westcliff. You'd increase the value overnight. A man in Sacramento does it. There's a picture in a magazine downstairs.'

'They wouldn't let you do that here.'

'Ron Bishop would do it, I bet. I think I'll give him a call.'

Clive snorted. He could tell when she was trying to frighten him. And she knew she could push him in impossible directions because he would always stop her just before things went too far. He was useful to her like that.

'I've got some news – good news,' said Clive. 'They've offered me early retirement.'

Christine sat up and turned round to look at him. 'Oh, Clive,' she said at last.

'It's all right. Peter Robson called me into his office. There's this new machine they've got. And they're going to do without bicycles.'

Christine was watching him closely. Water dripped down her face. He hadn't noticed her growing older. These few minutes in the evening when their schedules crossed were the only times they ever really saw each other. When he was retired he'd have more time for things like watching his wife grow older.

Christine sank slowly back into the bath. Her nipples rose to the surface. She said: 'Congratulations.'

'Thank you.'

'No, I mean it. You can't deliver letters for the rest of your life.'

'No.'

'It's great news, Clive.'

'Yes, that's what everyone says.'

'You deserve it. And the traffic is getting so bad these days, I worry about you on your bicycle. Have you thought what you're going to do?'

'What do you mean?'

'Well, what will you do with all the time?'

Clive pretended his mouth was full as he searched for an answer, but then he said, 'This and that.'

'Maybe Ralph can get you a job at Superburger.'

She stood up. Clive put his bowl down and held up a towel for her. As she stepped out some of the bathwater dripped into his lentils. Christine said again: 'You'll have to find something to do if you're going to be retired.'

She rubbed herself hard. She was thinking. 'We could do this place up properly, then move it like I suggested, and sell it. We could make a start at the weekend if you wanted. We could do this bathroom together.'

It was ten o'clock. Clive and Christine went into the bedroom. Clive undressed and put on his pyjamas, took off his glasses and climbed into bed. Christine dressed in her

21

nurse's uniform, put in her contact lenses and went to work.

# 4

THE RAIN MUST have come during the night. The front gate dripped and the tarmac had a deep gloss. Clive oiled his chain and cycled off through the puddles. Christine passed him in the car on her way home and she slowed in case he wanted to say something, but he only waved so she drove on.

When he reached the hospital entrance Stanley the porter stepped out from the lodge with his hand up. 'Sorry, sir,' he said, 'you can't cycle through here unless you have an identity card.'

'It's me, Stanley,' said Clive.

'I know it's you, Clive, but there's a new policy. You can't come through here unless you have a computerised identity card with an up-to-date picture on, sir. I've got to call everyone sir as well.'

'Stanley – it puts another two miles on my journey to go round the one-way system.'

'Don't blame me, sir. It's this new security firm,' and he pointed at his hat. 'They even gave me a medical examination. Unpleasant, that was.'

So Clive cycled right round the one-way system, which left him with no alternative but to negotiate one exit on the ring road. A lorry with French licence plates went past in a cloud of spray. Clive cycled on the hard shoulder but there was no shelter. A van came so close to him the slipstream made him totter. He shouted at it; it was a Post Office van.

When he arrived at work late Peter Robson said: 'Soon be able to lie in every morning, eh, Clive?' and he smirked, and Clive annoyed himself by smirking back.

He sorted out his first delivery. 'Did you see that programme about ants last night?' asked Margaret Rogerson.

'No,' said Clive. 'I must have missed it.'

'I videoed it,' said Nigel Sweeney. 'You can borrow it if you like.'

'Great,' said Clive. 'Thanks.' And he promised himself he would watch more TV when he retired, documentaries about ants and things.

He cycled out of the depot, round the one-way system again, and down to the harbour. The sea and sky met like an old saucepan and lid, and Clive thought: I love this town. They can build as many humps as they like; they can send all the blue cars one way and all the red ones the other; they can plant mini-roundabouts and dig under-passes and roll out ring roads and man everywhere with a security guard, I don't care. I will always love this town. And he pedalled up Beaconsfield Hill Road without notic-ing it.

First letter of the day was an airmail to Mrs Drake. For Mr Hadden, Clive had an envelope that read 'Photos – Do Not Bend'. The letterbox was too small, so he knocked on the door and Mrs Hadden opened it in her dressing gown – the blue one with the white piping. She's had that dressing gown fifteen years, he thought.

For Mr Parfitt on Tarr Avenue a letter from DVLC in Swansea. As Clive walked down the path Parfitt opened his front door, held out a clipboard and said: 'I wonder if you wouldn't mind signing our petition – for residents-only parking restrictions on Beaconsfield Hill.'

'Certainly,' said Clive.

Another manila envelope for Mr Hardy-Lewis, brown this time. Clive put it carefully in the metal-plated cavity in the wall and a Doberman bounded up to the electric gates and curled its lips. Mr Hardy-Lewis had lived in this house for as long as Clive had been a postman. Clive had seen the house gather alarms, and the wall grow higher and higher, until the electric gates and the intercom system were introduced. Clive hadn't seen Mr Hardy-Lewis for years, but now he pressed the bell. The Doberman steamed with rage.

24

The intercom crackled into life. 'Who is it?' yelled Hardy-Lewis.

'It's Clive Peacock, Mr Hardy-Lewis. The postman.'

Clive felt self-conscious talking to a wall; he started to blush. That was another thing he'd try to stop doing when he retired: stop being so self-conscious, and stop blushing so much.

'Something to sign?' said Hardy-Lewis.

'No, no . . .' Clive put his mouth right up to the grid. 'I just wanted to tell you that I'm retiring.'

A dustcart was growling up the hill. Hardy-Lewis said: 'Speak up, there's a good chap.'

'I just wanted to tell you I'm retiring. I wanted to let you know because I've been your postman for thirty-five years. I wanted to say how much I've enjoyed being your postman.' Now I'm grovelling, he thought.

'Well. Thank you very much,' said Hardy-Lewis. 'I've enjoyed having my letters delivered by you.'

The other dog came bounding down the path and pushed its nose through the gate; its teeth were dripping. Clive said: 'I don't know who your new postman will be. He might even be a robot, huh.'

'What's that? Are those dogs annoying you?'

'No, no.' Clive imagined Mr Hardy-Lewis sitting in his armchair, reading the paper and just speaking into thin air.

'They're noisy, I know. Bloody good at what they do though. Don't suppose you want a puppy, do you?'

The dustcart disappeared over the hill munching rubbish. Clive shoved his face against the wall. A caterpillar crawled through a crack in the brickwork towards his nose. 'No, thank you, Mr Hardy-Lewis.'

'Never mind. Now listen. Retirement. It can be a problem. Get yourself a hobby. Look at Leonard Bernstein. He didn't have a hobby. He retired on the Tuesday and he was dead on the Friday. They showed *West Side Story* on the television twice that month. Me, I got interested in UFOs. I'm a damn sight busier now than I ever was when

I worked. I'm going to Warminster on Friday on a UFO-spotting weekend. More UFO sightings in Warminster than anywhere else in the country. They've chosen Warminster for some reason.'

'Thank you very much for the advice, Mr Hardy-Lewis,' said Clive.

'You're welcome,' said Hardy-Lewis.

Clive cycled through the rest of his round. He was a witness to a road accident in which a D reg. Escort clipped the side of Mr Hovis's G reg. Astra.

He found a ginger cat which he was sure was Mrs Tidy's Bruce, whose disappearance had been advertised on telegraph poles throughout the area for the last month. He spent a long time persuading that cat to come home. When he got to Mrs Tidy's she said it was nothing like Bruce.

On Spring Road he took a photo of the Gill twins aged eighty-seven with their own camera as they stood proudly in front of their roses.

At the end of the round Clive stopped at the mailbox on Waverley Road, unlocked it and took out the collection. There were never more than a handful of letters at this time of day. He read the addresses dreamily; each one was like a journey. In this batch alone were tickets to Wales, to Newcastle, to London and one airmail about to set off on a voyage to New Zealand. He cycled back to the depot with the envelopes feeling hot in his bag, and again he had to stop and shake his head to remind himself that this really was all coming to an end the following week. He had never imagined a life without letters. He needed to post letters.

The Optical Speedsort machine had begun to throb that morning, and it looked more bloated now. People had started to call it the OS but Clive didn't want to become familiar with it. He gave it room as he passed, as if it were another Doberman on a leash.

He went to the canteen and sat next to Rolf Milne. Rolf smiled at his newspaper and said: 'Listen to this. It says here that according to a new poll taken by a leading coffee manufacturer, sixty-five per cent of couples would rather have a nice hot drink and an early night than sex.'

Clive struggled with the wrapper round a handy-pack of Royal Scot. It tore and two of the three biscuits fell on the floor and shattered. He ducked beneath the table to pick up the bits and noticed Rolf had odd socks on. He heard him say: 'I don't believe it – have you read this?'

There was never any need to buy a newspaper if you sat next to Rolf Milne.

'It says here that the Chinese are going to build an exact replica of Benidorm off the Canton coast. "We looked at all European resorts and Benidorm impressed us the most," said Lee Chan, from the Chinese Ministry of Tourism.'

Clive said: 'I've been meaning to tell you something, Rolf. I've been meaning to tell you I'm retiring. I'm being given early retirement.'

'I know that, Clive.' Rolf closed his paper. 'I've been meaning to say "Congratulations". Congratulations.'

'Thank you. How did you know?'

'It's up on the newsreel there, look. You're getting a retirement breakfast.'

Up on the digital newsreel, after the news that all employees wanting to go shopping to Boulogne on the Bank Holiday should have their names on the list by Wednesday, came the announcement of Clive's retirement. 'Clive Peacock, Postman of the Year 1967 and '68, is retiring next week. Well done, Clive. Three cheers. Breakfast on July 18th in the canteen at 9.00 am. Everyone welcome.'

'I'll be there,' said Rolf. 'You can count on me. When Kelvin Parker retired everyone clubbed together and got him a Stripper.'

Clive's first thought was of that tool of Christine's that you plugged in and it vibrated the wallpaper off the wall.

'They got him a golf iron as well, of course,' said Rolf.

On the way home Clive called in at the Job Centre and the library. In the Job Centre sixteen people stood with their hands in their pockets, browsing: 'HGV Class III

27

wanted immediately.' 'Car Park attendant needed.' 'Traffic Warden required.' 'Vacancy exists for Garage pump attendant.' Clive wanted a part-time job that would bring him in a little extra, that was all.

A giant of a man stood gormlessly in front of the catering vacancies. He said, 'Shit,' and walked to the door. The room filled with the sound of traffic then fell hushed again.

Clive ended up at the Just Arrived board, which was empty, and then he found himself at a desk with a computer and a packet of Rolos.

He sat down and rehearsed the speech he'd give at his retirement breakfast. 'I've had so many happy times here at the Post Office . . . In my time I have seen many changes . . . Since I've been a postman the postal service has of course been revolutionised.'

The first speech he'd ever given in his life, and it was his retirement speech. There was something sad about that, he reflected. 'I'll be able to spend a lot more time on hobbies now.' That was what they wanted to hear.

A door at the rear of the office opened. The ranks of the unemployed looked up and examined the smartly dressed woman walking towards her desk. She sat down and slipped a name tag in her display case: Ms H. Kinsella. Then she pressed one button on the computer and smiled at Clive. Clive smiled back.

'How can I help you?' said Ms Kinsella.

'I'm after a part-time job,' said Clive.

'Fill in one of these, please,' she said and pushed him a card.

Outside a lorry ground its gears and everyone winced. Clive filled in the form and slid it back to Ms Kinsella.

'You're interested in delivery?'

'That's right.'

Her fingers tapped the keyboard softly. Clive could see orange stars jumping in her eyes. 'You can't drive?' she said.

'No.'

She tapped the keys again. 'Keyboard skills?'

'No, sorry.'

'And you don't drive, you say?'

'No.'

'Any languages?'

'Er . . . no.' Clive could see jobs scrolling through her eyeballs.

'And you're sure you can't drive?'

'No,' said Clive.

'Not even a fork-lift?'

'No.'

She gave the keyboard a firm poke. 'Shame,' she said.

'Mmm,' said Clive.

Then the computer buzzed back and Ms Kinsella said: 'Ahh! Here's one for you. The *Link*, that new free newspaper, they want a delivery man three hours each evening. That would be perfect, wouldn't it?'

'Well . . .'

'When can you start?'

'Well . . .'

'Wednesday?'

'Well . . . I suppose.'

'Good,' said Ms Kinsella, and she picked up the phone and popped a Rolo in her mouth.

The library was much noisier than the Job Centre. The main reason for this was a large and florid man whose clothes were torn and smelled of decay, who swayed on his feet, and who pointed a dirty finger at a librarian as he shouted, 'You've upset me, you have.'

Clive wandered round the aisles. Two schoolgirls were arm-wrestling in Reference. A toddler was running around pulling books off the bottom shelves. Behind a desk marked Information a librarian talked about tennis on the telephone. Retirement would give him time to read, Clive had told himself, but he felt out of touch with things like books; surrounded by so many he felt overcome by indecision.

He sat down by the shelf marked America. Between the bookcases he could see a couple kissing in the private study area. A row of books on the American West caught his eye.

He pulled out *The Story of the Pony Express*. On the front cover was an old advertisement – 'Wanted: Lean and wiry fellows. Expert riders willing to risk death daily. Orphans Preferred. Wages: $25 a week.'

The book fell open and Clive read: 'With news of President Lincoln's inaugural address in his saddlebag, Pony Express rider Bob Halsam was just past Cold Springs, Nevada, when Paiute Indians ambushed him. One by one he picked them off with his twin revolvers, but then an arrow embedded into his arm, hit the bone and remained there quivering. Bob galloped on, but then another arrow tore into his cheek, knocking out five teeth and breaking his jaw. His faithful pony Old Buck carried him into Middle Gate relay station. There he spent a few minutes tending his wounds and finished his run to Fort Churchill. He covered 120 miles in eight hours in a fastest ever Pony Express ride that took the mail from St Joseph, Missouri, to Sacramento, California, in seven days seventeen hours.'

Clive could feel his pulse racing. He took the book straight to the front desk, where the large drunken man with the stale clothing was saying, 'I'm not leaving until I have a personal apology from the manager.'

The Beaconsfield Hill Neighbourhood Watch met that night, round at Mr Denbigh's house on Tarr Avenue.

There were eighty-three members in total. Only fourteen ever turned up – the same fourteen. The Neighbourhood Watch was just one part of a community club that organised barbecues, outings, Christmas parties, talks on public safety. Fourteen people always turned up to these events: the same fourteen.

Mr Denbigh let Clive in. 'We've not started yet,' he said. 'Only five here so far.' Clive took his jacket off. Ralph's metal detector was propped against the wall.

He followed Denbigh into the living room. Mrs Tidy and the Haddens were there. Clive said hello without looking at anyone and sat next to Ralph. Ralph grunted. He was reading the Distant Dream holiday brochure he'd found on Mr Denbigh's coffee table; he looked confused by it. Clive played with the change in his pockets.

The Drakes arrived in their Toyota, even though they only lived round the corner. And then Mrs Atherton limped in with her towel and washbag. She was sixty-nine and lived in the only house on Beaconsfield Hill still without a bathroom. She sat down and said: 'I'm having my new hip put in on Thursday.'

'Wonderful,' said Clive.

'I'll be able to do anything but go horse-riding, the doctor says.'

'Never mind,' said Ralph.

The Lemsfords arrived. Mrs Lemsford was carrying a tin with a picture of Prince Andrew and Sarah Ferguson on the outside and thirteen flapjacks inside.

Mrs Wheatley arrived and entertained everyone by setting off her anti-assault alarm. And then Mr Parfitt showed up with his petition for residents' parking.

'Only Mr Pitman left . . . so we'll start,' said Denbigh. 'Anyone with any news to share?' He looked round the room. Everyone looked at everyone else. Mrs Tidy said: 'I've still not found my cat Bruce, but that's not really news.'

'I reckon it's cat thieves,' said Mr Drake. 'They steal them for the fur.'

'They export them. I read it in one of the colour magazines,' said Mrs Hadden.

'Let's not start this again,' said Denbigh.

'I've a question,' said Mr Lemsford. 'Anyone know what size batteries a smoke alarm takes?'

'I'm doing away with alarms,' said Mrs Wheatley. 'I'm enrolling in the self-defence course for the over-fifties down at the College.'

There was a knock on the door. Denbigh went and let in Mr Pitman – Detective Sergeant Pitman of the local police force – who lived on Rockley Road, who always attended Neighbourhood Watch meetings and who was always fifteen minutes late.

31

'We're just having question time, Mr Pitman,' said Denbigh.

'I was just saying that I think we should do away with alarms and such niceties and all enrol on the martial arts course down at the College,' said Mrs Wheatley.

Detective Sergeant Pitman stuck his lower lip out in response. In the opposite corner of the room Clive was trying to think of a hobby he could take up. But I've got a hobby, he kept telling himself; delivering letters is my hobby.

Denbigh said: 'Well, if we're all through with questions . . .'

'I've a question,' said Pitman. 'There was a theft the other night in the Beaconsfield Hill vicinity. Eighty-five traffic cones disappeared from the road works on Enderby roundabout. I just wondered if anyone saw anything that might help police with their enquiries?'

'Why steal eighty-five traffic cones?' said Ralph.

'Why steal a cat?' said Mrs Tidy.

'We don't have a motive,' said Pitman.

'Hmm,' said Clive.

Pitman smacked his lips. 'So no one saw anything?'

Everyone looked at everyone else again. Mr Drake said: 'There are some new people moved in opposite us. Bit suspicious. I don't know much about them except they're from Colchester, and they've got two cars and three children, and she works as a dental receptionist in the Health Centre, and they haven't put any rubbish out since they've been here. They've got a satellite dish as well. You could check them out.'

Pitman glanced at him tiredly. Denbigh filled the gap in the conversation. 'Right, then,' he said. 'Next item on the agenda, the Beaconsfield Hill Neighbourhood Watch annual outing.'

'Oh, good,' said Mrs Atherton.

'How about Stratford-upon-Avon and a matinée at the Royal Shakespeare Theatre?' suggested Denbigh.

'You want to watch for the foreign tourists in Stratford-upon-Avon, I've heard,' said Mr Hadden.

'Yes, they smash the car windows and steal your handbag while you're stopped at traffic lights,' said Mrs Wheatley.

Denbigh was undeterred. 'I can organise transport, a lunch in a restaurant called La Langoustine which I've heard is very good, and a ticket for *The Tempest*, all for £34 a person.'

'I could make some scones for the journey,' said Mrs Lemsford.

Pitman stood up and patted his pockets for his keys. 'You don't mind if I leave, do you? It's late-night shopping at Asda.'

'Of course not, Mr Pitman. Any special advice now that the holiday season is upon us?'

'Um . . . no, not really, just tell a neighbour if you're going away, and cancel the newspapers.'

'They still shove four of the things through your door every day,' said Mrs Wheatley.

Denbigh showed Pitman out and returned rubbing his hands. 'Stratford-upon-Avon it is, then. Any more questions?'

'Will the water be hot enough for my bath now?' said Mrs Atherton.


Clive wandered home. He never said anything at meetings. He'd been like that even at school – the quiet one at the back of the class. He had a knack of nodding knowingly and convincing teachers he was brighter than he looked – an impression that lasted until exam-time, when he failed everything. His problem was he only ever thought of the right thing to say when he'd fully digested the information, weighed up the evidence for and against, and then come to an opinion by a process of elimination. By that time two weeks had normally passed.

He walked down Tarr Avenue and turned up Rockley Road. A car came screaming round the corner at speed, swerving across the road and riding up the kerb as it skidded into Wyman Crescent and roared off. 'Baby on Board' said the sticker in the rear window.

# 5

ON SUNDAY CLIVE got up at 4.45 as usual. He left Christine beneath her cloud base of covers and went downstairs. By the kitchen door he tripped over the antique umbrella-stand, newly moved from the hallway. He kicked it and hurt his foot. Then he made some tea and stood at the sun lounge window watching the mudflats turn from dark grey to light grey.

A magazine lay open in the middle of the floor. Clive picked it up and disturbed a plate lying beneath. On the plate were toasted crusts indented with teeth marks, Christine's teeth – he would have recognised them anywhere.

The magazine was folded open on a picture of a man from California, a man named Mark Giannini who had a big moustache and sunglasses and now had a smear of butter and toast crumbs across his face. Below him was a picture of his three-storey house being towed away on a trailer to its new location on 25th Street. 'I just got tired of my neighbourhood,' said forty-four-year-old Giannini.

It was a joke, surely, thought Clive. No one dug up their house and moved it down the street. But this was a very serious magazine. The picture on the front cover was of a woman in overalls applying the finishing touches to a wall that looked as though it was covered in fungus. The by-line read 'How to distress your house'.

He listened to the local six o'clock news. Mayor Eddie Hicks said: 'I've lost ten pounds so far, so obviously I'm fairly confident of going the whole way, Barry.' The woman who had been sneezing for two weeks was now only five weeks away from the world record. She was interviewed and every other sentence she punctuated with a well-oiled sneeze. 'Does it hurt?' asked the interviewer. 'Only when I laugh,' said the woman and laughed and sneezed and groaned.

Clive tuned to some classical music. Classical music – that's what he would give more time to when he retired. A composer a week. And outings. Christine and he would have more outings; get to know each other again. They'd have outings to classical music concerts.

He washed up Christine's plate and then went into the cupboard under the stairs, and for the next two hours sorted through a box containing a mixture of nuts and bolts and screws that were all meaningless to him, but which he divided into sizes then put into individual boxes and labelled. It was a job he had been saving for Sunday.

At nine o'clock Clive made some more tea and took Christine up a cup. She reached out a bare arm, sleepily. He climbed back in bed with her. Sunday morning was the morning they might have sex. Their foreplay was a cup of tea and a bourbon biscuit.

Clive Peacock had met Christine Irvine in the Wessex Cycling Club on 16 June 1958. A picture of the club members had been taken on that day; it still stood in a frame on Clive's tallboy. The black and white print was fading but the scene was clear enough: a picnic among sand dunes, some bicycles lying intimately in a heap, a tablecloth spread over a patch of grass, and five prime specimens of local youth sat around with their toes in the sand, or lying on their backs with blades of grass in their mouths, all smiles and haircuts.

There was Trevor Price, six foot of bones and freckles. His ambition had been to fly jet aeroplanes. Now he was landlord of the Duke of Wellington, a pub known for its variety of filled baked potatoes.

In front of him was Lizzie Docherty, West Country road race champion (girls) three years running. Four years after the picture was taken she married an American serviceman and moved to Illinois from where she'd sent Christmas cards to everyone. She reappeared only once, years later, on holiday. The following Christmas there were no cards from Illinois and no one heard from her again.

Lying on the grass next to Lizzie was Ralph with sharp creases in his flannels. He lounged on one elbow, oblivious to the twenty years that lay ahead. How could that lineless face have ever expected the five children, the bankrupt roofing business, the vasectomy, the appearance on *Take Your Pick*, the sixth child, redundancy from Securicor, the job in a burger bar, and the search, morning and evening, for a way out with a metal detector?

In front of Ralph was Chris Blair, a boy with a kiss curl in his blond hair and mischief in his eye. He had once given Clive an anatomical dictionary and made him test him on the different parts of the female genitalia. The vulva, the labia, the mons – Chris Blair knew them all. One afternoon as the club were cycling to Weymouth he had explained all about the clitoris to Clive. 'The only organ on the human body, male or female, designed solely for pleasure, that's the clitoris,' said Chris. 'That proves it, doesn't it?'

'You bet,' replied Clive. Although what proved what he wasn't precisely sure. The only hint his libido had so far given him was that the most satisfying position to ride in on the club outings was right behind Christine, even if it did mean he had always lost his appetite by the time they stopped for the picnic and he would have stale, squashed sandwiches the next day for lunch.

There she was in the photo, just sixteen years old, hair in a ponytail, face fatter than now but with two sharp edges where the cat's-eyes frame of her spectacles peaked. The black and white picture didn't show it but her bike was hand-painted three different colours, a colour-washed BSA.

And there was Clive, nineteen, his thick horn-rimmed glasses shining in the 1950s sun like headlights, his arms folded tightly, thin legs pulled up against his chest, his mouth frozen in a smile he had always hoped was wry.

It was the summer before he went off to do National Service, and all the free time he had he spent with the club cycling around the coast and the hills inland. Normally the meets were well attended, but one wet Sunday only Clive and Christine were there on the harbour wall at the departure time. They waited ten minutes, Christine hoping – she later told Clive – that no other member would turn up; Clive hoping the same but uneasy of what they would talk about on their own. No one else showed, so they cycled off to Chapman's Pool.

At Corfe Castle they sheltered from the rain in a bus shelter, and for an hour they talked about their eyesight and the disadvantages of wearing glasses. After that Clive found himself saying anything that came into his head. Christine wasn't pretty, but she was bright and had an impulsiveness that, Clive came to realise, she was frightened of. She was a nurse; she smelt vaguely of hospitals – which Clive found reassuring. And she had beautiful brown legs, smooth and long, ending in white socks and blancoed tennis shoes with the laces threaded in a complex latticework.

More than anything though, Clive could remember the enormous relief he felt in finally meeting Christine, just to know that a woman like her really existed. At last here was someone he found attractive and could be of use to. Clive was a plodder who always got there. Christine was charged like a piece of elastic and would often fly right past where she was heading unless someone grabbed hold of her. Clive decided he would be that someone. And he was successful most of the time. Only on occasions was he unable to stop her and then he was carried along by her momentum. They were the best times, when they were flying, hanging on to each other.

They reached Chapman's Pool and left their bikes on the cliff. A path led them down to the beach and then around the coast just above the waterline to a point where a landslip had crumbled into the water. There was no way round, but Christine had seen a prize she wanted on the other side of the obstruction: a piece of sun-bleached driftwood, gnarled and fragile and weathered in the shape of a bird. And she wanted it badly – she was trying to scramble round on the crumbling cliff.

Clive said she was stupid even to think about it. She said there had to be a way. Clive just wanted to go back to the bikes and cycle back to Corfe and sit in that bus shelter again. He didn't want this sort of excitement on a club outing. She slipped and slid back to the beach with her legs grazed but that didn't discourage her. She just looked for another foothold.

And then Clive saw how to do it. If he was to jump in the sea and swim round the belly of the landslip, he could easily climb up back to the path that continued on the other side, and then reach that damned piece of wood. He kept the idea to himself as he tried to think of everything that could go wrong, but it seemed as long as his timing was right, so that a wave didn't throw him against the rock, he'd be quite safe. And there were no waves.

'I've got to have that driftwood, Clive,' said Christine, and she dug her toes into the landslip again.

'It's all right,' he said. 'I see a way; I'll get it for you,' and he pulled off his clothes down to his underpants, so grateful he hadn't worn the string pair his grandmother had knitted him, and with as little fuss as possible he jumped into the water as if it was a typical thing for him to do. He quickly swam the ten yards around the landslip, and pulled himself out and up the cliff on the other side, where he tore the piece of driftwood out of the ground and threw it down to Christine, then he dived in the water again and swam straight back. The entire operation took minutes.

They were married three summers later. Their wedding present to each other was a tandem. They made plans to cycle across the Alps; that was their favourite conversation for two years. Then Christine went on an interior design evening course. Her mother died and, with the money left them, they managed to buy a crumbling cottage right on the A35. There they lived for three years, and that driftwood was the centrepiece of the living room. While Clive

39

delivered the post, Christine stripped the house bare. She took a book out of the library and rewired the place from top to bottom. Another book out of the library and the place was plumbed. Another book and the beams were exposed. She sank a septic tank and patched up the roof. Inside she furnished it with materials from dumps. Her hands grew hard. When they came to sell they got three times the original cost.

Clive was glad they moved. The house had never seemed finished to him. But soon he realised that no house Christine lived in would ever be finished. There would always be cement sacks in the front garden; there would always be rooms with restored cornices on one wall and damp patches on the other. Christine liked to live in a half-built state. As things neared completion she would grow anxious.

They had tried for a family, and twice Christine became pregnant but both times she lost the child, the second only weeks before the due date. After that they never talked of children again. They moved from house to house, buying cheap and selling at a good profit. Christine decided to work nights so she could spend her days knocking down walls and building extensions. And Clive was happy as long as he was working, delivering the post. Then they bought the house overlooking the mudflats, and after eight years Clive had thought that at last she'd settled. But now she had that sparkle in her eye; now she wanted to phone up Ron Bishop to ask him to dig up the house and move it out; now was the sort of time that Clive knew he had to reach out and grab her reins.

By ten o'clock they were up and dressed and Clive was tying L-plates to the car bumpers. Christine said: 'Why do you want to drive? What are you trying to prove?'

'I'm not trying to prove anything. I feel like driving, that's all. I want to learn to drive now I'm going to be retired.'

They were going to Superself, the DIY hypermarket. Christine had a plan for the bathroom. She'd announced it when she came downstairs that morning. She said she wanted to distress it; it was a style she'd read about, she said, and she showed Clive that stupid magazine.

'A bathroom with a sort of died-in effect is what I'm after. Bare floorboards; a big old mirror; exposed plumbing. Together we can do it. You'll enjoy it.'

Clive had made sure his eyes jumped with enthusiasm. She was trying to involve him. She rarely consulted him on anything to do with the house and he was quite happy with that arrangement, but from now on he wanted to involve himself. He'd said: 'How can I help?'

She bit her lip and replied: 'You'd better watch to start with. You can pass me things.'

Clive checked his handbrake, checked the gears were in neutral, looked in his mirrors and then pulled out carefully into Rockley Road. He sensed Christine stiffen. She disapproved of Clive's driving, just like all the instructors at the El Paso driving school had done, and all those driving test examiners, not to mention all the other drivers he'd terrorised over the years, and the pedestrians. Clive had special driving glasses which he claimed gave him adequate vision, although he still drove extremely slowly. He cycled faster than he drove.

Superself was on Northacre, an industrial park full of supercentres on heathland to the north of town. Clive threaded the Peugeot estate into the line of traffic that crawled towards the bypass. Everywhere there were road signs with sacking over their heads, hiding themselves until the new one-way system came into effect on Tuesday, when they would leap out and refuse entry or enforce left turns.

Clive said: 'You remember that tandem?'

Christine hadn't thought of the tandem for years. 'Yes, I remember the tandem, of course I do,' she said. Then, sensing what he was going to suggest, she laughed and added: 'We were a lot younger then.'

They passed the Episcopalian church. On a notice board the poster read: 'Even the blind have stars in their eyes.'

And next to it was another sign: 'Sold by Harding and Sons, Sole Agents'.

'I'd have liked that church, you know,' said Christine. 'Too pricey though. I really think we should buy a piece of land up on Westcliff – I've seen just the site – then move the house like I told you. It's such a good idea. Let's go up there this afternoon and I'll show you where I mean.'

Clive turned and looked straight at her and spoke slowly as he always did on these occasions. It was the way he let her know he was in command. 'Listen. We're not digging up the house. It's a stupid idea. Just forget it. No one in their right mind would dig up their house . . .'

Christine didn't answer. But that was because she had her hands over her face. When Clive looked back to the road he saw why. He was in fact no longer on the road; he was in the middle of a flowerbed, itself in the middle of an ornamental roundabout that consisted of a circle of neat beds sloping down to a fish pond.

It took them both a moment to realise what had happened. How had Clive managed to leave the flow of traffic and plant the car up here so smoothly?

Then Christine screamed at him: 'What are you doing? What have you done?'

The engine stalled. 'We've . . . hit a roundabout,' announced Clive.

The other traffic was paying little attention to them. The cars edged round one by one, the occupants merely glancing at this strange couple parked in a flowerbed. 'But there isn't a roundabout here,' protested Clive. 'There's never been a roundabout here.'

Christine was beginning to panic. 'Get off it, for heaven's sake!'

Clive opened the door. They were surrounded by pansies; it was as if the car was floating on a sea of flowers. He knew he had to move, and yet it was so very peaceful up on this mound out of the traffic. He felt like having a picnic.

'Get off the thing!' yelled Christine and Clive started the engine and stalled again. He started up once more, let the revs climb, and slowly let out the clutch. The wheels went spinning round in the mud as multi-coloured petals flew past the windscreen. Then one back wheel gripped and the car spun round and flattened a row of baby conifers. Clive slammed into reverse and backed into the fish pond.

'This is an ornamental roundabout, Clive! What are you doing?'

It was clear what Clive was doing: he was pumping that gear stick for all he was worth. But now the wheels were skidding on lily pads and throwing water about like a paddle boat. Vision was disappearing as the windscreen grew a layer of slime. The engine choked as the filters inhaled mud. And now smoke was beginning to rise from the heater vents.

Clive jumped out into the pond and tried to push the Peugeot back on to dry land. Christine helped and the car eventually rolled forward over a bed full of petunias. Clive revved up the engine once more and two wheels held while the other two dug a trench, digging up bulbs that wouldn't normally have seen the light of day for another nine months. The windscreen was covered in top-soil now. Clive put the wipers on, and suddenly the wheels found traction and the car sped off the roundabout over a geranium display. Through the mirror he could see an aftermath reminiscent of both a wedding and a rugby international. 'I'm sure there isn't a roundabout there,' he said. 'I'm sure there isn't.'

They continued to the industrial park in silence. Both wanted to believe the incident on the roundabout had never happened, and the best way to achieve that was not to mention it.

In the car park Clive parked next to two cars the same colour as theirs only without the layer of compost and frogspawn. A banner overhead announced the opening of a new extension at Superself that day. The England cricket captain was doing the honours; a picture of him hung over the entrance.

Inside the store there was a crowd; whole families had

43

dressed up and turned out for the event. A child was crying. Clive banged his knee on a wheelchair. And there on a platform was the England cricket captain flashing his white teeth, and declaring the new extension open. There were cheers; and then balloons fell from the ceiling.

Christine picked up the paint and sanding papers she needed and insisted that *she* drive back. Clive sat there in disgrace, gazing out of the window at the model aircraft that flew above the bypass. Everyone had ideas of what to do with their Sunday. Clive closed his eyes and tried to think of where he'd like to be above all else, and he saw himself on that old tandem cycling over the brow of a hill with letters in his saddlebag. There were mountains in the distance, snowcapped and blinding white, and when he looked behind him there was no one on the back seat.

Only when they were back home and rubbing down the old paintwork in the bathroom did Christine relax again. She balanced a plank on two chairs, climbed up and surveyed the wall. Clive stood beneath her with brushes, paint-pot and rags.

'Right,' said Christine. 'Brush, please,' and Clive handed her the brush. She stroked the wall a few times with strawberry emulsion, and then said, 'Rag,' and Clive took back the brush and handed her the rag, and she dabbed the wet paint and drew the rag across the wall reproducing precisely the marbled effect on the cover of that magazine.

'Turn the radio on,' said Christine. 'It's Malcolm Dixon and his emotional phone-in.'

Clive switched the paint-splashed radio on and Steven from Blackburn said: 'My wife has a very low opinion of me.' Clive blushed and felt uncomfortable. He handed Christine the rag when she asked for the brush.

Malcolm Dixon's response was: 'Why do you think she has a low opinion of you, Steven?'

And Steven from Blackburn said: 'I've a feeling it's because she's always seen herself as a victim.'

44

Christine said: 'He helps people to help themselves, that's what I like about Malcolm Dixon. Brush.'

Clive wanted to tell her that she wasn't to worry; this period would be hard but they would weather it. But he decided that would have been a worrying thing to say.

The wall was completed. It looked really distressed; it looked three hundred years old. It looked as though it had a disease. Clive suddenly started to feel dizzy. He sat down on the toilet seat. 'It's just the paint,' said Christine. 'You'll get used to it.' She stood back and said: 'I like it. What we need to do now is distress the fixtures. We need an old Lloyd Loom chair with paint splashes in the corner, and some hard lavatory paper and some 1950s taps. The effect has to be complete to work. I think it gives warmth.'

Clive wanted to say, 'You're running away with yourself as usual, aren't you?' But he'd leave her be for a while.

Downstairs there was a knock on the door and Ralph popped his head round. 'I knocked,' he called out and walked inside, neatly sidestepping the antique umbrella-stand (now at the foot of the stairs). He wore an anorak with Sporting Club Santiago written across the back. In each hand he carried a metal detector.

'Nice anorak,' said Christine and winked at him.

'Superman summer sale,' said Ralph and beamed, but then he became more serious – he was here to speak metal detectors.

'I've brought you a C-Scope Metadec II, Clive. Thought you might like to try it for feel. It's got pre-programmed discrimination.'

The mudflats sucked and spluttered as Ralph and Clive slowly covered a grid of land. They both had headphones on, and now they both shouted.

'You've got to be able to tell the difference between buried treasure and a ring-pull top. That's the biggest problem facing metal detectorists, I find,' yelled Ralph.

The needle swung between green and red. Clive concentrated on the crackle of interference, but it made him sleepy, and soon he was watching the herons and the gulls glide on the evening light over the cool river, and the tide rolling in to swallow all. 'Tomorrow's my last day,' shouted Clive.

'I'm aware of that,' replied Ralph. 'And I asked down at the burger bar if you could have a job but they said it was difficult at the moment. I was lucky, to be honest: my boy Tony works down there, you see; he got me my job. They said they might want someone on boxes but not just yet. You'd be all right on boxes. You have to flatten them. It's not difficult. I started on boxes. I'm on cheeseburgers now. When the order comes in I slip the cheese between the bun. I don't start until ten o'clock and I get off after lunch. Don't get paid much, of course. They pay my boy Tony more than me; but he works out front. They don't allow anyone over forty out front. It's all oldies in the back, you see. There's a real camaraderie.'

Clive breathed in deeply, the air was like a fuel injection. 'This King Raedrik,' he yelled. 'Have you seen anyone else out here looking for him, ever?'

'No. This is my theory. You're the only person apart from me who knows. I want to share this with you, Clive. You and me deserve it.'

'What happens when we find him?'

'We give him to the British Museum . . . We're not like that lot who roam the beach after bits of jewellery and lost purses. We're doing this to connect ourselves with history: metal detectoring as archaeology, this is.'

Clive's earphones screamed at him. The needles swung over into the red zone. 'I've found something,' he said and his heart sat up.

Ralph crouched over the mud, took out his trowel and dug slowly and meticulously for twenty minutes, until he unearthed another ring-pull top.

They walked back in the dark. The mudflats merged with the sky, bats darted in the gloom.

'It was a Diet Pepsi ring-pull, that was,' said Ralph.

'Was it?'

46

'Yes. Ninety per cent of the ring-pull tops I find are Diet Pepsi. My kids drink it. Can't stand the stuff myself.'

When they reached Beaconsfield Hill televisions flickered behind net curtains. A car with aerofoils and chrome wheels and a jacked-up rear roared past, flames spitting out of the exhaust. Ralph waved at the driver, who honked. 'That was my boy Roy,' said Ralph. 'I wish I could get him interested in metal detecting.'

Clive and Ralph stood in a pool of streetlight. Ralph said: 'So, tomorrow, last day and all that.'

Clive nodded, and smiled into the distance. Ralph wasn't going to hug him or anything, was he?

'Meet you same time tomorrow afternoon?'

'Okay,' said Clive, and gave that nod of enthusiasm he was becoming familiar with. He handed back the Metadec II.

'Keep it,' said Ralph. 'Get the feel of it, until you want to buy one of your own.'

'Okay,' said Clive. 'Thanks.' And now he felt the urge to hug Ralph, but he resisted. 'See you tomorrow afternoon, then.'

As he walked home a window opened and someone shouted into the night: 'You never phone me; why do you never phone me?'

# 6

CLIVE WATCHED THE numbers on the digital alarm clock tremble and trip from 1.44 to 1.45. It was a warm and thick night and he'd lain awake since 'God Save the Queen' had woken him from a TV set across the way. Christine had come to bed at 1.28. He'd pretended to be asleep, but now he turned over and looked at her bare back in the glow from the streetlight.

She was already asleep. He reached out and lightly drew his finger down her spine. Her back was rippled like a relief map of England. She had a Pennine Chain of vertebrae that stretched up to the border of her neck. And there on one flank was the ridge of the Cotswolds and on the other the lowlands of East Anglia. He loved her back, as much as her front he thought. Clive lay there wide awake at 1.50 and imagined how hard it would be to choose between Christine's front and her back. If, just say, someone came into the bedroom now and put a gun to his head and said he had to choose between Christine's front or back or be shot between the eyes, it would be a difficult decision.

The streetlights were turned off and Christine became a blank screen; 2.01 flicked to 2.02 and Clive scratched his belly then got out of bed and padded to the window. In a house opposite another lone figure stood in the same position. It was the policeman Pitman, just standing there looking at the cars squeezed together in the gutter. He was dressed in an open shirt but he was still unmistakably a policeman. Suddenly the car outside his window began to scream like some injured animal and its lights flashed in distress. The outburst lasted for thirty seconds, until the alarm cut out. By that time Pitman had drawn his curtains. There wasn't a soul on the street.

Clive went back to bed. His legs throbbed with tension. He felt hot and took his pyjama jacket off; then he felt cold and put it back on again. He was normally such a good sleeper.

He dozed, and dreamed he was dressed in uniform, wheeling his bike along a street, letters in his hand, when without warning he was hit from behind by a robot postman, a matchstick man on rails, just two foot high, chugging down the street vomiting mail. Clive ran after him gathering up the letters but the robot postman was coughing them up in drifts in the gutter, and now everyone was running out into the street picking up any letters they could find and tearing them open and Mrs Atherton and Mr Denbigh and Mrs Drake were all squabbling . . .

He woke as a car pulled up and stopped. Clive could hear the engine settle down, hiss and drip. He could hear the driver shut the car door and walk up a path then fumble with door keys. Then he was dreaming again, on his bicycle, his pannier full of letters, cycling up a hill, effortlessly, but when he reached the top it was a false summit, and so was the next one and the next. He woke again as two cats wailed, and now he felt exhausted.

At four o'clock he got up and made tea. He went out into the garden and in the light from the kitchen checked his vegetable patch for weeds. The sun rose. He watched the sky closely. This is your last day, he kept telling himself. He felt he should be paying more attention to details.

In the bathroom he shaved very carefully, but looking only at his skin, never at his face. Once his hand started to shake but he managed to control himself by looking at the freshly distressed wall. We did that, he said to himself, and then out loud: 'God knows why.'

Back in the bedroom Christine turned and mumbled: 'Are you all right?'

'Couldn't sleep. Tea?'

He went downstairs and boiled the kettle again, and pumped up his bicycle tyres while the pot brewed. Then he returned to the bedroom and sat on the edge of the bed and dressed.

49

'I've got a splinter in my hand,' mumbled Christine. 'It's really painful.'

Clive sat by her and pulled her hand under the bedside light. The palm was calloused and coarse, nails short and broken, and her index finger scarred. Clive's hands were so smooth after thirty-five years of envelopes.

There was a splinter, a big one too, thick and black, and the skin all around was inflamed. 'I'll pick it out for you,' he whispered.

From the bedside cabinet he took a traveller's sewing kit marked Holiday Inn – their present from Christine's brother when he went on holiday to Florida. He pierced Christine's skin with a needle and as gently as he could began to tear open the tunnel the splinter had bored into her flesh. Christine winced and sucked sharply.

'Sorry,' said Clive. 'It's in deep.'

He picked underneath the black sliver to gain some purchase but it snapped as he tried to pull it out. He dug again and tore the flesh a little more. Christine had her eyes closed in pain but he kept picking, until he could slowly draw it out. It was half an inch long.

'There,' he said and offered it to her in his palm.

She said: 'You've got some blood on your shirt. You should wear a clean one on your last day.'

He kissed her forehead and smiled. She squeezed his arm gently in reply, then curled under the bedclothes again.

At five-fifteen he wheeled out his bike and cycled off down Rockley Road. His whole metabolism was racing; he felt as though he needed to hold on to himself. At the back of his throat there was an ache trying to escape, something he wanted to swallow but couldn't. He had tears in his eyes, he realised – just the cold morning air, he told himself.

When Clive arrived at the sorting office everyone was gathered round the Optical Speedsort machine. They were stood there with hands in pockets watching Desmond the personal technician lying underneath his care, grunting.

The machine was silent, its lights off. It lay there like a doped animal.

'What's up?' asked Clive.

'It was switched on last night,' said Nigel Sweeney.

'And it broke down this morning,' said Margaret Rogerson.

Clive licked his top lip and played with the change in his pocket.

'Teething problem, nothing more,' said Peter Robson.

Desmond the technician crawled out holding a horribly chewed letter. 'Here's the culprit,' he said and pulled a paperclip out of the envelope. 'The OS is a sensitive machine; it can't be dealing with paperclips.'

The OS would be out of order all morning. It needed a part that would have to come from Swindon. 'That's the cost of progress,' said Peter Robson.

Clive sorted what mail he had and headed back to Beaconsfield Hill. He completed his round with his head down; he didn't want to speak to anyone. He didn't even notice they were painting single yellow lines along Tarr Avenue.

Back along the bypass a lorry from Robertson's cesspit-emptying service narrowly avoided him.

And then back at the sorting office he walked into the canteen to be greeted by thirty postmen and -women assembled for his retirement breakfast. Clive had forgotten all about it. He thought: Retirement? I'm only fifty-two, for heaven's sake.

Ethel Branston the canteen manager had done a buffet with sausages, bacon and tomatoes, eggs done three different ways, and her special baked beans with curry powder. Clive sat at the head of the table. Rolf Milne read the paper and said: 'I don't believe it. They're going to build a tunnel under that new motorway to preserve a two-hundred-year-old badger run. It says here. Listen . . .'

Clive wasn't concentrating properly. 'You look tired,' said Pauline the facer-canceller. 'You'll enjoy being retired. My father didn't know what he was going to do but then he discovered eggcup collecting.'

Fresh pots of tea were put on the table. Rolf dug his elbow into Clive's ribs as Peter Robson stood up and said, 'Well, Clive, your retirement is the end of an era really. Still, ends of eras are all part of progress, and you would be the last person to stand in the way of progress, I know that.'

'I hear we'll be having robots delivering the mail by the year 2000,' said Nigel Sweeney and everyone chuckled respectfully, including Peter Robson, who wasn't going to have it said to him that he couldn't take a joke.

'Quite,' said Peter Robson.

'Anyway we want to give you this as a reminder of your days at the PO, and so . . . here it is.'

Peter Robson handed Clive a box. Inside was a carriage clock.

'Thank you very much,' said Clive.

'And another thing, the Post Office have decided that you can keep your bike, as a sort of memento.'

'Thank you very much.'

'Speech!' shouted Nigel Sweeney.

Clive stood up. The canteen staff were all gathered behind the counter, arms folded over aprons. The postmen and -women were all watching him smugly. Peter Robson was picking his teeth.

Some witty remark to make about the standard of apple crumble over the years, that was what he wanted. Some prophetic comment concerning the future of the Royal Mail. Some memory that would capture the deep respect and love he felt for his job and for the postal service. But all he could feel was that ache climbing up his throat again and trying to spill out. He looked at Peter Robson, who looked away. Barney Loxton coughed. Margaret Rogerson said: 'We know how you feel, Clive.'

And Clive said: 'I'd just like to say: can I keep my jacket as well?'

Everyone laughed, and suddenly all attention was on the young woman in high heels and raincoat, who had left the swing doors swinging, and was now skipping towards them playing with her pigtails. As she reached the table she flung her coat open to reveal her schoolgirl uniform.

'He's over here,' shouted Rolf and slapped Clive's back.

'You always have to go and spoil it, don't you?' said Ethel Branston.

The girl sat down on Clive's lap and giggled horribly. Her suspenders dug into his leg. She had freckles applied with felt tip. She looked straight through Clive and said:

'My name is Susie and I'm only sixteen,
But I'm advanced for my age if you see what I mean.
I'm here today to give you a thrill
To make your retirement happier still.
So wherever you go remember this,
There's nothing so bad can't be bettered with a kiss.'

She leaned down and, with her face at right angles to Clive's, she kissed him full on the lips. He caught a smell of cigarettes and a taste of lipstick and wasn't aware of where his hands were. All he could hear was the cheering and laughter of the other postmen.

The Kiss-o-Gram wrapped herself back up in her raincoat and sat down like a doll, as if she was waiting for another coin to be put in. The postmen looked at the floor and mumbled to each other, all embarrassed at the thought of having to say something to her. Clive said he was going to the Gents, but he hurried down the steps back into the sorting office, took his carriage clock, grabbed his second delivery and mounted his bicycle on the run. He went over the humps on the depot road so fast his hat fell off.

At top speed he cycled out to Beaconsfield Hill and was up it in one breath. 'Lovely day, Mrs Wheatley,' he said, which confused Mrs Wheatley walking under her brolly.

For the next hour he delivered letters with that old Peacock panache. He leaned back and flicked them through the boxes. He tossed them from hand to hand and he swayed his hips as he strode down garden paths. He lifted his hat to everyone he saw, and he whistled his way through the round, making Mrs Tidy open her window and say, 'What are you so happy about?'

Then at 11.48 he dug his hand in his bag and there were no letters left. 'At least I went out in style,' he said to no one.

He freewheeled down to the pillar box on Waverley Road and made the twelve o'clock collection for the last time, picking the letters out one by one, feeling them, flicking them through his fingers like playing cards: Yorkshire, Scotland, Wolverhampton, Shropshire, a number for London, a handful of locals, one for Italy.

One of Ralph's boys, Robert, came down the hill clutching an envelope. 'Can you take this to the BBC?' he said. 'It's to *Points of View*. It's about Jimmy Savile.'

'Certainly,' said Clive. 'I shall make sure it reaches there personally.'

Clive added the letter to the pile and slowly pedalled back to the harbour. When he passed Winchester Avenue he slowed. One of his collection was for number 22. Why didn't he make sure it reached there personally?

He popped it through the door. It was breaking all the rules, but it was his last day! He did the same for the letter addressed to Latimer Road and for the one on Oster Street. The letter for the surgery on Court Road was out of his way, but it was no bother, and it was marked Urgent. He'd show them just how good the postal service could be. And no Optical Speedsort machine could get the mail delivered this quick, only a postman could.

In the end he worked his way through all the local mail, returning via the High Street where he delivered letters to the Halifax and the NatWest Bank, cancelling the stamps himself with a ballpoint. The last local one was to Folly Road, a greeting card for Mrs E. Rutherford: collected at twelve o'clock, delivered by one. Clive gave himself a snigger of satisfaction. He was Clive Peacock the people's postman.

At one-fifteen he reached the roundabout on the bypass, and there he had to stop. Red PO vans sped past him and bumped over the humps back to the depot, but he couldn't summon up the will. He leaned against a crash barrier and sorted through the rest of the collection. Maybe there was one for somewhere not so far out of town, one he could deliver and be back by two o'clock before they noticed.

The letter to Shropshire caught his eye. It was addressed to Mr and Mrs Flint, Mynd Farm, near Church Stretton. Church Stretton? The cycling club had been up that way years ago on their summer rally. Ten days they'd gone for. Clive had lain in a tent one night near Ludlow with Chris Blair, and Chris had said how he'd like to get hold of that Christine and run his tongue from the bottom of her leg right to the top.

A wave of hot air blasted Clive as a lorry loaded with another lorry rumbled past. He squinted through the cloud of dust at the road back into town, then at the access road to the industrial estate and the depot, then the road leading off the roundabout heading north.

The letter to Mynd Farm had a second-class stamp on it. It could take three days to be delivered – he could cycle there in the same time. And there was a lump in the corner that could only be a paperclip. The Optical Speedsort would have it for lunch.

He put the letter back in his bag and secured the Velcro straps, then cycled round the roundabout, past the road to the depot and set off north for Shropshire.

# 7

IT WAS THE day the new one-way system was to be introduced, and Detective Sergeant Pitman needed some new
trousers, maybe a suit, he'd see.

A number of obstacles stood in his way though. The first
was the traffic into town which, according to the radio, was
at a complete standstill. The second was that he had lost
his car keys, which was why he was rummaging around in
the fridge. He didn't really think his car keys were in the
fridge – he was almost sure he had left them in the ignition
all night – however, he knew that if he didn't look in the
unlikely places – like the fridge, and the rubbish bin, and
the bathroom cabinet, all places where he had, over the
years, found his car keys – if he went straight out to his car
he knew he wouldn't find them there. It would be one of
the occasions when they had somehow got into the pocket
of a jacket he'd not worn for three weeks, or into the bread
bin perhaps. He checked the bread bin.

Only when he was satisfied they were nowhere in the
house did he go out to the car, and there they were, dan-
gling safely in the ignition. And of course the times he did
leave his keys in the ignition were always the only times he
remembered to lock his car. Pitman stood on the pavement
and thought: It's hard being me.

He tried to force down the window, but backed off when
he saw a kid coming up the road, one of what's-his-name's
boys – the bloke with the metal detector. The kid stopped
and said: 'Trying to break into it?'

'Yes,' said Pitman, and he turned away as the kid pulled
out a comb. He didn't want to see this. He just heard a
grunt and click and the door sprang open.

'There you go,' said the kid. 'Give us a lift into town.'

Ralph's boy got out at the harbour. He decided it was

quicker to walk. Lights all over town were changing from red to amber to green, but it didn't matter what colour they tried, they couldn't get the traffic sorted. People were climbing out of their cars and sitting on their bonnets reading the newspaper. The driver of the car in front of Pitman turned his engine off and went to buy a pack of cigarettes. The High Street was a two-lane car park, a monster of a jam whose head was choking on its tail.

By the time he reached the multi-storey by the shopping precinct it was ten o'clock and Pitman was already telling himself to calm down. He parked on level D, and took the lift down to street level. His mood dropped alongside him. What was it about multi-storey car parks that depressed him so? An eighteen-year-old girl had hanged herself in such a place just after Christmas – this one or one of the others in town, it didn't matter which. The fact was she had chosen a multi-storey car park to commit suicide in. Pitman could think of nothing more desperate.

He emerged in The Lanes, once a derelict warehouse district, now a pedestrian shopping precinct. It was ten-fifteen. He couldn't dawdle; he had Robert Tripp in the interview room at eleven. Robert Tripp who had got drunk, stolen a car and driven it into a travel agent's. The most interesting feature of the case was why, out of all the shops on the High Street, he had chosen a travel agent's.

Pitman stepped through the doorless entrance of Superman into a supermarket of clothes hung on wooden cacti. Posters of cowboys in tight jeans and ten-gallon hats papered the walls. Music from *The Magnificent Seven* dripped from the ceiling. An assistant dressed in a snake pattern shirt and a sheriff's badge switched off the Hoover he was pushing, took one look at Pitman and said: 'Let me guess; thirty-two waist?'

Pitman hated these shops, but there was always a sign in the window that yelled, 'Sale, Genuine Reductions', and there was no doubt, Superman was the best value in town. Pitman was fifty-five years old and had maintenance to pay on a wife and two teenage sons. He didn't want to be fashionable, but he couldn't afford not to be.

'Thirty-six, with a long leg,' mumbled Pitman. Man had landed on the moon; some clever bastard had found the *Titanic*; but some things, like Pitman's waist, never ever changed.

'All these on the bottom row with the orange tags are thirty-six,' said the assistant. 'Here's a nice Victor Padrone from Italy, only £70 in the sale.'

Pitman winced. The assistant winked at him and switched his Hoover back on. Pitman stepped into one of the line of changing booths and stood staring at himself in front of a full-length mirror. And it didn't matter which mirror Pitman stood in front of, he always saw a policeman staring back. No matter what expression he adopted, what posture, what clothes he wore or how he combed his hair, his reflection said 'policeman'. He held in his stomach and smiled – policeman. He curled up his lip and sneered – policeman. He dropped his trousers and stood there in shirt tails and socks – policeman in shirt tails and socks. He might as well have had a blue flashing light on his head.

He straightened himself up. Nothing wrong with being a policeman. You got interesting people like Robert Tripp to interview when you were a policeman. Robert Tripp who had got drunk and had driven into a travel agent's. Why the hell had he gone out of his way to get the travel agent's? There was nothing but brochures inside. The case had no obvious motive, and to Pitman this suggested there was more to it than there seemed. Surely there had to be more. No one could appear as guilty as Robert Tripp did.

The Hoover poked its nose under the curtain and sucked at Pitman's trouser leg. He kicked it and it retreated, then he tried on the Victor Padrone suit. It wasn't a bad fit. It did have pockets the size of a clown's, and silly thin lapels, and no vents and a stupid label on the outside, but otherwise it could pass off as a perfectly good unfashionable suit. He stood up and examined himself in the mirror. Policeman in a Victor Padrone suit. Who the hell is Victor

Padrone anyway? he mused and patted his old jacket pockets for his Access card.

He hurried back through the precinct to the multi-storey and climbed to level D. His car had gone. 'I left it on level D, I know I did,' he said out loud as he walked down a level to check C. No sign of it down there either. He went up another level to E – nothing. He walked round the cars, turning in ever-decreasing circles, winding himself up into anger. Twenty minutes he was gone and some bastard had nicked his car.

Down at the pay booth the attendant was watching cartoons on a miniature TV. Pitman rapped too loudly on the glass and said: 'Have you seen a blue Escort drive out of here in the last fifteen minutes?'

The attendant looked blank and said: 'Nope.'

'Are you sure? I parked it on level D and it's gone.'

'Happens all the time,' said the attendant. 'Are you sure it was level D? People mistake E for D very easily.'

'Course I'm sure.'

'Been stolen then, hasn't it? Call the police.'

'I am the police,' hissed Pitman.

He couldn't report his car stolen again. They'd come out to pick him up and find it on level D½ or something, like they did the last time, and he'd be a laughing stock again. He decided on one more look, from top to bottom.

Down into level A he strode, into the bowels where there were few vehicles at all, just supermarket trolleys lying on their side in puddles. And then up through all levels, looking behind every pillar, finding four other Escorts the same colour as his but not his own. Finally he surfaced in the sunlight of level G.

A breeze blew up here. There seemed to be an enormous amount of sky, and the noise and smell of the traffic was left behind in another life. Pitman felt nearer heaven.

He went to the edge and leaned over the concrete wall. That suicide victim had probably spent all day looking for her car and then said, 'What's the point?' and strung herself up.

He felt like staying up on level G all day, not bothering with Robert Tripp and his smashed-up travel agent's. He breathed in the view. The spire of St Benedict pierced all the new development, that was reassuring. And there was the old Customs House, the elegant brickwork rising above the new British Home Stores. The rest of the view was obscured by another concrete and metal sandwich that stood just across the street, another multi-storey car park . . .

Pitman sighed and his shoulders dropped as he slouched off back down the ramps.

Look on the bright side, he said to himself. You had the right level, you just had the wrong car park.

A stack of No Waiting signs, wrapped in protective poly-thene, stood in the porch of the police station. The building was at bursting point. CID had been promised relocation away from Traffic, but the promise was a year old now and the two departments were still sharing. 'Mng,' said Pitman to Desk Sergeant Keogh, who sat surrounded by Give Way triangles.

The whole station was in turmoil. The foul-up in the one-way system had been caused by One Way No Way, the anti-one-way-system lobby which consisted largely of taxi drivers who claimed the new system was unworkable and refused to take any notice of it. They were going to go one way they said, but not necessarily the same way as everyone else. They would have been arrested but no police car could get out of the compound to arrest them.

Pitman entered the office he shared with Woman Detective Constable McMahon. A stack of traffic cones piled behind the door tottered and fell gracefully to the floor. Pitman stacked them up again.

On his desk were five reports of cars stolen during the night. There was also a missing person form. Pitman grabbed it with excitement. He didn't want a serial killer on his patch, nor an arsonist, nor a drugs baron, but the very idea of dealing with someone who hadn't got drunk and stolen a car was a real thrill these days.

He glanced through the form. The Post Office had reported a postman disappeared with mailbox keys. Pitman snorted. A crooked postman – wonderful. What sort of town was it where you couldn't even trust your postman?

Hold on, he checked himself. Don't prejudge the man. He could have been attacked or abducted. He could at this very moment be lying in a ditch somewhere. So what sort of town was it where a postman couldn't walk the streets without being attacked and abducted and left in a ditch?

A memo from the Detective Chief Inspector was stuck to the bottom of the form. It read: 'Deal with this, but quickly. I'm not really interested. Just put it on the computer.'

Of course he's not interested, thought Pitman. There was no car chase involved.

WDC McMahon came in. 'There you are, Lawrence,' she said and the pile of traffic cones collapsed again. 'Robert Tripp has been waiting thirty minutes.'

Pitman followed her down the corridor to the interview room, and there sat Tripp with his nicotined teeth and conker of an Adam's apple. Pitman sat opposite him, crossed his legs casually and said to himself: Remember, you are here to help this man.

'Mr Robert Tripp?'

'Yeah.'

'Maybe you'd like to tell me exactly what happened on the night of July 10th?'

And without reservation Tripp proceeded to recount how on that night he did drink seven pints of lager at the Swan public house and did steal a Ford Fiesta and did break into Four Seasons the travel agent's on the High Street.

Pitman nodded sympathetically. He had just one question: 'Why, Mr Tripp, did you break into the travel agent's?'

Tripp thought carefully about this, then said: 'Well . . . I haven't had a decent holiday for years.'

'I understand,' said Pitman.

# 8

WHEN HE ARRIVED at the Royal Mail sorting office Detective Sergeant Pitman asked to see Peter Robson and was shown to a group of what turned out to be local businessmen on a tour of the system. They were all gathered before a silver-grey machine the size of a piece of artillery, and Peter Robson was the man tying his hands in a knot, trying to explain the complexities of this: 'Optical Speedsort machine, a computerised eye that will deal with 45,000 letters per hour.'

No one in the group showed any emotion at this piece of news. Peter Robson had made the mistake of giving them their sandwiches and drinks before the tour rather than after. To wake them up he said: 'There's even talk of robot postmen by the year 2000,' and he slapped the OS playfully. The OS responded with a metallic cough, then it choked and shuddered to a halt. A red light came on overhead.

Now there was some interest among the tourists. 'That's buggered it,' said Donald Silcoates, representing the local branch of Dewhursts.

Peter Robson slapped the OS again. The red light went out, so did every other light on the machine. He grinned. 'Teething problem.'

Desmond the engineer arrived. 'This is Desmond, personal engineer for the OS,' said Peter Robson. 'What's the problem, Des?'

Desmond didn't answer. He ducked underneath and came up a few minutes later with a crumpled and oily envelope. 'Someone put a stamp on upside down,' he said. 'It's no good having sophisticated machines if people are going to put stamps on upside down, is it?' and he flung the letter in a bin.

The group looked at Peter Robson and his red face.

'Desmond's a character,' said Peter Robson. 'He's from Swindon, Desmond is.'

At this point Pitman decided to step in to the rescue. 'Mr Robson?'

'What!'

'Detective Sergeant Pitman. I telephoned earlier.'

The OS sprang into life again. Peter Robson's grin reappeared. 'Yes, of course,' he said. 'Be right with you.' He turned back to his businessmen with a flourish. 'Well, gentlemen, I hope you've enjoyed your tour. If there's any way the Post Office can help the business establishment please don't hesitate to . . .'

The OS ground to a halt again. Donald Silcoates from Dewhursts shouted, 'Desmond!' and engineer Desmond ducked underneath the OS once more. He flung out another butchered letter. 'I thought so,' he said; 'Rochdale. It always chokes on letters to Rochdale, don't know why.'

'My sister lives in Rochdale,' said the representative from Carpet City.

Detective Sergeant Pitman sat in Peter Robson's office beneath a picture of Norway. It reminded him of the days when he used to smoke menthol cigarettes. Peter Robson had made a cup of tea and now he was taking a packet of biscuits out of a Tupperware box kept in a locked drawer. 'Shortcake?' he said.

'Thank you,' said Pitman.

The biscuit packet was put back in the Tupperware container, the container returned to the corner of the drawer, the drawer locked and the key put back in the pocket on a bit of string.

'That's interesting,' said Pitman.

'What is?'

'That device you have for keeping your keys handy.'

'String, you mean.'

'Right,' said Pitman. 'I'm always losing my keys. String. I'll remember that.'

Robson flashed Pitman his U-bend smile.

'Right, then,' said Pitman.

'Yes,' said Peter Robson.

'Clive Peacock. Postman gone missing I understand, with a set of keys to a postbox and a collection of mail.'

'That's right. He never came back after the second delivery, never returned his mailbox keys. We couldn't find them this morning. We're very careful with our keys, you see. I phoned his wife and the alarming thing is she's not seen him since he left for work yesterday.'

'And he never brought his collection back either?' asked Pitman.

'Not that we know of. He was retiring yesterday. We had a little celebration in the canteen earlier. That was the last anyone saw of him.'

'How did he feel about retiring?'

'He was a bit emotional, I suppose. He loved his job, you see. He was a model postman.'

'Why was he retiring, then?'

'We offered him early retirement. He couldn't drive. He was the last of the cyclists and the new technology has made bicycles redundant. Progress, you know. He was the end of an era. That's what makes it all so upsetting. He isn't the sort of person that things like this happen to.'

'Things like what?' asked Pitman puzzled.

'Kidnapping, or mugging.'

'What makes you think he's been kidnapped or mugged?'

'Well, it's the way this town is going, isn't it?'

People who said that always annoyed Pitman, as if the town wasn't anything to do with them. Pitman wanted to say: 'The way this town "is going" is due entirely to the people who live in it.' Instead he gave Peter Robson a hopeless gaze. Peter Robson looked hurt. Pitman said: 'Just where is this letterbox to which the keys are missing?'

'At the bottom of Waverley Road. Up on Beaconsfield Hill.'

'That's where I live,' said Pitman.

'Clive was your postman, then. He did that area for

years. You must know him: lean chap, bottle-bottom glasses.'

'Oh, him,' said Pitman. Now it was his turn to squirm. He hadn't got a clue who his postman was.

Pitman asked to speak to some of Clive's colleagues. Peter Robson called in Barney Loxton, Nigel Sweeney, Margaret Rogerson and Rolf Milne. They all squeezed into Peter Robson's office; Rolf Milne knocked over the model of Concorde. Pitman asked them one by one what sort of a man Clive Peacock was.

'He was diligent,' said Barney Loxton.

'He was thorough,' said Nigel Sweeney.

'He was very reliable,' said Margeret Rogerson. 'And very tidy.'

'I agree with the others,' said Rolf Milne.

'How did he feel about retiring?' asked Pitman.

'Very happy,' said Barney Loxton.

'He was over the moon,' said Nigel Sweeney.

'He had bags under his eyes,' said Margeret Rogerson.

'Yeah, bags,' said Rolf Milne.

'Any idea about what might have happened to him?'

They all thought this over.

'It's unlike him but I reckon he's been attacked.' Barney Loxton spoke up.

'That's all I can think of too,' said Nigel Sweeney.

'I think he's been attacked and mugged as well,' said Margaret Rogerson. 'He wasn't the sort, but it's the way this town is going, isn't it?'

'I agree with the others,' said Rolf Milne.

Peter Robson led Pitman out. There was something about the whole sorting office process that reminded Pitman of the chicken farm he had worked on when he was fifteen. When they got outside, the sunlight made them both squint. Peter Robson said: 'The boys from the PO internal investigation department will want to be involved, of course.'

Pitman nodded. 'We'll put it all on the computer and see what turns up. He won't have gone far. Where does

Peacock live anyway? I'll want to send someone round his house.'

'He lives up on Beaconsfield Hill as well. Up there on Rockley Road.'

'Rockley Road, that's where I live,' said Pitman.

'Number 42 he lives at.'

'I live at 45.'

'He's your neighbour, then,' said Peter Robson, and Pitman squirmed again. Then it dawned on him just who Clive Peacock was. 'Oh, it's him,' he said. '*That* Clive Peacock, my neighbour – of course.' But he was thinking: Him! That little man who sits in the corner of the room at the Neighbourhood Watch meetings and says nothing. That's Clive Peacock? Surely not. He's not the sort to go missing.

The traffic was bumper to bumper as Pitman turned on to the bypass. It took him an hour to crawl to his exit, an hour of gazing at the car in front with the sticker in the rear window: 'I'd rather be in Florida'.

He came round the back of the mudflats and passed the pillar box on Waverley Road. If someone steals a bag of mail they must assume there's something valuable in it, he mused. But no one puts anything of value in letters these days – certainly not cash, or jewellery or important documents. He yawned. He shouldn't even have been making this call. He should have asked WPC McMahon to do the interview with Mrs Peacock. But Pitman felt involved somehow. As if some distant relative was in trouble – someone for whom you always wanted to do more but never got round to it. He was Clive Peacock's neighbour, for goodness' sake. As he parked outside the Peacocks' gate he felt guilty because it was the first time he'd been to this house and it was as a policeman rather than as the man who lived opposite.

The tiny front garden was lost under building clutter, but when Pitman thought about it the Peacocks' house had always looked like this. He squeezed past the concrete mixer, and knocked on the door. Inside, a radio was on very loud. He knocked again but the only response he got was someone saying: 'I don't really think my problem is very important; not compared to the problems that most people on this programme have, it's nothing really . . .'

Pitman stepped round and peered through the bay window. In the sitting room a woman dressed in overalls was lashing an old table with a bicycle chain. He watched in astonishment. Maybe he'd never spoken to the Peacocks much before because he'd always thought they were a bit funny. She was always dressed in paint-splattered trousers, and he was the sort of man you always forgot to include. Pitman watched Christine for longer than he should have done, then rapped on the glass. She turned and he smiled and pointed to the porch.

The door was pulled open with a scrape. 'Hello, Mrs Peacock,' said Pitman like an old friend. 'It's me. Detective Sergeant Pitman,' and his hand automatically patted his pockets for his ID.

'Yes,' she said.

'I live over the road.'

'Yes, I know.'

'I wonder, could I have a word?'

They sat in the living room. There was a plate with crusts on it poking out from under his seat and one from under hers. A coffee cup stood on every surface. Pitman wasn't completely sure this wasn't deliberate.

The table in the middle of the room was scarred and scored from the bicycle chain. Pitman eyed it so that Christine clearly felt she had to explain. 'I'm distressing the table,' she said, which turned out to be no explanation to him at all.

Pitman refused tea. He sat forward and struggled to look sympathetic, an expression he had learnt at police college thirty years previously in the days before his face had set. Then he asked Christine if she knew where her husband was. She picked the dirt from under her fingernails and

68

said: 'I don't know. I'm assuming he's gone off on his bike somewhere.'

'Have you any idea where?'

'I really don't know where.'

She seemed very calm. He had been expecting someone more fraught. He said: 'I'm surprised you haven't called the police, Mrs Peacock. He has been gone overnight.'

'Well, he sometimes does go off like this. It's not the first time.'

'When were the other times?'

'At times of stress.'

'Such as?'

'When his father died was one, and when . . .' She was suddenly wary; his question had touched a nerve.

'When what, Mrs Peacock?'

'The time I had a miscarriage, he went off then as well. But only for the day. You're right, he's never been away overnight. He has had a lot on his mind recently though. He's been given retirement, you see. But he'll be back soon. He's just sorting himself out. Cycling to Clive is like therapy.'

Cycling as therapy – that sounded nice, thought Pitman.

'Sorting himself out he may be, Mrs Peacock, but I'm afraid the Post Office don't see it quite so innocently. It appears your husband disappeared with a twelve o'clock collection, plus the keys to the Waverley Road postbox.'

'Yes,' said Christine.

He waited for her to say something more, but she'd settled down again.

'How did Clive feel about retiring, Mrs Peacock?'

'All right, or so he said. Although I've a feeling he was more put out than he let people think. He loved his job. This is what I mean about being under stress recently.'

'How about money?'

'We have all the money we need. I work, and Clive will get a pension. We don't spend much anyway.'

Her answers were dismissive. Pitman abandoned his

sympathetic approach. 'Did Clive have any enemies, Mrs Peacock?'

The question amused her. 'No. No, why?'

'Well, there is a possibility he might have been assaulted or abducted . . .'

'No,' said Christine and she even smiled. 'Not Clive. He wasn't the sort.'

Pitman asked to look round the house. As she led him from room to room he was reminded of the time he went backstage at a theatre. The house seemed to be a collection of backdrops. She led him into the bedroom. The window was open and the room billowed. On one bedside cabinet was a book: *The Story of the Pony Express*. 'Lean and wiry fellows. Expert riders willing to risk death daily' read the front cover. Pitman fingered it.

'Clive's,' said Christine.

He opened it at the bookmark and read: 'Crouching low in the saddle Sam Hamilton spurred his mustang and outpaced the Indian horses as he rode through the wet muddy night over the pass to Placerville Station.'

'Do you know if your husband took any spare clothes with him?' asked Pitman.

Christine looked confused. 'How would I know that?'

'Well, are there any clothes missing from his drawers?'

'I don't think so. I don't really know where he keeps his clothes. He looks after that department.'

She opened a few cupboards round the house but seemed as surprised as Pitman to see what was in them. 'Oh,' she said. 'That's where we keep the ironing board.'

Afterwards they stood in the doorway. Pitman would normally have told her not to worry, but she'd been the one telling him that. Instead he said: 'What are we going to do, Mrs Peacock? The Royal Mail has been interfered with. It's a serious business. And a man is missing. All sorts of theories spring to mind.'

'He'll be back soon. I know it.'

'Maybe. In the meantime I want to tell the local newspapers,' said Pitman. 'We need to settle this matter quickly. Do you object to publicity?'

'No, if you think it will help,' said Christine without thinking.

Pitman drove back around the mudflats. The afternoon light gave them a sticky sheen. A lone figure stood out there with the sun reflecting on his metal detector – what's-his-name with all those children. Pitman could feel a surge of relaxation as he gazed over the estuary, the kind of buzz he never normally felt until he was home and reaching out for the scotch bottle. Minutes later he was back in a line of cars waiting to join the ring road. Now the sun shone on four lanes of multi-coloured metallic roofs, and the screw at the back of his head that had been working loose was tightening again.

After work Pitman drove to Asda, to the Late-Night Shopping Spree, where he hurried round the aisles on one of his flash forays. He shopped at Asda because he knew where everything was. He could pull his supplies mechanically from the shelves – shopping without thinking. Only once did he hesitate, when he caught his reflection in the mirror above the vegetable section: 'Policeman out on a late-night shopping spree,' it said.

He reached the tills and made straight for checkout number 6 where Sonia sat. Her queue wasn't the shortest but that didn't bother Pitman. Sonia was the fastest checkout girl in town. Within minutes she was feeding his goods smoothly through the bar-coder, an expert at work. Not once did she call the manager, or query a price, or go for a teabreak or ring the bell for more change. She had long eyelashes and painted nails and had never once smiled or spoken to Pitman in his long association with Asda, and that was just the way he liked it.

The Musak and hot lights lulled him. By the door he saw the man who used to be Sergeant Brewster, now retired and for the last year an Asda security guard. Pitman waved; Brewster waved back, the wave of a man with time to spare. He always reminded Pitman of a horse put out to grass. More than that he reminded him of his own retirement only two years hence, and the thought appalled him.

The total was rung up: £12.40. Pitman patted his pockets and handed Sonia his library card. 'Sorry,' he said. 'Miles away.'

It was an effort to open his front door when he got home. One of the two free newspapers lying on the doormat had jammed it. He forced it open, ripping a free sample sachet of shampoo and smearing goo all over a Wickes catalogue.

There were two pieces of mail. 'You too can be a Laura Ashley Family,' announced the first. The second was a large envelope, marked Airmail, with a hand-written address and an Italian stamp. It was another correspondence from Signor Masserella.

Pitman poured a whisky and felt himself melt into his chair. How had he ever come home to a wife and two rampant boys? They'd lived apart eight years now and got on far better than they had ever done when they lived together. Thank God they hadn't tried to work it out or anything stupid like that. After they'd left, Pitman realised that home was a place he would only ever feel comfortable in on his own.

He opened the letter from Signor Masserella. Inside was a local newspaper from Livorno. The headline was something about a multiple pile-up on the autostrada.

'My Dear Mr Pitman,' began Masserella, 'thank you for your last letter. I was also impressed to see you catched the man who attempted to injure the Woolwich Building Society. So, he was drunk and stolen a car. I have never been to England, as you know, but I want to come one day.'

Masserella and Pitman had been corresponding ever since their towns became twinned – it was part of a twin-community scheme in which Pitman had been happy to participate. He was no linguist but Masserella was and loved to write long, long letters. The trouble was, from the start it had been clear that the man was a complete pillock.

He was a policeman too, and he filled sides of A4 with details of Livorno police procedure. After three years of correspondence Pitman felt confident he could arrest someone in Italian if he ever wished to. He groaned when he saw Masserella's latest ten pages. The last paragraph was: 'Write soon. I enjoy your letters each time. And Please not to forget the copy of the *District Herald*.'

Pitman swigged his whisky. His replies were never more than three pages long, took him two months to write and always consisted of the same news of one-way systems and traffic offences. He'd tell him about Clive Peacock this time. At least Clive Peacock was a bit different; at least finding a missing person was helping someone. The man needed therapy, his wife had said. Well, that was good because therapy was exactly what Pitman set out to give anyone who strayed into crime. They would have laughed at him down at the station had he suggested that but it was true. Pitman had no interest in criminals who didn't want therapy. And if they did want therapy then as far as he was concerned they weren't criminals, just misguided.

He sat gazing into space until it grew dark, then took a piece of writing paper out of a drawer and wrote: 'Dear Signor Masserella, thank you for your letter. Not much has happened here recently. A new one-way system has opened, some traffic bollards have been stolen and today a postman went missing . . .'

He tore it up and threw it in the bin. Another free newspaper was pushed through the door. One of these days he'd stitch that letterbox up.

As soon as Pitman got to work the next morning the DCI rang down and told him he wanted to see him. Before he went Pitman called the *Examiner* and give them the details of the Clive Peacock story. The reporter said: 'I think we'll call him Clive Peacock the Missing Postman. That's got a feel to it.'

In the DCI's office Pitman stood as far away from his superior as possible in an effort to avoid being sneezed over. The DCI had hay fever again. He spent April to October inside a tissue, and when he spoke he sounded like a railway station announcer.

He said: 'I've got a report here concerning the Fleetway ornamental roundabout. It was attacked at the weekend by a rampant Peugeot.'

'Really, sir?'

'I know this roundabout, Pitman. It's one of my favourites. It's brand new. It's covered in floral displays and has a fish pond in the middle. And now it's been ruined. Do you know what this means, Pitman?'

'It means . . . No, sir.'

'It means that even the fish in this town are being run over. Doesn't that sound bad to you?'

'Yes, sir.'

'It means even the flowers in this town aren't safe from hit-and-run drivers.'

'No, sir.'

'Something has to be done, Pitman.' The DCI sneezed three times.

Pitman took a step further back and said: 'There are so many traffic violations, sir.'

'Traffic is all you've got to do, Pitman. For God's sake. We've just invested in a multi-million-pound traffic system. The fish and the flowers on the ornamental roundabouts are an integral part of that system. I don't want people on my roads who run over fish. I don't want people in my town who run over flowers.' And he blew his nose on the report and handed it to Pitman.

Pitman had a copy made, and when he got back to his desk he gave it to WDC McMahon. She put it on her neat pile. 'Leave it to me,' she said. 'This is nothing. When I worked in the Met we had a separate pile for roundabout abusers.'

'I'm glad to hear it,' said Pitman, but he thought: We're not the Met; this isn't London; this is a conurbation of controlled growth on the South Coast. This is a town for people not cars. And yet he knew he was only fooling himself. He used to tell people how he could remember playing in the streets when he was a kid. These days kids could spend all morning trying to cross the street to get to school.

The late edition of the *Examiner* arrived at five o'clock. The Missing Postman story was on the front page. There was a picture of Clive Peacock as he appeared on his Post Office security badge. The caption underneath read: 'Police called in as Slimathon Mayor opens new kiddies' paddling pool'.

On page two was a picture of the tubby Eddie Hicks with his trouser legs rolled up splashing about in the water with a six-year-old. The caption read: 'Fun for all as local postman goes missing'.

It was at seven o'clock that evening, just as Pitman was about to leave for home, that the call came in from the *Chronicle* in London, from a reporter named Sarah Seymour. She said to Pitman: 'I've heard about this Missing Postman. It sounds like an interesting story. I'd like to come down and speak to you. I'll bring a photographer. I'll be down first thing tomorrow morning. Is that all right?'

'Yes,' said Pitman. 'If you really want to.' Although later, as he sat in the blood donor trailer in the police station car park, he wished he'd declined the interview. This was a local matter. The nationals? he thought. What do the nationals want with my Missing Postman?

# 9

Lean and wiry fellow willing to risk death daily, cycling north. Clive put his head down and pedalled into the wind, watching the chain run smoothly through the gates, watching the tarmac run under his feet. He was going to have to push himself to reach Church Stretton in three days, but pushing himself was no problem. Cycling was a drug that soothed him, helped his body maintain a rhythm, and stopped him puzzling over what he was doing. As long as he was moving and that letter was beating in his bag he could cope.

When he left town that afternoon he cycled all the way into Wiltshire without stopping. Where the A303 cuts the A350 he rested in a Little Chef for five minutes with a mug of tea. A man with Hunt and Crayford Haulage Ltd written on his breast pocket had peered at him from behind his newspaper and whispered: 'Where are you headed?'

'Shropshire,' he said.

'Well, watch out for the contra-flow between junctions 19 and 20 at Bristol.'

Into the night he'd cycled. He thought about finding somewhere to stay, but whenever he stopped he didn't feel comfortable until he was moving again. In Trowbridge he called in at a chip shop. He wasn't hungry but felt he should have something. He ate standing in front of a row of televisions in a Radio Rentals window. The local news was on although he didn't recognise the newsreader. He thought of Christine watching TV at home with an empty plate on the floor beside her. She probably thought he was still out on the mudflats with Ralph. She'd realise he was gone when she came home from work and found her previous night's plate and crusts under the sofa. Her life would operate in much the same way without him. It would just be messier, that was all.

He crunched a piece of batter and watched the reflection of a traffic light change to red. A police car stopped and he thought: They'll be looking for me. There was a branch of his bank with a cash dispenser nearby and he took all £180 out of his account.

The TV sets were switched off. The chip stop shut and Clive was alone on a chilly summer's night in Wiltshire, but all he had to do to feel better was climb back on his bicycle.

Around midnight his road met a motorway and ran alongside for a distance. The sound of the traffic above became the sound of the night and Clive began to feel safe in the flood of yellow light. It was like swimming along with the rest of the shoal.

He stopped in a service area where whale-like trucks stretched themselves in the car park with their engines still running and their exhaust writhing in the mist. The drivers were drawn to the glow of the cafeteria like moths to head-lights. They were fixtures, these drivers, and the truck stops were like dens. The smell of diesel was intoxicating.

The tea woman gave Clive a mug without asking. The steam rose and his glasses misted up. He couldn't see the face of the person who spoke to him from the booth behind.

'Where are you headed?' asked the mystery voice.

'Shropshire,' said Clive.

'Watch out for the spilt load just south of Cheltenham.'

'Thanks. Where are you headed?'

'Newbury.'

'Watch out for the contra-flow between junctions 19 and 20.'

'Thanks.'

He put his head back into the cloud of the tea. Next thing he knew, a waitress was nudging him. 'You can't sleep in here,' she said.

So he pushed his bike down an embankment of wood-chips and heather to a service road where he found an underpass and a road-workers' red and white striped shel-ter tucked under the bridge. Inside was just a paraffin stove and a bench, but that was all he needed. With his jacket zipped up to his eyes, he curled up in a corner and was soon sent to sleep by the rhythm of the wheels overhead.

Some footsteps echoing in the concrete tunnel woke him. He pulled open the flap of the shelter and saw a man in a dirty camel coat clutching a holdall that said 'World Cup Spain 82'. He was walking around Clive's bike.

'Evening,' said Clive. There was a smell of damp clothing, and damp skin.

'Your bike?' enquired the man.

'Yes,' said Clive.

'That's a good old bike.'

'I was almost asleep.'

'It's the cars; they're like counting sheep. Whenever I can't sleep I count cars.' He paced up and down and rubbed his hands together. 'My name's Michael,' he said.

'Clive.'

Michael stepped inside the shelter. They sat on opposite ends of the bench. Clive thought he would get used to Mike's smell but he never did.

'Want a mint?' said Michael and offered him an Extra Strong. 'Here, I'll take the top one with the fluff on it. You can have the clean one underneath.'

They sat and sucked their mints. Then Michael said: 'You know, I've been thinking. If they made a film, a motion picture of your life story – just say – who would you choose to play you in the title role? Go on, have a think.'

Clive jangled the change in his pocket. 'Dustin Hoffman,' he said.

'Dustin Hoffman? No, no, Dustin Hoffman wouldn't play you at all well. You want someone like Stan Laurel.'

'Stan Laurel? He's dead.'

'Well, I know, but that sort. Ronnie Corbett – there you are. He could play you beautifully.'

Clive didn't know whether he wanted to play this game.

'Who do you think should play me, then?' asked Michael.

'Boris Karloff,' said Clive.

'Don't be stupid. There's only one person who could play me properly. Bob Hoskins. Not the way he is these days but when he was in *Pennies from Heaven*. I'm a salesman, you see. I can identify with Bob Hoskins. Richard Dreyfuss, he could play you as well. If Ronnie Corbett turned the part down.'

'No, Dustin Hoffman would be better,' said Clive. 'Dustin Hoffman gives the impression of depth.'

'Now that's interesting. That's exactly why I chose Bob Hoskins. Basic sort on top, but underneath you're not quite sure what's going on.'

A Long Vehicle passed over the bridge and the concrete shuddered.

'What are you doing here?' asked Clive.

'Me? I'm going home. I've been on the road too long. I've done my bit. Had a good time but I know when to stop.'

'Where's home?'

'London. Willesden. Up the A4 to the North Circular and then turn down the A1. How about Tim Brooke Taylor? He could play you. He could do you beautifully. What's in that bag?'

'Nothing.'

Michael sat down and folded his arms. A motorbike whined overhead. Michael stood up and walked around the stove again.

'I've got shoes in my bag. I'm a shoe salesman, you understand. People always need shoes. I've been selling shoes all my life. Good times, bad times. Time to slow down now though. Where are you off to then, with your bike, and your bag with nothing in it?'

'Shropshire.'

'What, up the A466 to Monmouth, the A49 to Hereford and on to Ludlow?'

'That's right,' said Clive.

'I've been there hundreds of times. Whereabouts in Shropshire?'

'Near Church Stretton.'

'Church Stretton? What, up the A49 again past Wenlock Edge?'

Clive nodded.

'I used to have a ladyfriend in Church Stretton. We split up though; she wanted to get married – not to me, of course. She had her eyes on someone more reliable. I'm here today, gone tomorrow.'

'Humphrey Bogart,' said Clive. 'He could play you.'

'Lots of people say that. I'm not sure whether I fancy the idea though. I don't know if he could capture the essential me.'

Clive could feel himself dropping off but he wanted to be careful his letters and bike weren't stolen. His head kept nodding and he'd jerk up and see Michael walking round the shelter, nattering. 'Canterbury, now that's a good place. I enjoyed Canterbury so much I almost decided to stay. I was all for phoning up the missis and telling her to pack up and move on down. I'd get a job in a chain store or something. Sell fridges – fridges are good to work with. Something more settled, but I wasn't ready, see. I am now though. This time next week, I'll be in my armchair at home in Willesden just off the A1 watching *Newsnight*. Peter Snow! Now there's a good idea. I mean if Bob Hoskins turned down the part, then I'd be more than happy to have Peter Snow play me.'

A lorry woke Clive with a shudder. His hand reached out for his bag and found it, and he could see his bike outside untouched. But Michael was gone, had been for a while. His mildew scent had been replaced by the familiar paraffin.

Clive's back felt stiff after the previous day's exertions but he had only to cycle a few miles and he was back in rhythm. And he cycled even harder on the second day than on the first. He crossed over the Severn bridge into Wales and followed the River Wye north through the gorge. Holiday traffic and caravans filled the visitor car parks and caused queues, but Clive wasn't stopping for anything. He wasn't looking at any views.

He thought of Christine once in Chepstow, when he saw some workmen on the church roof, and again in Ross-on-Wye, when he stopped at a café and the tables hadn't been cleared of dirty plates. She would be wondering what had happened to him by now. He'd never gone off overnight before. Clive could see a policeman sitting in the living room and Christine saying, 'He'll be back soon.'

He stopped just twice that day, the first time near Tintern when he had a puncture and while traffic thundered past him he operated skilfully with spoons and patches, chuckling as he ran his fingers round the tyre and picked out the shard of glass. It was years since he'd had a puncture, a proper one on the open road.

The second time was in Monmouth where he pulled into a Happy Eater, and a truck driver leaned across and said something in Welsh. Clive said: 'Pardon?' and the driver said: 'Where are you headed?'

'Church Stretton.'

He nodded and said: 'You get the best bed and breakfast this side of the Pennines at the Black and White House in Hereford.'

At the Black and White House the woman at the door said: 'What's your load?'

'Royal Mail,' said Clive, and she pouted but handed him a pair of sheets and asked for £4.50. 'Breakfast at six-thirty, you're in room 6 with two other gentlemen.'

'Anywhere I can put my bike?'

'Under your bed,' she said and disappeared through a door marked Private and covered in fingermarks.

Dick and Tony were the other gentlemen. Dick lay on his bed in his vest, snoring. He had tattoos and ingrowing toenails. Tony sat reading a comic. 'How do?' he said as Clive struggled through the door pushing his bicycle.

'Evening,' said Clive and he kicked his shoes off and lay down on the bed, exhausted.

'Fancy going to the pub?' said Tony.

'Okay,' said Clive and put his shoes back on.

They walked into town. Tony said: 'Looks familiar this place, doesn't it?'

In the Bell they had pints of cider and Tony played the Trivial Pursuit machine. 'What is the highest lake in the world?' he'd ask out loud and then answer himself: 'Titicaca, you bonehead.' A conveyor belt of cultural debris ran behind his eyes as the questions sprang up in front. Geoff Hurst, Michelangelo, penguins, Darwin, penicillin, they all featured at some time during the evening until Tony announced: 'This is it, kid, next question and it's the jackpot. Who introduced pillar boxes to Great Britain: Robert Peel, Anthony Trollope, Lord Mountbatten? What sort of a stupid question is that – how the hell should anyone know who invented the bloody postbox . . . ?'

'Trollope,' said Clive.

'What?'

'Trollope,' and Clive reached out and pressed button B and the machine choked and spat out £16.

They went to an Indian takeaway and then sat on a bench overlooking the river where they ate their onion bhajees and chicken tikkas. Tony said: 'This is probably the cider talking, Clive, but don't you find it funny how when you're a kid you think you'll grow up and everything will be all right, and then when you get to twenty-five you think: Well, I don't feel any different but I suppose when I'm thirty I'll get myself sorted out. And then you get to thirty and you feel just the same, and then forty. And then you start to wonder if it will ever happen.'

'You're right,' said Clive. 'It's the cider talking.'

Back at the Black and White House Clive climbed into bed. His bicycle pedal poked him affectionately through the mattress. Tony said: 'How did you know about Trollope anyway?'

'I'm a postman,' said Clive.

Then it was the third day and he was bypassing Ludlow, and Church Stretton appeared on the road signs. The wind and blue sky had dried him out and he could feel the sun starting to pick at his face, but he was on the last leg of the journey now and picking up speed, and that thump in his bag was getting stronger.

When he reached Church Stretton it was almost dark and a mist was gathering in the valley. There was no one on the streets; the town felt wrapped in cotton wool. He wanted directions to Mynd Farm so he knocked on a door and asked. A man tried to explain in detail, but as soon as he pointed towards the hill behind his house Clive was gone.

The hill was steep and narrow and there were no road signs any more. The day faded; Clive's lights bounced back off the mist and he seemed to be surrounded by moorland. Below him in the valley there was a low groan of some animal in labour. I don't want to be left alone in this, was all Clive could think of.

Then he emerged from the gloom and found himself on a summit under a clear starry sky with the smothered valley below. And he breathed hard and threw his head back, letting the moment invigorate him, then he gave his bike the reins and it leaped down the hill back into the mist.

Suddenly there was a creature darting out from the bank into the road. Clive braked and swerved but his front wheel went straight over the dark shape. There was a bump and a scream, and Clive was thrown over the handlebars. He landed on grass and heard his bike hit the tarmac.

His glasses were gone, but he remembered not to panic – that was how you trod on them. He methodically patted the ground and quickly found them, although the frame was buckled and one lens cracked.

The first thing he saw was his letters spilt over the road. He grabbed at them, and then he saw the brown bird he had run over, a pheasant or something, writhing on the cold black tarmac, blood oozing from its breast.

Clive stuffed the letters back in his bag; some of them had blood on them. Then he turned to the wounded bird.

He would have to kill it – it was gasping and in agony. He found a piece of wood and tentatively prodded the creature. It spasmed, and coughed blood. Its eyes rolled and one foot clawed at the ground. Clive had never done this sort of thing before. He could feel sweat trickling down his back. He looked away, raised the stick and swung.

He missed. The pheasant lolled its head and a drop of blood appeared on its beak. What beautiful feathers, thought Clive, and swung again. This time he hit the bird's neck. It split and blood splashed up and hit his anorak and still the bird clawed at the ground. He swung again and again and once more and the head came off and rolled a short distance down the hill.

Clive was breathless. He picked the corpse up by the feet, held it at arm's length, and was about to fling it into the ditch when two headlights pierced the mist close by. He'd heard the engine for some time if he'd thought about it, and now he froze like a rabbit in the beams. An old black Mercedes covered in muck loomed. Out stepped a man in gumboots and patched jacket, a shotgun under his arm.

'Caught you red-handed,' he said and pointed the barrels at Clive's chest.

# 10

CLIVE SAT RIGID in the passenger seat. He was thinking that this was the most frightening situation he would ever find himself in: in a car in a wild and misty valley, miles from anywhere, with an ugly farmer pointing a shotgun at him. Do something, he kept telling himself; take action before it's too late. He fastened his seat belt.

The farmer drove with one hand on the wheel and held the gun with the other. He looked nervous too. But a nervous man with a shotgun was a bigger threat than a calm one, thought Clive, and these hill farmers had a reputation for being trigger happy, didn't they? They were always shooting dogs and foxes, anything that annoyed them or their livestock. What was the penalty for running over a pheasant? Clive tried to reason with him again.

'I'm just a postman,' he pleaded. 'I'm not a poacher. I've no use for your pheasant. I ran it over accidentally, I was putting it out of its misery.'

The farmer spoke slowly and took his eye off the road for long periods. He said: 'I've lost thirty pheasants at least this year to the likes of you. I'm not letting you go.' He prodded the air with the gun barrel. 'They used to execute poachers, you know.'

The car lunged into a pothole and the shotgun jumped out of the farmer's arms. Clive squirmed in his seat. This wasn't happening to him. He was at home really. He'd fallen off his bike on that last morning at work. He'd banged his head and since then he'd been in a coma. His picture was in all the local papers with the headline 'Coma drama for local Postman'. Christine was at his bedside. So was Ralph with his metal detector. They were trying to bring him round. He just needed another bump on the head and he'd be conscious.

The farmer was peering through the mist looking for the

road. Clive held his bent glasses on to his ears with one hand and clung on to his mailbag with the other. 'Where are you taking me?' he said.

'To my farm.'

'Which farm?'

'Mynd Farm.'

'I'm looking for Mynd Farm,' said Clive. 'I've got a letter for Mynd Farm. Are you Mr Flint?'

This familiarity annoyed the farmer even more. 'I'm calling the police as soon as I get in,' he said. 'I'm not letting you go.' Clive could see his white knuckles round the gun.

The Mercedes hit another pothole. In the back Clive's bicycle bucked and a handlebar knocked the farmer's cap over his eyes. Clive let out a shriek, and the farmer reeled. 'Don't you try anything, this is loaded, you know.'

It had never occurred to Clive that the gun wasn't loaded. He wasn't experienced in situations like this. It was time he got his life in order. There was something wrong if he was finding himself in battered Mercedes, in mist-filled valleys – probably in Wales by now for all he knew – with a man threatening to shoot him. He must be brave; he must act. They probably didn't have police round here. They had their own laws; he wouldn't stand a chance of justice. He mustn't be a coward. 'Listen,' he said, 'I'll give you money. How much for a pheasant?'

'I don't need your money,' said the farmer.

'£180,' pleaded Clive. 'That ought to cover it.'

'Shut up, we're here.'

Out of the mist lights appeared, swinging in threads across a farmyard; trees leaned over an old stone farmhouse. The Mercedes rumbled across dung-coated cobbles. The farmer stopped the car by stalling it. He sounded his horn.

'Right, out with you, and no funny business. This gun is loaded, you know.'

Clive climbed down. The mud was dry and didn't smell but from the house came an aroma of curry that made his mouth water. It annoyed him the way his stomach could be so selfish at such a difficult time.

The farmhouse door opened, activating a light above the porch, and there stood Mrs Flint in an apron that said, 'Come and get it.'

'I've caught a poacher,' said the farmer, 'caught him red-handed.'

Mrs Flint took a step back and trod on the dog, who howled. As Clive passed her she took her apron off and said: 'Come in and make yourself . . .'

'Inside,' growled Flint, and Clive was marched into a well-equipped kitchen. He stood against a microwave at the far end and looked across a big formica-topped table at the Flints, who stood together against a tumble dryer atop a washing machine. 'Have you got bullets in that?' said Mrs Flint.

The farmer scowled at her. Then he waved his barrels at Clive. 'Right, stand where you are and don't try anything. Angela, phone Dan Ellison.'

'You phone him,' she said. 'I couldn't,' and she passed him the cordless phone. She was looking at Clive's broken glasses with interest.

Flint fumbled with the phone while trying to keep the gun steady.

'You can put the gun down,' said Clive. 'I'm not going to try to escape. I'm a postman. Look, I've got a letter for you.'

He put his hand in his pocket – an unwise move. The farmer panicked and dropped the phone, and maximising the drama of the situation said: 'Stick 'em up.' Clive stuck his hands in the air and felt his legs buckle. Finally he screamed: 'I've got a letter for you, for God's sake! I'm a postman!' And he pulled out the envelope and flung it down on the table. 'Look, Mr and Mrs Flint, Mynd Farm, Nr Church Stretton, Shropshire SY6 8BJ. That's the only reason I'm here. I'm not trying to poach your pheasants. What do I want with your stupid pheasants?'

The Flints thought about this for a moment. Then Mr Flint said: 'You can tell that to the police.'

'Yes, you can tell that to the police,' said Mrs Flint; although now she was staring at the envelope on the table, and then when she picked it up nothing else in the room mattered. Clive could see she was trembling as she opened it.

'It's a letter for you, see,' he said. 'I'm a postman.'

'You're not our postman,' said Flint.

But now his wife was looking at a photograph paper-clipped to a letter. She sat down and her whole body seemed to relax. She curved into the seat, and something left her as she turned the page over. She smiled and then her eyes began to shine.

'Morris,' she said.

'There's no bloody answer. He'll be in the pub. I'll phone 999. That'll frighten him.'

'Morris.'

'What?'

'It's from Patricia.'

'What?'

'She's all right. She says she's found a place to live, and she's even got a job, in Boots. Here's a photo of her, look.'

Flint turned to her; Clive was unimportant now. Flint took the letter from his wife and read it and Clive could see his eyes redden too. 'Thank God,' he said, and he put his arm round his wife and she buried her head in his trousers.

They let Clive stay the night. They put him in Patricia's room. The door had a ceramic plate with her name on it. On the bed was an old stuffed polar bear and on the wall a picture of Don Johnson.

Mrs Flint gave Clive a dressing gown and took away all his dirty clothes. After he'd changed he was called back into the kitchen where a plate was rotating in the micro-wave. The machine pinged and Mrs Flint pulled out curry on rice. The Flints left Clive alone then, but he could hear them in the other room, on the telephone. She was talking so excitedly and he was prompting her.

Later he took a shower and climbed into Patricia's bed between sheets that smelt of talcum powder. On the bedside table next to him glowed his retirement carriage clock, and he lay there with his whole body warm and replete and his blood galloping through him. This was really delivering the mail.

Mrs Flint marched in with a cup of tea at five-thirty. She had make-up on and a clean apron. She pulled open the curtains with a flourish and said: 'I thought you'd like to be up early. Breakfast whenever you're ready.'

Downstairs she hovered over him as he ate. Clive wanted to ask her about Patricia. The letter he had delivered was on the mantelpiece propped up in a toast rack and he was tempted to take a peek, but it wouldn't have been professional he decided. His role in all this was to deliver the mail, that was all, and he had performed that task admirably.

'Patricia's bed is very comfortable,' he said, and Mrs Flint smiled and pretended something needed attending to in another room. She had her head turned away as she passed him and she was sniffing, but Clive could tell that a cloud had lifted from her life that morning. When she was out of the room he did take the letter from the toast rack, but not to read it, to cancel it. He wrote his initials, CP, over the stamp.

Mrs Flint returned clutching a sack. 'Morris had an early start,' she said. 'But he said to say goodbye, and to give you this.' She held up the sack. 'It's the pheasant. He says he's sorry about last night, but you can't be too careful round here these days.'

'Thank you very much,' said Clive.

'I've washed and pressed your clothes, by the way,' she said, and pointed to the Aga where they were neatly folded. 'And I've mended the tear in your shirt sleeve.'

'Thank you very much,' said Clive.

He packed up and dressed then stood on the porch and smacked his lips.

'Right, then, I'll be off. Thank you for . . . you know . . .'

'You're welcome. I'm not sure who you are. You don't look like a friend of Patricia's.'

'I'm not. I'm the postman.'

'Yes. Anyway, she seems to be all right. It's nice down there, isn't it? By the sea.'

He wheeled his bike a little way down the drive. "Bye then.'

"Bye.'

Out in the fields he could hear a tractor, but it was lost in the tall crops. He wondered if he should stay a little longer, but when he turned back to Mrs Flint the door was closed. So he cycled down the lane out of the farm, feeling revived, and when he got to the junction with the A49 he stopped and jangled the change in his pocket and thought: So, what do I do now?

There was nothing else he could do. He stuck his hand in his bag and pulled out another letter. Gulliver and Morton, Solicitors, Pakenfield Road, Wolverhampton. He looked at his map: he could make that in a day.

Lean and wiry fellow cycling up Wenlock Edge and down into Bridgnorth. He bought some plums for his lunch and ate them on the steps of a cinema. Dustin Hoffman was in the main feature. Maybe he would be a bit miscast as Clive. Maybe Richard Dreyfuss would have been better. He had the 'little man who could only be pushed so far' image, and Clive was beginning to identify with that character.

He pushed on to Wolverhampton, and found Gulliver and Morton the solicitors without any trouble. He strode up to the reception and put the letter down in front of a secretary who was reading her horoscope.

'What happened to your glasses?' she said.

'Nothing,' said Clive. 'What's Aquarius?'

'A good day to make decisions concerning financial matters. Don't worry about your relationship taking a turn for the worse, all will correct itself before the weekend. Beware of the colour blue.'

'Perfect,' said Clive.

Later that evening, the landlady at the Fairview B & B in Lichfield twisted her lips in suspicion when the guest in the Post Office jacket gave her a pheasant and asked her if she'd like to cook it for supper. But business had been slack and she led the man into the living room to watch *Coronation Street*.

She called him when the bird was ready. She'd set just one place at the table, but she was very pleased to eat with him when he asked her to. He had a face that grew on you, this postman did.

'My name's Clive,' he said.

'I'm Lesley. And I've never cooked pheasant before. I had to follow a recipe.'

They ate in silence. Lesley produced an apple pie to follow.

'Do you like horror?' said Lesley.

'Pardon?'

'Horror films. Only there's one on later and I don't like to watch them on my own. I normally ask guests in to watch TV after and you're the only one staying tonight, so if you want to watch I'd be grateful.'

They watched the horror film after the news. Shortly before midnight Christopher Lee had a stake buried in him, but Clive was fast asleep. He woke at five o'clock and he was still on the couch. Lesley had put a blanket over him. On the TV was a note: 'I tried to wake you but you wouldn't budge. Breakfast at eight.'

Clive dressed and left. He cycled idly for two hours in no particular direction until he came to a bridge and looked down on a motorway. The lines of rush hour traffic were all heading into Birmingham. Everyone was trying to push their way into the fast lane and the result was that the middle and slow lanes had less traffic and were moving faster.

In a nearby village he found a park where he sat and ate the rest of his plums for breakfast, and watched a groundsman roll the cricket square. He wondered whether Christine was cooking meals for herself or living off snacks. The plates would be concealed under every piece of furniture in the house by now. There'd be two or three teacups by her bedside, newspapers piled up by the door, a rim round the bath, another splinter wedged in her flesh. He looked on his shirt-cuff – Mrs Flint hadn't managed to wash the bloodstain out.

There was a phone box at the edge of the park. Clive leaned his bike outside and would have called Christine but the phone was broken. When he held the receiver to his ear it was screaming.

He stood there in the kiosk for a while enjoying its cosiness, wondering what he was going to do next when he knew exactly what he was going to do next. He pulled out another letter: Mr R. Pickering, 12 Greenaway Street, Shipley, Yorkshire. Clive smiled – this was fun. And he was feeling more and more in the grip of a force he knew he couldn't control, but which he sensed he was drawing strength from. Later that morning he caught his reflection in a shop window as he stood astride his bike at traffic lights. He saw a windswept face, but taut and with a sharpness in its eyes. He had blown-back hair, and his back was straight and he was poised at the handlebars like a sprinter at the blocks. The lights turned to green and he was away before all the traffic. Later he thought of the letter to Italy in his bag and tried to calculate the distance, but he hadn't really any idea.

It was late afternoon when he stopped in a Little Chef on the A38 near Derby. He drank coffee and ate a steak and kidney pie and took glances at the newspaper lying on the seat next to him. 'Man Leaves Wife and Marries Mother-in-Law' shouted the *Chronicle* headline, and curiosity got the better of Clive. He skipped through the pages – other people's lives, but then he saw a face he recognised.

It was, of course, his own, although his first thought was how different this picture was from that reflection he'd seen in the shop window earlier. How smug he looked here.

Two columns were given over to the story of the Missing Postman. Clive squinted at it through his cracked lens. The report was written by someone named Sarah Seymour and she was outraged, that much was clear. She wrote: 'Shocked is the best way to describe the people of this South Coast town today. How else, they say, are they supposed to feel when their postman as well as their postbox has been interfered with?'

Clive closed the paper and looked round the café. Two other drivers were propping up the *Chronicle* on their bellies. His picture was in every one of them.

He turned towards the window and opened the paper again. 'What exactly happened at the Waverley Road postbox on Monday no one knows, but the fact is Clive Peacock has disappeared and so has the twelve noon collection. "What is happening to Britain?" this community is asking.'

A face pressed itself against the window. A little boy pointed at him. Clive turned away. Someone tapped him on the shoulder to ask if the seat next to him was taken and Clive jumped up and pushed his way out to the Gents.

He sat there with the seat down. Sarah Seymour continued: 'Theories of what has happened to Clive Peacock are numerous. While Mrs Christine Peacock, his wife, is sticking by her man saying, "He'll be back shortly, he often goes off on cycle rides," the rest of the community has different ideas. Mr Denbigh, the spokesman for the local Neighbourhood Watch, said: "We all knew Clive and we considered the man to be beyond reproach. But who can tell in this day and age? We're all a bit stunned. Mrs Atherton is keeping an eye on the postbox at the moment from her living room window, but she's sixty-nine and is having a hip replacement next week. It's the way this town is going of course." '

A man entered the next-door stall to Clive and sat down. He had trousers from Burtons. Clive closed the paper and a trickle of sweat slid down his cheek. He dropped his own trousers for authenticity's sake, and opened the paper again.

'The police officer on the case is Detective Sergeant Pitman. He said yesterday: "Let's not jump to conclusions here. There's a possibility of course that Clive Peacock has stolen the mail, but equally he could have simply fallen off his bike and received a head injury and be lying in a ditch somewhere quite innocently." '

Someone hammered on the door. Clive had been in there half an hour, reading and rereading the article. He took one last look at the picture – one last look at that life – and shoved it down the toilet. Then he pulled his hood up and walked out of the Gents a wanted man. "Bout bloody time too,' said a driver from Birds Eye.

He tucked himself into a telephone booth to try to make a call to Christine, but the line was engaged. He tried a number of times but left when a queue started to form. He noted a sense of fate connected with everything to do with home, and then when he pointed himself in the opposite direction he felt the breeze fresh on his face.

He wheeled his bike down the service road away from the highway. A car passed and splashed him. He hadn't noticed it had been raining. The car had a sticker in the rear window: 'Don't follow me I'm lost too'. Clive decided it was best to stick to back roads from now on.

'Have a good weekend,' someone shouted back in the car park. Clive presumed it was Friday night although it made no difference to him. An image of the DIY centre flashed into his mind and out again as he checked the straps on his bag and set off up the B5023.

# 11

Two men in council overalls were working on the road outside the house. They were building road humps in accordance with Section 90c of the Highways Act 1980.

Christine could see them from her perch up a ladder in the living room. She was painting a crack in the plaster along the main wall. Her original plan had been to have just a hairline, a metre long, in one corner, but the idea had run away with her and now an illusory crevice sliced the wall at an angle of sixty-five degrees from the ceiling until it disappeared behind the TV. It gives the room something, she said to herself. A past maybe? A crack in a wall was something you could peer into.

There was a knock on the door. She sighed. Since that newspaper article in the *Chronicle* she'd had people knocking on her door day and night. She'd had to take the phone off the hook as well. Out of the corner of the window she could see one of the workmen waiting on the porch, the bigger of the two, the one with the little moustache and the big feet. When she opened the door he stood there grinning and offered her a kettle. 'Would you mind, love?'

'No, of course not.'

'It's taking us longer than usual. We normally get three hours per hump, you see. Two humps is a day's work. But these are ornamental jobs. Not just your lump of tarmac slapped in the middle of the road. These are cobblestoned and have little flower tubs in the corners, and Victorian bollards. So we get a day on each. We'll be done by tomorrow though.'

Christine took the kettle into the kitchen. It wouldn't fit under the tap for the dirty plates. Whenever she looked in the sink she thought of Clive. He had been gone for over a week now and as the dishes had begun to pile up, as the garden had sprouted a crop of weeds, and as she'd become increasingly more unable to find things in their usual place, she'd missed him more and more. This had seemed cynical at first but it was just the way her love for him surfaced, she rationalised. If this week had taught her anything it was that Clive had the sort of presence you didn't appreciate until it was gone.

She returned the kettle to the workman. He said thank you but didn't move. He made a face and said: 'This is where the Missing Postman lives, isn't it?'

Christine fumbled for an answer. 'Yes . . . of course it is.'

'What's he up to, then?' said the workman, but Christine slowly closed the door. Slowly because she was beginning to feel that sooner or later she would need to talk to someone about all this, someone who would let her talk. Not the hump builder though. She locked the door and went back to her crack.

The neighbours had been as supportive as they were able. Mrs Wheatley had stood on the doorstep and said: 'I'll not come in because I expect you want to be alone with your thoughts.' Mr Parfitt had stood in the hall and said he hoped Clive was all right, and since he was here would she mind signing the residents-only parking petition?

Mrs Tidy had paid a visit and said she knew how Christine was feeling. Her cat was still missing after three months and it didn't get any easier. She added that she wasn't comparing Clive to a cat, but a loss was a loss.

Then Mrs Lemsford had come round and given Christine a lemon curd cake. She ate most of it that night, instead of cooking. What was left she put on the floor by the couch, and the following day Detective Sergeant Pitman called round and trod in it.

Christine had been burning holes in the chest of drawers at the time. She'd laid lighted cigarettes on the top and was letting them scorch the wood. 'Distressing again?' Pitman had asked.

'Ageing,' said Christine.

She asked him to sit down and that was when he put his foot on the cake. He spent a moment deciding the best action to take and in the end opted for removing his shoes and holding them in his hand. He sat there unaware of the threadbare soles to his socks, saying how sorry he was about the newspaper reports, how he had been severely misquoted, how she wasn't to believe all that she read, and how the national press didn't really care a damn about how they upset local communities. Christine couldn't take a policeman in stockinged feet seriously though.

Then Pitman said: 'The good news is, however, reports have come in that Clive has been seen.'

'Where?' she said in a voice she'd never heard before.

'A number of places. It appears he's safe and well. We've heard from a farmer in Shropshire where Clive actually stayed a night, and from a firm of accountants he visited in Wolverhampton.'

'And what did they say?' demanded Christine.

'They all said what a nice chap he was.'

'But what's he up to? When's he coming back?'

'I'm afraid they didn't seem to know anything about that. You see, Mrs Peacock, it appears – and this might sound far-fetched – but it appears he's delivering letters.'

Christine was confused. 'What letters?'

'Well – the ones in the bag that he stole. It seems he stole them . . . in order to deliver them.'

There was a silence. Christine stared at the wall. That was when she had got the idea for the crack. Then she said: 'Well, that's cleared that up, hasn't it?'

She climbed back up the ladder and switched on the radio. Malcolm Dixon would be on in a minute. He was the man to talk to, of course – the one rock in her life. When that journalist from the *Chronicle* had said to her, 'How are you coping, Christine?' she'd thought about saying, 'I listen to Malcolm Dixon a lot.' But she didn't say that. Instead she said she was redecorating; it helped keep her mind off things, she said. You had to be careful what you told that journalist. She spoke so nicely but she was a thin woman who never looked at you, and she wriggled a lot. 'Did your husband spend a lot of time on his own?' she'd ask and before you could answer she was writing in her notebook.

She'd been round three times now, most recently the previous afternoon shortly after Pitman. She already knew about Clive delivering the letters, and she asked: 'I wonder if you'd mind awfully if I looked round the house?' Christine had taken her upstairs and shown her the bedroom and she'd bent down and looked under the bed. 'You find all sorts of things under beds,' she'd explained. She made Christine laugh but each time after she left, Christine had a strange taste in her mouth.

Malcolm Dixon came on the air. His first caller was Margaret, who said: 'It's a shock because, although my husband and I never had an intimate marriage, I thought we understood each other.'

Christine remembered when it used to be songs on the radio that caught her out when she broke up with boyfriends, but now it was problems on emotional phone-ins.

She checked herself. What was she thinking? Clive and she weren't breaking up, for heaven's sake. He'd just gone off on one of his cycle rides.

'What do you think you could do to be able to understand each other better?' delved Malcolm Dixon.

'I'm beginning to think we might be happier apart,' said Margaret.

Christine shivered. She saw Margaret all alone by the radio, having to search for instincts she had long ago packed away in some loft of her memory. The thought of parting from Clive had never entered Christine's head. They needed each other – for sure they did. They might have lived their own lives, but they were living within the same framework. They might have been pulling in different directions, but that effort was keeping the frame standing.

She hurried down the ladder and, on an impulse, picked up the phone and called Malcolm Dixon; he was engaged. Before she could stop herself she had dialled Ron Bishop's

98

number; his answerphone was on. Christine said: 'Ron, I want to speak to you about that idea I had for digging up the house and moving it. I want to know what you think.'

She stood back from the wall. The crack she had painted looked authentic enough, but she knew she was going to have to commit herself completely to this style if it was going to work. She couldn't let herself hold back. What she needed now was an old grand piano in the corner, one that didn't work properly, one with some duff notes, and with a giant candelabra coated in fallen wax standing on top of it. A large oil painting would hang well over the fireplace. And in the far corner she needed a different concept altogether. Something wooden would work, but not furniture – nothing so boring as furniture – something more basic. A tree! That's what was required. And a real tree, not an ornamental job, something big and deciduous. A sycamore growing out of the floor would be perfect. Meanwhile the opposite wall would be improved with that damp patch and fungal effect she'd seen. She dragged the ladder across.

Nigel from Stoke-on-Trent got through to Malcolm Dixon and said: 'We didn't hit it off in bed for a long time . . .'

Christine was never really sure if she and Clive had 'hit it off' in bed, although she assumed they hadn't.

'. . . But then my wife and I discovered self-indulgence was the best therapy. So now we have sex-and-cooking weekends. We spend two days cooking nice meals and eating them in bed. It does us the world of good.'

The idea of that just didn't appeal. Christine could have stood for a sex-and-DIY weekend at a pinch, but it would have been an effort. When she had been trying to become pregnant she could remember each moment of their love-making, but after the two pregnancies had failed she had lost her drive, and with her drive, her memory.

She sponged grey paint over the white wall and stippled it to raise the mouldy effect she wanted. A pattern emerged – it was a face, surely a child's face. She drew the sponge across it again and it was gone.

He'd gone off cycling, that was all. He'd always gone off cycling at difficult periods in his life. Cycling had helped him get over his father's death, and the loss of the first pregnancy; although, strangely, he never went off after the second – after the stillbirth. That episode ought to have been more traumatic and yet he never showed any emotion; and they never talked about it, of course – that wasn't their way. Clive just did more overtime. She was proud of him – the way he held himself together during that period. It was then that she began to realise just how glad she was to be married to a postman. She loved telling people – it just felt right. And whatever house they moved to, it felt right that he should live there with her. He was the one part of every house they'd lived in that she didn't want changed.

She sponged the wet paint again and the child's face re-emerged. He'd just gone off cycling; retirement was bound to be difficult, but he'd get over it.

There was a knock on the window and Christine wobbled on the ladder. Ralph had his face pressed up against the glass. She held her chest to show him he had startled her.

When she let him in he said: 'Sorry to make you jump. I knocked. The door's locked.'

'I had the radio turned up. I've had too many callers. I want to get on.'

Ralph stood his metal detector upside down in the antique umbrella-stand and bounced into the kitchen. He was wearing a red jacket with Traditional Clothing embroidered on the back. 'Another new jacket?' said Christine.

'Superman sale,' said Ralph. 'Those humps are coming on, aren't they? They're ornamental ones, you know. Shall I make some tea?'

'Not for me. Have one yourself.'

'Might as well wash up while I'm at it.'

'No, leave that!'

'Right,' said Ralph, recognising a sensitive area when one poked him in the eye.

They sat at the kitchen table. 'So, what about this?' he said and patted his pocket where a newspaper stuck out.

'What?' said Christine.

'Have you not seen the newspaper? I don't believe you've not seen the newspaper.' He spread the *Chronicle* out for Christine. She found herself gazing at Clive's picture again, but in a larger spread now, and all around him were pictures of people she didn't recognise. She read: 'He watched the late-night horror movie with me but fell asleep before the end,' said Lesley Protheroe from Lichfield.

Christine closed the paper. 'I don't want to read it.'

'You've got to read it,' said Ralph. 'Clive's become one of those media sensations. It turns out he's delivering . . .'

'I know, I know all about that.'

'It says here: "Clive Peacock, the Missing Postman, may have stolen the mail, but it seems the circumstances are rather different than first imagined . . ." '

'I don't want to hear,' said Christine.

'No. Of course not.' He folded the newspaper up, then unfolded it again. 'But just listen to this: "It turns out Clive Peacock isn't a simple thief. He's a man of action, forced into this situation by the machine that took his job. Clive Peacock has stolen the mail only to deliver it.

' "Just where the Missing Postman is now no one knows. Detective Sergeant Pitman, the officer in charge of the case, said: 'The police are baffled, to be honest.'

' "Meanwhile at home, the Missing Postman's wife, Christine, is coping with the strain by redecorating . . ." '

'I don't want to hear, I said,' snapped Christine.

'No. It's fantastic though, isn't it? I used to go to school with him!'

Christine had had enough. 'We never had an intimate relationship, you know. Even so I felt we understood each other. But there's not a word from him.'

Ralph scratched his ankle in embarrassment. Christine had never seen him do anything quite so awkward. 'Well,' he said, looking at the table. 'Men are strange creatures, Christine.'

'You knew him better than anyone, Ralph.'

'You're right, of course. I couldn't imagine life without Clive. We were like *that*.'

'Tell me what he's up to.'

'I don't know.'

'You must have a clue.'

'He's protesting against being replaced by a machine, it says so in the paper.'

'Clive never protested against anything, you know that. I just wish for once he could have told me what he was up to, and then we wouldn't be having all this stupid newspaper business,' and she lashed out at the *Chronicle*. It scattered over the floor. The England cricket captain looked at her from the back page. He had been caught drinking and driving.

'Well done,' said Ralph. 'You should release your aggression more often. You need an outlet. I think that might have been Clive's problem. I mean, I've got my metal detector. I've heard Stefan Edberg likes to play the guitar. But poor old Clive had nothing, except for his bike.'

'We never really hit it off in bed, you know?'

Ralph scratched his ankle again. 'No, I didn't know that, Christine. Clive and I, I have to admit, never talked about sex. We never talked much at all, to be honest. We were mates.'

'He belongs back here. It's like a part of the house has disappeared.'

'Yes. I'm sure it's . . .'

Ralph didn't know what to say now. She had disarmed him, talking about sex like that. She said: 'Ralph, I want you to know how much I've valued your friendship this past week. I look forward to your visits. I feel I can talk to you.'

'Good. Good,' said Ralph. 'I'll always be here, Christine, you know that.' Then he touched her on the elbow and she sensed he wanted to hug her, but she wasn't sure if she could cope with that, not without warning.

That night she decided to cook a meal – a cottage pie. She

stood over the sink peeling onions. They brought tears to her eyes, and when the tears turned to real sobs she was grateful for the excuse and she didn't try to stop herself.

There was a knock on the door. It was Ron Bishop. He came in and left dusty footprints on the floor. 'You're crying,' he said.

'No, I'm peeling onions,' she sniffed.

Ron Bishop looked around the house with his mouth open. 'What the hell have you been doing to this place?'

'Distressing it; what do you think?'

'It looks dreadful. You should open an interior design consultancy.'

'Do you think so?'

'Yeah. Stick an advert in that new paper. It goes through every house in the town. They'd lap this crap up over on Westcliff. Is that a damp patch?'

Christine blew her nose. 'That's where I want to move to Ron, Westcliff,' and she showed him the magazine cutting, the picture of the house on the back of a trailer being towed down a street in Sacramento, California.

Ron Bishop chuckled and said: 'You'd have problems getting up to Westcliff.'

'It's not far.'

'It is now they've made Pallister Road one-way. You'll have to tow your house through the High Street, then down Folly Lane to the ring road, and up round the back of the golf course.'

'But it could be done?'

'I don't know. I suppose we could have a bash.'

'How much?'

'I haven't got a clue. You'll have plaster cracks on all your walls, you know.'

'Wonderful,' said Christine.

Ron Bishop left; he'd give her a quote, he said. Her tears forgotten, she was suddenly excited by the prospect of digging up her home. She didn't cook after all. She had a sandwich, and although she was determined to wash her plates up afterwards she shoved them under the chaise longue as usual. She didn't even go to work at the hospital that night. She called in sick. She stayed up late and began to feel herself soaking up an energy from somewhere, an old energy, like water from a tap that hadn't been turned on for years but which tasted just as pure and refreshing as it ever had. She tried to check herself, to rationalise the feeling once more – it was just her way of coping with trauma, she assured herself. But then she thought: If this feeling of excitement isn't real, why is it so scary? She knew why, and as the dawn brightened the mudflats, she took her contact lenses out and gazed into the blur and said quietly: 'You'd better come back soon, Clive, or I'll roll away, I know I will.'

# 12

WEDNESDAY NIGHT, Neighbourhood Watch night, and Detective Sergeant Pitman rode the new humps on Rockley Road without even noticing them. He was late, and he was angry. The DCI had just told him to stop posing for the newspapers, stop wasting his time with the Missing Postman and concentrate on jobs that mattered. 'Bring me the head of that bastard who knocked down the Welcome To sign on the bypass this morning,' he'd said through a Kleenex.

Pitman parked outside the Tidys'. When he rang their bell he kept his finger on the buzzer longer than was polite. When Mr Tidy let him in he didn't wipe his feet.

Mr Hadden and his pipe were standing in the middle of the room, talking about padlocks. Pitman sat down heavily on the sofa next to Mrs Tidy. She handed him the Prince Andrew and Sarah Ferguson tin with one ginger biscuit left, and a copy of the *Beacon*, the neighbourhood newsletter. 'My cat's still missing,' she said and pointed to the lengthy description at the bottom of the page. Pitman wanted to say, 'Good,' but restrained himself.

Mr Lemsford now had something to say, something about pyjamas. '. . . in my pyjamas, eating breakfast, when I remembered it was dustbin day and I'd forgotten to put the bins out. So I took them down to the street, and when I got back to the front door it had slammed shut . . .'

Pitman tried to massage his own neck but it made his arm stiff. It was all the fault of that newspaper report. 'The police are baffled.' He was sure he'd never said that. You couldn't trust these nationals. They helped no one but themselves. Mrs Tidy leaned over and whispered to him: 'The only other news is Mrs Atherton's hip operation has been postponed for a fortnight.'

'. . . so I picked up a ladder that was lying by the hedge,' continued Lemsford, 'and climbed up on the garage roof, still in my pyjamas, remember. Then I hauled up the ladder and pushed it across to the windowsill of my bedroom and managed to scramble across and force open the window. I crawled through and landed on the bed none the worse for the experience.'

And just what was Peacock up to anyway? Was he just going to work his way through his letters and then come home, or what? He'd emptied his bank account but that wasn't going to last him long. 'He's one sandwich short of a picnic,' Desk Sergeant Keogh had reckoned. 'Forget it!' the DCI had said. 'Just shove it on the computer.' But Clive Peacock couldn't be dismissed as easily as that, and Pitman certainly wasn't going to forget it. He hadn't joined the police force just to keep his desk tidy.

'. . . It wasn't until afterwards that I realised the lesson to be learnt from my little adventure,' went on Lemsford. 'All the time while I was trying to get back into my house there were people walking by below, but no one thought to stop and question me. They all assumed: Poor chap, he must have locked himself out, why else would he be on the garage roof in his pyjamas?

'So it struck me: if I was a burglar why not dress up in pyjamas. Then if anyone saw me forcing a window they'd think: Poor chap, he's locked himself out. Moral of the story: beware of anyone wandering around in pyjamas.'

The members of the Beaconsfield Hill Neighbourhood Watch sat in an amazed silence until Mr Tidy said: 'Well.'

And Mr Hadden proposed: 'May I suggest that everyone carries ID in their pyjamas from now on?'

'And nightdresses,' said Mrs Atherton.

'Well, of course,' said Hadden.

There was general consent, followed by Mr Denbigh rising to his feet. 'Now – the outing. I want to confirm I've booked the community van and reserved seats for the matinée performance of *The Tempest* in Stratford-upon-Avon for two-thirty on August 31st.'

Pitman attempted to groan inwardly but didn't succeed.

Denbigh looked at him over his glasses. Mrs Wheatley sat up and crossed her legs. Sod them, thought Pitman. He wasn't going to stay longer than he had to. He wanted to catch the late-night spin at the Posh Wash.

'Listen,' he said, 'before we go any further I'd like to know what we're going to do about Clive Peacock.'

Denbigh shook his head and said: 'I'm sorry, but if he's not got his name on the list by Friday he can't come.'

Pitman answered rather too firmly: 'I'm not talking about the outing, Mr Denbigh.' Mr Drake shuffled his bottom into his seat. Ralph Nugent scratched his ankle. They needn't worry, thought Pitman, I'm in control.

He smiled genially. Mrs Wheatley looked away. Pitman said: 'The case is concerning me because he's our neighbour, and I think maybe we should be doing more than we are to help find him.'

'We could put notices up on telegraph posts like I did for my cat,' said Mrs Tidy.

Pitman tried to smile at her as well. He said: 'I know you've all been asked this before, but I want you to think again if any of you posted a letter into the Waverley Road postbox before twelve noon on the day Clive Peacock disappeared, July 18th.'

The whole group thought long and hard. Then Mrs Drake said: 'No one asked me before.'

'Didn't a policeman come round and ask you?' said Pitman.

'One came to my door,' said Mrs Wheatley. 'I remember, he looked like President Kennedy.'

'Well, no one came to mine,' said Mrs Drake.

Pitman clenched his teeth. 'It only matters if you posted a letter that day, Mrs Drake.'

'Well, I did post a letter that day, as it happened.'

'You *did*?'

'Of course I did, I post a letter every Monday morning.'

'Who to?'

'My daughter.'

'Wonderful,' said Pitman. 'Where does she live?'

'Livorno.'

'Livorno?'

'Livorno.'

'Livorno in Italy?'

'That's right. She teaches English on the twin-town cultural exchange scheme. She says she likes it there but she's put on too much weight.'

Pitman thought about this for a moment and then sat down and looked at the ceiling.

'Can I have my bath now?' said Mrs Atherton.

Down at the Posh Wash Pitman was the only washer for the late-night spin. He sat there watching his clothes clamber up the walls of the dryer. His ex-wife was always asking him why he didn't buy a machine. The answer was because he found the laundromat the most relaxing place in town. The tangle of clothing before his eyes mesmerised him and he began to think of Ms Willis, the young woman cashier at the bank with the false nails. He imagined her blouses spinning round in the same drier as his Superman shirts. Was that romantic or lecherous? He supposed it was lecherous.

The laundromat manageress sat in her booth reading a magazine. She was surrounded by postcards. Who would dream of sending a postcard to their laundromat when they go on holiday? thought Pitman. He never sent postcards to anyone when he went on holiday, but that was because he never went on holiday – another reason for the collapse of his marriage. He mused how, for someone who placed so much importance on the role in the community of the family unit, he had been so unsuccessful in his own attempt to create one. The day he was divorced he remembered as a far happier day than the one he was married on. If he and his wife were honest about it divorce had been the goal towards which they had strived so persistently during their ten long years together.

His buttons stopped rattling in the dryer. Pitman put another 20p in the slot and his clothing crawled up the sides of the cylinder once more. The smell of soap and heat reminded him of his mother's kitchen. He was standing on a stool at the sink while she hand-washed his father's shirts and said: 'It's always August under the armpits, Lawrence. Remember that.'

He yawned. The woman in the booth yawned. He could see the magazine she was reading. 'Distant Dreams', it said on the cover. 'Destinations Worldwide'. The picture on the front was of a very brown, blonde woman in a white bathing costume lying on a beach with fishing boats pulled up on the sand nearby, and distant mountains dropping into the blue sea. Maybe a similar picture had inspired Clive Peacock. You saw pictures like this all your life, places so distant only dreams could ever get you there. You worked hard and then you retired and the dream died. Clive Peacock saw the letter to Livorno as his last chance and grabbed it. Well, there were too many distant dreams in this life, that was the trouble, too many places to escape to. If people only improved the places they lived in they wouldn't have to escape.

The dryer sighed and died again and Pitman bundled his clothes into his blue laundry bag. Outside, the warm summer night smelled of dustbins. He began to pat his pockets for his car keys, then he remembered his new toy. He looked round to make sure no one was watching and then gave a low whistle. From the inside pocket of his jacket came a whistled reply. Pitman pulled out his keys. So simple. Why hadn't he thought of a whistling key-ring before?

A sample packet of six teabags was waiting for him on the doormat as he got home. Pitman trod on them and they split. He ignored the mess, poured himself a scotch, and switched on the radio. Traffic reports and sexual problems were all he could find. Whenever he switched on the radio these days it was traffic and sex; maybe the two were symbiotic. Not that he would know. Traffic problems he had aplenty, but he couldn't remember the last time he had a sexual one.

He put some cheese on toast under the grill. The smoke alarm told him when it was ready. Then he sat down to try to write to Signor Masserella. He wrote: 'Dear Signor Masserella, thanks for your letter. Sorry for the delay in my response. Since I last wrote I've been spending my time trying to trace a missing postman. A man who stole a bag of letters and is travelling round the country delivering them . . .'

He read it to himself then laughed out loud and tore the letter up.

After a fruitless hour lying in bed trying to sleep he came back downstairs and sat in his armchair again listening to someone talking about greenfly and their reproductive problems. When he woke it was six o'clock and someone was talking about traffic being at a standstill. He decided to take the bus into work. At the bottom of Rockley Road he waited half an hour. A woman next to him said to her friend: 'She's depressed but she's still sexy.' And her friend replied: 'I don't know where she finds the time to fall in love.' When the bus came it had Asda Superstore written on the front.

At the station Pitman went straight to see the DCI and said to him, 'I think, sir, since he has a letter to Italy in his bag, we should contact Interpol.'

The DCI looked at him, his mouth hanging open. 'I've got a better idea, Pitman. Why don't you fly out to Livorno, stay in a nice hotel on the sea front, hang around the beach and the bars and the restaurants and discos, and keep an eye out? Who knows, Clive Peacock might have got there by September. Take WDC McMahon with you. I've heard she's a goer.'

The computer was down, that was the official reason for the traffic foul-up, but everyone knew the one-way system wasn't working. Everyone knew it had made matters worse. Pitman sat at his desk with his feet on a pile of No Right Turn signs and read the *Examiner*. The local traders claimed their takings were down fifty per cent in the first week of the new system. They claimed it was unworkable. The residents of Folly Avenue announced that unless they were given humps within the next week they would sit down in their road and form a human barrier to traffic on Monday 12 August from eight am to midday.

Back in the office WDC McMahon was happily wading through the stolen car pro formas. She said: 'Lawrence, you do know I've got Nigel Heath in the interview room for you this afternoon?'

'Who's Nigel Heath?'

'An unusual case. He's the one who on the night of July 21st got drunk on light and bitter, stole a car and drove into the gas showrooms.'

'What's unusual about that?' asked Pitman.

'He got drunk on light and bitter rather than lager.'

Her phone rang and she answered it with cool authority. Pitman looked at her and thought: An island of organisation in a sea of chaos. She cupped the mouthpiece as she said: 'Guess what, the TV are here. They want to interview you, Lawrence.'

'What?'

'The TV want to interview you.'

'The TV? Why me?'

'It's about the Clive Peacock case.'

'Tell them I'm out.'

'They've a crew here. It's Simon Maugham. You know, from the Network News.'

'I don't care. I'm not . . .'

A man poked his head round the door, a sandy-coloured man. He said: 'Detective Sergeant Pitman? Simon Maugham, Network News. I wonder if we could have a quick interview?'

He strode in. Pitman noticed his shirt had eight pockets on it, all of them empty. Behind him came a cameraman with chest hair sticking out of the front of his T-shirt, and a soundman wearing Bermuda shorts.

Pitman stood up and said: 'No. I'm not talking to the media again. How did you get in here anyway?'

Simon Maugham looked as though he would burst into tears. He said: 'It's just that we've interviewed Mrs Peacock, and the staff down at the sorting office, and a few of Clive Peacock's neighbours, and now all we want is the police angle to make the report balance.'

'No, I was so misquoted in that newspaper. I'm sick of it.'

'The *Chronicle* is a dreadful paper, isn't it?' said Simon Maugham. 'The good thing about it is that no one really believes what they read in it, and so, since it's got such an enormous circulation, you couldn't wish for a better paper to be misquoted in.'

Pitman was growing nervous of all the technology being set up around him. He said: 'No, no, I don't want to be interviewed again. I don't understand what all the fuss is about anyway. Clive Peacock is a missing person, that's all.'

Simon Maugham was shocked. 'But he's becoming something of a national figure, Mr Pitman. This piece is lined up for the main evening news.'

'Listen, this is a local matter. It's not for the national press or the TV. We can clear it up. Just leave us alone. Are you recording this?'

The soundman and the cameraman stood on either side of Simon Maugham like acolytes. Simon Maugham now looked very concerned. He said: 'Excuse me for saying this, Detective Sergeant Pitman, but statements like that usually suggest some sort of cover-up.'

Pitman couldn't understand how he was suddenly up against a wall; he hadn't even been aware he was back-pedalling. He detected a tremble in his voice. 'Now you listen to me, this is not a cover-up, okay? It's *not* a cover-up! We're just trying to get him back here with the minimum fuss. Clive Peacock was a respected member of this community and it's back among his own people that he belongs. You are recording this, aren't you?'

'But Clive Peacock has interfered with the Royal Mail. Isn't that an offence punishable by ten years' imprisonment?'

'Oh, don't be ridiculous!'

'I think that's fine,' said Simon Maugham. 'Thank you, Detective Sergeant Pitman. Very good of you to cooperate; I know it's a nuisance. It'll probably go out tomorrow night, at the end of the news. You know, the slot they usually reserve for elephants stuck in moats at the zoo, that sort of thing. Nice suit, by the way. The public like a trendy policeman.'

Pitman spent the rest of the day at the station. The roads were too jammed to go anywhere. His last job was to interview Nigel Heath. As Pitman and McMahon walked down the corridor a crack of thunder made the building shake. McMahon said: 'I don't fancy walking home in this.'

Pitman said he'd give her a lift. She sniggered and said: 'People will get ideas.'

He couldn't understand what she meant by that. Then he remembered the DCI had said, 'I've heard she's a goer.' He mumbled: 'There's no need to worry.'

Nigel Heath had bad breath and outsized nostrils. Pitman sat down opposite him and said to himself: Remember you are here to help this man.

Nigel Heath, a young man of twenty-three, had his charge read out to him by WDC McMahon. The details were that on the night of July 21st, he did drink twelve pints of light and bitter in the Marlborough Arms public house, then steal a Ford Escort and drive it into the gas showrooms. He admitted the offence, only adding: 'They didn't have any lager.'

Pitman had one question: 'Why the gas showrooms, Nigel?'

'It was an accident,' said Nigel Heath.

'An accident?' said Pitman.

'Yeah, I meant to get the travel agent's next door.'

The rain was rattling the windows as Pitman and McMahon got back to their office. Pitman patted his pockets for his keys – not in his jacket, must be in his trousers. He grinned at her; she grinned back. 'I'm looking for my car keys. Must be in my mackintosh.'

He put his mackintosh on and checked the pockets. Then he patted his trousers again and his jacket. He grinned at her again. She grinned back again. Then he whistled and she took a step towards the door. 'I've got one of those whistling key-rings,' he explained.

'Oh.'

Pitman walked round the room whistling. He opened his drawers and whistled in them. He bent under his desk and whistled to the floor. 'They must be here somewhere.'

WDC McMahon began to whistle in his aid. 'How peculiar,' she said.

'Yes,' said Pitman and whistled into the filing cabinet. 'Maybe I left them in the interview room.'

They walked down the corridor and whistled into the corners of the interview room, but there was no response from the key-ring.

'Maybe in the Gents,' said Pitman. He left WDC McMahon outside and went into the Gents. The middle lavatory was engaged. Pitman whistled into the other two. The door of the third flew open and there was Desk Sergeant Keogh.

'I've lost my keys,' explained Pitman.

'Just watch it,' said Keogh and went back in the toilet.

Pitman crawled round the office once more. It was as he had his head in the wastepaper bin and was whistling at the screwed up rubbish that he remembered he had caught the bus into work that day.

He stared into the bucket. Maybe she'd see the funny side of it. No she wouldn't. She'd think he was an idiot. He continued whistling while he thought what to do. 'Maybe you should catch a bus home,' he said. 'It might be ages before I find them. You know what keys are like.'

'It's all right, I'll help you. They must be here somewhere. You couldn't have got into work otherwise, could you?'

'No.' He looked under a pile of papers for no reason, patted his pockets again and wondered how long he could keep this up. When the phone went. Pitman dived for it. 'Pitman!' he yelled.

'Hello, Pitman?' said the thin voice on the other end.

'Who is it?'

'It's me, Clive Peacock.'

'Who?'

'Clive Peacock, the Missing Postman.'

'Yes, I know who it is.'

'I thought I'd call you.'

'Yes. Yes, of course. Where are you?'

'Well, actually, I'm a bit lost.'

'Hang on a minute.'

He cupped the phone. 'Sorry,' he said to McMahon. 'This is rather important. I'm going to be caught up here for at least another half-hour.'

'Oh,' said WDC McMahon.

'I should take the bus.'

'Yes. Shame.'

'Yes. Don't worry, I'll find them.'

'Right. Another time maybe.'

'Of course.'

She left. Pitman was suddenly calm. He sat on a pile of Roadworks Ahead signs and spoke slowly. 'Sorry about that, Clive . . . Clive?'

But the line was already dead.

# 13

EVEN THE BLIND have stars in their eyes. Where did that phrase come from? It didn't sound like the Bible. It sounded like a line from a poem, or a song, or a nursery rhyme perhaps.

Even the blind have stars in their eyes. The words were caught in a loop in Clive's head. He closed his eyes and tried to count the stars, the flashes of sunlight trapped behind his eyelids. He was cycling to the brim of a hill, imagining what he would find over the other side, and in those flashes he saw a town, a mountain range, a cement works, a reservoir. But then when he looked again he saw none of these. Instead there was another valley, and another road climbing up another hill into the distance.

He was well out of the shelter of the South and the Midlands now. The accents had sharpened daily; the country had become stretched. Now he was in Derbyshire and cycling over a deep green skin pulled tightly over hills, broken by outcrops of rock and stitched together by seams of stone-walling. Above was always a frantic sky. There was no one else on the road, and he was travelling blind but with stars in his eyes.

A thick stubble stuck out of his chin now. The skin on his face had become crisp and then shattered with the wind and sun and now he had a dirty tan. He gripped his handlebars with crusted hands, fingers lean and with long nails. He would have felt streamlined were it not for his bicycle. It was caked in debris and the tubing groaned with all the effort. Clive could handle the steep Derbyshire gradients – as he climbed each one he imagined he was pedalling up Beaconsfield Hill – but his old bike was struggling.

He bought himself a sleeping bag in a War on Want shop and at night he found any shelter he could. Barns and bus stations were the best bets; one night he bunked down in a half-built house. He was never moved on from these places. He was always away before the first workmen appeared.

He'd cycle in the mornings and then stop and snooze at lunchtime in a library or park, and then cycle into the evening. He didn't need much food; tea and sandwiches and individual fruit pies kept him going. He lost himself in a world of back lanes and black and white signposts, of farm machinery and village shops, surfacing only occasionally to cross a major road or sit in a transport café. In one of these, just a converted caravan, a woman in a red leather jacket sat down next to him and asked him if he wanted a good time. Clive had his mouth full and didn't know what to say anyway. She pressed him. 'We can do it in your truck.'

He swallowed and said: 'I'm on a bicycle,' and he grinned at her, but the girl didn't see anything funny.

He thought about Christine every evening about dusk, when everyone else was heading home and he had nothing but the black carpet of the road ahead of him. He still hadn't contacted her. He'd thought of sending her a card, but the idea of putting it in a postbox seemed stupid. One evening, when he was lost, he saw in the distance the red glow of a phone box, miles from anywhere, like a buoy in the middle of the ocean, and he pedalled to it as fast as he could. As he breathlessly dialled his own number he was there in his own living room, waiting for the phone to ring, looking over Christine's shoulder as she too stood waiting. But the line was still engaged. He tried for half an hour, rehearsing what to say to her when she answered: tell her not to worry, tell her he was all right, ask her to water his vegetables. But she must have taken the phone off the hook. In the end he phoned Lawrence Pitman, just to hear what he had to say. But then he lost his nerve and hung up. It had been daylight when he went into the phone box and it was dark when he came out.

Even the blind have stars in their eyes. He made up a tune and sang the line over and over until he annoyed

117

himself. Maybe it was a poem he'd learned at school. Was it Blake or somebody? He cycled with his head down and it was written on the road.

He'd stopped thinking about what he'd done. Seeing his picture in the paper had made him nervous to begin with, but as long as he had a letter thumping in his bag he had a reason to keep going, and, although he was wanted by the police and the Post Office, in his postman's uniform he still felt part of every community he cycled through – people still said good morning to him – and that made him feel justified.

As he crossed into Yorkshire the warm weather broke, and he knew he needed another night inside. He found a bed and breakfast near Sheffield. The woman didn't ask questions. She just said: 'We mostly get construction workers staying here. People think they're noisy and go out to get drunk every night but that's not the case at all. They're mostly in bed before *News At Ten*.'

She sat in front of the TV and cut up vegetables. The newspaper was folded open at the TV page and some programmes were ringed in red biro. They watched a comedy and she cut up a cauliflower and a pound of carrots, and laughed along with the audience in all the right places.

Afterwards she took her bowl out into the kitchen and returned with some onions and a swede. She said: 'I like my TV but I can't abide sitting around and doing nothing,' and then she turned over to watch a documentary. 'So, the Kalahari bushmen have remained unchanged for two thousand years,' she commented afterwards.

She had a husband who worked nights in the steelworks – the ones you could see blazing in the valley – and they had a son of seventeen. After supper she sent him upstairs to study. 'He's doing computer studies. I know it's holidays but he wants to go to university, you can be sure of that. He's got ambition – all the kids have round here. There's a seventeen-year-old down the road with his own software company. Seventeen. What a future.'

When Clive went to bed at nine-thirty the lights were on

in the boy's room and Clive could hear the hollow tap of a computer console. He sat on his bed and retaped the broken frame of his glasses with some Elastoplast he found in the bathroom. The cracked lens was working loose; it wouldn't last much longer. There was a knock on the door and it swung open and the boy was standing there. 'I just want to get a book,' he said, and he ran his finger along the spines on the bookshelf. He had a round, smooth face, the kind Clive always imagined his own boy would have had. He didn't often imagine his boy grown up, but when he did the face was very vivid, a baby's chubby face but on a young man's body. Worse things have happened in the world, he always said to himself when the face wouldn't go away, and he thought of the pictures of starving children on TV.

'How far have you come on your bike?' asked the boy.

'From Dorset.'

'We went to Wales for our holidays. I want to go on a cycling holiday on my own, though. Where's good to go?'

'Shropshire was very nice.'

A voice called up from downstairs. 'Duncan?'

'Yes, Mum,' and he went back to his room. Clive woke in the middle of the night and the computer console was making more noise than the steelworks.

A mist sat on the next morning like a hangover and the day never properly recovered. Clive lost his way again and spent hours cycling in entirely the wrong direction. The damp crept under his skin and his bike hobbled like a rheumatic. He stopped and oiled all moving parts, balanced his wheels and greased his cables, but he was concerned for it.

The mist meant he stumbled across the countryside. He'd be cycling along with his head literally in a cloud and suddenly there would be a stately home in front of him, or a skeleton of a coal mine. The journey developed into a series of frightening images thrust into his face and then dragged away in the gloom. Once, a breaker's yard loomed ahead and a transporter turned right in front of him, it never even saw him. On the back of the vehicle were tied a number of bent and buckled dead motorcars all headed for the crusher. Clive pictured his bicycle thrown into those teeth. It would be chewed up and spat out as a metal box small enough to take home in a carrier bag.

As night fell the fog rolled over the moors and absorbed every sound. A soft rumble of trucks told Clive he was near a main road, and then suddenly he was on a bridge and looking down on another motorway. The motorways had meant security at the start of this trip, but now they seemed isolatory. The cars on them were bubbles in a tube, motoring through arteries, immune to all evil and pleasure. The fog didn't seem as thick over the motorway, as if the power of the headlights had burnt away the cloud, as if they'd beaten it back into the wild where it belonged. And there was a warmth rising from the smooth tarmac that was seductive; the fumes were like the perfume of an old lover. But Clive had broken that habit. He was a lean and wiry fellow willing to risk death daily so that the mail would go through, and he didn't need the protection of motorways any more.

He pressed on, his headlight ineffectual against the thick screen ahead of him. Shelter was what he wanted – he didn't think he could last a night out in this – but visibility was so poor now he could see nothing beyond the verge. No vehicle had passed him in thirty minutes and there hadn't been a road sign for miles. 'Even the blind have stars in their eyes,' he sang. 'Oh, shut up, for God's sake.'

Then just a few yards ahead was a stationary car and a woman bent over a wheel struggling with a spanner. She was smartly dressed and this made the scene look hopeless. She looked very vulnerable. The fog might have curtained off everything, but that didn't make the surroundings less menacing. You sensed that beyond this smoke screen were moors that were endless. When the woman saw Clive her body curled up like a hedgehog. 'Need any help?' he said. at his most avuncular. Now he could see her clearly, and the face was familiar, from TV or somewhere. It was Sue Lawley.

'Oh,' said Clive. 'Hello.' She looked damp and worried but it was definitely her.

'Yes, I do need some help, please. I've a flat tyre and I just can't get this wheel nut loose. I've been struggling for ages. There's no traffic on this road at all.'

It was her for sure. She sounded nervous, and annoyed with herself rather than calm and composed, but she presented herself just the way she would have done on TV with her hair brushed and her make-up faultless. She was out on a foggy moor but it was as if the foggy moor was out of place, not Sue Lawley.

He tried to remember what programme he'd seen her on but couldn't. She was one of those legless faces you saw on TV sitting behind a desk. 'Let me have a go,' he said jovially. He wanted to reassure her; he was conscious of his unkempt state.

Clive took the spanner and placed it over the wheel nut and tugged at it, but it wouldn't budge. 'It's probably been put on with one of those electric drills,' he said. 'Which is all very well, but you need an electric drill to get it off.' He dug out his adjustable wrench from his saddlebag.

'How I ever got into this situation I don't know,' she sighed. 'I just came off the motorway – the sign said petrol – and before I knew it I was surrounded by fog. I thought I was heading back to the motorway . . . And I'm supposed to be in Leeds this evening.'

Clive tightened his spanner and jerked it a couple of times. 'The motorway's the other way,' he grunted. 'You're going in the wrong direction. This goes on up over the moor.' The spanner slipped and fell to the ground; so did Clive. She helped him up; she was shivering.

This time Clive used one spanner to hammer the other and then he jerked it again, and finally it gave. 'There you go!'

'You've done it!' She shrieked with relief.

He loosened the other nuts, then slipped the jack into

place and pumped up the chassis. Sue Lawley took out the spare tyre and rolled it round, and Clive fitted it. But then when he let the jack down the spare was as flat as the punctured one he'd just taken off.

'Oh no! This can't *be*!' She had her hands up to her face.

'That's rotten luck, that is,' said Clive, although he couldn't deny that there was something thrilling about the situation. He was kneeling on the tarmac in the middle of Yorkshire in the mist looking at a flat tyre, but it was Sue Lawley's flat tyre and that added a frisson to the occasion.

'There's nothing we can do, I'm afraid,' said Clive. 'One of us will have to go and get help.'

'I can't believe this. Why should the spare be flat? All this can't go wrong on one night.'

He looked at her for a moment. Her eyes said she'd had enough. She shouldn't be left on her own. 'Maybe we'd both better go,' he said. 'I passed a pub about five miles back, by the motorway. We'll have to walk it.'

She pulled a tissue from her pocket and searched it for a dry bit to blow her nose. 'All right,' she said. 'Thank you.' She took a briefcase from the back seat and they set off into the mist; within seconds the car had disappeared.

'I hate cars,' said Sue Lawley. 'I hate the way I know nothing about them.'

'You can't blame yourself,' said Clive. 'It was probably the valve. They can work themselves loose. It happens on my bike.'

'I should have used the other car. I knew I should.'

Their steps had echoes. Clive's bike sounded like a box of loose bits. Every sound was amplified in the fog. A train passed in the distance but it shook the earth right here. They walked in silence. Clive didn't want to say, 'You're Sue Lawley, aren't you?' People would say that to her all the time. They'd ask questions like 'So what is it like being famous and recognised everywhere?' She'd much prefer he didn't mention it, probably.

'The fog's getting worse,' said Clive.

'Listen,' she said, 'I really appreciate you helping out like this. My name's Sue.'

'I'm Clive.'

'Were you on your way home?'

'No, I don't live round here.'

'Where were you going?'

'I'm heading towards Shipley.'

'That's up beyond Huddersfield, isn't it? Where are you going to stay the night?'

'I'm not sure. I'm just cycling really.'

This thought, that he was sleeping rough, unnerved her, he could tell. She stole a look at him and he could see her register his rough face and crumpled condition. It was her turn to say something and she jumped in with 'What happened to your glasses?'

'I fell off my bike.'

She laughed at this. Clive said: 'I come from Dorset. I'm just visiting Shipley. It's a sort of cycling break for me. I like cycling. I'd have found a bed and breakfast or something.'

This explained it. Sue Lawley said: 'You just up and go, do you? Cycle up through the country. You just need the excuse to go visiting?'

'Yes.'

She thought about this. 'Good for you. I wish I could do that.'

'Why can't you?' said Clive and wished he hadn't. Now she'd have to tell him about work.

'Work doesn't allow it. I don't get much spare time. When I get holidays I don't like to do anything exertive.'

Clive wanted to say, 'This isn't a holiday.' But he would have sounded too cryptic.

'It's funny, isn't it?' she said. 'I lead this busy lifestyle. I have to travel around the country – fly a lot of the time – I have this rigorous timetable, with many people depending on me, and then one flat tyre and that's it, the whole operation collapses.'

'You can't trust machines,' said Clive.

'I need a car phone. My children are always telling me

to get one. I say I don't like being on call all the time. I've got one in the other car, that's the stupid thing.'

Car phones can break down as well, thought Clive.

She was a good strong walker; she walked as if she had an appointment at this pub. She was regaining her composure. Her nose was red but Clive could see she was pretty, as pretty as she looked on TV.

They walked for an hour. Then they heard the sound of the motorway. There was no on-ramp nearby so there was no traffic, but the bridge loomed before them and they could feel that familiar rush of metal and air.

And there was the pub Clive could remember passing, its lights shining on vapour, the motionless sign depicting a man in a cloak holding up a stage coach: The Highwayman. Good Food and Accommodation.

They walked inside to a reception area. There was the Highwayman's bar to the left and the Coachman's restaurant to the right. Both had soft music playing; both were empty. Sue Lawley went straight to the phone booth.

Clive wandered into the Highwayman's bar. A collection of pistols hung on the exposed beam, and above the bar was a picture of the pub as it once was – back in the Fifties by the look of it. A motor rally was taking place. Young men in boiler suits stood by their cars – chromed MGs and Triumphs. Women wearing headscarves and sunglasses sat in the passenger seats. A main road ran right past the front of the pub and where the motorway should have been was a field. Clive jangled the change in his pocket and moved on to the menu. Gammon steak with pineapple rings; duck à l'orange; lamb chops in a Stilton sauce. He suddenly felt as though he hadn't had a meal in weeks.

'Are you all right?' said a voice behind Clive. A man had appeared behind the bar – the landlord by the look of him. He was dressed in a sports coat and cravat and was about sixty; he could have been one of the young men in the picture.

Clive nodded. 'Fine, thank you. My friend has broken down. She's just using the phone.'

'Not an accident?' He was looking at Clive's glasses.

'No. Just a flat.'

'What a night,' said the landlord. 'I haven't poured a drink since I opened. Have you been on the motorway?'

'No.'

'Big pile-up. Some fatalities. Motorway madness, they said on the radio. It's always been a fog pocket here. You want a drink?'

'Half of bitter, please,' said Clive and he sat on a bar stool. 'How old is that picture?'

'Thirty-three years. The motor-cross club used to meet here first Sunday of every month. The motorway changed all that. This place used to thrive – for four hundred years it thrived. It was a stagecoach inn, for heaven's sake. The trunk road north went right past the front door. Then whack! The motorway arrives and everyone bypasses the place. Stone the crows – Sue Lawley!'

Sue Lawley had come in and was sat on the next stool. She smiled at the landlord and said to Clive: 'National Breakdown say they'll come as soon as they can. They don't know how long though.'

'There's a pile-up on the motorway,' said Clive. 'Maybe it's lucky you came off and got lost.'

'Sue Lawley,' said the landlord. 'Pleased to have you at The Highwayman,' and he held out his hand.

She shook it and said: 'Is the restaurant open?'

'It can be,' said the landlord.

'Well, Clive, I'm going to buy you dinner.'

'Thanks very much,' said Clive. 'I'll have the gammon steak and pineapple rings.'


They had the Coachman's restaurant to themselves. The landlord was also the waiter. After they'd eaten, he cleared away the plates and made conversation. 'Staff couldn't get here tonight. You wait till I tell them we had Sue Lawley for dinner. You might have to stay the night, you never know. Well, don't worry, there's plenty of room. I was telling your friend earlier how we used to have a lot of custom here at one time. This building dates back to 1513. Famous people like yourself came here, in the days before the motorway. We had Richard Harris for lunch one time, he was a laugh. And George Best used to call in. Dame Peggy Ashcroft had dinner here once, although I have to confess I didn't recognise her, and then we had Roy Jenkins call in on a whistle-stop tour. Anything to follow?'

'Have what you like, Clive,' said Sue Lawley.

'I'll have the duck à l'orange, please,' said Clive.

She just had a coffee. She was probably a small eater. She was slim, and food quickly lost its appeal to people like her, Clive presumed. She leaned back in her chair and stretched her legs out so one of them brushed his. 'Sorry,' she said.

The music changed. The landlord had put on a classical tape. Sue Lawley leaned back in her chair and said: 'Ah Rachmaninov, Rhapsody on a Theme by Paganini.' And she closed her eyes and put her head back. Clive looked at her pale neck. She purred: 'I just melt when I hear this. When I want to relax at home I put Rachmaninov on and do the ironing.'

'Hmm,' said Clive.

'When I was a child my father owned a garage and I'd operate the pumps sometimes, and I used to fantasise that the cars were just driving from petrol station to petrol station. People drove to work every morning and then one day decided to keep on going. That's what I'd like to do; just keep going one day, escape the way you've done – I admire you for that. Are you a postman, Clive?'

'Yes. Yes, I am. I always wear the jacket when I go cycling.'

'Did you read that story in the paper the other day about some postman from Shropshire or somewhere who everyone thought had stolen a bag of letters but in fact he was driving round the country delivering them? I can't remember exactly. It was a funny story, but I could identify with him, you know?'

'Sounds a bit strange to me.'

'No, it was a good story. I used to work on a newspaper; I know a good story. I'd love to have interviewed him. He's a real person, an unlikely little man who just set off with a bagful of letters because he lost his job or something. No one really knows why.'

'Maybe . . . he couldn't help it,' said Clive quietly.

'What do you mean?'

'Well . . . there are some things that you can't explain. You just feel happier when you do them. There's no need to understand why. That's what I feel when I cycle. Other people can come up with all the explanations they want; it's none of their business.'

Clive blushed when he realised she was listening closely to what he was saying. 'The point I'm making is you shouldn't have to have a reason for everything you do,' he concluded.

'Do you believe in guardian angels, Clive?'

'Er . . . not really.'

'I like the idea of them. I like to think there's someone watching over me, just me and no one else, someone to make me stop and think, stop and say no, someone who's guiding me. I wonder; are you my guardian angel?'

'No, no. Not me.'

'Maybe I'll read about you in the paper tomorrow; the mysterious man on a bicycle who led all sorts of people out of the motorway madness through the fog to a friendly inn. Maybe you're the ghost of a highwayman who is bound to do penance, bound to help people on the road.'

'Ha! What an imagination.'

The landlord called out: 'Telephone call for Sue Lawley.'

She hurried off to the phone. Clive finished the cheese and biscuits and wondered if they would stay the night. If they would climb the stairs after their meal and she'd touch his arm and say: 'Thanks, Clive, I really needed to meet you tonight,' and then look at him in such a way that he would know she wanted him to kiss her . . .

She came striding back to the table – in control now. She said: 'That was National Breakdown. There are no trucks available within a fifty-mile radius; they're all in use on the motorway. So I called my producer in Leeds and told him I'm staying the night here. And I think you should do the same, Clive. I'll pay. This will be on expenses. I've arranged it all with the landlord.'

'Thank you very much,' said Clive. 'I'll do the same for you one day.'

The landlord saw them up the stairs. 'You're in room 5, Sue Lawley. That's the most historic room in the house. They say Mary Queen of Scots slept in it once. There's a plaque on the wall.

'And you, sir, you're in room 6 next door. It looks out over the motorway now, although at one time it looked out over a field.'

They stood in the corridor. Sue Lawley said: 'It's nice down in Dorset, isn't it?'

'Oh yes,' said Clive.

Then they said goodnight and quickly went into their rooms. Clive heard her lock her door.

He lay on his bed thinking of her pale neck. There were sirens speeding past outside his window, and then he heard the shower running in her bathroom.

# 14

ALL NIGHT THE lights of the motorway emergency vehicles spun around Clive's room. He could hear the straining of the lifting gear and the tearing of metal, and once when he pulled back the curtains he saw the cold blue flame of an oxyacetylene torch pierce the fog. He lay awake and read the hotel fire drill. Sue Lawley had said something about admiring the way he had just got up and left. She'd said she admired anyone who was able to escape. But I'm not trying to escape from anything, Clive said to himself.

He was up at first light and looking at himself in another strange mirror. With a disposable razor that he found in the bin he shaved his upper cheeks and neck, and now he had an incipient beard rather than an overgrown face. It was the first time in his life he'd had facial hair.

A radio was turned on downstairs and he could smell toast. But he wanted to get going. There was a chill in this place – the newly arrived ghosts of highwaymen who only last night were driving up the motorway. He dressed and made his bed so that the room looked unused. He had this urge not to leave any traces. He opened his door and was about to go downstairs when he saw Sue Lawley's door handle move and he ducked back into his room. He didn't want to see her again. He liked that idea of being her guardian angel. If he sat down to breakfast with her, the previous night would be lost. Breakfast at this hour of the morning was a bowlful of reality that could smother any candlelit dinner. There were no corners of the room to hide in at breakfast.

He heard her pad down the stairs and then the telephone in the lobby clicked and she was saying, 'Yes, I'm fine. It's been a funny old night.' Clive crept down the corridor to the Exit sign and found a fire escape to the backyard.

The road was still lost in the fog but he quickly climbed, and by the time he passed Sue Lawley's car the cloud had begun to thin. Then he was above it all, and flying. The whole valley lay drugged below, but up here the sun was already softening the turf. He tasted the air in the bottom of his lungs. The motorway still prickled the back of his throat, and when he closed his eyes he had to banish the grinding of metal on metal, but the nightmare was over up here. There were no fences, no white markings on the tarmac. Sheep wandered in the middle of the road. High above, a jet drew a pure white trail across the perfect canvas of the sky, and Clive's mission for the day, his contribution to the unravelling of the great tangle of life, was to deliver a letter to Mr R. Pickering, 12 Greenaway Street, Shipley, Yorkshire, and it was all going perfectly well until after one particularly steep incline his bicycle spasmed and ground to a halt like a derailed train.

Clive laid the frame down on the tarmac. A trickle of oil was seeping from the back wheel. He stood it on its seat and handlebars and examined its drive. When spun the wheel screamed in pain, and then he saw one of the rear forks had snapped where it joined its chain-stay. The thing was crippled.

'Problems?' said a voice from somewhere.

Clive turned and saw a man sitting on a bench. He hadn't noticed him at first. He wasn't camouflaged particularly, he just seemed to be a feature of the landscape, like the bench itself.

'Yes, problems,' said Clive. 'Didn't see you there.'

'You'll always see me here.' He was an old man with perfectly false teeth.

Clive tried to lash the fork with a shoelace but it was pointless. The slightest pressure and it collapsed again. 'Is there a bike shop near here?' he called out.

'Don't think so,' said the old man. 'But then I'm not the fellow to ask. I've never been out of this valley.'

'Really?'

'Thought you'd be amazed by that. Most people are.

They made a radio documentary about me once. A man from Broadcasting House came all the way from London and asked me questions about my personal life. It went out on April 16th 1983 at ten-thirty in the morning on Radio 4.'

'I must have missed it,' said Clive.

'I taped it if you want to hear it.'

'Is there a bike shop in the nearest town?'

'I wouldn't know, would I?'

'No,' said Clive. He tried to reattach the chain but the teeth on the freewheel were bent. He would have to continue on foot. 'How far is Shipley?' he asked.

'Couldn't tell you; never been there.' The man unwrapped a sweet and popped it in his mouth. 'My theory is: stay in one place and let the world come to you. That's how I met you, isn't it? That's what I told them on Radio 4. I get all my news from the radio. Doom and gloom I call it. There's been an earthquake in Turkey, by the way.'

Clive turned his bike the right way up again. It rattled like a bag of bones.

'And there's been a fire on an Italian ferry. Forty-four feared dead.'

'Nice talking to you.'

'You hurry too much. You just wear out your shoes hurrying. See these shoes – I bought them off a travelling shoe salesman eight years ago with the money from Radio 4. Oh, and I forgot to tell you there are going to be five hundred jobs lost in the motor industry.'

Clive pushed and dragged his bike through the afternoon. He would have tried to hitch a lift but there was little traffic up here. Very little moved on these open moors. All the activity was in the sky. A bird of prey hovered; clouds shot across the blue and mustered to the east; a range of mountains peeked over the horizon; a hot-air balloon sailed across the far end of the valley and as the sun dropped the balloon seemed to absorb the light and it rose effortlessly like a private moon.

He reached Shipley not long after the shops shut. He

could see the chimney of the old mill from a distance and was drawn towards it. Shipley had once been a mill town but now it smelt like a dry-cleaner's and had the echo of a museum. The grime had been scrubbed from the stone with chemicals. The Wesleyan chapel was now a craft shop, and when Clive stood beneath the Paradise Mill he saw it had been converted into office units. A busy mural on one side of the building was the only reminder of the textile years.

Clive found Greenaway Street, and the Pickering household at Number 12. It was a new bungalow, spotless and with aluminium window frames. He stood before the letterbox with the letter in his hand and composed himself. He'd come three hundred miles to do this. But as he reached out the door was pulled open and there stood Mr Pickering. 'How do?' he said.

'Hello,' said Clive.

'Funny time for a post.'

'Special delivery.' He handed the letter to Mr Pickering, who peered at it and said: 'It's nothing important, you should have saved yourself a journey.'

Clive inflated his cheeks. Mr Pickering said: 'But since you're here I wonder . . . we're having a bit of trouble with our letterbox.'

Clive pushed the letterbox. It squeaked and grated; it was stiff and out of alignment.

'I can fix that,' offered Clive.

'I'd be grateful,' said Mr Pickering.

Clive went to his bike and brought back some 3-in-One oil and his spanners. He oiled the spring and tightened the bracket that secured the frame to the door, and that did the trick. Mr Pickering was very impressed. 'I always say it's best to leave specialist jobs to the experts,' he said. 'Are you going to be our regular postman from now on, then?'

'No. I just do special deliveries.'

'Shame. Our normal bloke's like a robot. What happened to your glasses, if it's not a rude question?'

'Nothing,' said Clive.

He asked Pickering if there was a cycle shop in Shipley. Pickering shook his head. 'No. There used to be one on the Leeds Road but it got hit by an articulated lorry.'

Clive pushed his bike through town. It groaned at every pavement step it was dragged up. It sounded as though it wanted to be put out of its misery. He wandered aimlessly. There were few people on the streets to bother him. He glanced at the property prices in the estate agent's. He eyed the Italian cheeses in the delicatessen. He paused to admire the Oddfellows' Hall, which now housed a textile museum and art gallery.

Then, in a newly converted collection of shops and parking spaces called The Quadrant, Clive found a window full of bikes under the sign Bike Mountain. Inside were muscle-bound machines all with twenty gears minimum and tyres like a motorbike's, and they were hung from the ceiling as if they would escape the moment they touched the ground. They were for hire as well as for sale. A map on the door showed the various cross-country cycle paths visitors could follow. Shipley was the mountain bike centre of Britain, claimed the poster.

The shop was closed but there was a light on inside. Clive knocked on the window a few times, then he found a bell labelled Flat. When he pressed it he heard nothing, but upstairs a curtain was pulled open and a face appeared, chewing. Clive pointed to his bike.

When the man opened the door he looked at Clive closely. 'What can I do for you . . . ?' he said at last.

'It's my bike. I know you're closed, but . . . it's badly damaged.'

The cycle shop owner glanced at the bike but he was more interested in Clive. Clive looked away. The man said: 'It is you, isn't it?'

'What?'

'You're that missing postman, aren't you? I saw you earlier on the Six O'Clock News. They had a picture of you, no beard, but it's still you, isn't it?' He stood there grinning.

133

Clive said: 'It's about my bike.'

'Come in!' said the shopkeeper. 'I've seen you on the news, honestly.'

He led Clive into his shop: 'My name's Arnie. You're Clive, aren't you? What a surprise. There was an interview with your missis as well. It'll be on again later I expect.'

He lifted Clive's bike into a vice. Clive jangled his change nervously. 'What did it say exactly on the TV?'

'You're delivering letters, aren't you? This policeman was on saying how you should come home before it got out of hand, and then your missis said something, and some other people. It'll be on later I'm sure. It was one of those stories they have at the end.' He looked at Clive and grinned again. 'Good for you,' he said.

He turned his attention to Clive's bike. He poked it and said: 'This fella has had some stick, hasn't he?'

'I've had it fifteen years. It's Post Office issue.'

Arnie prodded the damaged fork. It was clear to both of them there was nothing that could be done.

'It's knackered I'm afraid,' said Arnie. 'I could weld it but it would make no difference.'

'I've had it fifteen years.'

'Aye. You'll not find replacements neither.'

Clive thought of home, of Ralph on the mudflats, of Christine up a ladder with a paintbrush.

Arnie said: 'Tell you what: stay here tonight. We'll see what we can do in the morning. I'm pleased to have you here. I'll put some lasagne in the microwave and you can watch the news. How's that?'

They went upstairs. Everything in the flat was a different shade of blue. Arnie said: 'It's my wife, she's going through a blue phase.'

Arnie put a frozen lasagne in the microwave. Clive bent down to look in the tropical fish tank. The fish were all blue. 'Nice looking fish,' said Clive trying to make conversation.

'Aye,' said Arnie. 'I never used to rate fish. I used to think it must be boring stuck in a bowl like that all your life. But then I read that fish have got no memories. Every

134

time that little fella swims to the corner of the tank it's like it was his first time.'

'Hmm,' said Clive.

'I lie awake at nights sometimes and try to imagine what it would be like if every time I looked out of the window and saw the allotments over there it was like the first time.'

'You'd probably get used to it,' said Clive.

The kitchen filled with the smell of lasagne. Arnie said: 'My wife's at her interior design course at the College. She'll be home later. We met cycling.'

'I met my wife cycling,' said Clive. 'We were members of the local club.'

'Lucy was a member of a racing team from Newcastle. I met her at an event in Halifax in 1966. I didn't fancy her at first – funny, isn't it? She'll be pleased to meet you. She saw the news earlier as well.'

The lasagne was delicious. It burned the roof of Clive's mouth. Clive said: 'Why is this the mountain bike centre of Britain?'

'The Tourist Board decided it was, don't ask me. Downstairs isn't my shop. I just manage it for some bloke in Bradford. He comes up at the weekends and works up a sweat. I used to work in the mill, until they closed it.'

Afterwards Arnie made tea and they sat down to watch the later edition of the news. They heard about the earthquake in Turkey and the Italian ferry that had sunk. During a report about the redundancies in the motor industry Arnie's wife Lucy came in. She wore a navy-blue jacket, pale blue skirt and sky-blue tights; her shoes were blue and white. Arnie introduced Clive, and Lucy said: 'I liked the decor in your living room. I'd like to distress our flat.'

'You'd like to do what?' said Arnie.

Then the newsreader said: 'And finally the story of Clive Peacock, the Missing Postman . . .'

'Here we go,' said Arnie. 'Sssh.' And they settled into their seats as if they were watching some new drama series.

'. . . Two weeks ago Clive Peacock left his home on the South Coast with a sack of mail. Theft, technically, but it seems that his motives amounted to rather more. Simon Maugham takes up the story.'

And then there was Simon Maugham resting an elbow on the pillar box at the bottom of Waverley Road. He said: 'It was on July 18th that postman Clive Peacock picked up the twelve midday collection from this box. It was the day he was to retire. New technology had made his job redundant. After thirty-five years' dedicated service at the local delivery office. But Clive wasn't going to give up that easily. He wanted just one last chance to prove his worth. Clive decided to deliver this last collection by hand.'

And there were the Flints, standing outside their farmhouse. She had taken her apron off and he had hosed down his wellingtons. 'Nice chap,' said Mr Flint. 'He brought us a letter from our daughter Patricia who we haven't heard from since she ran away from home six months ago. A man with a mission, that much was clear. Brave too. Didn't panic when I pointed my shotgun at him. It wasn't loaded, of course.'

And there was the secretary from the solicitors in Wolverhampton. She said: 'He had a thick pair of glasses with a crack right down the middle. He didn't look like a man on the run. He looked a bit comical, to be honest. He was an Aquarius.'

Simon Maugham was now standing outside the sorting office.

'He's nice looking, that Simon Maugham, isn't he?' said Lucy.

'Ssssh,' said Arnie.

Simon Maugham said: 'This crusade, as it were, against the threat of new machinery, has, of course, won Clive enormous respect from his colleagues . . .' And the camera cut to Margaret Rogerson, Nigel Sweeney and Rolf Milne.

Margaret said: 'He was always a man of action, was Clive. Quiet, but he was a doer.'

'A loner but a man of action all right. We feel very proud of him down here,' said Nigel Sweeney.

'That's right,' said Rolf Milne. 'Proud.'

Next up was Lawrence Pitman, sat at his desk looking bewildered. Behind him was a stack of traffic cones and a road sign that said Salisbury 25. Simon Maugham's voice-over said: 'The police seem to be at a loss as to how to deal with Clive Peacock and his determination that the mail will go through. Detective Sergeant Pitman, the beleaguered officer in charge of the case, is rather sensitive about the whole affair.'

Lawrence Pitman shook his head and blurted: 'This is not a cover-up, okay? It's *not* a cover-up! We're just trying to get him back here with the minimum fuss.'

'But Clive Peacock has interfered with the Royal Mail,' said Simon Maugham. 'Isn't that an offence punishable by ten years' imprisonment?'

'Oh, don't be ridiculous!' retorted Pitman.

And then there was Christine, with a caption underneath her: Christine Peacock. She was sitting casually on the chaise longue. Clive looked for dirty cups and plates in the picture but couldn't see any. What caught his eye was a damn great crack running along the length of the wall. 'What the hell has happened to the living room?' he gasped.

'I love that distressed look,' said Lucy.

'Sssh,' said Arnie.

'Sorry,' said Lucy.

'Sssh,' said Arnie, 'that's his missis.'

Simon Maugham said: 'Why has Clive done this, do you think, Mrs Peacock?'

Christine blew the hair off her forehead. 'I think he was under a lot of stress. He doesn't often do things like this but when he does it's for a good reason. I think he should come back now though. This is his home.'

Well, it doesn't look like my home, thought Clive. What was she up to? He went away for a couple of weeks and she'd wrecked the place. And she had that look in her eye, the one she used to have, the one that called out: Someone, stop me.

Simon Maugham was back on screen: leaning against the pillar box on Waverley Road. 'And so Clive Peacock continues on this oddest of odysseys through the summer, charming everyone wherever he goes. Just what the appeal of a Quixotic postman is, is uncertain, but maybe in times when champions are all self-centred and superhuman, the Missing Postman – a man in his fifties, redundant and with bad eyesight – is the kind of non-hero we can all identify with, a man who is doing what everyone else only talks about doing. Perhaps Mrs Catterall who runs a B & B near Sheffield where Clive stayed two nights ago, summed it up best.'

And there was that woman who had cut up vegetables all evening, sitting on the couch with her son next to her. She said: 'He's the man who refused to give up work. Nothing wrong with that. All power to his elbow. You've got to be cheeky to get anywhere these days.'

The newsreader reappeared and shuffled his news reports, smiled and said: 'Watch out. He might have a letter for you.'

Arnie flicked the TV off and said: 'Right, let's go to the pub.'

'I'd like to use the phone, please,' said Clive.

'Of course,' said Lucy.

Clive rang his number, but it was engaged. His head was pounding. He hung up and said: 'I don't know what I'm doing here. I'm going to give myself up. I've got to go home.'

'No. No. You don't want to do that,' protested Arnie.

'I'm wanted by the police. I can't keep going like this.'

'You've got to keep going, Clive. Everyone's rooting for you.'

'I want to go home.' Clive was putting on his jacket.

'You can't go home, Clive. You can't let people down.'

Clive took his jacket off and sat down again.

'If he wants to go home he can do,' said Lucy. 'He's missing his wife.'

Clive put his jacket back on again.

'I know he can do, of course he can do. He just shouldn't, that's all. You heard what they said: he's a non-hero.

138

C'mon, Clive. I want you to come down to the pub with me. I want you to meet some people.'

Clive zipped his jacket up. He felt like a drink.

They walked along the canal towpath. The water was stagnant and reflections of lampposts yawned over the surface. A line of restored narrowboats were moored. One was a restaurant, one was an art gallery, one was a plant shop. 'Good investments, narrowboats,' said Arnie. Clive looked in the canal and saw his reflection struggling to keep its head above water.

Presently they reached the Navigation. 'Cheer up,' said Arnie. 'We'll get you back on your feet.'

# 15

THE NAVIGATION HADN'T missed out on the heritage boom. The bars had been knocked into one long room. Character and charm had been installed. A collection of narrowboat memorabilia was on display. Canal artist Jenny Broadbent was available for private commissions.

On one wall was a flight of photographs of a flight of locks taken in 1901. Opposite was a portrait of James Brindley, pioneer of waterway engineering. Poems by Canal Poet Adrian Dromgoole were framed and hung in corners – a collection signed by the author was available for £4.99. Above the bar was a large framed picture of people dressed up in smocks and holding wet rags and buckets. The caption underneath read: 'Navigation Arms Dwyle Flunking Team, District Champions 1988'.

'This place has changed of late,' Arnie said to Clive. 'They sell Pub Grub now; but I've heard it's horrible.'

The bar was busy. They sat down at a table with three other men all squashed on to a bench with their arms folded under their chins. They wore polo shirts and slacks but they had ruddy faces and watery eyes. Arnie said: 'Frank, Ted, Nelson.' And in turn they replied: 'Arnie.'

Then Arnie coughed and said in a loud voice: 'May I introduce a personal friend of mine. Clive Peacock, the Missing Postman.'

Ted, Frank and Nelson studied Clive. Ted smacked his lips. Frank paused with his pint halfway from the table to his mouth. Nelson put his hand out to shake Clive's and knocked his beer over Ted's lap. Arnie added: 'And he's staying in my living room the night, on the fold-down couch.'

Nelson said: 'What happened to his glasses?'

'Never mind what happened to his glasses,' said Frank.

'Shift over.' Then he called to the bar: 'Bernie, a pint for me and a pint for the postman.'

Everyone in the pub was soon gathered round Clive. Arnie acted as his manager. 'Clive, tell them that story about the farmer and the shotgun.'

And Clive would sup from one of the eleven pints of beer lined up in front of him and keep the audience enthralled with his mastery of the understatement. 'It was nothing really, although I have to admit it was probably the most frightening episode of my life.'

They all laughed and slapped him on the back and in turn called out: 'Bernie, a pint for me and a pint for the postman.'

'He kept driving over potholes,' went on Clive. 'And his head would hit the roof and his hat fall over his eyes. I only wanted to deliver his letter.'

'Bloody good for you, that's what I say,' said Nelson and slapped the table and spilt beer all over his own lap.

A man named Pat who wore a Save the Rain Forest T-shirt said: 'You're the man who refused to give up work, you are.' And he plonked a pint on the table in front of Clive. 'I lost my job when the mill closed. Now I have to work in an estate agent's.'

'I used to work in the mill an' all,' said Ray. 'Now I have to manage a narrowboat cruise fleet.'

'Me too,' said Bob, 'I spend my time making gourmet sandwiches at the delicatessen counter of Pam's Pantry.'

'And me,' said Ronald, 'I've ended up working for the bloody National Trust.'

'We all got good redundancy but that's not the point,' said Ray.

'No, it's not the point,' said Bob.

'We should have refused to give up work like you did,' said Pat.

'I'll drink to that,' said Nelson and knocked the ashtray over Arnie's coat.

The landlord called last orders, then he locked the doors and said: 'Right, who wants another drink?'

141

Arnie said: 'Tell them about having dinner with Sue Lawley, Clive.'

'It was nothing, really,' smiled Clive. 'I was cycling over the moors in the fog and suddenly there was Sue Lawley and she said: "Can you help me change this wheel?" So I did and then she bought me dinner and we stayed the night in a hotel.'

'And . . . ?' said Ronald.

'And I had gammon steak with pineapple rings,' said Clive.

'And . . . ?' said Bob from Pam's Pantry.

'And what?'

'Then what,' said Ray. 'You know . . . ?'

'What?'

'They mean did you . . . *you* know?' said Arnie.

'No. I didn't.'

They pondered on this for a moment.

'That means you did,' said Bob.

'Aye. Good for you,' said Ted.

The landlord brought a round of drinks over on a tray and said to Clive: 'I used to work in the mill. Now I have to be nice to tourists all day long and it's bloody murder.'

An old man called Young Vic downed his pint and spoke without ever taking a breath. 'I was in my allotment the other day when one of them Americans comes up to the fence and took a photo of me. "Do you do cream teas in there?" she says, waving her *Walking Tour of Shipley* at my greenhouse. I said: "Bugger Off." '

'Good for you, Young Vic,' said Bernie the barman.

'Mind you, it's not a bad idea,' said Young Vic.

Nelson put up his hand to make a point and knocked a pint of beer over Clive's lap. 'I've forgotten what I was going to say now,' said Nelson.

Ronald leaned over to Clive and said: 'You can call in at my wife's dry-cleaner's tomorrow and have your clothes done, express, for free.'

'Aye,' said Bob. 'And if you want a picnic for the journey

142

you can come down to Pam's Pantry and I'll give you a prawn and avocado sandwich. They're very popular.'

'They're horrible,' said Arnie.

'I know, but they're popular,' said Bob.

'You'll find all the support you need in this town, Missing Postman,' said Frank. 'We know what you're going through. There's not a man in here who wouldn't have his job back at the mill if he could. Not even Danny over there, who only works four mornings a week selling advertising space over the telephone and makes a bloody fortune. He'd rather be back in that mill – isn't that right, Dan?'

'Oh aye,' said Dan. 'It's quality of life we're talking about here, not money.'

'It's gone clear out of my head,' said Nelson.

'The thing is,' said Clive, 'I've no money left.'

'Here's a tenner,' said Harry Brampton, who used to work in the mill but now ran a guesthouse recently awarded three stars from the English Tourist Board.

Suddenly everyone was throwing money on to the table. The pile quickly came to £258.70.

'That's very kind of you all,' said Clive. 'But the other thing is my bicycle's bust.'

'That's true. It's knackered,' said Arnie. 'He needs a new one.'

All were silent. No one looked at Danny who sold advertising space over the telephone. Then Danny's hand slowly went to his jacket pocket, and he pulled out his chequebook and said: 'Arnie?'

'Yes, Dan?'

'What's the best bike in your shop?'

'The Mercury Drifter, Dan.'

'How much?'

'Five hundred and fifty pounds.'

'Bloody hell!'

'It's worth it, Dan,' said Arnie.

They all watched as Danny scribbled out the cheque and handed it to Arnie.

'Thank you very much,' said Clive.

'You can't fool the likes of us, Clive Peacock,' said Danny. 'You may be a card with all your stories about farmers and shotguns, and your dinners with Susan Lawley, but I know why you're delivering letters. Every time you pop a letter through a box, it's one in the eye for management – am I right?'

'Well . . .' said Clive.

'I can tell an honest man when I see one.'

'Thank you very much,' said Clive.

'They may be chasing you, but we all want you to keep going until that bag is empty.'

'The other thing is,' said Clive, 'I'm worried about Christine.'

'His missis,' explained Arnie.

'What about her?' said Ray.

'She needs me home,' said Clive.

'She seemed like the kind of lass who could hang on a bit,' said Ted.

'Aye,' said Bob.

'Aye,' said Nelson. 'She can hang on.'

'Well, the other thing is,' said Clive, 'I'm wanted by the police . . .'

Danny interrupted. 'For heaven's sake, where's your moral fibre? You've stolen nothing but what is rightfully yours – your job. Now get on with it.'

Everyone downed their pints in solidarity. Nelson stood up and knocked over the pint of beer held by the man behind him. It dripped over his own head, but it didn't bother him. He said: 'Get on with it – that's what I wanted to say.'

In the early hours Clive and Arnie tottered back along the towpath; beer slapped the sides of their stomachs.

'You'll love the Mercury Drifter, Clive. It was voted best bike in *Mountain Bike* magazine. You can cycle up walls on a Mercury Drifter. What colour do you want – blue, red or black?'

'Black,' said Clive.

'Good choice,' said Arnie.

144

They walked back to the flat. 'They're a good bunch down the pub,' said Arnie.

'They are, aren't they?'

'You're a political postman now, Clive.'

'I suppose I am.'

'Delivering letters for the working man.'

'Yes.'

But later as he lay on the foam bed-settee and watched the tropical fish explore the tank again and again, with awe and fascination, he was thinking: No I'm not.


Next morning Clive was fitted for a Mercury Drifter. Arnie weighed him and measured various bits of his body and then wheeled the machine in. It was black all over with straight lines rather than the curves Clive had been used to. It didn't have mudguards but it had a compass. It looked raw. There was something unfriendly about the Mercury Drifter.

'How does it feel?' said Arnie.

'Uncomfortable,' said Clive.

'That Post Office bike was like an old armchair. You'll get used to it.'

His old bike lay out in the yard. A dog was sniffing it. Clive picked it up and sat on it one last time. 'Don't go getting sentimental over a bicycle, now,' said Arnie.

Panniers were attached to the rear wheels of the Drifter. A waterproof pouch for Clive's letters was secured to the front. A container with tools and spares was clipped to the down tube. Then Arnie handed Clive a plastic bag. Inside was a collection of clothing – cycling gear, short and long, bad weather and good, tracksuit and shorts, a pair of cycling shoes, some fingerless gloves, a cap that converted into a balaclava, a rain cape, knee supports, goggles.

'What's all this?' said Clive.

'It's a complete kit,' enthused Arnie. 'Danny said you were to have it,' Clive pulled the touring jersey over his head. 'Time for a Tetley's' was written across his chest. He looked puzzled.

145

'Oh aye, there is that,' said Arnie. 'Dan said he reckons that since he was supplying the new bike he ought to have the advertising space. Seems fair enough? Tetley's are one of his clients, see. Tetley's sponsor the Pennine road race. I went in for it once myself. I came thirty-eighth. You don't mind, do you?'

'I suppose not,' said Clive.

'You look like a proper cyclist now with sponsorship on your chest.'

'I suppose so,' said Clive. He picked up his postman's uniform and examined the tears and frayed edges and said: 'I guess I'll dump this.'

'No, don't do that,' said Arnie. 'Let me keep it and I'll raffle it at the church fête in September. The Missing Postman's uniform – should be worth a bob or two. I'll do the same with the bike. Proceeds to the church roof fund.'

Clive smoothed down his jersey, pulled on his skin-tight shorts and sat astride the Mercury Drifter.

'How does it feel now?' said Arnie.

'Feels great, I suppose.'

Lucy came down to say goodbye. She wore violet trousers and a turquoise blouse.

'You've both been very kind,' said Clive.

Arnie shook his hand hard and long. Lucy kissed him on both cheeks and made Arnie take a picture of her and the Missing Postman.

'Go carefully,' she said.

Clive dipped into his waterproof pouch and pulled out the next letter. 'Appleby in Westmorland.' He smacked his lips in anticipation.

'You'll be there before dark,' said Arnie.

'I think it's a birthday card, judging by the size of it,' said Lucy.

'I think you're right,' said Clive.

And he cycled out of town with a wave to everyone he saw, stopping only once to pick up his prawn and avocado sandwich from Bob at Pam's Pantry. 'Time for a Tetley's,' said Bob. 'That's a good idea.'

146

The Mercury Drifter was firm and quick. Clive cycled forty miles that morning with ease. He felt refreshed and invigorated and by lunchtime Shipley already seemed days away. Going home, indeed – what was he thinking about? He was a postman, damn it! With letters to deliver. In fact he was more than just a postman. What about that time he had given mouth-to-mouth resuscitation to Mrs Gomm from Tarr Avenue? And what about the time he had foiled an attempted robbery at the off-licence on Harbour Heights? In thirty-five years the only complaint about his work had come from the union, who were concerned he was doing his round too quickly and showing up the other postmen. He was a lean and wiry ex-Postman of the Year two years running, braving Indian attack, swollen rivers, mountains and deserts so Penny Griffith in Appleby could get her birthday card.

Clive stopped just once all day, when he saw a phone box. He dialled his own number but it was engaged. It didn't bother him. He was feeling good and he just wanted to tell someone. He stood in the box eating his prawn and avocado gourmet sandwich that collapsed as soon as he bit into it, and out of mischief he decided to call Detective Sergeant Pitman again. When Pitman came on the line Clive said: 'It's me, Mr Pitman – Clive Peacock.'

'What are you up to, Clive?' Pitman said.

And Clive replied: 'I'm flying,' and then he hung up.

At three o'clock the Cumbrian mountains appeared to the west. At four it began to drizzle and he put on his new black cape. At seven o'clock he reached Appleby in Westmorland.

Penny Griffith lived at 43 Penrith Road. Clive cycled to the town centre and then followed the road signs for Penrith, and there was number 43, a grand house with two cars in the gravel drive and a double garage.

But the letterbox was too small for the card. He tried to slip it under the door, but in the end he had to ring the bell.

Through the frosted glass he could make out a little girl

come to the door and climb on a chair to reach the catch. She pulled it open and took one look at Clive and shrieked: 'Mum! It's the Missing Postman. Come quick, it's the Missing Postman.'

The girl's mother came running and put her arm around her daughter.

'It's the Missing Postman, Mum. I've seen him on telly.'

Clive blushed and would have jangled the change in his pocket but his cape didn't have pockets. He said: 'I've got a letter for you, ma'am.'

The woman smiled nervously. 'Hello,' she said.

'Hello,' said Clive. 'I've just got this letter here for Penny Griffith.'

'I'm Penny Griffith,' claimed the little girl. Clive handed her the card and she tore it open.

'Would you like to come in?' said the woman.

'No. No, thank you.'

'It's a birthday card, Mum, from Auntie Clare and Uncle Paul. It's ten days late as well.'

'Sorry about that,' said Clive. 'Couldn't be helped.'

'Are you sure you won't come in?' said Mrs Griffith. 'We're about to eat.'

'I'm a bit pressed,' said Clive and, rather more dramatically than he intended, he threw his cape round his shoulders.

Penny jumped up and down. 'Give him some birthday cake, Mum. I'm going to give him some birthday cake.'

'There are some cold chicken legs in the fridge – bring some of those as well, Penny.'

'Thank you very much,' said Clive. A house that had cold chicken legs in the fridge – he'd heard about such places but had never come across one. He was mixing in those sorts of circles now. He thought about staying, but he knew the more he stopped in places like this the more chance there was of being caught. He was going to have to be careful from now on.

'If you'd been here ten days ago you could have come to the party,' said Mrs Griffith.

148

Clive grinned and tried to think of something to say.

'Where are you going next?' asked Mrs Griffith.

'Not sure. Scotland, I think.'

Penny came back with a piece of cake wrapped in silver foil and some drumsticks in cling-film. She handed them to Clive. 'Thank you very much,' he said and took a step back. 'Right, then.'

'Are you sure you won't come in?'

'No, I've got to go,' said Clive. He gazed up at the sky. 'It's warmer, isn't it?'

'Yes,' she said.

'Right, then,' said Clive.

''Bye,' said Penny.

''Bye,' said Clive and walked backwards down the drive.

'Everyone thinks you're wonderful, by the way,' said the woman. 'Everyone in my husband's factory is rooting for you.'

Clive turned and bumped into his bike, and his glasses fell off one ear. He fumbled them back into place and then put his cake and chicken in his pannier and wheeled his bike away.

'Even my husband thinks you're a brave man,' the woman called.

Maybe I should have stayed a bit longer there, he said to himself as he walked down Penrith Road. He pulled the next letter out from his pouch. He was right: it was the long haul north up the west coast of Scotland, to Mallaig.

He set off again immediately, but he didn't go far from Appleby that night. He found an old railway station to sleep in. The sky cleared; the moon was huge and the night blue. The railway cutting was clearly visible as it curved past the station, but the lines were long gone and the vegetation thick.

The ticket office and waiting room were still standing although rotten, but that made the floor soft to lie on. Clive rolled out his sleeping bag on the splintered boards and lay there eating his chicken legs. When he unwrapped the

149

birthday cake he saw the word 'Happy' written on it in green icing.

He lay there very still; the whole room was like a big pillow. He felt almost as drunk that night as he had the night before. 'Blind but with stars in my eyes,' he hummed.

# 16

THURSDAY, LATE-NIGHT shopping at Asda, and Detective Sergeant Pitman was caught in a trolley jam, a sheer-volume-of-traffic situation that stretched from the fresh fish counter to petfoods. They'll have a one-way system in here before long, he reflected. Put in a mini-roundabout at the junction of fresh fruit and frozen veg, and a no-left-turn by the soft drink shelves. It was people who parked their trolleys in the thoroughfares who were the biggest culprits – just left them and went off to browse. Unattended trolleys would be towed away if Detective Sergeant Pitman had his way.

He did a U-turn, took a right down aisle 6, and a left by washing powder and household aids. If he turned left again by the bakery he should reach aisle 2 at Cottage Cheese Corner, and that was his destination.

Two women with trolleys blocked his path; they were chatting, wasting time, and Pitman blasted a passage through them. That made him feel better. It was wrong to relieve his stress on innocent fellow-shoppers, he knew that, but he was beyond caring. The DCI had said to him that afternoon: 'Pitman, what has happened to your brain? I'm seeing you on TV and you're making a bloody fool of yourself. I've told you: forget all about that postman. Leave him to the media, they deserve him. The man's a freak.'

But Clive Peacock wasn't a freak, Pitman was convinced of that. 'I'm flying,' Peacock had said to him on the tele-phone that morning before hanging up. And left there, with an earful of dialling tone, Pitman had for the first time begun to see his man as the innocent victim in this whole charade.

He moved with the trolley traffic down past tinned fruit. A man at toiletries caught his eye and smiled at him. That had happened a number of times, since his TV appearance.

Pitman ignored him and took a sharp left to bring him to Cottage Cheese Corner. Or what used to be Cottage Cheese Corner. Instead he found himself facing an assortment of biscuits. He sighed and slumped over his trolley. Why did they do this? Why? Just when you'd got to know your way round the supermarket, when you could plan your route and be in and out within minutes (providing Sonia was on the till). Why, for no reason, did they go and rearrange everything?

He stood there looking for an assistant. A jogger went past and turned left at pasta and rice. Across some freezers Pitman spotted a girl with a name-tag. He hurried down aisle 2 and up aisle 3 and confronted Pauline with short, sharp speech. 'Do you know where the cottage cheese is?'

'Aisle 2,' said Pauline.

'No it isn't,' Pitman said, too emphatically. 'It used to be in aisle 2 but it's been moved.'

'Try aisle 6 at the deli counter then.'

Pitman rejoined the flow. The larger they built these supermarkets the busier they became. Where did all these people shop beforehand? That was what he could never understand. It was as if demand grew to meet supply in this game. A man was perusing the boot polish shelf and blocking the entrance to aisle 6. Pitman rammed him from behind, knocking him off balance. 'Excuse me,' he said, 'so sorry,' and he flew past with his mackintosh tails flying.

He turned right at fresh meat, clipping a mother with a baby perched on her trolley. The baby started to cry. This chaos was what the Missing Postman had left behind, it was what he was flying above. This thought made Pitman jealous, and being jealous annoyed him. Then he became annoyed with himself for being annoyed. Clive Peacock had said, 'Enough is enough,' and got out. Clive Peacock, Mr Sit-in-a-Corner-and-Say-Nothing, was hundreds of miles away, and flying, and that was annoying.

He got to the bottom of aisle 6 – no cottage cheese. Pitman was beginning to lose his temper. He gripped the trolley handle and tried to control himself. When a man in a red jacket and tie and a name-tag that said Derek marched past, Pitman grabbed his arm.

'Excuse me,' syllabified Pitman. 'You've moved the cottage cheese. It used to be in aisle 2. Now it's gone and I can't find it. Where have you moved the cottage cheese to, Derek?'

Derek tried to smile, the way he was trained to. Pitman squeezed his arm until the smile disappeared. Derek said: 'Cottage cheese, sir?'

'Cottage cheese, Derek.'

'I think you'll find it in the cold cabinet in aisle 10, sir. Next to yoghurts and cream.'

'Show me.'

'Pardon?'

'Show me, Derek.'

'I'm afraid I'm . . .'

'Or I'll arrest you, Derek.' Pitman patted his pocket for his ID and flashed his phone card.

'Yes, sir,' said Derek, and with Pitman's trolley poking him in the bum he provided an escort to aisle 10 and the cottage cheese.

'There you are, sir,' said Derek.

'Thank you, Derek. And may I make a suggestion? The next time you decide the cottage cheese should move, make sure it leaves a forwarding address.'

Derek smiled as he was trained to and hurried off. Pitman rummaged through the cold counter. There was an impressive range of cottage cheese. There was cottage cheese with pineapple, cottage cheese with chives, cottage cheese with olives and cottage cheese with onion and green peppers. No plain cottage cheese though. No good, honest, ordinary cottage cheese with nothing added. 'So – no plain cottage cheese, eh?' said Pitman too loudly, drawing attention to himself. He grabbed four tubs, one of each variety, and threw them into his trolley.

Other shoppers gave him all the room he needed now as he marched up aisle 10, babbling: 'Doesn't bother me. I'll pick all the olives and the other crap out when I get home.'

He turned sharp right and emerged at checkout 3 – and there he stopped, his jaw drooping bonelessly. There was no sign of Sonia.

Pitman felt all his organs sink to the bottom of his stomach. How could she do this? How could she just walk off? She had been there when he came in. He had made sure. But now her checkout had a Closed notice at the entrance, and there was no sign of her. But she never took tea breaks; she never went off duty. She must have been taken ill. Maybe she'd fainted. Or maybe she'd resigned. While he was hunting down the cottage cheese Sonia had been given a better offer.

He hung his head and stood in the queue at checkout 4 – and he stood there for fifteen minutes. The cashier moved like a puppet. Her eyes were glazed, her movements leaden. The queue edged forward. Pitman closed his eyes and saw himself flying. The earth revolved underneath him; any obstacle he encountered he rose gracefully up and over and on into a blue, empty beyond.

Someone shoved him in the back with a trolley. You see, it wasn't that simple. Clive Peacock had tapped into a drug, some liberating, escapist drug that was in fact available to anyone. You just needed to be pushed enough to plunge that needle in, to swallow that pill. But it didn't end there. The problem was you had to come down sometime. Clive Peacock was flying, but only because he had jumped off a cliff.

The checkout girl was labelled Doreen. She plonked a Next Customer bar down and Pitman's groceries tumbled down the ramp away from him. '£14.45 please,' Doreen monotoned and tossed a carrier bag in his general direction. Pitman patted his pockets for his credit card.

The carrier bag wouldn't open. He tried to peel it apart but the wafer-thin polythene sides were locked together with static. He picked at them with his thumbs; they wouldn't separate. He tried rubbing the edges. He blew on them. He licked his fingers and tried to drag them adrift. The next customer was waiting, looking at Pitman as if he was an imbecile. Well, I'm not budging, he thought. If the supermarket chooses to give their customers bags they can't open they can pay the consequences.

'I can't open this bag,' he snapped at the cashier and handed it back to her.

Doreen didn't flicker. She was on a yacht sailing round the Aegean, lying on deck, with Eric from Wines and Spirits at the wheel. She wasn't coming back from her daydream for the likes of Pitman. She reached down and handed him another bag. Pitman fumbled with it a few times but he was speaking his mind now. 'These are stupid bags. So stupid I want to see the manager about them.'

'What?' sighed Doreen, a cloud now blocking out her sun.

'I want to see the manager.'

Someone in the queue let out an exaggerated groan. Doreen pressed the bell under her seat and sat back and folded her arms; a mauve-lipsticked smirk twisted her lips.

'Smirk at me and I'll arrest you,' warned Pitman.

The assistant manager came hurrying down the aisle. It was Derek. He slowed when he saw Pitman.

'Ah, Derek,' said Pitman. 'Me again. It's about your bags.'

'Yes?' said Derek.

'I can't open them. In fact, I don't see how any reasonable human being can be expected to open them.'

Derek took Pitman's bag. 'They can be tricky, I agree,' he said. 'But they are very strong and biodegradable, you see.'

'But useless if you can't open them.'

Derek tried to smile and blew on the sides of the bag. A voice at the back of the queue shouted, 'Get on with it!'

'Shut up,' shouted Pitman.

'Just because you've been on TV doesn't mean you can be a nuisance,' said another shopper.

'You can shut up, too.'

Derek was beginning to panic. He was grabbing bag

after bag. 'Here, I'll do it,' said the woman next in line. 'I find if you rub them on your coat it absorbs the static.'

Pitman stood back and let this little woman rub his plastic bag up and down her thigh, and it was there, at eight-thirty on a Thursday night, in checkout 4 at Asda, that Pitman resolved that no matter what else he did in his remaining time on the force, he would find the Missing Postman and bring him back to the bosom of his community. Clive Peacock wasn't flying, he was falling; and he hadn't jumped, he'd been pushed. Pushed by everyone in this supermarket, pushed by everyone at that moment caught in a queue in the one-way system. Pushed by those Distant Dreams. Well, it wasn't too late. He hadn't hit the ground yet, and it was Pitman's job, not as a policeman but as a citizen, to catch him before he did hit the ground. Clive Peacock was worth saving, he must always remember that.

'It doesn't matter about a goddamn bag, forget it!' he yelled at them, and stuffed his cottage cheese tubs into his voluminous trouser and jacket pockets. 'I don't need a stupid bag. Can't you see I'm wearing a Victor Padrone suit?'

He drove home and drank more than enough whisky. It kept him awake, but he knew he wouldn't sleep anyway, and whisky soothed him the way little else could, made him see the funny side. He had caused a scene in a supermarket. So what? he chuckled. He'd eased his tension. Some people did it in the gym, Pitman did it in the supermarket. At least he didn't take it out on his wife any more.

That reminded him. He was taking the boys to a basketball match at the leisure centre the following evening. He might have been a lousy husband but he could make up for it by being a good father. It must have been months since he'd taken them on an outing somewhere.

At midnight he picked up his letter to Signor Masserella and tried again. 'You may be interested in the case of the missing postman . . .' he wrote, then leaned back, closed his eyes and thought of Clive Peacock curled up somewhere in an outhouse with a deep sea of sleep rolling over him, and waking up tomorrow with nothing to do but cycle. And as he sat there in his armchair, a rogue wave hit Pitman and turned him over and over until he too was drowning in sleep. He struggled but he'd been caught unawares. He went under for the third time and was gone.

When he reached the station the following morning Pitman was satisfied his good temper had returned. Although when Desk Sergeant Keogh said to him: 'A man from BBC radio called. He says the Missing Postman was seen in Shipley last night, in Yorkshire. He wants an interview,' Pitman replied: 'Tell him to go and boil his head,' and he realised he was still a little edgy.

His first appointment was in the interview room, with Kevin Miles, aged twenty-four, the man WDC McMahon had traced and then charged with the destruction of the Welcome To sign on the bypass.

Miles sat before him. He had a grey face, and he spoke slowly, pausing to search for the right word, never finding it. Pitman reminded himself: Remember you are here to help this man all you can.

Kevin Miles admitted to drinking eight pints of lager and then stealing a Ford Sierra and driving it straight at the Welcome To sign. Pitman leaned forward and said: 'Why, Kevin, why did you do it?'

Kevin Miles thought for a moment and then said: 'I was keeping up with the flow of traffic.'

'I see,' said Pitman.

Back in his office he balanced a coffee cup on a pile of No Entry Unless For Access signs and looked at the picture of Mayor Eddie Hicks on the front page of the *Examiner*. The story concerned a Board of Commerce scheme to create a Clive Peacock Town Tour that would include the sorting office and the now famous postbox on Waverley Road. The Mayor was quoted: 'Clive Peacock has gained this town a lot of publicity; we should reward that.'

Pitman shook his head in disbelief. And then another

story at the bottom of the page caught his eye. It read: 'Christine Peacock from Rockley Road, the wife of Missing Postman Clive Peacock, has opened an Interior Design Consultancy. Peacock Design will specialise in the distressing of interiors.'

WDC McMahon strode excitedly into the room. The traffic cones collapsed but she ignored them. She was waving a bit of paper. 'Look at this, Lawrence, look what I've found,' and she thrust a witness pro forma into his face. A man on his way to the Northacre industrial park two Sundays ago had seen a Peugeot with L-plates on, registration D 859 PKY, driving all over the Fleetway ornamental roundabout. It was that business the DCI had been so displeased about. Pitman read the report without interest until he saw the name of the Peugeot owner: Christine Peacock.

McMahon said: 'I called Christine Peacock. She admitted that it was her car. But she said that Clive Peacock was driving – the L-plates were for him.'

They both marched straight to the DCI's office. The DCI had an almost empty box of man-size tissues on his desk. Beneath that box was a full box.

'It's about the missing postman,' said Pitman.

'I'm warning you, Pitman. I am warning you!'

'But look at this, sir,' and Pitman showed him the witness pro forma. The DCI read it tiredly, then his red eyes narrowed. 'The bastard. The Fleetway roundabout massacre – you're telling me it was him?'

'It looks that way, sir,' said Pitman.

'Well, I'm not standing for it. Stealing the Royal Mail is one thing, running over innocent fish is another.' The DCI leaned back in his swivel chair. For a moment he looked like the Duke of Edinburgh. 'This Clive Peacock has got to be found. Where was he last seen?'

'Yorkshire, sir, last night,' said Pitman.

'Take a car and get up there fast.'

'Right, sir.'

'And be back by this evening.'

'What . . .'

'That's long enough. He's on a bicycle, for heaven's sake; you've got a Ford Granada. McMahon, you go with him.'

Pitman signed for a pool car and they left immediately. The reception of Radio Estuary grew gradually weaker as they headed north. The news was that the Town Surveyor had resigned over the failure of the one-way system. His successor had already announced that another new system would be introduced as soon as possible. The last news item they heard before the signal was lost concerned Jason Adams, a ten-year-old paperboy, who had been knocked down on Russet Avenue, a well-known rat run used by cars in the morning rush hour to avoid the new No Left Turn down Silver Street. The boy was in a coma on a life-support machine. The driver of the vehicle involved was in shock. A spokesman for pressure group One Way No Way said: 'It was just a matter of time really, wasn't it?'

# 17

Pitman and McMahon joined the motorway and continued north all morning. The road had a film of drizzle. The wipers weren't needed, then they were, then they weren't. It was that sort of journey.

They conversed freely from junction 16 to junction 8 – policework entirely. WDC McMahon expressed her concern at the increase in the number of road tax dodgers and how difficult to enforce the present scheme was. Pitman agreed – he could do little else, his own tax disc was six months out of date.

Between junction 8 and junction 2 they were silent. As they passed a Motorways Merge 1 mile sign, Pitman yawned the kind of yawn one would normally control in company.

'Do you want me to drive?' asked McMahon.

'No, no, I'm all right. You don't mind missing lunch, do you?'

'No, let's get there.'

Good for her, thought Pitman. She was a good officer, was WDC McMahon. She was precise and keen and she called him Lawrence, and he would have liked to call her by her first name but he could never remember what it was, so he didn't call her anything. He wondered how old she was. She must be in her late thirties. No wedding ring though. That was the first thing he noticed about a woman – his eyes always drifted to their ring finger. He didn't know why. He never acted on the information. His father had suggested he do it. It was the only sexual advice he'd ever given him.

Pitman stifled another yawn.

'I'll talk to you and keep you awake,' said McMahon.

'I am awake,' said Pitman. What did she mean, she'd talk to him? He didn't like the sound of that.

'How long have you been in the force, Lawrence?'

'Getting on for twenty-nine years now.'

'Up for retirement soon then?'

'That's right.'

Pitman had a vision of himself in a security uniform, patrolling the aisles at Asda.

'Are you married?'

'What? No,' said Pitman. He coughed and checked his rear-view mirror while he composed himself. 'I was married – two children, teenagers now. We got divorced a long time ago. It's hot in here, isn't it?' and he checked the heater control. It occurred to him how he never took the trouble to get to know people any more. He'd shared an office with this woman for three months now and didn't know the first thing about her.

'How about you?' he said. 'Are you married?'

'No. I'm single,' said McMahon.

Pitman nodded. They passed junction 30 without incident. Then McMahon said: 'Any girlfriend?'

'Pardon?'

'Do you have a girlfriend . . . ?'

'No,' replied Pitman flatly. No one in his twenty-nine years on the force had ever asked him such a personal question. Before he could stop himself he'd said: 'How about you?'

'What?' said McMahon.

'Do you have a girlfriend . . . I mean boyfriend. I mean . . . partner.' That was the word they used.

'Why do you want to know that?' she said.

'What? . . . Oh, no reason. Let's listen to the radio.' He checked his mirror again. A truck was coming but Pitman pulled out all the same and overtook the car in front. The truck let rip with a blast on the horn and flashed his lights.

'Are you sure you're okay?' said McMahon.

'Fine, thanks,' said Pitman. 'We should be there in an hour.' He turned the radio up. Pop music blared. Pitman tapped the steering wheel.

'Do you like this?' shouted McMahon.

'Love it.'

Two junctions further she said: 'Can I find a different station?'

'Sure, suit yourself,' said Pitman, and she pressed a button and the cracked voice of Jane from Kent said: 'What hurts is the way we stayed together through the bad times and then, as soon as we pulled through, he left me.'

'How do you think you can begin to repair this hurt, Jane?' said Malcolm Dixon.

'Talking to you is the biggest help, Malcolm,' said Jane from Kent.

They made good time and reached Shipley shortly after lunch. They went to the local police station and met young Constable Burton. He looks about fifteen, thought Pitman. What did they say? You know you're getting old when the policemen start to look younger. But that didn't apply if you were a policeman yourself, did it?

Constable Burton sat in the back and directed them to the Pickerings on Greenaway Street. He said: 'I saw him myself last night, and I knew he wasn't local. I would have checked him out but the computer's down.'

Mr Pickering answered the door. He showed them into his front room and introduced his wife. He wore a shiny blue suit and golf club tie and she wore a horrid pink frock with matching shoes. She said: 'Where do you want us to sit?'

'Wherever you like,' said Pitman.

'Only the cameraman from the television was very particular about where we sat. He wanted us to sit by the cocktail cabinet; the light's better there apparently.'

'Although the director disagreed,' said Mr Pickering.

'Just sit where you like. All I want you to do is tell me what happened when you met Clive Peacock.'

'You don't want to know what sort of man he was?'

'No.'

'The woman from the *Chronicle* did.'

'Just tell me what happened, Mr Pickering.'

'It's very boring. I could tell you about the look of determination mixed with sadness and a hint of fear he had in his eyes.'

Pitman didn't respond.

'All right. He posted the letter. I tell a lie, he didn't post the letter – he handed it to me. Because my letterbox wasn't working that well, you see. Then he mended it for me – the letterbox. He didn't say much at all. It was my impression, though, that he was a cut above your normal postman.'

There was a pause while Pitman thought to himself: This whole trip is going to be a complete waste of time, I know it.

Mrs Pickering said: 'Do you not want to know whether he looked like the sort of man who would fight to the bitter end?'

'No,' said Pitman.

'He didn't, as it happened, but the man from the BBC radio seemed to think he must have done.'

'Any idea where he was going next?' said Pitman.

'No,' said Mr Pickering. 'Well, that's not the sort of thing you ask a postman, is it? You don't say: "Thanks for the letter, where are you off to now?" Likely as not he'll say, "Next door," and then you just look daft.'

They left the Snowcemmed bungalows of Greenaway Street and Constable Burton led them to Bike Mountain. 'This is where he spent the night. He seemed to make a lot of friends very quickly. He was that kind of bloke apparently – one of the lads.'

Pitman thought: Clive Peacock? One of the lads? He was wallpaper, for heaven's sake.

They parked in The Quadrant next to a car marked Radio Pennine. In Bike Mountain Lucy was in charge. She stood behind the counter in faded blue-jeans and a dark blue pullover. When they asked to speak to Arnie, she said: 'What paper are you from?'

'We're police officers, madam,' said McMahon.

'Oh. Well, he's in the pub with the woman from the *Chronicle*.'

Constable Burton led them down the canal towpath to the Navigation; his gangling gait belonged in a playground. They passed a floating restaurant with a blackboard menu that advertised 'Piquant liver in a sherry sauce'. McMahon's stomach rumbled at the sight of it. 'Good heavens!' she said. Outside the Navigation a sign read 'Pub Grub: Liver and bacon casserole'. This time Pitman's stomach responded. 'Mmm,' he mumbled.

Inside the Navigation everyone was either holding a microphone or talking into one, was either taking a picture or posing for one. Arnie, Ted, Frank, Nelson, Danny, Young Vic, Ray, Bernie, Pat, Ronald and Harry Brampton were all sat round a long table recounting the visit of the Missing Postman. Sarah Seymour took notes while her photographer poked people with his Pentax. Simon Maugham looked beautiful while his cameraman argued with his soundman. The man from Radio Pennine stuck his microphone so close to people's faces it had soup stains on it. A reporter from the *Shipley Gazette* wanted to know where everyone went to school. As soon as Pitman and McMahon entered, the reporter from the BBC spotted them and said: 'Good afternoon, Rodney Freeman from the BBC.'

'I remember,' said Pitman.

'I got your message about going and boiling my head . . .'

'Good.'

'Anything to add at this point?'

'Don't tempt me, son.'

Arnie was talking to Simon Maugham. 'He was a laugh a minute really, but he was very determined.'

'Aye, determined,' said Nelson.

'He struck me as a rebel, sort of,' said Ray the narrowboat cruise manager.

'There should be more folk like the Missing Postman around,' said Bob from Pam's Pantry. 'This country needs more Missing Postmen.'

Arnie said: 'I could tell straight away him and me would

hit it off. He was a laugh, but there was a serious side to him as well.'

'Aye, and he could tell damn fine stories, that's for sure,' said Frank.

Clive Peacock, tell good stories? Pitman looked unconvinced. 'What stories . . . ?' he asked.

'Well, he told us this one about the farmer and the shotgun. This farmer picked him up in his Land-Rover and . . .'

'It wasn't a Land-Rover,' said Harry Brampton. 'It was a Mercedes and he was taken back to the farm at gunpoint. But he had a parcel, see.'

'It wasn't a parcel, it was a letter,' said Bernie the barman.

'It was a letter from their son,' said Nelson.

'From their daughter,' said Young Vic.

Pitman interrupted them. 'Did anyone ask him what his motives for all this were?'

There was a silence.

'Did anyone ask him if he was all right, or try to understand why he had run off and was delivering letters?'

'Not exactly,' said Arnie.

'Did none of you think to ask?'

'We all know why he did it: as a protest, a protest against being replaced by a robot.'

'Clive Peacock wouldn't protest if you set fire to his trousers,' said Pitman.

'Ah, well, you don't know the man like we do. He sat right there and told us straight: "I'm doing this as a protest against the undermining of the workforce in the face of increased deployment of technology." '

'Bollocks,' said Pitman and walked out.

Pitman and McMahon adjourned to Pam's Pantry and ordered gourmet sandwiches. Pitman opted for a bacon, lettuce and tomato. McMahon had a prawn and avocado. Whenever anyone ate avocado Pitman thought of bathroom suites.

They took their sandwiches to a table in the middle of the room. As soon as they bit into them, both sandwiches collapsed and fell on their laps. Pitman controlled himself. He said: 'You know, I don't think I'm a particularly nostalgic person. I don't long for the days when the summers were warmer or anything like that. But there were some things that were better years ago. Weren't there? Have you noticed that?'

McMahon had her mouth full of avocado. When she opened her lips to speak her teeth were pale green. Before she could answer the Network News crew came into the café.

'I'll have the salami and cheese,' said the cameraman.

'I'll have the egg and anchovy,' said Simon Maugham.

'I'll have the egg and anchovy as well, please,' said the soundman.

'Why do you always side with him?' said the cameraman.

They sat down. Simon Maugham acknowledged Pitman. Pitman shook his head in disapproval.

Sarah Seymour and her photographer strode in. 'I'll have a houmus and cress on wholewheat, please,' said Sarah Seymour.

'I'm just going to smoke,' said the photographer.

The BBC reporter came in, smiled at everyone and ordered nothing.

Detective Sergeant Pitman finished his sandwich, wiped his mouth, sipped from his tea and said to the assembly: 'What are you all doing here? – that's what I'd like to know.'

No one replied. Pitman looked round the room but no one would meet his eye. 'I mean, what's the fascination? Answer me that. What's the fascination with a postman who's gone missing? I know it's the silly season, but you must be bloody hard up, that's all I can say.'

The soundman belched in the corner.

'You know what I reckon? You're all just a bunch of vultures.'

'Flock,' volunteered the reporter from the BBC.

'Shut your mouth,' snarled Pitman.

Sarah Seymour took out a pen and started to make notes.

'You don't give a damn about the man really. All this business about the Missing Postman being the sort of character this nation needs, a man who stood up for what he believes in – it's all a load of crap and you know it.'

The *Chronicle* photographer swallowed smoke and began a coughing fit. Without looking up Sarah Seymour said: 'Can I quote you on this?'

'You can quote me on what you bloody well like,' said Pitman, and Sarah Seymour wrote it down.

He was on his feet now. 'Have you ever thought that Clive Peacock is a victim? Has that ever occurred to you? No, of course not. Wouldn't make any difference to you if he was, would it? All you want is a good chase.'

Simon Maugham's Vodaphone rang. He answered it in a whisper.

'You're not interested in his welfare one jot. You just want to find him because you think he's a bit . . . weird. Well, I know Clive Peacock. He's a member of my community. He's my neighbour. And I know he's not running away as a protest or anything like that. I know he's not a hero, and I know he's not a character who tells stories no matter how much you want him to be. What I do know is that this is a cry for help. A cry from a man who more than anything is in need of support . . .'

Simon Maugham swigged down his tea and jumped to his feet. 'C'mon,' he said. His soundman and cameraman followed. They ran to their van in the Quadrant car park and drove off at speed.

Pitman continued: 'And what are you going to do if you do catch him? You'll whip his feet from under him. Then you'll feed on the juicy bits and leave the rest to rot.'

Sarah Seymour's Vodaphone rang. She answered it fluidly; she said: 'Yes . . . When? . . . Okay.' Then she stuffed the rest of her sandwich in her mouth and made for the door. Her photographer followed. They climbed on his motorbike and roared off down the Huddersfield Road. The windows in Pam's Pantry rattled.

Pitman turned his attention to the lone BBC radio reporter and said: 'I just hope I find him before you do, for his sake.' The BBC radio reporter said, 'Good afternoon,' and left.

Pitman and McMahon were left with their sandwiches. The man behind the counter came round to clear away the mess and said to Pitman: 'Don't forget to say something about Pam's Pantry in your article, will you? We could do with some publicity.'

Pitman was on his feet with clenched fists when McMahon took him by the arm and led him outside. He leaned against a phone box with his eyes closed while she called the station.

'The Missing Postman has been spotted in Appleby,' she said when she came out. 'It's just gone on the computer.'

They went back to the car. Pitman said: 'Let's go home; there's no point in hanging around. He'll be miles away from Appleby by now. It'll just be a repeat performance.'

They drove back down the motorway. They didn't speak between junctions 19 and 5. At junction 4 Pitman said: 'They'll never find him, you know. They'll always be one step behind. They'll always arrive long after he's gone. If we're going to catch him we need to be a step in front. We need to know where he's going next.'

They stopped for petrol. Pitman paid cash and got a free wristwatch in his change. Then he called his ex-wife and told her he wouldn't be able to take the boys to the basketball game that night as planned. She asked why not.

'Because I'm in Birmingham,' he said. When she started yelling at him he put the phone down. She would never give him a chance to explain, that was her problem.

They continued south, silent for a long time. Then McMahon said: 'Do you really think Clive Peacock is a victim?'

'I think he's been forced into a situation,' replied Pitman.

'And rather than face up to it, he's sort of jumped off the edge.'

'I feel like that sometimes,' said McMahon.

Pitman turned to look at her. Her face was lit intermittently by the lights of passing cars. He mumbled: 'Yeah, well, we all do at times, don't we?'

She sat back and smiled as she said: 'You know what I do when I want to jump off the edge?'

'What?' said Pitman, not really sure if he did want to know.

'I go into a crowded pub and take a step backwards.'

'Really? . . . And that helps, does it?'

'It depends whom I step on.'

They drove on in silence. When they reached home it was midnight and there was a traffic jam the length of the High Street.

# 18

THE AFTERNOON SKY was a washed-out blue, left out in the summer sun too long, and Clive Peacock the Missing Postman with the nutbrown forearms and the 'Time for a Tetley's' T-shirt was heading through Scotland towards the empty part of his map. The distances were longer now but the effort still soothing. He'd had this fantasy that the journey north would be an uphill struggle, but he was cruising.

Into the long, long evenings he rode. Loch Lomond appeared and he followed the shoreline ever north, beginning to sense just how far he'd come, and when he dug out the letter to Italy from the bottom of his collection he looked at it and thought: Of course I can do it. The address was Miss Emma Drake, 39 Via Bergamo, Livorno. Emma, Mrs Drake's daughter, although the name was unimportant, the address was the thing. As long as he had the address there was a corridor leading straight there from everywhere in the world. He fingered the envelope, and noticed in the top corner the words Air Mail. Guilt nipped him, and he promised himself he would cycle until midnight.

He came out of the shelter of the Lowlands and into wide and empty country. There was no fat of the land here, and he would have felt conspicuous had he not also felt so lean – reduced to muscle and bone. He knew he had lost weight simply because his clothes hung on him. His knuckles had rolls of skin. His legs were made of tough and dark meat. He had a permanent hunger, and yet big meals didn't appeal. He enjoyed his hunger.

He left Loch Lomond behind and slept the night in a telephone kiosk on a stretch of moor that didn't offer one light in any direction. All was calm, but there was a sense of the land just simmering. Clive lifted the telephone receiver and heard the comfort of the dialling tone. He put a pound coin in the slot, pushed the buttons of his own number, and sat back against the glass and heard his phone ring. It was just midnight but hardly dark.

After five rings his call was answered.

'Hello,' said Christine's voice.

'Hello. It's me.'

'This is Peacock Interiors. I'm sorry, there's no one here to take your call right now, but if you'd like to leave your name and number and any message I'll get back to you as soon as I can.'

He didn't leave a message. He dialled the number again and listened to her voice and realised that that sound was all he wanted. They wouldn't have had much to say to each other had she answered in person. He dialled again and again until his money ran out. What the hell were Peacock Interiors anyway?

The kiosk was like a nest and Clive huddled into his bag and was asleep in minutes. But then a flash in the sky woke him, and as he rubbed the sleep from his eyes he could make out a line of lights jumping out of the earth far to the north. He put his glasses on and the broken lens fell out, but he could still see the lights dancing like elves on the horizon. Even when he closed his eyes the flashes crept behind his eyelids. He laughed when he realised they were the Northern Lights, the edge of the world on fire, and he didn't need glasses to appreciate this.

The phone rang. He answered it but it was a wrong number, a woman wanting to speak to Eric. She apologised.

'That's all right,' said Clive.

'I'm so sorry, it's past one o'clock.'

'That's all right, really.' He would have spoken to her all night if she'd wanted. After she rang off he had the urge to phone the first number that came into his head and say, 'It's Clive Peacock here, the Missing Postman.'

The next morning a Land-Rover drove past with snow on

its roof. The country was becoming less predictable but Clive trusted his Mercury Drifter. He was heading to Fort William, about fifty miles away around the lochs, but when he passed a track that led off directly to the north with a sign, West Highland Way, he recognised it as a short-cut, and felt confident enough to follow it.

The going was rough in places and some of the inclines tortuous, but he knew the Drifter could cope. And when he reached a good height the path linked a run of ridges and he was riding on top of a treeless land where water seeped through every crack and there wasn't so much as a shadow to shelter in. The feeling of slumbering power was so great up here it should have been frightening, but instead Clive felt his senses made keener. He just kept heading north, head into the wind, never looking behind him. And that was the attraction of this kind of travelling: the lack of revision. The traveller kept going until the end of the road, and the only true experience was the one he had. Throughout his life, Clive had come to realise, exploration had taken him only to places where he'd sat on sofas and behaved politely. His bicycle rides had given him his few true tastes of freedom, the few surprises he'd had, as now the clouds ahead parted and there was a monster of a mountain, scarred with rock and snow, and roaring like a tethered animal. Then the hole was filled; the mountain was locked away again, and in its place what looked like a giant bird of prey was flying straight towards him, coming in stiff-winged, fast and so low Clive instinctively ducked. Behind it it dragged a noise like a shift in the earth's crust, a piece of the sky being ripped out. The Drifter seemed to startle and rear; Clive struggled to hold on. But then he saw the bird was a jet fighter, and was already past him and climbing straight up into the sky like a rocket. It disappeared as suddenly as it had arrived and within seconds the silence of the moors had recovered.

In the late afternoon he came down into forestry and found a loggers' track. There were walkers here and other mountain-bikers, and he was one of a crowd winding down into Fort William. It was a change to approach somewhere on a track rather than a road. Instead of roundabouts and traffic lights he sneaked in past the backs of houses and freight yards and then down an alleyway into town. Fort William turned out to be a familiar collection of grey banks and building societies, but Clive felt he'd arrived out of the clouds.

The town was full of visitors who didn't want to stay long; they were there to stock up and get out. Clive found a café off the main street and he sat inside trying to stick his glasses together with Sellotape, but it was hopeless, they were going the same way as his old bike. He held the menu up to his nose. The lens dropped out again; so he ordered a fried egg sandwich.

A motorbike pulled up outside. The two riders came into the café and sat down in the booth behind Clive. The woman ordered a cappuccino; the man said he would just smoke. Clive heard a newspaper being opened, and the woman said: 'That's a wonderful picture, Stephen. You got the little girl perfectly. And the smile, and the birthday card. It's just right.'

'I guess so,' said Stephen. 'When we find him it will be a front, I bet.'

'We should put a book together when this is all over. The search for the Missing Postman. I knew it would be a winner. It's exactly what they want.'

Clive buried his head in his sandwich, then got up and sneaked through the door marked Toilet. He sat there for fifteen minutes. When he came out the café was empty and his fried egg sandwich was cold.

'We're closed now,' said the café owner. Clive peered through the window. In the square opposite was a camera crew from Scottish television. A man with a tape recorder over his shoulder was stationed on the street corner holding people up with his microphone. The two motorbike riders were spread out on a bench. She had her feet up on his lap. Clive said: 'What's all the fuss about?'

'It's that Missing Postman fella,' said the owner.

'Someone said they saw him near here. The TV and newspapers are after him. The same thing happens in Inverness when anyone sees the monster.'

They were guarding the only road out of town. They'd be bound to see him if he tried to make a run for it. A police car pulled up as he watched. The thought of going home was suddenly appalling.

He edged out of the café and wheeled his bike away from the square. At some traffic lights he crossed the street with a group of shoppers while a white van with the words Network News on the side pulled up. In the cab were three people; they seemed to be arguing over a map. One of them looked up and Clive turned the other way, but through the van's open window he could hear; 'That was him. I'm telling you, that was him.'

Clive tried to hide himself in the crowd, but as the lights turned green there was a chorus of car horns and everyone turned to see the white van do a U-turn and head back up the street. Clive saw a narrow turning to his left and he nipped down it, but when he looked behind him he saw the van pass and then heard it screech to a halt and the doors slide open. His heart was climbing up his throat. In front of him was a big wooden door with two noticeboards outside. One advertised times of services at St Matthew's. The other advertised that the maintenance in progress was the work of Twist and Sons Ltd, Building Contractors. Clive bundled himself and his bike through the door.

His eyes were useless in the sudden darkness. All he could make out were shapes kneeling in pews to one side. Then he heard some footsteps coming down the aisle towards him, and a voice boomed: 'For goodness' sake, there's no need to bring your bike into the church. What's wrong with you? This is the house of God. Chain it to the railings like everyone else. If I catch you again it'll be fifty pence in the poor box.' The voice could only belong to a clergyman. The man pushed past Clive and headed towards the occupied pews.

Clive went back up the aisle until he passed a purple

veil that hung from ceiling to floor, and he tucked his Drifter behind there. Then he knelt down among the others. He was trying to work out what sort of church it was. There was a light burning on the altar, a pulpit, a font, and here, where five or six people were kneeling, a row of cubicles each with a green entrance curtain. One person came out and another went in. Of course, they were confessionals. Catholic.

He held up a prayer book and peered from behind it. All around, scaffolding climbed the walls. 'Please pray for the soul of Gerald Anderson' read the plaque before him. Clive thought he would hide in this dark tangle of metal and souls for a while. He couldn't face the thought of being interviewed. And if the police got him he'd be home this time tomorrow.

One by one the line went in to confess. No one had so much as looked at Clive when he had knelt down; there was an unwelcoming chill here rather than a sense of comfort. Around the walls were pictures of agony. Every sound echoed until it was lost in some dark, dusty corner. And the work being done on the roof made the whole place look uncertain. A notice from Twist and Sons apologised for any inconvenience to worshippers caused by repairs. Clive imagined prayers being caught up in the web of scaffolding on their way to heaven.

A woman went into the confessional and spoke too loudly. The man next to Clive covered his ears but Clive listened and could hear her plainly. 'Bless me, Father, for I have sinned,' she said. And then: 'I've used bad language, Father.' So have I, thought Clive, but nowhere near enough.

Her voice was lost as the church door opened on hinges that could have used a dose of 3-in-One. Clive turned slowly and could make out three figures standing in a beam of dusty light. He stuck his head in his book as Simon Maugham and his crew walked casually down the far aisle past the purple veil from where two bicycle wheels peeped out. They sauntered round the altar with hands in pockets and then turned towards the confessionals. The woman who had used bad language emerged and a young boy waited a moment to let the priest get his breath back before he took his turn. But suddenly Clive was scrambling over the backs of legs to the front of the queue, and as the young boy rose Clive pulled him back and bundled himself into the cubicle. His glasses fell off. He knelt on the floor, patting round for them.

'What in God's name is going on out there?' said the priest from behind a grill.

'Nothing, Father.'

'Doesn't sound like nothing. Have some respect, will you? In the name of the Father and of the Son and of the Holy Ghost.' He ended on an upbeat. Clive suspected it was his turn now.

'Bless me . . . Father . . .' Clive muttered. He was on all fours still trying to put his hands on his glasses. The priest put his nose to the grill. 'Will you kneel where you're supposed to and stop behaving like an animal?'

'Yes, Father. Sorry, Father.' He knelt on the stool and felt his glasses crush beneath his knee. 'Oh shit!' he hissed.

'Well, that's ten Hail Marys for a kickoff,' said the priest. 'Now, how long is it since your last confession?'

'I can't remember, Father.'

'Could be a record breaker. What are your sins?'

Through a crack in the curtain Clive could just make out the carefully layered hair of Simon Maugham bouncing past the confessors' pews.

'C'mon, man, I don't have all night.'

'I have stolen something . . . Father . . .'

'What have you stolen, my son?'

'Nothing.'

'What?'

'Nothing . . . that wasn't rightfully mine.'

'Will you talk sense?'

'I've stolen letters.'

'Whose letters?'

'I don't know whose. I stole them from a pillar box.'

176

'Well, put them back, for goodness' sake – you can't go round stealing other people's letters.'

'Yes, Father.'

'Are you sorry you did it?'

'No, Father.'

'What do you mean, no?'

'I'm glad I did it. I'd do it again.'

'I can't forgive a sin for which there is no repentance.'

'No, Father.'

'It's a crime as well. If the police catch you you'll get ten years for penance, you know that?'

'Yes, Father.'

'Will you give them back?'

'Yes, Father.'

'Any other sins?'

Simon Maugham and his crew walked back towards the entrance. Clive heard the door swing shut after them.

'Pardon, Father?'

'Any other sins?'

'No.'

'You're sure, now? That doesn't seem much for someone who hasn't been to confession since the days of Pope Pius.'

Clive was confused: 'What? You mean . . . any sins . . . ever?'

'I mean any other sins you want to confess for which you've never received forgiveness.'

Clive was thinking of that ladder, the way the rung had broken when he stepped on it, and the way he just wedged it back together and left it. Then the cry as the heavily pregnant Christine fell and hit the floor, and the way three weeks later they were holding a stillborn child.

'No, Father,' he said. 'No other sins.'

It wasn't his fault. She shouldn't have been decorating at that stage in her pregnancy. It wasn't his fault. It was twenty years ago, for God's sake.

'Make a good act of contrition, now. It's written up there on the wall if you can't remember it, which I'm sure you can't. And give those letters back.'

'I'm going to deliver them, Father. Will that be all right?'

'What? Yes, fine.'

'Good.'

Clive held the only sizeable piece of lens he could find up to his eye and read the act of contrition from the wall.

'Go in peace now, my son,' said the priest.

And Clive came out of the confessional with a completely buckled and broken pair of spectacles but with a dispensation from God to deliver his mail. The other confessors all looked at him, appalled. He bowed out, apologising, 'Sorry, I was desperate to go.'

# 19

THE MEDIA POSSE was still there, waiting, as good as a road-block out of town. Clive crept round the back streets looking for another way out but could find none. And now it was five-thirty; the shops were closing; the visitors were leaving in their caravans; soon he'd be without cover.

Then he found himself outside an optician's. It was still open and he stood outside for a moment enjoying the glow he had known since childhood. Inside he could just make out assistants in smart blue cardigans. The room was in motion with mirrors and shiny display cases that sparkled with assorted frames. There were comfortable chairs and carpets, and pictures on the walls of people pouting sexily in spectacles. Clive had always looked forward to visits to the optician's. It was the only place where they had asked him questions he alone knew the answers to. The assistants in there were friends, he knew that, and he needed a friend.

He pushed open the door and the smell of spectacles catapulted him back forty years with an effortlessness that stung. A young woman with long eyelashes greeted him with a smile and a clasp of her very white hands.

'Can I help you, sir?'

'I'd like to see the optician. Please.'

'Have you an appointment, sir?' Her accent was like a song.

'No, I'm passing through. I'm on holiday.'

'You have to have an appointment.'

Clive felt confident in an optician's, and he was determined. 'Yes. But I need to see an optician, badly.'

'I could fit you in tomorrow.'

'Tomorrow won't do.'

'Our opticians are finished for the day; we close in fifteen minutes, sir.'

Clive surprised himself by raising his voice. 'Listen to me. I have to see an optician, now.'

The shop was silent. One customer edged for the exit. 'Sorry,' said Clive. 'I didn't mean to . . .'

The consultancy room door opened and a tall man in a leather-patched jacket came out. 'Who's shouting out here?' he demanded.

The assistant spoke softly. 'This man says he has to see an optician.'

The optician confronted Clive. 'Who the hell do you think you are?'

'I'm on holiday and my glasses are broken.'

Now the optician was peering at him. 'Who *are* you?'

'I need something temporary, that's all.' Clive held up his bent and broken frame. It was pathetic.

The optician relaxed and said: 'Come this way. I'll see what I can do.'

He led Clive into the consultancy room and closed the door. 'Don't you have a spare pair for on holiday?'

'I left in a hurry,' mumbled Clive.

'Aye, I know you did.' Then he held out a big hand. 'Robert Peterson.'

Clive shook hands. 'Pleased to meet you. I'm Ralph Nugent.'

Peterson smiled. 'You're Clive Peacock. I know who you are.'

'No I'm not.'

'Yes you are. There's no use denying it.' He had a look at Clive's broken lens and then shone a pencil torch into his left eye. 'Your eyes really are bad, aren't they?'

'They're not getting any worse,' said Clive.

'No, the damage is done.' He put the torch away and sat on the desk. 'Relax, Mr Peacock. I'm not going to inform anyone of your whereabouts. If you really want to know, I'm pleased to have you here. I heard you were in the area but I never thought to see you.'

He fingered the buckled frame of Clive's glasses. 'But much as I'd like to help you, I don't know what I can do. I can't mend these, and I can't get you new ones right away. You should have contacts, an adventurer like yourself.'

'I'm not an adventurer. I'm a postman.'

'Aye. Have you got a prescription?'

Clive took the prescription he always carried with him from his wallet. The optician shook his head. 'It would take at least a week.' He began to flick through files on his desk. 'They do it with computers now, but it takes longer. I have to send them all to Dundee, and there's a waiting list.'

'My eyes have let me down all my life,' said Clive. He felt he could talk to opticians.

'Yes,' said Peterson. 'You can blame your eyes for a lot. But you're not letting your disability stand in your way. A lot of people are impressed by that. Those pictures of you in your – how shall we say? – ample glasses have inspired many a visually impaired person, believe me. They need someone like you, Mr Peacock, someone motivated by anger, someone who refuses to be discriminated against. We haven't had the likes of you up here since blind Mrs Mirren did a parachute jump.'

Peterson had been running through the files; then he found what he was looking for. 'I thought so. I thought I had someone with a similar prescription to yourself. Mr Gordon up in Fassfern. He's got your glasses. I'll call him up. Maybe he has a spare pair he can loan you.'

He telephoned Mr Gordon. There was no reply. 'He's a bit deaf as well. Maybe he can't hear the phone. Which way are you heading?'

'Mallaig,' said Clive.

'It's on the way. Call in and tell him I sent you.'

'Thank you very much,' said Clive.

'A pleasure,' said Peterson. 'You'll find we're a well-organised group in the General Optical Council. We like to help each other. I'll tell you what I can do. I'll contact head office – get them to alert all members. If ever you're passing by an associated branch on your travels, call in. They'll help you all they can.'

'What I really need is to lose the TV and newspapers out there. I don't want them to find me.'

'Aye, I've been thinking about that. Let me call my friend Ivor in Pitlochry, see if he can cause a diversion.'

'I can't think what they want with me.'

'Have you not seen the paper recently, Mr Peacock?' Peterson folded open a copy of the *Chronicle*. Clive held it at arm's length and could just make out his face and the headline 'Missing Postman Made My Day'.

'What does it say?' said Clive.

Peterson put his own spectacles on and read: ' "Little Penny Griffith had the best birthday present she could have wished for this week – a letter delivered by the Missing Postman. 'It was ten days late but it didn't matter,' said nine-year-old Penny. 'My mum is going to get it framed and hang it on my wall over my bed.'

' "Meanwhile Clive Peacock is rumoured to be heading north into Scotland, having discarded his GPO uniform and riding a Mercury Drifter mountain bike. Dressed all in black, this mercurial mailman seems to have written himself into the legend books. A letter from the Missing Postman is what everyone wants to brighten up their lives this summer . . ." '

'Hmm,' said Clive.

Peterson made his call to his friend Ivor. Ivor called back and said he'd spoken to someone at Network News and informed them there had been 'a definite sighting of Clive Peacock in Pitlochry'. Shortly afterwards Clive and Peterson watched from a window as Simon Maugham and his crew got news and drove off, followed shortly by the rest. The commotion was over and the town looked empty.

Mr Peterson walked Clive to the main road. He slapped him on the back. A lot of people are slapping me on the back these days, thought Clive.

'Thanks for your help,' said Clive.

Peterson stood to attention. 'My pleasure. Remember, if

ever you're in trouble call an optician. Opticians are a good bunch.'

'I'll remember that,' said Clive.

Fassfern was on the banks of a loch about ten miles west of Fort William. Clive cycled there carefully, travelling blind now. But he found Mr Gordon's house easily enough and knocked on the door. There was no answer. 'He's a bit deaf as well,' Peterson had said, so Clive lifted up the letterbox and peered in; there was a light on but no sound of anyone home.

Round the back of the house he found another door, which opened when he tried it. He poked his head into the kitchen and called out – still no response. He stepped inside; he needed these glasses.

The cottage was an old stone building with alcoves and angles that made you want to lean just a little further round each corner. Clive felt like an animal prowling and sniffing at everything. The fridge turned itself on and the hair stood up on the back of his neck.

He passed through the kitchen into the hall and opened the door into the living room. There was the vague smell of gas. A newspaper lay scattered on the floor. In the armchair were dented cushions. Clive turned up the stairs and called: 'Mr Gordon.' But still no response.

These were the sort of situations he hated. The fear was, of course, that you would open a door and find a corpse slumped on the floor. Clive had never found a dead body – never even seen one before – but there was something lukewarm about Mr Gordon's house that had him worried. It had a look and a feel about it that people like Christine spent a lot of time and effort trying to recreate in a breezy fashion, whereas the original, in reality, was always deathly gloomy. Mr Gordon's house smelt of old newspapers, and the lino had rotten corners. Clive was trying to block out the picture of the man leaning awkwardly across a piece of furniture where he had fallen, but the state of the house reinforced the image.

He called out again, just to relieve the tension; he didn't

expect an answer. All he heard was himself swallow. As a postman he knew it was his duty to check on old people living on their own, but he also knew it was the one area of the job in which he was deficient. He usually left it to the milkman.

There were two doors on the landing. His hand went out to one and it stuck as he pushed, but then swung open wide and he fell in. The room was empty, just a single bed with a green counterpane. He crossed the landing to the one remaining room. He held his breath, closed his eyes and pushed the door, then stood there daring himself to look.

A car parped outside. Clive was feeling dizzy. He opened his eyes and saw a bed. And there it was, the body lying neatly on top, looking marooned and bloated, fully dressed, shoes on, even, and the room smelt sweet.

Clive couldn't go in. He was rooted to the rotting lino. He felt himself sway slightly; the floorboards creaked beneath him. The window was closed but the breeze was coming through the frame and the curtains were moving. The room was more alive than the person in it. Clive squinted at Mr Gordon's chest, just to see if it was moving – maybe he was just asleep. Of course, that was it. His eyes were closed, weren't they? He had just dozed off. Clive could make out no rise and fall, and the face was very pale, and he was making no noise, but that didn't mean he was dead, for heaven's sake. 'Mr Gordon,' he said, and the body didn't move. 'Mr Gordon,' he said more loudly. Then he shouted: 'Mr Gordon!' But there was no response. Just how deaf *was* he? Clive wondered.

And then he saw them, the glasses. They were there just where they should have been over Mr Gordon's eyes. Clive held his breath and took a step backwards. He couldn't do it; he couldn't just steal the man's glasses and run; it was shameful. Outside, the wind was picking up; the wires on the telegraph were whistling. At times like this when he was unsighted he realised how good his ears were, so good he knew he'd have been able to hear Mr Gordon's breath if he was alive. He shook his head clear. It was time to stop deliberating. He took three steps to the edge of the bed, reached over and took the glasses off the face. Mr Gordon didn't reach out and grab him. Clive turned away and tried them on. He was able to read the label on a Milk of Magnesia bottle on the chest of drawers.

He took the glasses off again and turned back to Mr Gordon. Slowly he reached out and held the man's index finger. Stone cold, and Clive was out of there.

On the table at the bottom of the stairs he found a wallet, and looked through it for a phone number to call a friend or relative. The wallet contained little other than Green Shield stamps. He did find an organ donor's card though, and that made him feel better.

With a freshly painted white line to follow, Clive set out on the road to Mallaig. The cycling concentrated his mind as usual, enabling him to put all distractions to one side. He had the weather to occupy his attention now as well. The sky ahead was black with rain. The land stirred as if waking and stretched like a giant on the night shift. Clive pulled his waterproofs on and bent over the handlebars. After ten miles his back was stiff and painful, after twenty he'd ridden through the barrier and felt he could cycle all night.

The rain came driving in from the west, blowing him into the middle of the road and soaking him in minutes despite his protection. No cars passed him now, and the road twisted so much he felt he would never have been able to find his way back had he needed to; the only way was forward. At one point he saw a refuge of some kind and thought he might take shelter. But inside he found the rotting carcass of a sheep. It was just one of those nights, he told himself, and pressed on.

Darkness fell earlier than usual. But then fork lightning lit the sky as bright as day and Clive could see the desolation around him. Another bolt of lightning speared the mountain ahead and he thought for the first time: I could die out here.

The Mercury Drifter followed the road on automatic

pilot. It was a hero that night. Its tyres sucked at the tarmac. Its lights threw an arc ahead that pierced the wall of rain and poked at the cat's-eyes. Clive rode like a passenger, watching in awe the night's display taking place around him and instead of dampened he felt exhilarated. He felt he could do no wrong. At one point when he reached the top of a hill he took his hands off his handlebars and let the bike go free, and as it raced down the hill, he thrust his head back and his arms out and screamed into the rain at the top of his voice. The next thing he knew the whole earth flashed white. A lightning bolt had torn the night in two and split a solitary tree ahead of him completely in half. The shock threw him into the air and when he landed the bracken was hot to touch. His bike lay on the ground with wheels spinning and tyres smoking. A dagger of pain stabbed his knee. He wasn't sure what exactly had happened, but he had the sense to take the hint. He remounted his warm bike and pedalled away from the smouldering wreckage as fast as he could.

Finally he reached the coast and a furious sea. Great sweeps of sand took the sting out of the waves, but every fixture on the land was cowering. A car passed him, the first for hours. It slowed and the driver peered at him through weary wiper blades.

It was two o'clock in the morning when he finally saw the lights of Mallaig and came down the hill towards the harbour. The wind was behaving like a hooligan in an empty street. Water tumbled down the gutters, and when he reached the harbour, waves were throwing themselves over the wall. Out on the water boats were lashed together shaking in the gale. Lamps still lit the streets, but then as Clive passed along the harbour they were all switched off, as if the town had waited up for him. Now that he had arrived he felt numb with exhaustion. He just had to find Harbour View House and deliver his letter, and the night's work was done. He didn't care what happened to him after that.

A row of guesthouses faced the harbour. Outside one an

old sign was being slapped by the wind until it squealed. Harbour View House B & B, it read. Clive climbed off his bike and stumbled to the ground, such was the pain in his knee. He dragged himself to the porch and leaned on the doorbell. Presently a light came on; Clive saw he was covered in mud. The door was pulled open and there stood a woman in a dressing gown with her hair down and sleep in her eyes. She looked at Clive with the door on the latch.

Clive said: 'It's me. It's the Missing Postman.'

Without a word she opened the door fully and Clive fell inside.

## 20

'ROCKALL, MALIN, WESTERLY six to gale eight, rain at times, moderate to severe . . .' The shipping forecast lapped at Clive's consciousness, a soft voice rising in waves from the room beneath him. It would swell and then recede, and return with a '. . . Lundy, south-westerly five, fair to moderate, falling more slowly . . .'

He put a hand out and explored the bedside table until he found his glasses. Daylight framed some curtains, but there were corners of this room that never saw light. There were shadows and cobwebs, and the wallpaper was peeling in places with damp. Every now and then the whole house creaked like an old boat. Downstairs there was the solid tap of footsteps on flagstones, and outside the sound of that B & B sign, still hanging on.

'Plymouth, westerly four to six, rain at times, moderate to good.' He tried to get out of bed but the dagger twisted into his knee again. He looked under the covers. The flesh was swollen and hot to the touch. He was lying in a strange bed with a strange knee and someone else's T-shirt on. Across his chest was written 'I'd rather be fishing'.

By lifting his leg he managed to swing himself out, and he hobbled to the window and pulled back the curtains. The rail came off the wall. It wasn't attached properly, just balanced there by the last person who knocked it off so that the next person to touch it would knock it off. Clive laid it on the floor.

He was looking out over a choppy harbour. The grey water smacked the grey walls, and the grey sky met the grey water. You could only see clearly as far as the ice factory but, across a channel, out of the mist a land mass loomed and peaked. The Western Isles. They rose out of the sea like a challenge. Clive eyed them like a mountaineer. He wished he had a letter to deliver there.

'Light Vessel Automatic, light to variable, rising, five, good.' The shipping forecast ended and the time signal followed. Clive heard footsteps on the stairs. He hopped back into bed, pulled the covers over him and rewound the events of the previous evening. He'd stolen Mr Gordon's glasses (the man probably wasn't dead, just asleep). He'd managed to cycle from Fort William, despite the lightning bolts. He'd knocked on the door of Harbour View House, handed the letter to Mrs Taylor and fallen inside. She'd said: 'I had a feeling you were coming.'

She'd led him up the stairs and he could remember lying on the bed as she tugged at his wet clothes. The light had been switched out and it was as if the plug in his head had been pulled.

Now the door was pushed gently open. A head peered round. Mrs Taylor smiled at him and said: 'Sleep well?'

'Yes, thank you very much. Where are my clothes?'

'In the airing cupboard, drying.'

Mrs Taylor had appeared stern and disciplinarian the previous evening. She had tutted a lot and everything she took off him she had shaken her head at. Now she had a yellow cardigan on and blue tracksuit bottoms and running shoes. Her hair was in a ponytail rather than tied up and the grey in it now looked like highlights rather than dead wood. She must have been forty-five he guessed.

'How do you feel?' she said, and put her hand on his forehead.

'Fine, thank you very much.'

'You had a temperature last night. You were in a state.'

'I'm all right this morning. I needed a good sleep.'

'You could hardly get up the stairs with that leg. I've called the doctor.'

'No, don't call the doctor. I'll be all right. I should really think about getting going.'

'You're not going anywhere until the doctor's seen you. He's a friend. We're all friends here.'

She sat on the bed and stuck a thermometer in his mouth. He lay there, helpless. Mrs Taylor smiled and said: 'All

189

people look the same when you stick a thermometer in their mouth.'

'Hmm,' said Clive.

'You'll like it here. You can stay until you're better. I had a feeling you had a letter for me – when I heard about you on the radio. Isn't that funny?'

She took the thermometer out – 'slightly above normal' – and felt his forehead again. 'I'll get the breakfast on. You can have a day indoors. Last night hasn't properly blown over yet. None of the boats went out.' She walked to the window, replaced the rail and drew the curtains again, as if there was something out there that Clive shouldn't see.

As soon as she left the room he was up. He needed to find two things: his trousers and his bike. He couldn't stop here. It wouldn't be long until they found him. All he needed was a cup of tea and he'd be ready to get going, back south to London. Cycling was the panacea.

He found his trousers in the bathroom on the boiler, just about dry, and his socks were crisp. He thought about washing them but he was learning to live like this.

He dressed and limped down the stairs. Through a window he could see some outhouses across the yard, and the wheel of his bike poking out. He found a back door and would have left without a word, but at that moment he was knocked over the head by the smell of mushrooms and bacon. His nose dragged him to the kitchen; this house looked as if it had been expecting him.

It was in fact a much bigger house than he had thought. But it was full of boxes and they took up all the space. There were piles on every surface; everywhere was half-painted, everything half-assembled or broken.

'I was going to bring you breakfast in bed,' said Mrs Taylor.

'Exercise is what I need. The leg will respond to exercise. It's just a sprain – the best thing for it would be a cycle ride.'

'You're going nowhere, I've told you. You've been cycling too much. All the way up here from Dorset; you've a screw loose.' The radio faded and died. Mrs Taylor slapped it and it sprang back to life with news of the situation in Namibia.

She sat down at the table and put two plates of eggs and black pudding down. 'That's the sort of breakfast I give my husband before he goes off to work.' She put a forkful in her mouth and chewed slowly. She didn't look as though she had a husband. Clive hadn't heard a husband.

A solitary piece of mail flew through the letterbox and slid along the stone floor of the hall into the kitchen and stopped by Mrs Taylor's feet. She kicked it away. 'Tch, TV licence renewal. And it doesn't even work properly. I write a letter a day, I do, and I rarely get anything interesting in return.'

'Who do you write a letter a day to?' asked Clive.

'All sorts of people. My MP, British Rail, Tesco's, a friend I have in Canada, Oxfam. The other day I wrote to Lyons Maid, congratulating them on a new ice cream they've just launched. I believe in writing letters.'

Clive nodded in solidarity, although he never wrote letters himself. He'd had a penpal in Italy once, a postman in Livorno when the twin town business got going. But their correspondence had faltered. It was a waste of time; he could speak no Italian and Eugene could speak no English.

'That reminds me,' she said. 'I want to write to Zanussi today before I go to work. There's a design fault on the powder-dispenser of the machine I've just bought. The seal round the drawer doesn't fit properly and it leaks. They ought to be made aware of it. It could easily be altered.'

Here was an unusual woman, Clive decided; best let her do the talking.

She said: 'You come from Dorset, don't you? It's nice down there.'

Clive nodded.

'You've led them on a wild goose chase, haven't you?'

'I suppose so.'

'You're all right here though, don't worry. We respect

privacy here. We all know each other but we respect privacy. You know what that letter you brought me was? It was a booking. I do a bit of bed and breakfast, see. I thought we'd be open now but the renovation still isn't finished. Someone wants to stay here for one night on September 3rd. I'll have to say no.'

The radio died again. She slapped it again and they ate their breakfast and listened to the news story of a budgie that had been left £10,000 in a will. Then Mrs Taylor said: 'I know why you're doing what you're doing, by the way. My husband's just the same.'

Mrs Taylor gave him some clothes that were too big for him, then she threw all his cycling gear in the washing machine. The doctor came just after midday. He took one look at Clive and winked. 'You've had a lark, haven't you?'

Clive smirked and sat up straight. The doctor examined his leg and said: 'It's a bad sprain. You cycled thirty miles on that?'

'It didn't hurt at the time.'

'You need to rest it for a few days; then the exercise will do it good. I'll wrap a support bandage round it.'

The doctor knelt down and looked up at Clive. 'I wonder if I could have your autograph?' he said. 'It's for my boy, he's a keen cyclist. He's been following your route.'

Clive signed a prescription for the doctor. As he stood by the door to go the doctor said: 'My father was a GP. The NHS said he had to retire; all they'd let him do was locums. So he travelled all over taking any locum he could, staying in guesthouses, and working in local hospitals. It was the only thing that made him happy. He was seventy when he stopped, and he was dead within three months.'

Clive said: 'I'm not sure if you're advising me to stop or to keep going.'

'It's probably too late to stop.'

'Yes.'

'But you can't keep going for ever.'

'No.'

Mrs Taylor worked in a chemist's in the afternoons. She wrote her letter to Zanussi and put her jacket on and said to Clive: 'Casa mia, casa tua,' and then she left him in the sitting room with his leg supported on a box. He sat there watching clouds being hurled across the sky. People trusted him so implicitly these days. He had stolen letters; he was wanted by the police; he was a stranger. But he was the Missing Postman, and all he had to do was announce himself and he was a house guest.

The box under his leg was full of books. Clive glanced at the covers. He picked out a biography of Lord Nelson, a copy of *The Cruel Sea*, some Hornblowers – a seaman's library. There was a notebook as well, a leatherbound volume that had a keyhole clasp. It wasn't locked though and Clive carefully opened the cover. The book belonged to Howard Taylor, skipper of the *Lovely Linda*. Inside were passages of neat handwriting:

*I banged the table, called for the bottle and said to them: 'Oh youth! The strength of it, the faith of it, the imagination of it. To me she was not an old rattle-trap carting about the world a lot of old coal for freight – to me she was the endeavour, the test, the trial of life. I think of her with pleasure, with affection, with regret, as you would think of someone dead whom you have loved. I shall never forget her.*

*'Oh, the glamour of youth! Oh, the fire of it, more dazzling than the flames of the burning ship, throwing a magic light on the wide earth, leaping audaciously to the sky, presently to be quenched by time, more cruel, more pitiless, more bitter than the sea – and like the flames of the burning ship surrounded by an impenetrable night.*

*'But you here – you all had something out of life: money, love – whatever one gets on shore – and, tell me, wasn't that the best time, that time when we were young at sea; young and had nothing, on the sea that gives nothing, except hard knocks – and sometimes a chance to feel your strength?'*

*They all nodded at me over the polished table that like a still sheet of brown water reflected our faces, lined, wrinkled; our faces marked by toil, by deceptions, by success, by love; our weary eyes looking still, looking always, looking anxiously for something out of life, that while it is expected is already gone – has passed unseen, in a sigh, in a flash – together with the youth, with the strength, with the romance of illusions.*

Clive turned the page to find a blank, as was the rest of the book. He read the passage again. He hadn't thought of Mrs Taylor's husband as a man of such passion. Then he yawned and put the book back in the box and gazed out over the harbour. The wind was dying, the seagulls were less resolute. And now the scene looked more familiar. The ice factory, the harbour office, the row of shops up the hill from the slipway, the visitors walking round the harbour and the cars waiting for the ferry – the place was perfect. Everything leaned towards the sea here, in a way it had never done in his own town. There he had felt tied to the land; the sea was simply the direction in which he gazed. That was how he had spent his youth, as that frightened boy patrolling the beach, waiting for something to happen. And then by the time he'd felt at ease with his youth it was over. He'd always imagined that the vagaries of the sea were the labours of the more courageous, those people who committed themselves, those like Howard Taylor. Although being courageous didn't seem to have done him much good. Looking anxiously for something out of life, that while it is expected is already gone, he had said. He sounded as much a sea-gazer as all the others, only he was gazing from a boat. Some men, like his old friend Ralph, had done better. They'd managed to confront their youth once more in their own children, and been able to lay it to rest that way. Others, like Howard Taylor and himself, were destined to search blindly for youth's meaning and might never recognise it even if they found it.

He tried to read the passage again but this time fell asleep, and didn't wake until Mrs Taylor banged the front gate. He saw her coming briskly up the path with her head up. She had a long face that, caught unawares, made her look secretly sad. Clive thought of Howard in his wheelhouse, looking out to sea under a starry sky, thinking of her. She was very attractive.

He pretended to be still asleep – that would make her happy. He heard her come in and then busy herself in the kitchen, but quietly so as not to wake him. Then she brought a cup of tea and a plate of cinnamon toast and knelt by the fireplace. Clive tried to think of how to enact a slow awakening. In the end he just opened his eyes and looked at her blankly.

'Hello,' she said.

'Your accent,' said Clive after a pause. 'I've come right up the country and heard all the accents, and here is the clearest and most friendly. I couldn't imagine anyone with your accent getting angry.'

She smiled smugly and reached up to feel his forehead again. 'You're cooler now. You're on the road to recovery. And I've some mullet for supper.'

'I can smell it.' Clive liked the house because outside it was hardened and weather-beaten but inside was full of sharp tastes and smells. He said: 'Linda?'

'Yes?'

'Nothing. I just wanted to see if your name was Linda.'

She knelt by him building a fire and shaking her head. 'August and you need a fire,' she muttered, then lit the paper, and the smell of burning pine mixed with the fish.

When the soup was ready she brought in two bowls on a tray with a bottle of wine. Her eyes were widening in the heat. She said: 'You've not asked me about my husband.'

'Where is he?'

'He's a fisherman.'

'It's a hard life, fishing.' Clive wondered if she was expecting him to be more exciting than he was. He had arrived in a storm, like the Black Magic man. He was on the run and she had looked at him now and again as if she was desperate for him to take her away from all this. I'm only Clive Peacock, he wanted to tell her. Being a runaway postman didn't alter that. If you were unexciting, you were unexciting wherever you were.

'It's a hard life all right,' she said.

'Is he at sea now?'

'He's missing – missing at sea. He has been for eighteen months now.'

'That's terrible.'

'Oh, he says he hates the job. He says he can never wait to come home, and then whenever he comes home he can't wait to get back again. He's going to work as hard as he can for three years and then he'll retire, he says. I don't think he will though.'

She looked around the room. 'We'll do this place up properly when he does retire, open a hotel.' She emptied her glass. 'I don't speak about him in the past. He's missing, not dead. I mean, I'm not deluding myself. There's every chance he *is* dead, but there's a chance he's not.' She smiled. 'It's fun when he *is* here though.'

Clive smiled back. She was lovely. She had her knees clenched together to support her bowl and he could see what she would have looked like as a young girl. She swept the hair out of her eyes with her spoon still in her hand.

'All the jobs round the house that need doing I write down on a bit of paper and then put them in a sweet-jar in the kitchen. And then when he's home he dips his hand in and pulls out a job and we spend the evening doing it together. Jobs like retiling the bathroom, or repairing the cracked windowpane in the porch.'

Clive said: 'My wife does all the DIY in our house.'

'It's not DIY that we do. It's DIO – do it ourselves. But he's been gone eighteen months; the place is falling apart, and I spend my evenings writing letters. I could do the work myself, I suppose. He must be dead, if I'm honest with myself. His problem is he can't live with the sea and he can't live without it. That's why I know why you're doing what you're doing.'

Clive could see Howard in his wheelhouse again, thinking of his lovely Linda, but his engine was dead, and he was drifting hopelessly.

They finished the soup and finished the wine. Then Mrs Taylor produced a bottle of single malt whisky. 'I drink

196

too much,' she said and poured two large ones. 'But I got a case of this sent me. You know how? I bought a bottle once last year and it got me over a difficult period – Howard's birthday, in fact – and I wrote to the company saying how helpful their whisky had been to me in my hour of need and so they sent me a case. Cheers.'

Clive held the whisky in his mouth, but it took the initiative and crawled down his throat. He wanted to return to the subject of DIY; he felt he was working something out here. He said: 'I tried to help my wife with the jobs around the house but I think she'd rather do it alone. She'd rather have the radio for company when she works. I just get in the way.'

'She's never showed you how, has she?'

'No.'

'How do you expect to be any good if no one ever shows you how?'

'I could learn from books if I wanted. She did.'

'There are some things you don't learn from books, some things you have to learn by experience. The best way to learn DIY is to have someone show you. You'd soon pick it up.'

More whisky sneaked down Clive. Mrs Taylor got up and went to the kitchen and came back with a big sweet-jar. Toffee Crunch, the label said. Inside were bits of folded paper. She pulled her chair nearer to his, then shook the jar and unscrewed the top. She was about to dip her hand in, but then she said: 'No, you do it,' and she offered him the jar.

Clive blushed. 'This is silly. I'm really no good at this sort of thing.'

'Go on,' she insisted.

He put his hand in and pulled out a piece of paper. He unfolded it and laughed and then folded it again.

'Well, what does it say?' she asked. She was getting excited.

'It says: Erect cling-film dispenser in kitchen.'

Mrs Taylor took her cardigan off and put her hair up,

then gathered her toolbox and led him into the kitchen. She marked the wall in four places, then with the electric drill fired short bursts into the plaster. She plugged the holes and moved aside so that Clive could slot home the cling-film dispenser. Then she handed him the electric screwdriver.

'I've never used one of these before,' he said.

'There's nothing to it. Just push.'

He pushed and the screwdriver hummed and spun the screws into the holes. Four times he did it: four times the screws were driven home unerringly. Mrs Taylor passed him a roll of cling film and he slipped it into the grips. A perfect fit.

Clive felt a thrill. She poured him some more whisky and then offered him the sweet-jar once more. He dipped his hand in. 'Repair curtain rail in bedroom,' he read. 'That's a good idea. I pulled the curtain right off this morning.'

She helped him up the stairs. In the bedroom she examined the wall and said, 'We'll need to fill these cavities with Polyfilla first, then drill new holes for the rail.'

They mixed the Polyfilla. Jobs that Clive had always imagined took hours took them minutes. She gave him the drill and he drilled four holes at nine-inch intervals along the top of the window frame, then he plugged them and screwed in the rail. Mrs Taylor ran the curtains along and attached buffers on each end.

Clive sat on the floor with his back to the wall and started to giggle. She giggled with him and then helped him up on the bed. They fell back and this time he stroked her forehead, and his fingers ran down her bare arm. She rolled over on top of him and he undid her hairclip so that her hair fell forward over her face, and when he pulled her towards him to kiss her it fell down and enveloped them both like a curtain. Her tongue poked through the veil and slipped into his mouth. He wasn't a tongue-in-the-mouth sort of person normally, but tasting of whisky the way she did he felt as if he was swallowing flames.

They rolled over and his knee twisted making him shriek. But when she pulled back he said: 'There's nothing so bad can't be bettered by a kiss.' So she smiled coyly and swung his injured leg up on the bed, then sat astride his waist. He ran his hands down her sides and then up inside her shirt over the electric surface of her underwear until he found warm flesh at the top of her back. He could see the tips of his fingers poking through her clothing.

She sat up and unbuttoned herself. Clive was watching, trying to concentrate, but she was going too fast and in seconds she was pulling straps down and undoing clips, and then she was pressed down on top of him once more. She struggled out of her tracksuit and pants; he tugged at his trousers. There was no time to remove any more clothing before their bodies were slotted together.

It was a sprint, but that was all right. They lay motionless on top of the covers for a long time afterwards, moist and warm, her head plunged into the pillow. Outside, he could hear a wave slapping the harbour wall, and he thought: What sort of place *is* this?

# 21

In the middle of the night Clive lay awake with his arm deadened under Mrs Taylor's head. She was sprawled over half of him, sleeping with her mouth open, wheezing slightly. He had to move, but he didn't want to wake her. He knew she was dreaming of Howard leaning over the rails of his *Lovely Linda* – the ghost of her husband on the ghost of his ship.

He rubbed her shoulder in the hope that she'd turn over, but she just burrowed her head further into his neck. Then out in the harbour a fishing boat gave a diesel cough as it pushed its way through the oily water past the ice factory, and Mrs Taylor woke, her eyes suddenly wide. She pushed herself up on an elbow and listened intently for a moment as the engine noise faded and the boat slipped into the channel. Then she turned over and was asleep again, and Clive had his arm back.

Despite the success of the new rail they'd not drawn the curtains, and now, with the moon high, a ribbon of pale light was reflected off the water into the bedroom so that the walls shivered, and the face of Clive's retirement clock on the bedside table rippled as it glowed. He lifted his arm through the beam of light to drain the pins and needles. He was the Missing Postman and this was his delivery arm; he ought to look after it. He would need it in London and in Livorno. Emma Drake and many others were waiting for their letters; people depended on this arm.

A car alarm screamed and shattered the peace. Mrs Taylor woke again. 'What on earth is that?'

'Just a car alarm. Have you never heard one before?'

'No.' She cringed. 'Hadn't we better do something, if it's an alarm? It must be a tourist.'

'Don't worry about it,' said Clive, and after thirty seconds the alarm cut out, and they both fell back to sleep.

That morning they repaired a broken window in the out-house. Mrs Taylor cut glass to fit and Clive became expert at applying putty. She switched on the radio. Malcolm Dixon and his emotional phone-in came on but Mrs Taylor said: 'I can't stand hearing other people's problems,' and she turned it off.

She wrote a letter to Marmite, congratulating the company on the design of their new jars – 'stylish and practical' – and then she went to work in the chemist's again. Clive defrosted the fridge and began to rearrange the bookshelves in alphabetical order, but his heart wasn't in it and mid-afternoon he went out for a walk to test his knee.

A rough track led from behind the house over moorland to a hillcrest, then fell into an empty valley and headed off to the mountains beyond. Clive stood on the crest in his 'Time for a Tetley's' jersey and let the wind bully him. There were wilder places on earth but this was enough for anyone. The terrain was like a blanket thrown over a body; it rose and fell with each puff of wind. The clouds bounced from peak to peak; one mountain cleared as another became obscured. Clive longed to see the whole jigsaw of town, mountain, islands and ocean laid out around him, but it was as if there would always be one piece missing.

He walked back through the town, where cars were queuing for the ferry over to Skye. Visitors filled the bars and bought the fishermen drinks and listened to their stories. The fishermen drank Bacardi and Coke and most could hardly stand. One said to Clive: 'It's a dangerous business fishing, you know. And it's never more dangerous than when I'm driving the boat.' He roared and the tourists all wanted to take his picture.

Clive sat on the harbour wall and watched the ferry out in the channel ploughing towards the mainland. The first car in line was a silver BMW, and the driver was looking hard at Clive. Then the window slid down with a hum. A face with sunglasses and a long forehead poked out and said: 'It's the Missing Postman. Right?'

Clive turned away.

'I know it's you.'

Clive started to walk away. The man got out and followed him. He wore a white suit and red shirt and he stood out on the quay like a lifebuoy. 'Trevor Ramsey, of Trevor Ramsey Public Relations. A pleasure to meet you.' He held his hand out right in front of Clive's face so that he had to shake it.

'Hello,' he mumbled.

'I don't believe this. A real stroke of luck. I'm based in London. I'm just up here to visit a client of mine. Palace Hotels – you know, the luxury chain? They've got a property over on the island, lovely place, got its own loch. And who should I bump into but the Missing Postman. Here, let's have a late lunch, I've been meaning to get in touch with you.'

'You're going to miss your boat,' said Clive, pointing to the ferry, slowing now as it approached the harbour entrance.

'I'll catch another one. Let's have an evening together and we'll talk business. I'm on your wavelength, Clive. I know what you're up to, you know. And you've done well, there's no denying that. If you string them on long enough you can make a pretty penny out of this. I just hope you know when to cash in. That's the tricky bit; timing is essential. You know what you need, of course?'

'It's docking, look.' Clive pushed Trevor Ramsey towards his car.

'An agent, a publicity agent. That's what you need, Clive.'

'Are you one of those media blokes?'

'Don't insult me, Clive. I'm a business manager. I'm on your side. I use the media – just like you've done. I want to help you, because I know what you're up to. From the moment I saw your story in the paper I thought: That lad is a lot brighter than he's let on. But like I say, this is a tricky business; you need an agent. I mean, I'm sure you've thought of selling your story to the newspapers, and doubtless you've got a book lined up or something. And you've got yourself a sponsor, I see, although Tetley's isn't exactly the image I'd create for you. But all that stuff is chicken feed. Have you thought about a recording contract?'

Clive looked confused. 'A *what* contract?'

'Recording contract. I could get you one tomorrow.'

'What, for a record?'

'They had the Whistling Postman, didn't they?'

'I can't sing a note.'

'I love it. Listen, it doesn't matter what you can or can't do, the public will buy anything with your name on it. They love you. Haven't you been watching the telly? I know people who would kill for that sort of coverage. You really *don't* know it, do you? I love it; I really love it.'

He started to laugh. Clive was watching the cars roll off the ferry. The ones waiting in the queue were starting up their engines, and now they were hooting at the empty car at the front. Trevor Ramsey was dragging Clive back to his car and still talking. 'And Missing Postman T-shirts. Have you thought of that? The merchandising opportunity is enormous.'

'I've got to go now,' said Clive.

'Where to?'

'None of your business.'

'Okay, Clive, get this. Off the top of my head. The Missing Postman board game. Perfect for Christmas. A game for two to six people. One player is the postman, the other five are the police or press or whoever. They have to catch you before you post all the letters. We could sell that to the States.'

Clive was laughing now. 'Stop talking rubbish,' he said.

'I'm not talking rubbish, Clive. I'm very serious. I'm always very serious. I could get you on *Wogan* tomorrow night. Not tomorrow – tomorrow's Sunday – the day after tomorrow.'

He was holding Clive's hand as he climbed into his car.

'Come with me now, Clive. We'll stay the night at this fancy hotel and talk things over.'

'No, thank you,' said Clive and closed Ramsey's door.

The ferry crew were shouting at Ramsey to get moving. Ramsey started his engine and slipped a business card into Clive's pocket.

'We'll talk about it. In the meantime keep me posted. Call me if there's anything you need. I don't suppose you've got a Vodaphone, have you? No. Anyway, my home, car and office phone numbers are on there. Tell you what, any time you want to stay in a Palace Hotel just give me a ring and I'll fix it up, anywhere in the country. Luxury restaurants, minibars in the room, health club in each hotel.'

'I'm just delivering the mail,' said Clive.

'I love it, I really love it,' and Trevor Ramsey drove down the ramp on to the ferry. Clive watched the other cars board. He felt sticky suddenly. The ferry quickly filled and closed its doors then backed away from its moorings, and there was Trevor Ramsey up on the deck shouting at Clive across the water. 'How much did Tetley's pay you, Clive?'

'Nothing.'

'Nothing! Bastards! Right, that's it. I'm not having one of my clients treated like that. I'll get you fixed up with Distant Dreams. I handle them – a prestige account. You'll get a much nicer vest as well. I've got all the contacts, see. So call me.'

When he got back to Harbour View House Mrs Taylor was already home making a fire. She said: 'You should be resting that leg.'

'It feels better with exercise,' he said and sat down in the armchair.

She lit the paper. The flames jumped and her face became drawn. 'You're going to disappear on me, aren't you?'

'I am the Missing Postman, you know.'

That night she brought out her photograph album. The pictures weren't arranged in any sort of order. She had to read the backs of them to remember who they were of, or where they were taken. Her life needs organising, thought Clive.

'There we are on holiday in North Wales in 1976. That's my brother Steve. And here's a picture of him getting married the following summer in Motherwell. He met Sarah in a queue for the January sales.

'And there's one of my mum's dog and my Uncle Peter, taken at my mum's funeral – 1979 she died, in Edinburgh. It was a really hot July day, I remember.'

It seemed strange to have pictures of your mother's funeral, but Mrs Taylor had lots of strange pictures. 'Here's one of a car accident we were all involved in. My Uncle Raymond broke his leg. I just happened to have the camera handy – lucky really.' She showed Clive a picture of a group of people gathered round a buckled car, and a man being stretchered into an ambulance. No one in the picture was smiling.

'Here's one taken at Christmas '81, the time we were snowed up for the whole holiday – it was wonderful. The roads and railway were all blocked. The boats didn't go out for days – there was no point. Howard was home for two weeks and we replastered the stairwell.' She passed Clive a picture of a man holding a blowtorch and looking nothing like Clive had imagined. He was wearing the pullover Mrs Taylor had given Clive to wear. There were Christmas decorations everywhere.

'And this is me just after he left that Christmas.' Clive noticed she had a bruise on her forehead. 'What happened to you?'

'Howard hit me. He gets bored if he's home too long. He was drunk. I thought about it and decided that I'd give him another chance. He drinks too much when he's home. They all do.

'Look at this one. This is the time a whale was washed up on the shore.' She handed Clive a picture of the scarred creature. It made the beautiful white beach look ugly.

'And here's a favourite.' She passed him a picture of a fishing boat, freshly painted. The name was the *Lovely*

*Linda.* Howard stood on the stern waving with a paint-brush. There was a beautiful blue sky above.

The pictures kept coming. 'There's the dog again. And that's me quite recently when I was very depressed. It's about three in the morning and I've been drinking. I was on my own.'

Clive hardly recognised her. She had red eyes but not because of the flash. 'I took it on the self-timer,' she said. Then she closed the book. 'I like photos to show all of a life. I've had such happy times and such bad ones. The danger, I think, is trying to forget the sad ones – pretending they didn't happen.'

'Mmm,' said Clive.

'Sorry,' said Mrs Taylor. 'I don't want to get all serious.'

Clive caught himself playing with the change in his pocket. He drew a thin breath and went into the kitchen for the sweet-jar.

'You devil,' she said.

He unscrewed the lid and offered it to her, and she dug her hand in and rummaged about in the bits of paper until she was sure she had a good one. 'De-scale the shower rose in the bathroom,' she said.

He carried her to the bathroom. 'Your leg, be careful,' she shrieked, but he felt fine.

He dismantled the rose and soaked it in de-scalant, then she scrubbed it with a wire brush. When it was replaced the water came out in a powerful jet. They watched it for a minute in satisfaction, then Clive was unbuttoning her cardigan and they were in the shower together with steam rising from their skin. He caught the outline of their reflection in the mirror. Lean, wiry fellow willing to risk death daily, taking a shower with his hostess.

Later they lay in bed with the lights off and listened to the radio. 'I sleep much better if I hear the shipping forecast,' said Mrs Taylor. 'It's the most soothing and cosy sound I know.'

After each area she would pass comment. 'They've had a good week down in Plymouth,' she'd say, or, 'I pity those poor souls off Humber.' Only when Area Hebrides came round was she quiet. 'Ssh,' she said, and listened carefully for the B & B sign. 'A very gentle swing tonight. Force three, no more.'

They pulled the covers over them. Mrs Taylor could be saucy when she wanted. 'I've been thinking. If I write a letter to Brazil will you take it there for me?'

'Yes, all right.'

'Then I could come along for the ride, couldn't I?'

'Have you got a bicycle?'

'I didn't think of that. Maybe we could get a tandem.'

'Who do you know in Brazil?'

'No one. I'd have to write to the Poste Restante.'

'The Royal Mail isn't to be abused, you know.'

'All right. I'd write to the Tourist Office in Rio de Janeiro asking about accommodation in middle-price-range hotels, in rooms with own bathroom and a view of Copacabana beach.'

'That sounds reasonable.'

She snuggled down and said: 'We could travel the world. I could write letters to exotic places and give them to you and you'd have to take them. I'd write off for a job at a Jamaican chemist's and you'd have to deliver my application. I'd send a birthday card to the Egyptian Minister for the Interior and off we'd go to see the pyramids. I'd get myself a penpal in Thailand, and we'd cycle across continents to deliver each letter in person. The only cost would be a book of stamps. Delivering letters is so sexy.'

'I'd quite like just to stay here,' said Clive.

He could tell she was smiling in the dark. She kissed him. 'Good,' she said.

Clive began to sleep in late, but his work rate never faltered. Over the next two days they repaired the TV aerial, replaced some of the cracked quarry tiles in the kitchen floor, and fitted new cords on the sash windows. They mixed cement and repaired the garden wall. In the wash-room they replaced a rotten sill and changed some leaky washers. In just one morning they painted the whole living room yellow and white.

Finally they serviced the Harbour View B & B sign. She painted one side and he painted the other, and with his can of 3-in-One he oiled the hinges.

That evening Mrs Taylor made a poppyseed cake and they took it to bed with them and watched an old movie on TV.

'It's nice to have the TV working in the room again,' said Mrs Taylor.

'It is, isn't it?' agreed Clive.

They made love in a bed of cakecrumbs while Peter Snow introduced *Newsnight*. Afterwards Clive thought of the shoe salesman he had met under the bridge in Bristol weeks ago. He said to her: 'Here's a question for you: if they were going to make a film of your life who would you have play yourself?'

She was thinking. The room was silent. There was no squeaking coming from the B & B sign now.

'I'd have the woman who drives the bus over on Skye,' said Mrs Taylor.

'That's an interesting choice.'

The night was calm and warm, but Clive woke at 4.45 and felt uneasy. His knee was no longer painful and he was rested, but all his muscles were coiled.

He went downstairs to make tea and while it was brewing he walked in his stockinged feet across the yard to the outhouse where his bicycle was kept. He pumped up the tyres, oiled the chain and greased the nipples. In his front pannier his remaining letters were still stowed. He sorted through them. The London bunch: Tottenham, Islington, Kensal Rise, a number for the City and the West End, St John's Wood, one for the BBC in W12. And there at the bottom of the pile was the pale blue envelope to Italy. If he popped them in the box at the local post office they'd all be at their addresses by the end of the week.

The dawn sky was crawling over the hills. He flexed his leg; his knee was fine. In fact he'd felt strange the last few days not having cycled anywhere. He'd have a ride today somewhere, just to keep himself in trim.

Back inside he carried a tray upstairs. Mrs Taylor stirred. 'You're an early bird today.' He got back in bed beside her. 'Cold feet,' she yelped. This was the first time he'd ever been unfaithful to Christine, but it didn't feel like infidelity.

Clive switched on the TV with the sound turned down. A man in a safari suit stood in the middle of a desert talking to the camera. The picture cut to a man in a patterned pullover sitting on a couch in the studio with a jug of orange juice on the table; then off to a woman outside the Houses of Parliament then back to the man in the pullover. There was something relaxing about the news with the sound turned down. You could make up your own stories.

Now the man in the pullover leaned forward with his hands between his legs and carved an expression that tried to convey amusement but not so amusing as to be frivolous. A raised eyebrow denoted that the following item was not only amusing with serious overtones but also spiced with a hint of irony.

The picture changed and suddenly there was the face of Clive Peacock, still that security pass picture, that unrecognisable man from a month or more ago. Clive sat in bed with a teacup poised at his lips. Mrs Taylor lay dozing at his side, and there on the screen was that man he used to be. Photos should show the saddest periods of your life as well as the happiest, she had said, and when he saw that picture of himself he knew it was from the saddest.

Another cut and there was Simon Maugham. He was talking to Sue Lawley. They stood in a car park somewhere; she was speaking through her coy smile. Then the camera cut to Mrs Atherton sitting in her garden, an old hand at this interview business. Another cut and there were the mudflats and a frame of Ralph in the distance with his metal detector. A close-up and Ralph was nodding knowingly. Clive sank back into the bed and pulled the blankets up to his eyes. The screen blinked and there was Christine lounging on the chaise longue in the living room. Behind her hung an oil painting that had a rent right down the middle. Her arms were flailing, and her eyes wild the way they used to be, the way he thought he'd never see again, and why was she dressed like a gypsy? She needed him badly, and here he was in bed with a stranger, in a fishing outpost nested among mountains and headlands and islands within a moat of mist.

Lawrence Pitman came on the screen and Clive reached out for the volume switch but instead hit the off button, and his life disappeared.

At that moment there was a knock on the door.

Mrs Taylor emerged from beneath the covers. 'It might be the postman with something to sign,' she said excitedly and pulled on her dressing gown.

Clive drank his tea. Another diesel chug drew him to the window, and there was another fishing boat sticking its nose out of the harbour and heading off hopefully. The gulls followed it a way, but then they returned to the harbour and the tight community huddled around the supermarket and the ice factory. 'A nice town this,' said Clive out loud, and a car alarm went off down the street.

But this time with reason. A van had nudged it into action, and the van was familiar. It was the white one that had chased him in Fort William. He stepped back from the window as Mrs Taylor stomped up the stairs and burst into the room. 'It's the TV people. They say they want to interview you. I told them you weren't here, but they know.'

Clive heard a motorbike pull up outside and there were the two leather-clad reporters from the *Chronicle*. Then a car with the words Radio Highlands arrived, skidding dramatically on the gravel.

'Tell them I'll be down in a minute,' he said calmly.

'Shall I ask them in?' she said. She was brushing her hair and fiddling with lipstick. She wasn't herself.

'No, I'll speak to them out on the harbour.'

'Right.' She hugged him. 'You're a good man.'

As soon as she was gone Clive pulled his cycling suit on, buttoned his gloves and tugged his balaclava over his head. Then he stuffed his belongings into his pannier and went silently down the stairs and out of the back door to the outhouse.

He could see them through the newly repaired window. They were all there: the TV crew, radio, press, a police car now as well. Mrs Taylor was standing there in her dressing gown answering questions. 'Just keep them talking, Mrs Taylor,' he muttered. His plan was to make a break for it to the track up over the moor, and then set off cross-country. He had the vehicle for it. They couldn't follow him up there.

He secured his panniers, then quietly propped open the outhouse door and straddled his saddle. He breathed deeply for thirty seconds, then, putting all his weight on his newly recovered knee, he burst out into the yard and pedalled as hard as he could for the open ground.

'There he is,' shouted Sarah Seymour, and her photographer kicked the motorbike into life. The policeman gave chase on foot and the TV crew tracked him with their camera, but no one was going to stop Clive on his Mercury Drifter. The policeman soon gave up. The motorbike struggled for a hundred yards but the surface became too rough. Clive could hear the machine choking and he turned to see it had stopped. The photographer was busy with his lenses, trying to get a picture.

'Give us a wave, Clive,' shouted Sarah Seymour. And Clive paused on the crest of the hill to see them all standing there helplessly, and he waved once before he pointed his bike down into the valley and off towards the mountains and the mist.

## 22

IT WAS AT the bank, in the queue for the cash machine, that Detective Sergeant Pitman finally got the break he needed.

His boys were coming for the weekend. He needed supplies and he needed money, and so he spent his lunch hour waiting in line, growing impatient, flicking his cash-card between his fingers, thinking of all the time he wasted in queues. If someone could invent a device that could do your queuing for you, he daydreamed, they'd make a fortune. People would be queuing up to buy one.

A graffitist had written 'I'm on holiday with my friend Bob' on the lobby wall. Pitman read it over and over again. Maybe all graffiti was written by people in queues who reached a certain stage of frustration and then could contain themselves no longer. It was either a swipe with a felt-tip or a spray with an automatic weapon.

The man in front unfolded a copy of the *Evening Echo*. Pitman read over his shoulder. The local women's hockey team had made the back-page headlines by losing every game of the season so far.

The man leafed backwards through car adverts to the centre spread, where he paused to study the plans for the town's *new* new one-way system, the one that would replace the now disgraced old new one. The latest idea was a web of ring roads, alternately one-way, all linked by a number of ornamental mini-roundabouts, beginning in the town centre and working their way outwards like ripples until they reached the bypass.

The man yawned and turned to the front page and Pitman was looking at another picture of Clive Peacock. His face had hardly been off the front of every local paper for the last month. At least they had a different shot of him now – the one from the day before's *Chronicle*. There was

Peacock on his bicycle, waving from a hilltop, and the headline as breathless as the *Echo* ever managed: 'Missing Postman Takes to the Hills'. Pitman sighed a helpless sigh. They were turning him into a cartoon.

The queue split between two cash-points. Pitman's turn finally came and he shoved his card in and entered his PIN number, 4875. The machine spat the card straight back at him. Pitman glared at it and said: '*What?*' The machine glared back and replied: 'Incorrect Number Try Again.'

'Trumped-up bloody shoebox,' he muttered and asserted himself by pressing 4875 again. Back came the card again with 'Incorrect Number Try Again' again. Pitman leaned on the console in despair. It was easier to get a small-business loan out of this bank than cash out of a cash-point. He tried another number – 4857. Back the card sprang. Someone from behind said: 'C'mon, we all want to go shopping, you know.'

'Well, you should have got up earlier, shouldn't you?' retorted Pitman.

The youth at the next point thumped the machine and it presented him with a pile of crisp notes. He turned to Pitman and said: 'Here, you're that policeman on the telly, aren't you?'

It was one of Ralph Nugent's boys. Pitman nodded and tried to smile. They were neighbours, after all. He tried 4578. The card shot out again.

'I've seen you on the telly. You and that nutty postman.'

Pitman smiled again and poked 4568 so hard it hurt his finger.

'Personally I hope no one catches him. I'm on his side. I support the Missing Postman, I do. I'd have one of those car stickers that says "I love the Missing Postman", but my car got nicked.'

'Really?' said Pitman. And he tapped in the first numbers that came into his head: 8429. The machine replied: 'Card Retained. Apply to Bank.' The shield dropped over the console. Pitman covered his face with his hands.

'What's happening up there?' said a woman behind, and

Pitman might well have swung round and socked her on the nose, had not Ralph's boy said: 'I don't care if he posts my letter or not, I support him. He's the working man's hero, he is.'

Pitman was suddenly paying attention. 'What do you mean, you don't care if he posts your letter or not?'

'He's got one of my letters. I posted it the day he disappeared.'

'Where to?'

'The BBC.'

'BBC what?'

'BBC Television. I wrote to *Points of View*. BBC Television Centre, Wood Lane, London W12 something, to be exact. I wrote complaining about Jimmy Savile – I can't stand him.'

Pitman was following the lad out into the shopping precinct. They navigated a path through the prams and collection tins. 'How do you know he's got your letter? What time did you post it?'

'I know he's got my letter because I handed it to him.'

'You handed it to who?'

'To bloody Clive Peacock, the Missing Postman. He was there emptying the box at twelve o'clock and I handed it to him and he put it in his bag.'

'Why didn't you tell me before?'

'You never asked. Don't get stroppy with me, mate. *I* haven't done anything.'

'Listen, this is very important.'

'I don't have to take police harassment from you, you know.'

'I know. I just want to make sure.'

'Make sure what?'

'Make absolutely sure that you gave Clive Peacock a letter and he put it in his bag, on that day, at that time.'

'I told you.'

'What did he say?'

'Thank you very much.'

'That's all?'

'That's all.'

'To the BBC Television Centre in London?'

'Oh, get lost!'

Pitman let the boy walk off. 'Ha!' he said and clenched his fists, and when a collector for Christian Aid rattled his tin under his nose Pitman put a pound coin in it.

Back at the station he went straight to see the DCI. He tried to be calm but couldn't control his excitement. 'Sir, I've got him. I've got an address for him. I know where he's going next. I know someone who gave him a letter the day he disappeared.'

The DCI blew his nose long and loud, sat back in his chair, blinked very slowly, sighed, let his mouth drop open and let his shoulders hang. 'Gave who a letter, Pitman?'

'The Missing Postman.'

The DCI blew his nose again. 'Where to this time? Hawaii?'

'To London, to the BBC TV Centre, sir. I want to take an observation van up there and do a stake-out. We've got him.'

'When's he going to be there?'

'I don't know exactly. He's on his way, though. He was spotted at the Scottish border heading south the day before yesterday. Soon.'

'Soon.'

'The weekend, I expect.'

'You want me to give you an observation van, another officer, no doubt, plus back-up should you need to make an arrest, for a loony postman who's coming, soon?'

'It's a cert, sir.'

'Give it to the Met.'

'He's ours, sir.'

'You're not having an observation van for this madman Clive Peacock. I'm sick of him. I hope he never comes back. I don't want him back. Besides, you're too busy here.'

'I'm not busy here, for God's sake!'

'Well, you bloody well should be. Some miscreant took the bulbs out of every Belisha beacon in the whole town last night.'

'Good.'

'What?'

'You heard.' And Pitman turned and left, slamming the door.

He went straight home and did something very unusual for him. He telephoned all the regular members of the Beaconsfield Hill Neighbourhood Watch and asked them to assemble at his house at seven-thirty that evening for an emergency meeting.

Meetings were never normally held at Pitman's house. The others never asked him, so Pitman never offered. But now he went round the living room plumping up the cushions and stuffing newspapers under chairs. He washed up the dishes and put some coffee cups on a tray. Only four had handles – it didn't matter, he didn't have any coffee. He'd give them whisky. That would show he meant business.

Ralph Nugent was the first to arrive. He stood on the doorstep with his metal detector under his arm. He had a jacket with the word Superman on the back. 'Glad you could make it,' said Pitman. He led him into the lounge and sat him down and without bothering to ask just handed him a whisky. Ralph licked his lips and looked round the room. Pitman was used to people not knowing what to say to him. He tried to look interested and said: 'Do you ever catch anything with that thing?'

'What thing?' said Ralph defensively.

'That,' and Pitman pointed to Ralph's Fieldmaster Searcher.

Ralph looked hurt. 'It's a metal detector, not a fishing rod.'

Pitman nodded. 'Ever detected anything interesting?'

Ralph looked suspicious. 'Bits and pieces. Nothing of any value. Ring-pull tops mostly.'

Before Pitman could stop himself he'd said: 'What do you do with them, throw them back?' He laughed. Ralph looked at the floor. 'Joke, sorry,' said Pitman.

The doorbell rang again. It was the Haddens and Mrs Lemsford. 'Emergency meeting, indeed?' said Mr Hadden. 'We've never had one of those before.' And he tapped his pipe on the porch step.

'I'm missing *This Is Your Life*,' said Mrs Tidy. And Pitman smiled and thought: If she mentions her cat I'll throttle her.

Mrs Lemsford thrust the Prince Andrew and Sarah Ferguson tin at Pitman. 'Swiss roll,' she said. 'I thought you might not have anything made.'

'Thank you, how thoughtful,' said Pitman, and showed them into the living room where he poured them each a large whisky.

Denbigh arrived, carrying a folder. 'About the outing, is it?'

'No, Mr Denbigh, it isn't,' said Pitman, leading him by the arm. 'To be honest, old chap, it's about something rather more serious, so I'd be grateful if you didn't talk about the outing tonight.' And before Denbigh could object he was sat down on a chair and handed a tumbler full of whisky and a lump of Swiss roll.

Mrs Atherton hobbled in with an Asda carrier bag and the news that her hip operation had been put back another week. Pitman gave her a whisky. 'I've never been in your house before, Mr Pitman,' she said and ran her finger down the wallpaper. 'Who's that?' she demanded, pointing to the picture of two teenagers on top of the TV.

'That's Matthew and Douglas, my boys,' he said as proudly as he could, and then remembered they were coming for the weekend. He'd have to cancel; there was nothing else he could do.

Mrs Wheatley arrived with the Tidys. And Mr Drake drove in his Toyota, even though he only lived across the road. The active members of the Beaconsfield Hill Neighbourhood Watch all sat in Detective Sergeant Pitman's living room on their first ever emergency meeting. Pitman presided. He said: 'Right,' and then he refilled all their glasses.

'I'll tell you exactly why I called you over tonight. Clive Peacock. That's why.'

Not a murmur from the Watch.

Pitman went on: 'I have to confess I'm worried about him. I'm worried he needs help. More specifically he needs the help of his friends and community. I've had a lead today which I believe will take me to him, and that's where you all come in. I want this to be a combined effort.'

The clock in the hall struck eight.

Ralph was confused. He said: 'How can we help?'

'Yes, exactly,' said Denbigh.

'I mean, we'd all like to help,' said Hadden.

'But how?' said Mrs Lemsford. 'That's the question.'

'I'll tell you how,' said Pitman and he turned to Ralph. 'I saw your boy in town today. I forget his name, blond with a cropped haircut.'

'Daniel,' said Ralph.

'Daniel. I saw him in the NatWest cash-point lobby.'

'That would have been Robert then,' said Ralph.

'Anyway, he gave me a piece of information regarding Clive Peacock that I have been trying to get for the last five weeks. He told me he posted a letter at twelve o'clock in the Waverley Road postbox on the day that Clive disappeared.'

'No!' said Ralph.

'Yes. In fact he handed it to him. It was a letter to the BBC, to *Points of View*.'

'With Anne Robinson,' said Mrs Hadden.

'So now we're one step ahead of him at last. And what I propose to do is this: we stake out the Television Centre. We wait there for him and, when he arrives, intercept him and bring him back where he belongs.'

'Good show, Pitman,' said Mr Tidy.

'Gooshow,' said Mrs Atherton and held out her glass. Pitman filled it again, so Mrs Atherton emptied it again.

Pitman continued: 'Now, how can you help? you're thinking.'

'Exactly,' said Mr Drake.

'I don't want to arrest Clive Peacock. I don't even want to involve the police. The best care is care in the community, we all know that. I want a select team of us, his friends, to be in the van waiting outside the BBC when he turns up. So, Mr Denbigh: I want the community van. I want the windows blacked out and I want it made as comfortable as possible. Then I want six volunteers, to take it in shifts, and to be prepared should Clive Peacock be confused about what is happening and . . . resist us.'

'Count me in,' said Ralph.

'And me,' said Mr Tidy.

'And me,' said Mrs Wheatley.

'And us,' said Mr and Mrs Hadden.

'Me too,' said Mr Denbigh.

'I'll make some devilled eggs for the journey,' said Mrs Lemsford.

'Good,' said Pitman, proud of this combined display of mettle. 'The latest information I have is that Clive is heading south, at speed. We need to get up to London as soon as possible. So we leave tomorrow morning, early, and spend the weekend up there.'

Pitman couldn't help but notice a shudder of disapproval pass through the Watch at this suggestion. There followed a silence that made him want to open the window.

'That would prove unpopular, I think, Mr Pitman,' said Denbigh.

'Yes,' said Mr Tidy.

'Yes,' said Mrs Wheatley.

'Indeed,' said Ralph shaking his head.

'Yes,' said Mrs Lemsford.

'Why?' asked Pitman.

'The outing, Pitman, that's why,' said Denbigh. 'This weekend is outing weekend: Stratford-upon-Avon, or haven't you been paying attention?'

Pitman looked at him without blinking. He was quite

calm, but in his mind Denbigh was an insect and he was pulling his legs and arms off. Denbigh said: 'There's a timetable advertised in the newsagent's with a menu from La Langoustine and the full list of those coming. I notice your name isn't on it, by the way.'

'Fuck the outing,' said Detective Sergeant Pitman, becoming the first person ever to use a four-letter word in the history of the Beaconsfield Hill Neighbourhood Watch.

There was a hush, then Mrs Atherton held up her Asda bag and said: 'Can I have my bath now? I've got my own towel,' and she got up and fell over.

Ralph didn't go directly home after the meeting. Instead he went to Christine's. He blamed it on the whisky.

He peered in through the Peacocks' front window and saw Christine up a ladder painting something complicated in a top corner of the room. He looked and looked and then closed his eyes and saw her legs on that bicycle all those years ago in Shropshire. Long legs, brown and smooth. Chris Blair had said how he would like to lick one of Christine's legs from top to bottom. Ralph had never forgotten that.

He opened the front door. 'Knock knock, it's me,' he called.

'Hi, Ralph,' called Christine. And he strode in and instead of leaving his metal detector in the antique umbrella-stand as usual he left it at the foot of the stairs.

'What are you doing?' he asked.

'Painting a cobweb.'

Ralph kicked an empty plate across the room. Was it the whisky or had he heard her say she was painting a cobweb?

She said: 'I don't know, though. There's nothing like the real thing. How do you get spiders?'

'I wouldn't know about that,' said Ralph.

'Spiders give a room warmth, and that's what I'm after. Not radiator warmth – that's not real warmth. I can't stand radiators; I'm thinking of having the central heating pulled out, to be honest. I mean warmth like you get from a pair of dark eyes, the warmth you get from second-hand crockery, from history. I've decided history is very warm.'

'You wouldn't like our house,' said Ralph.

'*Homes and Gardens* have asked if they can do a feature on me. "The Missing Postman's House" they want to call it. I said, "The Missing Postman doesn't live here," but they said I knew what they meant.'

Ralph felt a surge of confidence closely followed by a surge of guilt. But he was determined not to talk about Clive, even though he had Pitman's news.

'Anyway I can't turn down an opportunity like this,' said Christine. 'It's good publicity. Business is taking off, you know, Ralph. I've been asked to distress houses all over town.'

Ralph said quietly: 'You're different, you know, Christine.' It was the most philosophical thing he had said to anyone for years.

Christine made spaghetti for them. She burned the sauce and the spaghetti was undercooked. They sat in the sun lounge looking out over the mudflats as the sun set. The view was almost compensation for the meal.

They ate in silence. The stainless-steel forks scratched the Poole pottery plates. Then they both tried to speak at the same time.

Ralph said: 'After you.'

'No, no, after *you*,' said Christine.

'All right,' said Ralph and with the look of a man overtaking on a blind bend he said: 'I was going to ask if I could spend the night with you.'

'Oh,' said Christine, and let her tongue take the shock, twisting it round her mouth as she tried to prise loose a piece of embedded, undercooked spaghetti.

Ralph waited as long as he could for a response but then slammed on the brakes as his nerves failed him. 'What were you going to say?' he asked.

'Oh, I was just going to ask you if you'd seen in the

*Review* about the Mayor and his idea for Missing Postman Country.'

'Oh yes,' said Ralph. 'I've seen that. Why not? I think it's a good idea. Make a change from all that Hardy Country business. It's all publicity, as you say.'

'But I don't want that sort of publicity.'

'No, no, of course not.'

More stainless steel on pottery. A car alarm went off; they didn't flinch. Christine said: 'Ralph, when I said earlier the Missing Postman doesn't live here, what I meant was I don't want anything to do with this Missing Postman business. I want things to be as they were. I want him back before I do something stupid . . .'

'Like what?' said Ralph.

'I don't know. I've been thinking of lots of things.'

Ralph promised himself that after the count of three he would try again. One, two, three, and he swung out and this time his foot hit the floor. 'So. What do you think, Christine? About me staying?'

Christine got up and piled the plates. She gazed out of the window and said: 'Look at that garden. Clive's going to have a fit when he gets back. I should water it. I'm terrible.' Then without looking at him she said: 'I think you'd better go home now, Ralph.'

'Right,' said Ralph, and crawling from the wreckage he got up from the table and, collecting his metal detector on the move, he strode out of the house, but with his head held high: after thirty-two years he'd finally asked her.

Detective Sergeant Pitman said: 'Hello? . . . Hello?' and put the phone down. His ex-wife had just hung up on him again. 'I'll make it up to them,' he'd said. 'Soon,' he'd said. And he would have explained, but she'd called him a hopeless dinosaur and slammed the phone down.

He thought: I worry about her at times. She's so unreasonable. I'm not behaving like this to be awkward. I'd love to have my boys for the weekend. But I can't.

He swayed, beautifully poised on a cliff of whisky, balanced between anger and not giving a shit.

He dialled WDC McMahon.

'It's me,' he said. 'Detective Sergeant Pitman.'

'I know who it is,' she said. She was eating an apple.

'I mean, it's Lawrence.'

'Hello, Lawrence.'

'What are you doing this weekend?'

'Nothing special,' she munched.

'How would you like to help me find the Missing Postman?'

'All right.'

'It'll mean spending the day . . . and maybe the night, in an observation van outside the BBC Television Centre. With me.'

'Suits me.'

'And this is in our own time; it's not police work.'

'Fine.'

'Good. I'll pick you up tomorrow morning at eight-thirty sharp.'

'Right you are.'

Pitman put the phone down. She was keen all right, that WDC McMahon, keen and reliable. Keen and reliable and with an acute sense of duty. He poured the inch of whisky in his glass back into the bottle, spilling most of it, and went to bed.

Next morning he went down to the station at seven-thirty and against orders signed out an observation van. It had a mattress and sleeping bags in the back and smelt like a curry house.

He drove round to WDC McMahon's. She opened her front door before he could knock. She had on jeans and a T-shirt with the words Victor Padrone emblazoned across the front.

## 23

Lᴇᴀɴ ᴀɴᴅ ᴡɪʀʏ fellow, willing to risk death daily, banging on the door of an optician's in Pitlochry.

It was past closing time but Clive had had a day of it – cycling over moors and along railway tracks, and through hailstones the size of peppermints. Now though, a sympathetic-looking man in a tartan tie was unlocking the door.

'Sorry, we're closed,' he said.

'You're Ivor, aren't you?' asserted Clive.

'Yes,' replied the optician warily. Who was this person dripping mud on his doorstep?

'I'm Clive Peacock. The Missing Postman. Mr Peterson from Fort William said . . .'

'Come in,' said Ivor, and he locked the door behind them.

He let Clive sleep on the consultant's couch. He apologised that he couldn't keep him company – he had choir practice. Before he left, though, he went and bought Clive fish and chips. He had to wake him up to give them to him, and as soon as Ivor left Clive fell asleep again. He had the fish and chips cold the next morning at 4.45. He left a 'thank you' note and signed it: CP The Missing Postman.

He came down out of the Highlands and hid among the back roads again, hoping he could thread a discreet route south. But in a café just across the Firth of Forth he was recognised – a young lad asked for his autograph. Clive scribbled on a napkin and smiled at the boy's mother. In reply she held up the newspaper and there on the front was a picture of him waving as he set off from Mrs Taylor's. It took up the whole front page. He decided to travel by night from then on.

He explained this to the senior partner in the optician's

in Falkirk, as they sat in his office eating ginger cake and talking mountain bikes.

'I've always wanted a Mercury Drifter,' said Kelvin Rioch.

'They're dependable machines all right,' said Clive.

'Do you find the tungsten inert gas welding makes any difference to performance?'

'A bit,' nodded Clive.

'And how about the 650B tandem rims? Do they enable you to create the four-wheel-drive effect?'

'Sometimes, now and again, not often,' replied Clive.

'I see you've chosen the Bullmoose handlebars rather than the Slingshot.'

'It was a difficult decision,' said Clive.

The staff let him sleep in a back room on a couch until they closed at five-thirty. Then they woke him and gave him a flask of tea and some sandwiches for the night's journey. One of the assistants kissed him as he left.

The moon was becoming full again – he didn't have to switch on his lights. He was a silhouette gliding south, an overnight express, the mail-train with no time to spare. The letters were thumping in his pannier once more, and that was all he wanted to do now – deliver the letters. How could he think of staying in a Scottish fishing village? He was a postman, damn it! People depended on him. People in Italy depended on him.

He passed through towns at speed and with a well-oiled silence. At ten o'clock one morning he reached the border at Jedburgh. The opticians there had been warned he was on his way and were prepared. They had a camp bed in their storeroom made up. Again Clive slept until the shop closed. The optician woke him with tea and the paper. At the bottom of the front page was a story claiming that any letter delivered and cancelled by the Missing Postman was now worth £300. 'You're really famous,' said the optician. 'They'll have you on *Wogan*, I bet.'

He crossed into England and came down the east flank of the country, through the Vale of York. There were no mountains or fells to tackle any more, just wide horizons with pylons striding across farmland, and with fat power stations cooling their feet in rivers.

He was travelling into the season now and the vegetation bloomed and died within miles. In the evenings hover mowers hummed and the smell of fresh grass made him feel giddy. The countryside was familiar and it waved at him in the breeze. He felt as though he'd been away for years.

He slept in opticians' in Durham, in Goole, in Stamford and in Stevenage. In Stevenage his host said: 'I saw a sticker in a car today. It said "I love the Missing Postman".'

'Get away,' laughed Clive.

'It's true,' said the optician.

Then shortly after midnight one Friday Clive cycled under the M25 at Potters Bar. There was a glow to the south, a corona of orange light, that diluted the darkness and drew all traffic towards it. As the dawn spilt across the city leaving a pink and grey stain on the brickwork Clive was popping a letter through a door in Tottenham. From there he headed down into Islington and on into the City. The traffic was slight on a Saturday and the exhaust smelt fresh at this hour, but Clive wasn't taking it easy. He wanted to be done with London and be heading out of town to the coast. Harwich, Margate, Dover, Folkestone or even Portsmouth, his cross-channel options were wide-ranging; they couldn't cover them all. He didn't have a passport but he'd worry about that when the time came. According to the papers he was the Elusive Clive Peacock and he could slip through that sort of net.

He delivered four letters to the City and one to Dock-lands, then he set off for the West End. The traffic built and he was just another delivery man on a bicycle. London seemed to be choking with messengers bearing letters and packages that burst with importance, kids who cycled through the traffic as though their lives depended on it. Clive thought he should have felt a camaraderie with them but he didn't, he felt lost among them. And they were so purposeless he found they undermined his confidence. In one of the big hospitals, where Clive had a letter to deliver, a number of them were gathered around the reception – cyclists and motorcyclists – with radios and dirty faces; some even wore smog masks. They didn't recognise Clive. One asked him if he had any cigarette papers. Another said to him: 'See that secretary over there, she sits there licking envelopes all day long, and when I said to her I don't know how she could stand it, she says to me: "I love the taste of envelopes." Can you believe that?'

And Clive had thought about laughing with him but instead he'd said: 'Yes, I can believe that.'

The traffic became dopey and slow after lunch. This was London traffic though and it was as indigenous as mountains were to Scotland, a challenge to be taken up. Clive worked his way up to St John's Wood, ducking into subways and jumping lights; grazing his knees on bumpers, shouting at drivers and ignoring pedestrians. By late afternoon he had just two letters left. One was for Kensal Rise. He popped it through its box and heard a voice call: 'Not another letter from Maureen.' The other was for the BBC in Shepherd's Bush.

A summer storm trundled over the capital. Clive sheltered in a café, a busmen's haunt; he sat in the corner with egg yolk dripping on to his thumbs. The crews turned their buses round outside and then came in and crouched over newspapers and teacups. In the background on the radio Clive could hear Malcolm Dixon and his emotional phone-in. A caller was saying: 'I want us to wake up in the morning and look like that couple in the building society advert.'

Clive stirred his tea in time with the drivers and conductors and looked out into the steamy rain – summer in the city. He wondered if the people of Livorno had heard of the Missing Postman. He could see himself cycling in the sunshine down through France, through villages where

227

they would all line the street to wave and watch him pass. . . .

'I've a feeling an affair might do me good, you see,' said another caller to Malcolm Dixon.

. . . Like one of those cyclists in the Tour de France. . . .

'Why do you think an affair would help, Christine?' asked Malcolm Dixon.

. . . They'd have flags; they'd have ticker-tape. Vive Le Missing Postman! . . .

'It might help me decide if our relationship is worth saving,' said the caller Christine.

'And do you think your relationship is worth saving?' said Malcolm Dixon.

'I don't know. I'm so confused,' said Christine.

Clive's knee was knocking the bottom of the table.

'What do you think has made you confused?' asked Malcolm Dixon.

'Well, it's difficult. The thing is, I want him to come back, but what I really want is for him never to have gone.'

'You want the impossible,' said Malcolm Dixon.

'Yes,' whispered Christine, before Jack Remmington interrupted her with the weather.

Clive left the café without paying. He climbed on his bike and cycled, weaving his way through the traffic but with no notion of where he was going. The rain stopped but he wasn't aware. Of course their relationship was worth saving. He'd never thought that was in doubt. He'd just needed this time to work a few things out, that was all. Couldn't she see that? She was losing her grip, that was the trouble, spinning out of control, that was why she was behaving like this. And it was his fault.

'She needs me back. She said as much. She wants me not to have gone.' He talked to himself as he cycled. People on the pavement peered at him peculiarly. At some traffic lights a woman sitting comfortably in her red Volvo pulled up alongside him and he said to her: 'I was confused as well, Christine. That was why I left. I was desperate. I didn't realise how desperate. We need to talk and spend time together, that's all. Of course our relationship is worth saving, and who are you thinking of having an affair with anyway?' The Volvo pulled away as soon as the lights turned amber.

He cycled for hours. The yellow London night spread over the city like a damp patch. He didn't know where he was; he was cycling instinctively. Finally he came to a dead end, and when he looked around he saw he was on a new housing estate. A big sign said 'Homes for the Future', and he was surrounded by red-brick houses, a number of them still half-built, only a few with lights on inside. The gardens weren't planted, and the access roads were soft and smelt of tar. Even the cars parked on the crisp gravel were all new. Another sign, on the grass outside a show home, invited buyers to come inside and test the double glazing. Clive took up the offer. He tried the door and it swung open and he had a house to himself for the night.

He didn't turn on the lights. The streetlamps let him see all he needed to; he just ran his fingers over the shapes in the gloom. The ceramic top to the stove made him think of the Aga Christine had had installed in their kitchen at home. The nylon wall-to-wall carpets brought back the polished and varnished floorboards she had slaved over, and the rug she'd bought in the local auction (price £30; value, at least £250). Of course their relationship was worth saving.

Upstairs there were two bedrooms with foldaway walls to create more rooms if necessary. Clive slid back the doors of the fitted wardrobes, and ran his fingers down the cold paint. He saw his dark outline in the mirror move like a shadow.

There was hot water and so he drew a bath in the avocado and cream bathroom, and lay there breathing steam as a jet plane rumbled overhead. His head lolled; he was dreaming and he knew it. He saw Christine's bare back in the newly distressed bathroom at home. 'I want him to come back,' she had told Malcolm Dixon, and he wanted to be back now.

He wrapped himself in a bedspread and went back downstairs into the living room. The room was furnished with sharp black fittings. It looked as though it had too many corners. There were shelves and a cocktail cabinet, and a three-piece suite that would combine to make another bed that would sleep two. It seemed as though the whole house could fold down or up to accommodate any number one wished. Clive sat in an armchair and looked at the phone on the table. He picked up the receiver and couldn't believe it when he heard a dialling tone. I should be calling someone in Australia, he thought, as he pressed his own numbers. He didn't know anyone in Australia though.

'This is Peacock Interiors. I'm sorry there's no one here to take your call . . .'

Clive hung up. A light went on in the house opposite and he saw a couple enter the room and take their jackets off. They kissed each other playfully. He could watch them quite clearly framed in their front window. The cheap thrill of voyeurism was made cheaper still because, sitting there in an armchair, it was like watching the TV. He could hear music and then the couple were in each other's arms. She threw her head back and he kissed her neck and ran his hand around her waist and up the back of her blouse. Then they fell on the sofa and all he could see was the balding crown of the man's head.

Another jet flew low over the rooftops. The estate must be near the airport. The lights on the aircraft's wings and the airline markings were visible. Back across the road the man had stood up and was pulling the woman up with him. He led her out of the room. The light went off but then the one on the landing went on, and in the bedroom. They had no curtains in the house, it seemed. They must have just moved in. There were no pictures on the walls, and no lampshades even. This might be their first night in their new home.

Now they were in each other's arms again, smiling and pecking each other. They were both so young and beautiful, and didn't care about their lack of curtains. The man picked expertly at the buttons on the back of the woman's blouse and she kissed him hard and long and slipped her arms free from her clothing. He squeezed and kissed her shoulders then pulled her bra strap down and they fell out of sight again.

Clive wanted to hold his young wife like that. That was the way he had always wanted to make love – that was how he and Mrs Taylor had made love, he liked to think – and yet he had never touched Christine with anywhere near as much passion. Their sex had been undercover and always done by candlelight. Christine could do nothing romantic unless candles were involved.

The nearest they'd come to passion was during that intense period when she was trying to get pregnant; when every time he walked through the door after work the stairway would be lined with candles, and he'd climb to the landing and the flickering lights would lead him into the bedroom where Christine would be sitting in a chair by the bed wrapped in a shawl, and he'd be standing in the doorway in his GPO uniform. He'd throw his hat off and stride across the room and try to inject passion into her with every kiss and every grip. But they knew so very little about each other's bodies. They expected sex to look after itself, and it was struggling. As soon as the session was over Christine was up and out of bed, blowing the candles out and keen to get back to her rewiring. Sex was something she made room for in her timetable. Clive sensed it was a relief for both of them when she finally did get pregnant.

She didn't alter her routine much, she just did less strenuous work. They didn't talk about babies either, although Clive could tell their relationship was changing daily: they were going to have a child; there was no backing out now. When he looked at her he saw her leaning against the wall of his commitment, and that made him want to look the other way.

Christine found a pram in a second-hand sale. A Victorian

231

model: cost £6; value, at least £20. She stripped it and re-sprung it one weekend two months into her pregnancy. On the Sunday night they went to bed and Clive woke at three o'clock to find Christine bleeding and doubled up with cramps. He called an ambulance and she spent the next two days in hospital. Everyone said to her: 'Don't worry, you'll get pregnant again easily enough.' The doctor said: 'Sixty per cent of first pregnancies end in miscarriages; there's nothing to stop you trying again in a couple of months.' Christine lost weight afterwards and didn't go out of the house much. But then she started to repair the bedroom windowframe and Clive knew she would be all right.

He talked to no one about the miscarriage. He only knew he was in trouble by the way that knot in his stomach tightened for a few days afterwards, the same one as when his father had died. On that occasion he'd gone off on a cycle ride over the Isle of Purbeck and felt better for it. The weekend after Christine's miscarriage he went off on the same trip. He cycled clear across the peninsula, up and down the hills to Lulworth. It was almost midnight when he got home; he felt exhausted but still taut with helpless frustration. The next day he got up and did the same ride all over again. That evening he felt drained, and that was the feeling he wanted.

Two months after the miscarriage he came home from work one afternoon and found candles lining the staircase again. Four months later Christine was once more pregnant. This time she was determined to take it easy, she said: she would only do a bit of painting and decorating. Clive protested, but Christine claimed it relaxed her more than any breathing exercises. After five months the books all said they were past the danger period but Clive grew more and more tense. That wall of commitment stood firm, but he knew it was riddled with a vulnerability that he shared with no one. He decided to take up gardening. They only had a backyard at the time so he got himself an allotment, one he shared with three other postmen – a plot

232

twenty foot square each. Clive turned and tilled and fed his patch so lovingly that when he planted seeds the flowers sprang up with more vigour than even the packet promised. He was proud of the relationship he had with his garden. It was one of mutual respect: I do my bit well and you do your bit well and then we're all happy. He found himself looking at Christine lying in bed with her belly rising like a loaf under the blankets, and he felt a desire to climb inside that womb of hers with his gardening tools and check it over. He wanted to tidy it up ready for the blooming. Instead all he was able to do was bring her meals on trays.

The pregnancy was thirty-four weeks old when Christine stepped on the bottom rung of that ladder. It snapped and she fell – not badly, she said she felt fine. It was Clive who felt dreadful. He alone knew he had broken the rung himself the previous weekend when he'd used the steps to put a light bulb in, and he'd done nothing about repairing it, just idly slotted the two bits back together. He didn't admit to this now though; instead remorse made him pamper her to the point of annoyance.

Then on a routine visit to the hospital the doctor examined Christine with a frown. He left the room and returned with a colleague who carried out his own examination. Both doctors left the room. The Peacocks were called into a consultant's office and told there was no sign of life inside the womb. The foetus was dead and had been for a week or two.

They came home and Clive made a meal. Christine couldn't finish hers. She pushed the plate away and said quietly: 'It's just one of those things, I suppose,' and then she started to sob. Clive put his arm around her, but she wanted to be left on her own, she said. He didn't know which corner of the room to hide in. He sensed there was no escape from this, so much so that he didn't seek forgiveness or relief, all he sought was the blame he deserved.

Three weeks later, one windy night, Christine went into labour. Clive drove her to the hospital, reversing into a senior registrar's Vauxhall Viva as he parked. The labour was mercifully quick; he was by her side throughout. She screamed as the dawn broke, although the noise Clive would remember more than any other from that night was the gale blowing, rattling the windows. The child was delivered at seven-fifteen am. The midwives wrapped it in a sheet and handed it carefully to Christine. 'He's lovely,' said a nurse, and then Clive and Christine and their still-born baby boy were left in peace.

They were left in peace for fifteen minutes exactly. Then the bundle was taken from them and placed in a cot on the other side of the room; the child was grey and already growing cold. A nurse came and wheeled Christine away and the midwife led Clive out by the arm. The baby was left alone amongst the machinery.

Christine stayed in hospital overnight, in a separate part of the maternity ward, away from the other mothers. Clive left the car in the car park and walked home; he couldn't drive with L-plates unless another driver sat in the passenger seat. The next day he had planned to bring Christine some flowers from his allotment, but he didn't bother. He stepped in the lift up to Christine's ward and closed his eyes as he rose and it was like climbing a whole ladder of broken rungs.

They decided not to have a funeral. Clive had suggested they might give the child a name, but Christine didn't want to. 'There's no sense pretending,' she said, and that was the last time they spoke of it.

Now, nearly twenty years on, Clive sat wrapped in a bedspread in an armchair in the dark on a housing estate with the guilt finally climbing to the surface. Another jet screamed overhead and he covered his face with his hands and felt that ache in his throat overcome him and those tears brim again, and this time there was no attempt to dam them. Over the rim they came in a flood. His child was still locked in that room, and in no way frozen in a cold and grey limbo. Over the years the baby had grown, so that now he was swollen and livid, a twenty-year-old monster who roared every time you put your hand on the doorknob.

Clive threw himself back into the chair and howled. The wooden spine cracked and a seam in the fabric split. He stood up and kicked it and the arm came off. Then he turned to the wall and kicked that and the plaster burst with surprise. 'Real fireplaces can be fitted if preferred,' said a sign over a fibreglass lick of flame, and Clive kicked a hole in it and threw it across the room. He kicked the cocktail cabinet and a door fell off. He kicked the panelling along the staircase and it buckled. He punched the kitchen door and holed it as if it were made of cardboard. He sat on the stairs and lashed out at the banister and every baton snapped. He kicked the skirting board and it cracked from end to end. This was a gingerbread house, a real dream home.

He ran upstairs and booted the bath enclosure and it crumpled like a box. He barged his way into the master bedroom and the door split by the hinge. Then he climbed inside the fitted cupboard and put his head in his hands again as that monster in the sealed room roared, and he tried to fight his way out, kicking holes through the plywood doors.

Afterwards he leaned against a wall, panting. He pushed back a panel of double-glazing and let in the cool night. Not a sound came from it now, only his breath and his pounding pulse. He slid down the wall to the floor and sat there sweating. Everyone he'd met on this trip had given him a reason why he had run away, but no one had yet managed to convince him. All he knew was that he was running and that felt soothing. And he didn't want his life to be over yet – that felt soothing too.

He sat on the floor for some time, staring at a wall, stroking his beard. Then a smash of glass came from across the street and he was conscious of himself again, and of how his sweat had turned cold. Clive peered through the window and saw in the lamplight two men breaking in through the back door of the house opposite where the young couple slept upstairs. Every light in every other house was off. Clive held his breath, knowing he should act. He pulled on his clothes and went downstairs and phoned 999.

'A house is being broken into on . . . the Otley estate,' he read off a brochure. 'On Hollowoak Road. I don't know the number; there's a red car outside.'

The policewoman asked for his name and without thinking he said: 'Clive Peacock.' When she asked for his address he said: 'They're breaking in now, I'm going after them.'

The policewoman shouted: 'Stay where you are!' but Clive hung up. He didn't care what happened to him. He left the show house and crossed the road to the broken window. There was no one in the kitchen so he climbed inside, and now he could hear voices upstairs. A man said: 'Take what you want. I just don't want anyone hurt.'

Another man laughed and said: 'Don't worry, we'll take what we want.'

Clive could hear drawers being opened. 'C'mon, you must have some jewellery,' said another man.

Then a woman's voice: 'We've just moved in; all our belongings aren't here yet.'

'I want something that will make my trip worthwhile.'

'There's a trophy on the bedside cabinet. That's silver, take that.'

One of the burglars laughed and said: 'I don't want any trophy. I want money or jewellery. Oh look, a locked box. I guess you were lying.'

Clive stood at the bottom of the stairs. He tried to swallow but his mouth was dry. He could hear the woman crying now. 'Please leave that alone, that's not worth anything.'

'Well, why's it locked, then?'

Clive crept up to the landing. The sweet smell of alcohol was in the air. Peering through the crack in the door he could see one of the burglars on the bed – he looked drunk. The other was trying to force open a jewellery box with a Swiss army knife. That was his weapon, a penknife.

The box sprang open. The youth tossed his mate a brooch and said: 'Here, you can give this to Irene.'

'Yeah, that will suit Irene,' and he pocketed it.

The woman's voice was now trembling. 'That jewellery is my family's. It's of no use to you. It's of no value. Look, I'll give you my cash-card and my PIN number and you can draw out all the money you want from my account right now.'

The burglar on the bed said: 'I reckon this must be really valuable, you know – judging by how much you don't want us to take it.'

'It was my grandmother's,' cried the woman. 'It's of worth, but only to me.'

'Well, it's of worth to me now,' sneered the burglar.

Clive pulled his balaclava over his face. He knew he was about to do something, he just didn't know what. In the end he took a step back and kicked the door open. It came off its hinges completely and hit one burglar on the shins as it fell. He screamed. Everyone in the room screamed. Clive charged in shouting and waving his arms. 'Put your hands up; I'm a postman, I mean policeman, and we've got the place covered. You're under arrest.'

The burglar with the jewellery box came running. Clive swung at him but hit the jewellery box instead and that hit the lad in the face. He yelled; strings of gems spewed across the room. The other lad frantically scrambled for the door. Clive kicked his arse and he tumbled down the stairs. His mate had a bloody nose now and was cowering like a puppy until Clive screamed and charged at him and he bounced over the bed and rolled down the stairs after his partner. Clive chased them both out of the house. Another jet passed overhead but his screams were louder.

The man and woman came down the stairs wrapped in bedding, their faces stiff with shock. 'Who are you?' said the man.

'Me?' said Clive. 'Oh, I live over the road. You're new here, aren't you? It's a nice neighbourhood really. You

237

should join the Neighbourhood Watch. Put a little sticker in your front window. We meet every Thursday.'

'Here are the police,' said the woman. A blue light was spinning round the dark room. The couple went to the front door; Clive slipped out of the back.

He crept back to the show home, collected his bike and made for the trees at the end of the estate, where he sat for some time on the damp earth. Then he headed back into the city to the BBC.

# 24

IN A DARK blue Bedford van with shaded windows, parked opposite the gates of the BBC Television Centre, Wood Lane, London W12 7RJ, Detective Sergeant Pitman and WDC McMahon were talking about sex and Mexican food.

'It's the spiritual ingredient of sex that fascinates me so,' said McMahon.

'Goodness, these burritos are good,' said Pitman.

'Did you hear what I said, Lawrence?'

'Yes, yes, I heard what you said.'

Pitman had been trying to ignore her for the past two hours ever since she opened the two-litre bottle of Valpolicella. She always let her hair down a bit on a Saturday night, she said. He didn't mind, did he?

She was sitting in the front seat with her bare feet up on the dashboard, swigging from the bottle. 'Men just don't understand that though,' she sighed. 'The pleasure they derive from sex is so one-dimensional.'

'And that chilli sauce is just hot enough, isn't it?' said Pitman.

'Did you hear me, Lawrence?'

'Yes.'

'Do you agree?'

'How do you mean?'

It had been a long day, but they'd passed the time by taking it in shifts, by reading and listening to the radio, and by trying all the local takeaways. An hour ago, though, McMahon had gone out to Tortilla Flats in Shepherd's Bush and she'd come back with this selection of Mexican tasties plus the Valpolicella, and after two glasses she'd started saying provocative things about the male orgasm. All Pitman had been able to say to every theory she expounded was: 'How do you mean?'

'Well,' said McMahon and some wine dribbled down

her chin, 'what I mean is, men, it seems to me, experience sex on a purely instinctive basis, whereas women experience it on a number of different levels, spiritual as well as physiological.'

God, she's pissed, thought Pitman, and he gazed down Wood Lane for a lone man on a bicycle. The thought of spending the whole weekend here was appalling. He'd contacted the *Points of View* office and ascertained that they'd had no letter from Robert Nugent, so Clive Peacock hadn't made it yet, but he must be near. There were two sightings confirmed in Stevenage only the night before. He had to be in London by now.

McMahon said: 'Men are so wrapped up in role play. They're all little boys in the playground still. I like a man who ignores me, to be honest. I can't stand possessive men. The first thing I do if my man gets possessive is go right out and have an affair with someone, and it's stupid because I don't really want to, but I'm damned if anyone is going to think they can own me. That's why all the girls like you, Lawrence – because you're not the possessive type.'

'What?' said Pitman. He wasn't listening properly, but that last sentence pulled at his ear.

'That's why all the girls down at the station find you so attractive.'

'What are you talking about?'

'That was the first thing I discovered when I came to work there. They all know you're a Lothario, but they can't help but find you sexy.'

'Who's Lothario?'

'You and your bachelor existence. Every woman down there is frightened of you just to the right degree.'

'Frightened of me?'

'No, not frightened of you exactly. Frightened of your sexuality.'

Pitman was speechless. The chilli had made his nose run; he wiped it on a napkin.

'That's why I like you, Lawrence – because you don't treat women like trophies, like sexual objects. Why do men have to do that? Why do they have to be so proprietorial? It gets them nowhere. You'd think they'd learn from people like you who never make advances – just sit there and let the women come to them – but they don't. You can't help your natural sensuousness poking through, can you?'

Pitman checked his flies when she said that, and when he looked back she was pulling her Victor Padrone T-shirt over her head.

'What are you doing?' gasped Pitman.

'C'mon, you can be yourself, now,' she said and manoeuvred herself across the gear stick towards him. It suddenly dawned on him that he'd had an erection for the last fifteen minutes.

'I loved the way you ignored me entirely when we went to Yorkshire. Tell me honestly what did you do when we got back?'

'I went to bed.'

'I bet you did,' said McMahon, and she stroked his cheek and then climbed into the back of the van.

'And what about that time when you were going to take me home, and the phone went and you said you had to stay at the office? I bet that was a woman who called you, wasn't it? I could tell by the way you were behaving.'

'Is a Lothario a . . . womaniser?' asked Pitman.

'You're cute.'

'Down at the station they really think I'm a womaniser?'

'You bet.' She was wriggling out of her jeans now. 'The women do, anyway. The men are just jealous, I suppose. Do you know you've never once called me by my Christian name? No one's ever done that to me.'

Pitman said: 'You're getting some sleep, good idea. I'll keep watch until sunrise and then wake you up.'

But she was kissing the back of his neck now, and when he turned round he was looking at the very lovely body of WDC McMahon in nothing but her underwear. It was so long since he had had sex. He never saw women as sexual objects, that was true, but that was because he'd forgotten what sexual objects looked like. Now he couldn't help but gaze at her body and he felt the pangs of a hunger he thought he'd forgotten.

She said: 'I knew when you asked me up here we'd make love. I could tell by the nonchalance in your voice.'

'Yes,' said Pitman and he tasted refried beans in the back of his throat. 'Things aren't always the way they seem, you know.'

Now it was her turn to say, 'How do you mean?'

'Well . . . just because everyone thinks something is true, that doesn't make it true.'

'Come over here, Lawrence. You look like Clint Eastwood in that light.'

And so Pitman thought: On the other hand if enough people think something is true maybe that does make it true. And he climbed over the seat and took his jacket off and unbuttoned his shirt. She said: 'You're the first man I've ever been to bed with who hasn't bothered to hold in his stomach when he's taken his shirt off.'

Pitman unbuckled his trousers and undid his shoelaces, and it was then that he saw a single light coming slowly up Wood Lane from Shepherd's Bush. It was moving too fast for a bicycle surely, but it wasn't big enough for a motorbike, and there was no noise. And then Pitman saw the man in a balaclava in the saddle, and the panniers and the black cycling outfit, and he frantically pulled his trousers back up. 'It's him!' he shouted, and he kicked open the back door of the van and jumped out with his shoelaces undone and his shirt unbuttoned and ran towards the main gate.

There was a porter on duty at the barrier. Pitman saw him come out and speak to Clive Peacock, then shake his hand and lift the barrier, bringing it down again just as Pitman arrived tucking his shirt into his trousers. 'Open this gate at once,' he commanded. 'I'm a policeman.'

The porter moved slowly; a little smile crawled out of his mouth. People like Pitman made his night. 'Who did you say you were?' he said quietly.

'I'm a policeman. I want to get through. Clive!' Clive

was only a short distance from the barrier. He stopped and turned. 'Clive, it's me, Lawrence Pitman.'

'Have you got any ID?' enquired the porter.

'Yes, of course,' said Pitman and patted his pockets. 'Well, not on me, but I am a policeman.'

'I can't let everyone through here who says they're a policeman, now can I?'

'You let him through. He's a postman.'

'He's the Missing Postman, isn't he? He doesn't need ID.'

'I know he's the Missing Postman. I'm the policeman who's trying to catch him.'

'Well, you're certainly not coming through. He's one of us, is the Missing Postman.'

Clive came back to the gate. 'Hello, Mr Pitman,' he said.

'Clive. I just want to talk to you, Clive.'

'You can talk to him over the gate,' said the porter.

'What!'

'Talk to him over the gate if you want to. You're not coming in, not without ID.'

'Clive,' appealed Pitman and held out his hands to him. 'It's good to see you. I'm not going to arrest you or anything, don't worry. I'm here to speak to you, that's all.'

Clive peered silently out of his balaclava. Pitman leaned over the gate and tried to dislodge the thought of WDC McMahon's body from the front row of his brain. The porter said: 'Well, go on then, speak to him.'

'Yes.' Pitman was stumbling. 'I'm going to. Clive. Clive, I just want to ask you to think about what you're doing. I don't know why you're doing it. I don't think anyone really does except you . . . but now is the time to come back before it gets out of hand. If you came home now it would probably all be forgotten. I'd do my best to get you off. There's a lot of sympathy for you. But if you go on, then who knows what might happen? Don't listen to the press, Clive. I'm sure you're not listening to the press. They don't give a damn what happens to you. But back on Beaconsfield Hill we all do. We all want you back.'

'Don't listen to him. It's a trick,' said the porter.

'Shut up, you,' spat Pitman. 'Clive, believe me. Your wife wants you back; Mrs Atherton wants you back; your friend with the metal detector wants you back. We all do. Clive, there's something wrong, we know that. Maybe you're tired, or depressed, or just angry, I don't know, but we all want to help. The town needs you back. And I believe you need the town, Clive. The place is as crazy as always. They're introducing another one-way system, can you believe it? And all you have to do, Clive, is climb in my van over there right now and we can drive home, and I'll do everything I can to get things back to normal. But if you go on, if you go on to Italy, then I don't know what to say. You'll be caught for sure. You'll be arrested, and who knows what will happen to you? You've made your point, Clive, but now. . .'

It was then Clive peeled his balaclava off and Pitman couldn't believe what he saw. Clive's face was lean and tanned; his hair long; eyes bright blue. A black and grey beard sprang from his face with vigour. His teeth were bright white in the lamplight. That face that used to be a box, containing no expression of any note, now drew the light like a film star's. Pitman watched Clive as he ràn his fingers through his hair and he thought he had never seen a man so healthy. He looked as though he'd been dismantled, had all his worn parts replaced and then been reassembled. Pitman just stared. And then he felt that pang of jealousy he had felt before in the checkout queue at Asda, and countered with anger at the man for abandoning his responsibility and running. But now he gave way to the feeling and it filled him with excitement. 'What have you done to yourself?' he said.

'Nothing,' said Clive.

It occurred to Pitman that the only way he would get this version of Clive Peacock home would be by shooting him with a tranquilliser dart. Then he imagined the sleek and bright-eyed man before him struggling in a net and the thought made him falter. 'So what are you going to do?' he asked quietly.

Clive was in charge now. He said: 'I'm going to deliver this letter before I do anything,' and he pushed his bike up the hill towards the reception.

'Good for you, Clive,' said the porter.

'Clive. . .' called Pitman.

'Leave him alone,' said the porter. 'Keep going, Clive!' and they watched him as he went through the doors into the building. 'Damn,' said the porter. 'I meant to get him to sign something for me.'

'What's your name?' said Pitman.

'None of your business,' replied the porter.

'On Monday morning you can be sure that you will be without a job. I'll see to it personally.'

'Doesn't bother me, mate. I'm being made redundant on Friday.'

Pitman went back to the van and found WDC McMahon asleep with one foot hanging out of the door. He didn't wake her. He covered her with a sleeping bag and then climbed into the driver's seat. Back on the gate he saw the porter talking to a couple on a motorbike. One rider took her helmet off and Pitman recognised Sarah Seymour.

He patted his pockets for his keys. Until now Clive Peacock had always reminded him of a man in a bath groping round for the soap. He had never pretended to have any depth or extra dimension of any sort. He'd seemed quite content to be that little man people forgot about. But then he had gone and jumped off a cliff – jumped or been pushed, it didn't matter – and he'd discovered he really could fly.

Pitman burped and tasted coriander. Then he headed home with the empty bottle of Valpolicella rolling around in the footwell.

# 25

FROM OUTSIDE THE reception Clive could see them all gathering at the front gate. The Network News van pulled up and a crew jumped out and, like all the others, met the immovable barrier of the BBC porter. Clive was tempted to go and talk to them, let them take a few pictures. He felt in control now and he had nothing more to lose. As he sat on a wall watching the commotion his stomach throbbed as though it had been pumped. His head was clear as though some bump had brought him round. And he felt empty, wonderfully empty, as if he had his whole body to refill with whatever he wished.

He sensed Pitman was right: the time had come. But he also sensed this wasn't the way to handle it. He pulled a crumpled business card from his back pocket. 'Trevor Ramsey, International Management' it read, and he found a phone. He tried Trevor Ramsey's office, then his home and finally found him in his car. It was two am and Trevor Ramsey was in a motorway service area near Manchester.

'Clive!' yelled Trevor Ramsey. 'Great to hear from you. Where are you?'

'I'm at the BBC Television Centre.'

'What the hell are you doing there? You're not on a chat show, I hope?'

'No, I've just delivered a letter here. But they're all waiting for me outside. All the press.'

'Don't talk to anyone. Not until I can get down to you. Find a back way out – do you think you can do that?'

'Yes, I can do that.'

'Here's what I want you to do. Go to the Trafalgar Palace Hotel. I'll book a room for you. Stay the night there. Have what you want and put it on the bill, but lie low. I'll get down and meet you for breakfast, okay?'

'Okay,' said Clive.

'And we'll plan a proper strategy. Good boy, Clive. You're going to be rich, you know that?'

'Yes,' said Clive.

He went round the back of the building and found a Goods In entrance and slipped out there. Of course he could find a way out. He was the Elusive Clive Peacock, wasn't he?

The West End was full of bright lights but the light on the Trafalgar Palace was the brightest of them all. Clive wheeled his encrusted Mercury Drifter up the forecourt and offered it to the doorman. 'Would you park this, please?' he asked politely. The doorman didn't move, then Clive gave him a ten-pound note and it was as if someone had plugged him in.

He emerged from the revolving doors and strode to the reception. 'I have a room booked in the name of Trevor Ramsey,' he announced.

'Certainly, sir,' said the clerk and winked at him.

A porter led him to the lift. As the door opened it revealed a group of people in evening wear gathered around a man lying on the lift floor with a knife in his back. Clive peered through the curtain of dinner jackets.

'What's happened to him?' he asked of a woman wearing a tiara.

'He's been stabbed,' she said.

'Oh dear. Who is it?'

'Lord Huntley,' she said excitedly.

The porter showed him up to his room, which turned out to be a suite on the top floor looking over the river. He sat on the bed and felt small. A knock on the door made him jump. 'Come in,' he croaked, and two more porters entered, one carrying a bouquet of flowers, the other an ice bucket of champagne. A note was attached to the bouquet from Trevor Ramsey: 'Enjoy yourself, Clive. You've earned it. This is how it's going to be from now on.'

Clive did his best to enjoy himself. He had a bath and used all the individual shampoo bottles and the shower hat and the bath gel and all of the eight towels. He took a bite out of each piece of fruit on the welcoming fruit bowl, and he watched exactly thirty seconds of every television station he could find using the remote control from a reclining position on the king-size bed.

He called room service and ordered an avocado and prawn sandwich, and he called the front desk and asked them to send up a postcard of Trafalgar Square if they had one. When the porter came up Clive handed him the airmail letter for Emma Drake in Livorno and asked him to post it. He also gave him five pounds. Then he sat out on the balcony in a dressing gown and sipped his champagne and ate his sandwich, and looked out over the river, a cool corridor of sanity through the craziness of the warm city night. Below, a Post Office van wound its way through the back streets. The letter to Livorno would be all right; it didn't have a paperclip or anything in it. He picked up his postcard of Trafalgar Square and wrote: 'Dear Christine, by the time you receive this I will be home.'

As Clive entered the dining room the next morning at eight-thirty, the first thing he saw was a man rise from table 6, clutch his throat and collapse in a heap on the floor. A crowd gathered round him.

'What's happened?' asked Clive of a man in an MCC tie.

'Viscount Laverty has been poisoned, by the look of it,' the man replied with glee.

'Oh dear,' said Clive, and stood back as two ambulance men arrived and stretchered the unfortunate viscount away. He hadn't touched his breakfast, Clive noticed.

The head waiter led Clive through the pink and green restaurant to a table by the window, where Trevor Ramsey sat wearing his white suit, and a tie that looked like someone had spilt a drink down his front. He was talking on his Vodaphone. Clive heard him say: 'I think it fell off and rolled under the sideboard,' then Trevor Ramsey saw Clive and he whispered: 'I'll ring you back,' and he flicked off the phone and held out his arms. 'Clive,' he cried. And they locked hands and Trevor Ramsey shook Clive until his socks slipped down.

'What a star! What a star!' said Trevor Ramsey. 'I've just seen the latest editions,' and he held up a copy of the *Chronicle*. The front-page headline was 'Who was That Masked Man?'

Trevor Ramsey beamed and read: 'Sarah Seymour on the trail of the Missing Postman reports. "Clive Peacock the Missing Postman turned up again last night in Hounslow, and just when it mattered, heroically foiling an attempted burglary at the house of newly-weds Mr and Mrs Croxall.

' " 'I didn't recognise him at first,' said 28-year-old Lorraine Croxall. 'He didn't have a letter or anything. He just appeared out of nowhere and chased the thieves away. He was very brave.'

' "Her husband Bill Croxall said: 'He said he lived opposite – he obviously had a sense of humour.'

' "Police are still looking for the culprits, two youths, who also broke into, and mindlessly smashed up, a show home on the estate. Meanwhile the Missing Postman is back in the south of England after capturing the imagination of the whole country. The question is, where next?" '

'Fantastic, Clive. Fantastic coverage.' The phone rang. 'Excuse me a moment,' said Trevor Ramsey and flicked on the Vodaphone. 'I'm in a meeting. I'll call you back,' he said firmly. Then he leaned forward, and looked serious. 'So, Clive. My sources tell me you have a letter for Italy.'

'No,' said Clive. 'I'm going home.'

'Clive. The market over there is ripe. Look at all those footballers.'

'I don't have a passport.'

Trevor Ramsey chuckled. 'I love it! We could fix that, Clive. No problem.'

'My wife needs me.'

'But Clive, the country needs you.'

'I've posted the letter.'

Trevor Ramsey was shocked by this news. But he quickly recovered. 'I'll get you another one,' he said.

'I'm going home. I've made the decision.'

Trevor Ramsey chewed his lips and looked Clive in the eye. He was thinking. Clive watched him think. Trevor Ramsey said: 'You're right. A wise decision. You're not the tropical island sort of hero really, are you? You're more home-grown. Not the muscle-bound oaf, more the sensitive caring sort. Robin Hood, that's how I see you. We'll get you on *Wogan*, no trouble.'

Clive ordered a full English breakfast. 'Good,' said Trevor Ramsey. 'That's good. You're a full-English-breakfast sort of person. That says a lot about the Missing Postman. He stands for tradition. That will be our angle. Red telephone boxes, egg and bacon, village cricket. Perfect.'

Trevor Ramsey ordered a kipper and kiwi fruit. Every time he went to take a mouthful his phone rang. 'I'll call you back; I'm busy,' he answered each time.

'So, Clive, let's talk business. How's the book coming along? It would be nice to have a draft in by the end of the month. I've got a copy of the dustjacket here somewhere. *The Story of the Missing Postman* – I think it's a great title. I've sold serial rights already – to the *Chronicle*. They've been very keen over the last few weeks. I'm negotiating a deal for your own story. Should get five figures.'

As he spoke there was a gunshot and a man at the next table fell head-first into his fresh grapefruit. His tongue rolled out of his mouth. Everyone in the dining room except Clive and Trevor Ramsey rushed to help him. 'He's dead too,' exclaimed a woman with an Australian accent.

'Don't you love these Murder Weekends?' said Trevor Ramsey. 'They do ever so well. We get people from all over the world. My idea.' He picked a kipper bone out of his teeth and said, 'So – how many letters have you got left?'

'One,' said Clive. 'A postcard.'

'One, is that all? Where to?'

'My wife.'

Trevor Ramsey stopped chewing as he thought about this. Then he said: 'Clive, that's wonderful. I've got a tear in my eye, really I have. The letter that takes you home. I love it. That'll be another front page. I'll contact Sarah Seymour; she's a good girl. She's on our side.'

Trevor Ramsey pulled out a lap-top computer from his briefcase. 'Now, it's Sunday morning. What's your schedule?'

'I'm going home from here.'

'ETA?'

'What?'

'When are you going to get there? Home, I mean.'

'Oh, er . . . tomorrow morning.'

'Blimey, Clive, why not put the bike on the bloody train? No one will know. I mean, you've made your point. You could cruise back first class.'

'I want to cycle.'

'Of course you do. What time tomorrow?'

'Er . . . nine am.'

'Make it eight. We'll get you on the *Breakfast Time* news, live, they'll love it.'

'All right, eight,' conceded Clive.

Trevor Ramsey entered this information into the computer. Then he pulled a file out of his briefcase and his face tightened. 'Now listen, Clive. I want to say something. It's truth time. You've behaved like a pro so far. You've played the media beautifully. You stayed one step ahead. You've made them chase you, giving them tasters but never a mouthful. You've played the "the Missing Postman is only news as long as he's missing" card very effectively. But from tomorrow he's not going to be missing any more, is he? And that's when the tricky bit starts. So – if we're going to cream this little number for all it's worth you're going to have to listen to me. Am I right?'

Clive nodded.

'We need immediate impact, Clive. You're news, but not long-term news like, say, the Middle East. So we have

251

to pick our media. I think a pop song would be the best idea.'

Clive inflated his cheeks.

'I've got a few composers in mind. "The ballad of the Missing Postman" we'll call it. Get you on *Top of the Pops* that sort of thing?'

'I can't sing. I told you.'

'I love it. You've never thought of yourself as a sex symbol, I suppose.'

'No,' said Clive.

'Well, I'm afraid that's what you've become. House-wives all over the country are wild about you. You're enormous in the Thames Valley. It doesn't matter if you can sing or not, not as long as you dress right. We'll have to do a bit of work on that, of course. The SAS look is great, but you can't wear it when you go on early evening TV. We'll kit you out – get you some contact lenses as well, glasses aren't sexy, I don't care what they say.

'The other good news is I've got rid of Tetley's – blood cheek of that bunch. Distant Dream Holidays are your new sponsors. Big Money. So get rid of your Tetley's stuff, you'll be wearing this for the rest of the trip. It's quite tasteful.'

Trevor Ramsey pulled a waistcoat out of his briefcase. On the back was a seagull in flight. 'Distant Dreams' was written in longhand underneath.

Clive tried the waistcoat on. At the next table another ambulance crew stretchered away the corpse.

'Who was that?' Clive asked the waiter.

'I believe that was Lord Huntley's nephew, Jonathan, sir.'

Trevor Ramsey said: 'Now – what I need, Clive, is a list of all the places you stayed at, and all the places you delivered to. I want to issue wall plaques: "The Missing Postman delivered here" – that sort of thing. This was such a great money-spinner of an idea, Clive. I don't know how you came up with it. Was it a spur-of-the-moment job or did you have it planned?'

'Oh, spur of the moment,' said Clive. 'Could I have a prawn and avocado sandwich for the journey?'

'Have what you like,' said Trevor Ramsey, bashing away at his lap-top. 'So – money. As your agent I charge you forty per cent, fifty if an American deal is fixed. That's standard. Sound all right?'

'Fine,' said Clive.

'I've got a contract here which we should both sign just to protect ourselves. Read it if you like but buck up, we've got to get our skates on.'

Clive pretended to read the contract, then signed it. Trevor Ramsey signed it. The head waiter witnessed it; Clive noticed his name was Henry Potts. Trevor Ramsey pulled another Vodaphone out of his briefcase and said: 'I want you to have this from now on, so I can reach you on the road. How do you feel about opening department stores? It's a bit down-market, I know, but the money's good.'

'What are we going to do about the police, Trevor?' asked Clive.

'The police? – I love it! Don't worry about the police, Clive. They couldn't give a shit. You're a local hero. The police aren't going to do anything. It would be bad PR for them to arrest you. They've made the media do all the work, they can let the media have all the reward. Don't waste your time worrying about police. You should be thinking about your chat-show appearances. You've got to get lots of funny little stories lined up. People will say things like "So, Clive, tell us the funniest thing that happened to you." '

'How about a chat show with Sue Lawley?'

'*Desert Island Discs*, that's tricky; it's pre-recorded months in advance, you see.'

'I helped her change a wheel, you know.'

'Of course you did. That might swing it. They might do a special. I'll call her. Now, the book, Clive. I need to tell the publishers when to expect a draft.'

'Six weeks,' said Clive, getting the hang of this publici
business.

'Good. We'll rush-publish in the autumn and get th
Christmas market.'

The waiter delivered Clive's prawn and avocado sand
wich, then fell to the floor with a groan. He lay the
writhing. The other guests rushed to his side. An America
woman said to him: 'Are you dead?'

'Fantastic,' said Trevor Ramsey, as the waiter went pa
and started to foam at the mouth. 'What an actor.'

They adjourned to the lobby, and the doorman brough
Clive's bike from the garage. They'd had it cleaned. 'Than
you very much,' said Clive, and gave him all the loos
change he had in his pocket.

He polished his glasses and mounted. Trevor Ramse
said: 'Are you sure you don't want a lift?'

'No thank you,' said Clive.

'I love it!' said Trevor Ramsey and he straightene
Clive's Distant Dreams waistcoat. 'Looks very smar
You'll get some cheap holidays out of them. Probably. Yo
could go to Livorno; they do a package.'

So Clive cycled out of town, through Staines and alon
the A30. As he passed under the M25 he saw some graffit
'Keep Going Clive Peacock'.

He pedalled through the hot and humid day. In a layb
near Camberley, as he ate his prawn and avocado sand
wich, his Vodaphone rang.

'Clive Peacock speaking.'

'It's me, Trevor. Can you open a new DIY superstore i
Southampton next weekend?'

'Sure,' said Clive.

That night he slept in the middle of the New Forest.
storm broke the heat around midnight, but he was shel
tered under the arms of the giant trees, The noise of th
woods under siege was frightening, and lightning flashe
through the night sky and stabbed at the earth, but Cliv
felt safe. He slept and dreamt he was cycling up Beacons
field Hill Road. Christine was waving to him from th

upstairs window of their home. At first he recognised the house, but then he saw she'd added another storey and built new wings and towers and turrets. It was enormous. He rang the bell and a drawbridge was lowered. Christine appeared on the threshold, and now he could see she had extra storeys to her body. She had windows in her stomach and shoulders, stairways going up and down her back. She towered above him with outstretched arms supported by scaffolding.

He was woken by footsteps tramping through the leaves. He sat up, on his guard. 'What do you want?' he said, before the person trod on him.

'It's all right,' said the newcomer. 'I saw you. I was coming to join you. You don't mind, do you? I thought: That looks like a good place to kip, I mean, *he's* sleeping there, so it must be. I don't normally sleep out, of course. I'm a salesman. But it was such a nice night, never mind a bit of rain. My name's Michael.'

'Clive.'

'Pleased to meet you, Clive,' said Michael and he sat down. There was a familiar smell about Michael.

'Here's one for you,' said Michael. 'If, just say *if*, they were going to make a film of your life, who would you have play yourself? Go on, have a think.'

'We've met before.'

'Eh?'

'We've met before, a few months ago, under a bridge near Bristol.'

'What, down the A4?'

'That's right.'

'Oh, you're *that* Clive. It's all coming back to me now. Dustin Hoffman, you said, didn't you? Wasn't such a bad choice, I suppose.'

Clive said: 'I thought you were going home?'

'I did,' said Michael. 'But then I left again.'

'What happened?'

'Well, you've got to be careful going home. I was sat

there in my armchair, in my house in Willesden, all the creature comforts, but then I thought: People need shoes.'

'You're right,' said Clive.

'Also – and I never told you this when I first met you – my wife and I don't see eye to eye. If they made a film of her life then Joan Crawford should play her. She's difficult to live with, see. She said to me: "You ought to try looking at yourself, you ought to. You're blind." '

'Blind but with stars in your eyes,' said Clive.

'Blind with what?'

'Blind with stars in your eyes.'

'That's it. That's exactly what I said to her. I said: "I may be blind, my dear, but I've got stars on my eyes." '

Michael lay down next to Clive. The trees were dripping on their heads. Clive could taste sap. Michael said: 'I've got this plan though. Next time I go home I'm going to flummox my wife. Guess how?'

'How?'

'I'm going to pretend I get on with her. That'll confuse her. That'll win her round.'

They fell asleep. When Clive woke, Michael had gone. He wondered if he'd dreamed the whole episode. The rain had stopped and he was up and away with the dawn, cycling through a forest swaddled in mist. It was the most glorious morning of the whole trip, and when he finally reached the coast he was riding out of the sunrise.

It was Monday, seven-thirty am, the day the *new* new one-way system was to be introduced, and as Clive came into town along the cliff road and down towards the harbour, the traffic was already blocking off the High Street. The new layout took him by surprise, sending him round the back of Station Road and up the High Street instead of down. And yet, despite the many new arrows and multi-coloured signs and traffic lights, this new route didn't look so strange. Now that the High Street was two-way again, and the harbour approach was only one-way as far as Victoria Avenue (which was two-way and had lost those two sets of mini-roundabouts), there was something familiar about the whole set-up. When he thought about it Clive realised that the new one-way system was exactly the same as the first one-way system the town pioneered twenty-five years ago.

He followed the harbour round to the bottom of Beaconsfield Hill Road. Fifty yards before the incline he began to accelerate and went up it in one. No effort. He must have pedalled two thousand miles over the summer.

It was as he reached the brow of the hill, and his house came into view on Rockley Road that he saw them all, the ranks of the media, the line of vehicles from television, radio and press, parked and double-parked as far as he could see. There was a crowd of people milling around the house. There was a catering truck.

He ducked into Mrs Drake's front garden and peered over the hedge at the whole circus. A motorbike with that journalist and her photographer went by. Clive was panting with nerves.

He wanted to see Christine before he did anything. He went back down the hill and pushed his bike round the edge of the mudflats. A familiar figure in headphones came walking towards him. Ralph saw Clive and stopped in his tracks. He was wearing a new khaki jacket and clutching his Fieldmaster Searchman.

'Ralph.'

'Clive.'

'Huh.'

'You're back.'

Clive grinned. 'Yes, well.'

'You look . . . different – very different. Sort of . . . re-decorated.'

'It's been a funny summer, Ralph.'

'Christine will be pleased to see you.'

'It'll be good to see her.'

'I've been looking after her for you.'

'I know you have, Ralph. I knew you would.'

Ralph looked at the ground; Clive squinted into the clear, blue sky. The mudflats had never looked more fresh.

'There's quite a reception waiting for you, you know.'

'I know,' said Clive.

'Did you post all the letters?'

'All except Italy.'

'It's a hell of a cycle, Italy.'

Clive said: 'There's a new one-way system, I see.'

'Things have changed since you've been away.'

'I think it's the same as the first one-way system they introduced twenty-five years ago.'

Ralph laughed at this and leaned forward on his metal detector. 'You're kidding?'

'No.'

'That's funny.'

Clive breathed in the familiar air. 'That's a new jacket, Ralph.'

'Superman sale.'

Clive nodded and surveyed the mud. 'You haven't found King Raedrik while I've been away, then?'

'No,' said Ralph.

'It's nice down here this morning though.'

They watched a cloud bank as it was winched over the sun like a blind. 'You're right: it's been a funny summer,' said Ralph. 'My wife got salmonella – from a takeaway pizza.'

'Oh dear,' said Clive.

'And you know that woman who couldn't stop sneezing?'

'What happened to her?'

'She's dead.'

'Oh.'

'Car crash. She was two days short of the world record.'

Clive shook his head sadly.

'Nothing much else has happened – except you going and getting yourself famous. It's funny, we used to go to school together and now you're famous.'

On the ring road they could see the traffic crawling. A lorry was on the hard shoulder, steaming.

'Did you really go to bed with Sue Lawley?' asked Ralph.

'No,' said Clive.

'Good,' said Ralph. 'I knew she wasn't that sort.'

'Anyway,' said Clive. 'Maybe I'll come out with you later on. Is that Metadec still at my house?'

'You bet. It's been waiting.'

'Right, I'll see you this evening.'

'Get back to normal, you mean?'

'Right.'

Clive reached the cliffs at the back of his house, put his bike over his shoulder and scrambled up. The earth was slippery after the rain, twice his foothold gave way and he slid back. He was filthy by the time he reached his back gate.

The garden was hopelessly overgrown. The brambles and vines had had a great summer. Clive waded through the tangle to the back door. He didn't want to look at his plants.

He unloaded his panniers for the last time, then found the key under the brick and let himself in. The first thing he noticed was that the doormat had been changed. Gone was the standard-issue coconut hair; instead there were bare floorboards with the word MAT painted on the wood.

Clive stepped through into the kitchen and kicked over the antique umbrella-stand. He swore at it affectionately; it turned out to be the only feature in the house he recognised. Everything else seemed to have been stripped bare. The familiar overcoat had been scraped away to reveal this amazing underskin, like some painting lost for years.

He crept around in disbelief. One room was like a castle, another like a den. The walls were marbled and broken with cracks or had cobwebs painted in corners. In the hallway live mould had been grown above the skirting and then varnished over. Everything wooden had been stripped and then randomly charred. A picture frame hung above the stairs. The title was *Girls Playing in a River*, but there was no picture inside. He stepped into the living room,

took one look at the tree growing out of the floor an
stepped out again.

The stairs creaked a welcome. A bird, or maybe a ba
flew down from the landing and sent Clive sprawling.

Then he heard snoring; it was coming from the spar
room. He put his head round the door and peered into
scarlet darkness. A great Gothic wardrobe filled half th
floor-space, while the rest was taken up by a giant four
poster bed with barley-sugar posts and oak panels, al
wrapped in brown drapes.

A shuffle of bedclothes came from within. The drape
parted and Trevor Ramsey poked his head out.

'Clive! What time is it? Shit, I've overslept! Didn't ge
to bed until three. Are the TV here yet?'

'What are you doing here?' puzzled Clive.

'Your dear wife – a very nice woman, and very talented
if I may say so – suggested I stay here. She's arranged a
spread in *Homes and Gardens*, by the way: the home of th
Missing Postman. It's perfect. She's very on the ball.' He
got up and walked to the window. He was wearing a
nightshirt that said 'Distant Dreams' on the back. He had
pale legs, one with a varicose vein, and he stood at the
window scratching.

'Where is she?' asked Clive.

'In bed still, I suppose. Cor! Look at that turnout, Clive
Are you ready to face this lot?'

Clive went to his and Christine's bedroom. As he opened
the door a smell of roses lifted his head, and he saw a beam
of sunlight playing on the floor by the bed. Clive realised
now what the biggest change in the whole house was
everything was in its right place – even the sunbeams
Everything was part of the effect. There had been no dishe
in the sink, no plates under the chaise longue, and in the
bedroom everything was hanging where it should have
been. Christine had finally found a role for everything in
the house, and he had to admit it looked wonderful.

There she was under the covers: the bedrock, the life
and soul of the home. Her body rose and sank slowly

inhaling that sunbeam. Her hair was strewn across the pillow. Clive took his shoes off. He didn't want her to wake; he wanted this moment to last.

Out of his pannier he took his retirement clock. It looked a bit battered from its travels but it still ticked and glowed. He put it on the bedside table. It didn't look right there, he knew, but he'd find a place for it later. From his pocket he pulled out the postcard he had written to Christine, and he crept over to her bedside table and propped it up against her contact lens fluid. 'By the time you read this I will be home,' he whispered.

There was the sound of activity from outside now. Clive padded to the window and peeked through the curtains. There was Trevor Ramsey in his white suit talking to all the journalists. The TV cameras were set up and the crew were arguing about the light. The soundman threw a sandwich at the cameraman. Some local residents had gathered. There was Denbigh, and the Tidys and Mrs Atherton, and there were the Drakes climbing out of their Toyota even though they only lived across the street. A police car pulled up and Trevor Ramsey went over to deal with it.

Sarah Seymour from the *Chronicle* looked up at the window and saw Clive and blew him a kiss. Clive grinned and let the curtain go.

Christine stirred. As Clive crept back to the bed he caught his reflection in the big swivel mirror. Somehow the glass had got a crack from the top to the bottom. He touched it – the crack had been stuck on. He stood there a moment and studied himself. Familiar mirrors never told lies, and there stood a man he didn't recognise. A man with a taut face, weathered and leathered, but with every feature bursting through, nothing sunken any more. And shining above all were those two swimming-pool eyes that had never looked more alive.

He admired himself: lean, wiry fellow, willing to risk death daily, at home again and about to get into bed with his wife.

# 26

THAT WAS MONDAY. During the day a television interview with Clive appeared on the breakfast news, the lunchtime news and the evening news. When the interviewer, Simon Maugham, asked Clive why he had left home with his bag of letters two months previously, Clive said: 'Well, Simon, it was a protest, I suppose, a protest against being replaced by a machine.'

On Tuesday Clive went into a recording studio and cut a record. The song was composed by Dee Tiffen, who had been responsible for the runner-up in the Eurovision Song Contest of 1987. Clive's song was called 'The Missing Postman'. It sounded similar to 'The Ugly Duckling'.

On Wednesday morning he was interviewed on Radio 4. When he was asked why he had set off with the stolen mailbag, he said: 'Well, I suppose I did it to show that people with impaired vision who can't drive can in fact still lead perfectly normal lives.'

On Thursday morning the serialisation of Clive's story, as told to Sarah Seymour, began in the *Chronicle*. 'I did it to gain support for all workers cut off in their prime by premature retirement,' Clive was quoted as saying.

On the Thursday evening he appeared on *Wogan*. Wogan himself was on holiday, but Sue Lawley stood in. Clive was wearing his new contact lenses. They made his eyes water. Trevor Ramsey said: 'It looks as though you're crying, Clive; it's great. I love it.'

Sue Lawley told the audience how one night, earlier that summer, she had broken down in the wilds in the north of England, and a strange man on a bicycle had appeared out of the fog and helped her change her wheel. She had thought he was her guardian angel; he turned out to be her hero, the Missing Postman.

When Clive, dressed in a black double-breasted suit by

Victor Padrone, walked on camera, she kissed him on both cheeks, and then when she asked him why he had set off on his adventure, he said: 'To escape, I suppose, Sue.'

'Escape from what?' quizzed Sue Lawley.

'Pressure.'

'Were you under a lot of pressure, Clive?'

Clive thought about this and then said, 'No,' and the whole BBC Television Theatre erupted with laughter. Who was this joker, this postman from nowhere in particular, who had captured their hearts with such innocence and ease?

When they had settled down again Clive added: 'But there's a lot of pressure involved in having no pressure, Sue.'

And the audience laughed even harder. Sue Lawley laughed. The stage crew laughed. Everyone at home laughed. But that was probably the nearest Clive ever came to explaining why he had set off with the mailbag.

On Friday the 'Missing Postman' single was rush-released and entered the hit parade at number 24. Over the weekend Clive opened a supermarket in Salisbury and a new DIY superstore in Southampton. Trevor Ramsey introduced him as 'the kind of man we need more of in this country, a combination of guts, determination, and a strong belief in what is right and good. Ladies and gentleman, I give you Clive Peacock the Missing Postman.'

Clive came on to the platform waving self-consciously. He was handed a microphone. 'I'd just like to say thank you for all the support you've given me over the last few months. You don't know how important it was in keeping my spirits up. And now I'd like to declare this DIY superstore open!'

There was a cheer and a stampede for the stage. Clive shook all the hands he could. He signed all the autographs he could. Afterwards at the champagne reception, the DIY superstore manager's wife took him on one side and said he was the kind of man she couldn't resist and he could have an affair with her any time he wanted. She added that she enjoyed dressing up. Then she stuck a piece of paper with her phone number in his pocket.

'Thank you very much,' said Clive.

On Monday the police telephoned and asked if they could see him, but Clive had an appointment with the Mayor that day. He sat down to a luncheon in the Town Hall. Clive had avocado and prawn salad. Mayor Eddie Hicks, who was still on his Slimathon, had cream of mushroom soup, a pork chop with jacket potatoes, and the cheese board. He said to Clive: 'You've given this town a sense of pride – you know that, don't you?'

'Well . . .' said Clive.

'I want to put a blue plaque on your house. Something simple. "The Missing Postman lived here" – how does that sound?'

'That sounds simple.'

'And we'd like to include your house on the Heritage Walk. It's a bit out of the way, I know, and inconsistent with the general maritime theme of the town, but we should acknowledge the fact that you're a crowd-puller.'

Afterwards, as they stood on the Town Hall steps, the Mayor shouted above the noise of the traffic: 'Oh, and I've had a word with the police, by the way; there's no need to worry.'

On Tuesday 'The Missing Postman' had fallen to number 36 in the hit parade. The serialisation in the *Chronicle* finished a day early because of a story of a transatlantic yachtsman who claimed to have eaten his crew. Clive's only mention that day was on TV when the letter he had delivered to *Points of View* was read out. Ralph's boy Robert let Jimmy Savile know what he really thought of him. You got the feeling the letter was only read out because the Missing Postman had delivered it.

On Wednesday Clive was interviewed on local Radio Estuary. A young radio journalist came round to the house and stuffed a microphone right under Clive's nose and said: 'Well, Clive Peacock of Rockley Road, I understand that you are the legendary Missing Postman, the man who took a sack of mail and set off round the country delivering the letters by hand.'

'That's right,' said Clive, and if the journalist's next question had been 'Why did you do it?' Clive had made up his mind he would answer: 'For the money.'

But all the journalist from Radio Estuary asked was 'I wonder if you could tell our listeners which school you went to?'

On Thursday he went back to the sorting office; he had to finalise details concerning his pension. Peter Robson met him in reception without a word. He gave him a security pass and led him through the sorting office amid cheers from the staff. Clive waved to them all. Barney Loxton called out. Clive couldn't hear what he said but shouted back: 'You bet, Barney.'

Peter Robson wasn't so impressed. He said: 'I don't really know what to say to you, Clive Peacock, except that you're a complete bastard. And I've not fallen for any of this protest business. I know you've never protested against anything in your life. I reckon the reason you ran off with the mail was plain and simply because you're a weirdo.'

As they passed the Optical Speedsort machine Clive reached out and patted it. The machine screamed and retched and then stopped. Peter Robson didn't seem to give a damn.

On the Thursday night Clive was due to appear on *Top of the Pops* but 'The Missing Postman' had fallen out of the top fifty, never to reappear. So Clive went and gave blood instead. Afterwards he went to the Neighbourhood Watch meeting.

It was held at Mr and Mrs Drake's house. The usual bunch were there except for Mr Pitman and Mrs Atherton, who was convalescing after her hip replacement. The atmosphere was very subdued, but that was understandable. This was the first meeting since the outing to Stratford-upon-Avon – a day that had gone very nicely until the party returned home and found that everyone's house had been burgled.

'A crook must have copied the addresses down from the newsagent's window,' said Denbigh, and then he denied it was his idea to advertise the list there in the first place.

'I think we should install closed-circuit television on the lampposts,' said Mr Tidy.

Mrs Wheatley was for more drastic action. 'I think we should announce another outing and this time lie in wait for the buggers and then . . .' She drew her finger across her throat.

'I think we should all invest in corgis,' said Mr Drake.

'Corgis?' said Denbigh.

'Vicious little buggers, corgis. One bit the Queen the other day. She had to have three stitches and was late for a luncheon.'

Clive didn't say anything during the meeting; and they clearly didn't want to talk to him about his absence. Only Mrs Tidy and Mrs Parfitt spoke to him. Mrs Parfitt leaned across and said: 'You're a funny chap, aren't you?' And Mrs Tidy said: 'You know Bruce my cat's back, don't you? He was found down the docks on a freighter bound for the Caribbean.'

Before the meeting adjourned Denbigh stood up and said: 'I know it's a long way off, but I'd like to have numbers for the Christmas party. I've made a provisional booking at La Cruete in town: £12 a head for a five-course meal including coffee and after-dinner mint.'

On Saturday morning Clive took *The Story of the Pony Express* back to the library. The computer calculated he had to pay a fine of £23.60. On Saturday afternoon up in Shipley, at the annual church fête, Clive's old Post Office uniform and bike were raffled. Together they raised £258.70 towards the restoration of the church roof fund. On Saturday evening Clive spent a long time trying to find somewhere in the house to display his retirement clock. It looked out of place everywhere he tried.

Every morning Clive looked out of the window at his garden, mentally preparing himself to tackle the weeds and creepers. Every morning Christine went out to distress other people's houses.

One day a journalist and photographer from *Homes and Gardens* came round. They arranged Clive and Christine on the chaise longue under the tree that grew out of the floorboards. Clive checked that there were no dirty plates or coffee cups anywhere, but this was out of habit, there never was any discarded crockery any more. It was all on show on the kitchen dresser, specially pitted plates with a shattered pattern. Christine's proclivity to make a mess, Clive now realised, had been simply due to this search for a style. She'd not known where to put things, so she'd put them anywhere. That was all in the past now.

The journalist asked Christine all the questions. Clive sat there with his face stopped at a quarter to three. The occasional leaf fell on him. Christine was composed and well-informed. She talked fluently as she described how she created texture and form. She expatiated on her sense of warmth and her use of space and the importance of dust in a house. Clive listened with the same fascination as the journalist. Christine had never explained the reflective quality of naked plumbing to him before. It was wonderful to hear her so confident; maybe she hadn't been out of control at all. It was that afternoon that he sensed he would always feel a little like a lodger as long as he lived in the same house as Christine.

The Missing Postman and his interior designer wife sat there as the photographer took over. He asked them to move closer. Clive put his arm around Christine and felt her stiffen. She was really better left on her own with all this business, he thought.

When he'd come back home Christine had clearly been pleased, and she'd seemed keen to help him readjust. She wanted things to get back to normal, she said. She wanted to forget the summer had ever happened. She said that home was where he belonged, and that now he was back the house was complete once more. She said she'd always known he would come back. He'd had things to sort out, that was all, she understood that, and if he wanted to talk about them they could.

But they never did. He never told her the story of his adventure – she never really asked. He wanted her to quiz him, to demand: 'Why did you go?' and 'Why did you come back?' And he'd have answered: 'Because I needed to go,' and 'Because I needed to come back.' He had a series of rehearsed speeches, but they were never delivered. And so he began to say to himself: Well, maybe that's good. Because he was aware that whenever he did think about his journey he saw himself slipping off those rails again. So it was best left, he decided. He had wanted to ask her who she was thinking of having an affair with, but after a while he wasn't even sure that it was her voice he had heard on the radio that day in the bus crew café in Kensal Rise.

The burned smell of September was blown up the coast, followed closely by the first chill of autumn. Clive stood in his vegetable patch and scratched his head. Despite the summer's neglect, when he'd cleared away the overgrowth he found his carrots had never been more tender, his potatoes never more beautifully sweet. His six leeks were thick and sharp, and he couldn't remember his spinach ever being tastier. Christine claimed she hadn't touched his plot all the time he'd been gone, but she must have done – she must have done. He began to feel confused. One afternoon he sat on the mudflats for hours, sat there until the gnats came out, and he said to himself: I don't know what I want, but I know what I don't want now. I've learned that much.

Trevor Ramsey phoned him up once a week and asked how the book was coming along, and Clive would say he was finding it all a bit difficult. The truth was he hadn't even started it yet.

'I can get someone to ghost it if you like,' said Trevor Ramsey. 'That Sarah Seymour would be keen.'

'We'll see,' said Clive.

It would have been nice to have had something to fill in

268

his time. He had thought at first he could help Christine with her business, as she encouraged him to. He was good at holding things – she told him that. But he knew he just got in the way really, and he felt nervous working with her.

He'd been metal detecting with Ralph a few times, but Clive could sense a lack of spirit in his old friend. One afternoon he found Ralph looking at the sky as much as at the ground. 'Are you all right, Ralph?' he'd asked. And Ralph had said: 'Tell me, Clive, tell me really, why did you do it, you know, run off like you did?'

'Because I like delivering mail.'

'So everyone missed the point?'

'Entirely.'

The next day Clive was out on the mudflats first, and when Ralph did appear it was without his metal detector. He came striding over to Clive and said: 'Clive, I'm not going to beat around the bush, I've got two bits of bad news to tell you. The first is that I've been caught and charged with shoplifting from Superman. I've been doing it for five years, so I can't grumble.'

'No, you can't,' said Clive. 'What's the second bit of bad news?'

'The second bit of bad news – and this is more serious – is that I'm beginning to think King Raedrik the Viking isn't buried here on these mudflats after all.'

This was a shock. Clive let it sink in before he said: 'That's unlike you, Ralph.'

But Ralph was quite rational about his decision. He said: 'I think I'd have found him by now if he was here. I mean, enough's enough.'

'I know what you mean, Ralph.'

'It gets to the stage when you're only fooling yourself.'

Clive nodded. A lorry skidded on the bypass and there was a distant sound of ripping motorcar flesh.

Clive's metal detector began to beep. He switched it off out of respect.

One Friday – the same day that Mrs Atherton first walked

on her new hip and discovered that now her other one needed replacing – Clive went back to the Job Centre and asked if they still wanted delivery men on the *Link* free newspaper. They said they did and he could start on Monday. When he let Christine know she said: 'Why? We don't need the money,' although he sensed she was relieved.

'It's all right; it's only part-time,' he said.

So two evenings a week he went out on his bike, bumping over the new ornamental humps on Rockley Road and putting newspapers through letterboxes. It was mindless work. There was no involvement, no emotion, no mystery to the job. Every house got a copy; every house got the same news.

One evening, as he was passing home, he called in for a cup of tea and found Christine in the living room with Ron Bishop. They were discussing the removal of the house to Westcliff. Clive poked his head round the door. Ron was saying to Christine: 'I still think you're nuts, Mrs Peacock.'

Christine saw Clive, but she wasn't going to try and hide her enthusiasm for her project. 'It can be done, Ron – I know it can. You just slide steel rods under the foundations and then you hoist it up.'

'Anyone want tea?' asked Clive.

'She's nuts, Clive,' said Ron and he was laughing. 'Tell her she's nuts.'

Clive went into the kitchen and found a woman scrubbing the floor. 'Who are you?' he said.

'I'm the domestic.'

'We don't have a domestic.'

'I've been coming here for over a month.'

'Oh.'

He put the kettle on and went out into the garden. A bank of cloud was mustering out to sea. It looked identical to the one he'd seen long ago just before he had set off with his letters. It had gone round the world and was back again – the same shape, the same size. Did clouds do that? he wondered.

He hoped it would bring rain; the garden was dry and dusty. Although when he thought about this he didn't see the point in worrying about his crops any more; they didn't need him, that was evident. He'd just bung some seeds down for his winter veg and let them get on with it.

The telephone rang. The french doors in the living room opened and Christine handed Clive out the mobile phone. 'It's Trevor Ramsey,' she said.

Clive was momentarily dumbfounded, not at the prospect of speaking to Trevor Ramsey, but because he hadn't realised they had french doors in the living room.

Trevor Ramsey was uncharacteristically short. 'The book, Clive? I need to have a hundred pages by the weekend – keep the publishers happy.'

Clive said: 'Well . . .' and then he admitted he hadn't written anything yet. Trevor Ramsey raised his voice at Clive for the first time. 'I'm getting a ghost, Clive. You can't muck around like this! I'm getting Sarah Seymour. I'll tell her to come down at the weekend.'

'Fine,' said Clive.

'First thing Saturday. Get an early start.'

'Fine,' said Clive, and he went back to his newspaper round. As he passed the bus stop at the bottom of the road four out of the six people waiting were yawning.

## 27

DETECTIVE SERGEANT PITMAN sat in his living room, chewing his biro top and watching a spider attach the end of its web to his shoulder, linking him to the television, direct. 'Cheek,' he muttered, but he sat still and watched the little creature complete the job, anything rather than write this damned letter to Signor Masserella.

He tried again, 'Dear Signor Masserella,' he wrote, 'thank you for your letter. Sorry it's taken so long to reply. Things have been busy. Thirty-four cars were stolen last week, twenty-five of them white Vauxhalls. We suspect a serial car thief.'

He was distracted by a free newspaper being shoved through the door. He watched it crash to the floor and sit there as welcome as a steaming dog turd. If another was delivered tonight he might not be responsible for his actions.

He continued. 'You'll be interested to know another one-way system has been introduced. It turns out that it is identical to the first one the town had twenty-five years ago . . .'

He tore up the letter and went and stood at the window. He thrust his hands into his pockets and the fly split on his Victor Padrone suit – the end to a very forgettable day.

He'd arrived at work that morning to find a collection of cat's-eyes piled in boxes on his desk. He'd picked them up and thrown them out of the window. Then he'd gone to the interview room, where he had sat opposite an old age pensioner, a man who had got drunk, stolen a car and smashed into the travel agent's on the High Street.

The man admitted to the crime.

'Good for you,' said Pitman and left the interview room.

At midday the DCI had asked to see him. Pitman had been a bad taste in the mouth of authority ever since he took the observation van against orders. There were rumours about his future.

The DCI had lost his hay fever at last. His eyes were clear and mean now. Pitman decided he was more endearing with blotches and a runny nose.

The DCI sat back and said: 'We were talking about you last night in the senior officers' meeting, Pitman, and we all came to the same conclusion: you're a pain in the bum.'

'Yes, sir,' said Pitman.

The chief sat forward. Pitman crossed his legs and pulled up his socks.

'In spite of that I've got good news for you.'

'How nice, sir.'

'CID is being centralised. This station is becoming a traffic-control centre. They're installing a new multi-million-pound computerised traffic system – and guess where they're going to put it?'

'My office, sir?'

'Good guess.'

'And . . . what's happening to me, sir?'

'You're being offered early retirement, Pitman. Congratulations.' The DCI held out his hand. Pitman ignored it.

'What if I don't want to retire, sir?'

'I believe they need a custody sergeant in some station in the west of the county.'

'I think I'll retire, sir.'

'Good decision,' said the DCI. 'You could stay until the end of the month if you wanted but . . .'

He told no one, just packed up his desk and left. 'See you in the morning,' he said to WDC McMahon and she smiled ruefully.

Now he stood at his bay window and wondered whose was the new Audi parked on the street outside his house. A smart-looking car, that. He'd always wanted a smart-looking car. He'd told his boys he'd have one like that one day. He'd have to abandon such ambition now. He gazed at it longingly and the Audi responded with a fit of hysterics, flashing lights and shrill screams. Pitman drew the curtains and the alarm stopped. He felt flushed, as if he'd been caught looking down a blouse.

He returned to the letter. 'You'll be disappointed to hear that Mayor Eddie Hicks' Slimathon is not going too well. He has put on eight pounds since I last wrote.'

Another free newspaper was squeezed through the letterbox. Pitman flew at the door, pulled it open and flung the newspaper down the drive at the delivery person. He shouted: 'Go away and don't ever put another one of those damn things through my door again . . .'

It was Clive Peacock.

'Oh, sorry,' said Pitman. 'Didn't know it was you.' He rubbed the back of his neck in embarrassment. 'How are things?'

'All right,' said Clive.

Pitman nodded. The man was beginning to look more like the Clive Peacock of old. That was reassuring. He was wearing glasses again as well, and after the *Advertiser* had given half a page to the 'Clive Peacock Changes to Contact Lenses' story. 'You've got a job delivering newspapers, then?' said Pitman.

'That's right,' nodded Clive.

'Good. It's a good job. Local newspapers are the voice of the community.'

'You don't want yours though?'

'No. Well, yes, all right.'

He took the newspaper off Clive.

'You came back, then?' Pitman said.

'You told me to come back.'

'Yes. Well, you were in trouble. I thought you needed to come back, you see. I thought you needed the security of . . .'

'I *was* in trouble.'

'Were you?'

'Oh yes.'

'Good. I mean, I'm glad it all worked out for the best in the end.'

274

Clive didn't respond. Pitman was waiting for him to go, but Clive didn't look as though he was going to move. Pitman thought of how he'd looked outside the Television Centre: those piercing eyes and the look of hunger that had almost convinced him. Maybe it was just the light that night. He waved the newspaper at him. 'Well, thanks for this anyway.'

'You're welcome,' said Clive and took a tentative step backwards. Pitman took a step inside his doorway. Clive took another step backwards and Pitman closed the door, then he threw the newspaper in the bin.

'Dear Signor Masserella,' he began again, 'thank you for your letter. Sorry for the delay in replying . . .'

He sat back and folded his arms. 'This is important,' he said out loud. 'Why can't you say how you feel?'

'. . . I have been very busy all summer with the case of the Missing Postman, an unusual story which at times made me rethink the role the community plays in police work, but which in the end, I'm glad to say, reconfirmed what I have always thought . . .'

Pitman wrote until eleven o'clock. He wrote until he had filled twenty-five pages, until he had told the story of the Missing Postman in full.

'I was annoyed with the way this man felt forced to abandon his home,' he wrote on page 6.

'The media were out for his blood, and he was clearly crying for help,' he wrote on page 14.

' "I'm flying," he told me, but I sensed that he needed to come back down to ground more than even he realised,' he wrote on page 20.

He stopped halfway down page 25 and sat back and thought of Clive cycling over the Scottish moors and sleeping in woods and having dinner with the likes of Sue Lawley. He struggled for a last paragraph. He felt very tired. He wrote: 'I'm pleased to say that Clive Peacock is now at home again with his wife. It was a struggle but it was worth it. Care in the community has to be the best care there is.'

Something sounded unconvincing here, he knew, but he had had enough. He signed the letter with best wishes and folded it into a pale blue airmail envelope and addressed it to Livorno.

It was almost midnight when Pitman strolled down to the pillar box at the bottom of Waverley Road. He would get the boys up this weekend, he was thinking to himself. He could have them up for longer periods now. That was what retirement was all about.

Someone had written on the box 'Clive Peacock is innocent'. Pitman slipped his letter in the mouth and walked back. Ahead of him a bus stopped; a woman got out and walked up the hill. She looked over her shoulder when she heard Pitman's steps. Pitman was gaining on her. If he overtook her he'd frighten her, but if he slowed down she might think he was biding his time waiting to pounce. He opted to cross the street and put her completely at rest. But she opted to cross the street at the same time, and when she looked over her shoulder and saw Pitman had followed her she crossed back again by which time Pitman had decided to do the same thing. So he decided to overtake her and be done with it. He quickened his pace. So did the woman. She looked over her shoulder again and saw him striding towards her, and so she started to hurry. Pitman broke into a trot. And then the woman was running, and Pitman was running after her. The woman turned down Wyman Road, and as Pitman passed she popped out and kicked him hard on the shin. He doubled up in pain and a handbag landed on his head.

He sat on the pavement and heard the woman run away, and he thought: The trouble with people in this town is that they don't want to be helped. Then he limped home.

# 28

THAT NIGHT THE pillar box at the bottom of Waverley Road was broken into again, this time by force.

That night Clive Peacock disappeared again.

And that night Mrs Tidy's cat Bruce left home again, this time for good.

Ex-Detective Sergeant Pitman was woken by a knock on his front door. He couldn't believe it was nine-thirty and he'd slept through. He walked heavily down the stairs. Through the glass he could see the shape of a uniformed policewoman, WDC McMahon.

'Lawrence! Are you not well?' said McMahon, genuinely concerned.

'I'm all right,' mumbled Pitman. 'Come in.'

They sat in the living room. She seemed very jolly. He had spent the first week after their débâcle in the observation van trying to forget what had happened. Then he'd spent the second week trying to recall every instant of it.

'Would you like a drink of something?' he asked. He had no tea or coffee in the house but he felt like a gamble.

'No, thanks,' said McMahon. 'I've just come to ask a few questions.'

'Ask away.'

'That pillar box at the bottom of Waverley Road; it was broken into again last night. It was forced open. There were no letters in it when the postman emptied it this morning at eight o'clock. I don't suppose you posted a letter in there any time after five pm, did you?'

'No,' said Pitman. 'No. No.'

'We think it's Clive Peacock again.'

'I'm sure you do.'

'He's disappeared again.'

'He would have done, wouldn't he?'

'There's a DI in charge of the case now.'

Pitman nodded.

'By the way,' said McMahon, 'congratulations on your retirement. You deserve it.'

'Thank you.'

'And guess what. I've got promotion. I'm a Detective Sergeant now.'

'What can I say?' said Pitman and said nothing.

She hesitated, then stood up to go. In fact Pitman wanted to say so much. As she walked to the door he coughed and mumbled: 'I don't suppose you'd like to, one evening . . . you know.'

'No, it's all right,' said McMahon.

'I wasn't prepared before, you see,' explained Pitman.

She seemed confused, but she said: 'It's very sweet of you, Lawrence, but there's no need, really. It was my fault.' She turned away. 'I always fall for dangerous men.'

The CID, in cooperation with the Post Office internal investigations, was taking this latest interference with Royal Mail rather more seriously. They set up an incident room. The Waverley Road pillar box was cordoned off with white ribbon. The door had been forced open with a garden spade, Forensic decided. A uniformed policeman was positioned by the box, and everyone who passed was asked if they'd seen a person with a garden spade in the vicinity between five pm and eight am on the night of the 15th.

Interviews were far and wide-reaching. Christine's phone was intercepted. Press and TV camped outside her house. She refused to speak to anyone. She began distressing the cupboard under the stairs.

A week passed, then two, then three, and there were no leads, no sightings, no traces of Clive Peacock. The media lost interest. The police operation was scaled down. The pillar box on Waverley Road was withdrawn by the Post Office.

The nights drew in. Christine carpeted her house with fallen leaves. The feature appeared in *House and Garden*, and she was commissioned by a London hairdressing chain to distress three salons. The council never put the blue plaque up on the Peacock house though. It seemed the Missing Postman had gone too far this time.

Lawrence Pitman took a part-time job as a security guard at the Asda supermarket. He tried to enthuse, but the work was even more soul-destroying than he imagined it would be. He found it hard not being a policeman. He phoned up Malcolm Dixon one night and said: 'I feel as though I'm becoming disillusioned.'

'*You're* becoming disillusioned!' said Malcolm Dixon.

To tackle his problem Pitman decided to become more involved in local affairs. He decided to take more active interest in his Neighbourhood Watch, but the group disbanded when Mrs Wheatley was burgled and the police discovered Mr Tidy was the culprit.

Then one morning in November a letter arrived from Signor Masserella. Pitman opened it with his heart thumping. 'Dear Mr Pitman,' wrote Masserella, 'how is your belly off for spots? Thank you for the unusually long letter. It took so very long to get here, but I think I can explain why. Has your missing postman gone missing again? There was no postmark on the letter, you see, just the initials CP.

'And here is more proof if you need it. The day your letter arrived the postbox at the end of our street was robbed and all the letters taken. I was annoyed because I had just posted a long letter to my other penpal in New York. My Superintendent has given me the case to investigate. I think we should liaise. By the way, you forgot to enclose me a copy of the *District Herald*, how stupid of you . . .'

Pitman was distracted by a lot of banging and shouting across the road. There had been strange things happening at the Peacock house for the last two days. Workmen had been putting poles underneath the foundations and now a hoist seemed to have been attached. You would have thought they were going to lift the building up and move it.

Pitman stood there and closed his eyes and saw Clive Peacock cycling down the Adriatic coast with a hot bagful of letters. He had slept the previous night on the beach just outside Pescara. No one had bothered him; it was easy to live on the road here. The Alps had been spectacular, the Mediterranean coast a gem. Florence had beguiled him. The Apennines had taken their toll, but now he was warm, and on the flat, and heading down to Bari. And in his bag, at the bottom of his pile, was a ticket to New York. How he'd get there he hadn't a clue . . .

The earth rumbled and Pitman opened his eyes to see Christine Peacock walking down the street ahead of a huge truck towing her house. She waved to onlookers as she passed. That says it all about this neighbourhood, thought Pitman, and he went to his desk and dug out his passport. It was eight years out of date; he'd get a new one. If Clive Peacock wasn't going to hit the ground, then the only way to save the man was to jump off the cliff after him. The Missing Policeman – he liked the sound of that.

Warner now offers an exciting range of quality titles by both established and new authors. All of the books in this series are available from:
Little, Brown and Company (UK) Limited,
Cash Sales Department,
P.O. Box 11,
Falmouth,
Cornwall TR10 9EN.

Alternatively you may fax your order to the above address. Fax No. 0326 376423.

Payments can be made as follows: Cheque, postal order (payable to Little, Brown and Company) or by credit cards, Visa/Access. Do not send cash or currency. UK customers: and B.F.P.O.: please send a cheque or postal order (no currency) and allow £1.00 for postage and packing for the first book, plus 50p for the second book, plus 30p for each additional book up to a maximum charge of £3.00 (7 books plus).

Overseas customers including Ireland, please allow £2.00 for postage and packing for the first book, plus £1.00 for the second book, plus 50p for each additional book.

NAME (Block Letters) ...........................................

ADDRESS...............................................................

.............................................................................

☐ I enclose my remittance for _____

☐ I wish to pay by Access/Visa Card

Number ☐☐☐☐☐☐☐☐☐☐☐☐☐☐☐☐

Card Expiry Date ☐☐☐☐